The Caliban Trilogy is a searing examination of Asimov's Three Laws of Robotics, a challenge welcomed and sanctioned by Isaac Asimov, the late beloved genius of science fiction, and written with his cooperation by one of today's hottest talents, Roger MacBride Allen, *New York Times* bestselling author of *Star Wars: Ambush at Corella.*

CALIBAN

The First Law states:

A robot may not injure a human being, or, through inaction, allow a human being to come to harm.

INFERNO

The Second Law states:

A robot must obey the orders given it by human beings except where such orders would conflict with the First Law.

UTOPIA

The Third Law states:

A robot must protect its own existence as long as such protection does not conflict with the First or Second Law.

ISAAC ASIMOV'S CALIBAN

BY ROGER MacBRIDE ALLEN

A Byron Preiss Visual Publications, Inc. Book

ACE BOOKS, NEW YORK

This Ace Book contains the complete text of the original trade edition. It has been completely reset in a typeface designed for easy reading, and was printed from new film.

CALIBAN

An Ace Book / published by arrangement with Byron Preiss Visual Publications, Inc.

PRINTING HISTORY
Ace trade paperback edition / March 1993
Ace mass-market edition / September 1997

Cover art by Ralph McQuarrie.

For information address: The Berkley Publishing Group, 200 Madison Avenue, New York, NY 10016, a member of Penguin Putnam Inc.

The Putnam Berkley World Wide Web site address is
http://www.berkley.com

ISBN: 0-441-00482-2

ACE®

Ace Books are published by The Berkley Publishing Group, 200 Madison Avenue, New York, NY 10016, a member of Penguin Putnam Inc.

PRINTED IN THE UNITED STATES OF AMERICA

10 9 8 7 6 5 4 3 2 1

To five wondrous creatures,
named in the order
of their appearance
on this planet:

Aaron
Victoria
Benton
Jonathan
and
Meredith

Acknowledgments

This book would not have been possible without the support, and especially the patience, of David Harris, John Betancourt, Byron Preiss, Susan Allison, Ginjer Buchanan, and Peter Heck. There was many a slip between cup and the lip, but thanks to their collective efforts, never a drop of the good stuff was lost. The book stands as proof once again that every writer needs at least one editor, and sometimes five or six is no bad idea. Thanks are also due to Thomas B. Allen and Eleanore Fox, neither of whom had time to read the manuscript, and both of whom did.

I

A Robot May Not Injure a Human Being,
or, Through Inaction, Allow a Human Being to Come to Harm.

II

A Robot Must Obey the Orders Given It by Human Beings
Except Where Such Orders
Would Conflict with the First Law.

III

A Robot Must Protect Its Own Existence
As Long As Such Protection
Does Not Conflict with the First or Second Law.

. . . THE Spacer-Settler struggle was at its beginning, and at its end, an ideological contest. Indeed, to take a page from primitive studies, it might more accurately be termed a theological battle, for both sides clung to their positions more out of faith, fear, and tradition than through any carefully reasoned marshaling of the facts.

Always, whether acknowledged or not, there was one issue at the center of every confrontation between the two sides: robots. One side regarded them as the ultimate good, while the other saw them as the ultimate evil.

Spacers were the descendants of men and women who had fled semi-mythical Earth with their robots when robots were banned there. Exiled from Earth, they traveled in crude starships on the first wave of colonization from Earth. With the aid of their robots, the Spacers terraformed fifty worlds and created a culture of great beauty and refinement, where all unpleasant tasks were left to the robots. Ultimately, virtually *all* work was left to the robots. Having colonized fifty planets, the Spacers called a halt, and set themselves no other task than enjoying the fruits of their robots' labor.

The Settlers were the descendants of those who stayed behind on Earth. Their ancestors lived in great underground Cities, built to be safe from atomic attack. It is beyond doubt that this way of life induced a certain xenophobia into Settler culture. That xenophobia long survived the threat of atomic war, and came to be directed against the smug Spacers—and their robots.

It was fear that had caused Earth to cast out robots in the first place. Part of it was an irrational fear of metal monsters wandering the landscape. However, the people of Earth had more reasonable fears as well. They worried that robots would take jobs—and the means of making a living—from humans. Most seriously, they looked to what they saw as the indolence, the lethargy and decadence of Spacer society. The Settlers feared that robots would relieve humanity of its spirit, its will, its ambition, even as they relieved humanity of its burdens.

The Spacers, meanwhile, had grown disdainful of the people they perceived to be grubby underground dwellers. Spacers came to deny their own common ancestry with the people who had cast them out. But so, too, did they lose their own ambition. Their technology, their culture, their worldview, all became static, if not stagnant. The Spacer ideal seemed to be a universe where nothing ever happened, where yesterday and tomorrow were like today, and the robots took care of all the unpleasant details.

The Settlers set out to colonize the galaxy in earnest, terraforming endless worlds, leapfrogging past the Spacer worlds and Spacer technology. The Settlers carried with them the traditional viewpoints of the home world. Every encounter with the Spacers seemed to confirm the Settlers' reasons for distrusting robots. Fear and hatred of robots became one of the foundations of Settler policy and philosophy. Robot hatred, coupled with the rather arrogant Spacer style, did little to endear Settler to Spacer.

But still, sometimes, somehow, the two sides managed to cooperate, however great the degree of friction and suspicion. People of goodwill on both sides attempted to cast aside fear and hatred to work together—with varying success.

It was on Inferno, one of the smallest, weakest, most fragile of the Spacer worlds, that Spacer and Settler made one of the boldest attempts to work together. The people of that world, who called themselves Infernals, found themselves facing two crises. Their ecological difficulties all knew about, though few understood their severity. Settler experts in terraforming were called in to deal with that.

But it was the second crisis, the hidden crisis, that proved the greater danger. For, unbeknownst to themselves, the Infernals and the Settlers on that aptly named world were forced to face a remarkable change in the very nature of robots themselves . . .

—*Early History of Colonization,* by Sarhir Vadid,
Baleyworld University Press, S.E 1231

1

THE blow smashed into her skull.

Fredda Leving's knees buckled. She dropped her tea mug. It fell to the floor and shattered in a splash of brown liquid. Fredda crumpled toward the ground. Her shoulder struck the floor, smashing into the broken shards of the cup. They slashed into her left shoulder and the left side of her face. Blood poured from the wounds.

She lay there, on her side, motionless, curled up in a ghoulish mockery of the fetal position.

For the briefest of moments, she regained consciousness. It might have been a split second after the attack, or two hours later, she could not say. But she *saw* them, there was no doubt of that. She saw the feet, the two red metallic feet, not thirty centimeters from her face. She felt fear, astonishment, confusion. But then her pain and her injury closed over her again, and she knew no more.

ROBOT CBN-001, also known as Caliban, awoke for the first time. In a world new to him, his eyes switched on to glow a deep and penetrating blue as he looked about his surroundings. He had no memory, no understanding to guide him. He knew nothing.

He looked down at himself and saw he was tall, his body metallic red. His left arm was half-raised. He was holding it straight out in front of him, his fist clenched. He flexed his elbow, opened his fist, and stared at his hand for a moment. He lowered his arm. He moved his head from side to side, seeing, hearing, thinking, with no recollection of experience to guide him. *Where am I, who am I, what am I?*

I am in a laboratory of some sort, I am Caliban, I am a robot. The answers came from inside him, but not from his mind. *From an on-board datastore,* he realized, and that knowledge likewise came from the datastore. *So that is where answers come from,* he concluded.

He looked down to the floor and saw a body lying on its side there, its head near his feet. It was the crumpled form of a young woman, a pool of blood growing around her head and the upper part of her body. Instantly he recognized the concepts of *woman, young, blood,* the answers flitting into his awareness almost before he could form the questions. Truly a remarkable device, this on-board datastore.

Who is she? Why does she lie there? What is wrong with her? He waited in vain for the answers to spring forth, but no explanation came to him. The store could not—or would not—help him with those questions. Some answers, it seemed, it would not give. Caliban knelt down, peered at the woman more closely, dipped a finger in the pool of blood. His thermocouple sensors revealed that it was already rapidly cooling, coagulating. The principle of blood clotting snapped into his mind. *It should be sticky,* he thought, and tested the notion, pressing his forefinger to his thumb and then pulling them apart. *Yes, a slight resistance.*

But blood, and an injured human. A strange sensation stole over him, as he knew there was some reaction, some intense, deep-rooted response that he should have—some response that was not there at all.

The blood was pooling around Caliban's feet now. He rose to his full two-meter height again and found that he did not desire to stand in a pool of blood. He wished to leave this place for more pleasant surroundings. He stepped clear of the blood and saw an open doorway at the far end of the room. He had no goal, no purpose, no understanding, no memory. One direction was as good as another. Once he started moving, there was no reason to stop.

Caliban left the laboratory, wholly and utterly unaware that he was leaving a trail of bloody footprints behind. He went through the doorway and kept on going, out of the room, out of the building, out into the city.

SHERIFF'S Robot Donald DNL-111 surveyed the blood-splattered floor, grimly aware that, on all the Spacer worlds, only in the city of Hades on the planet of Inferno could a scene of such violence be reduced to a matter of routine.

But Inferno was different, which was of course the problem in the first place.

Here on Inferno it was happening more and more often. One human would attack another at night—it was nearly always night—and flee. A robot—it was nearly always a robot—would come across the crime scene and report it, then suffer a major cognitive dissonance breakdown, unable to cope with the direct, vivid, horrifying evidence of violence against a human being. Then the med-robots would rush in. The Sheriff's dispatch center would summon Donald, the Sheriff's personal robot, to the scene. If Donald judged the situation warranted Kresh's attention, Donald instructed the household robot to waken Sheriff Alvar Kresh and suggest that he join Donald at the scene.

Tonight the dismal ritual would be played out in full. This attack, beyond question, required that the Sheriff investigate personally. The victim, after all, was Fredda Leving. Kresh must needs be summoned.

And so some other, subordinate robot would waken Kresh, dress him, and send him on his way here. That was unfortunate, as Kresh seemed to feel Donald was the only one who could do it properly. And when Alvar Kresh woke in a bad mood, he often flew his own aircar in order to work off his tension. Donald did not like the idea of his master flying himself in any circumstances. But the thought of Alvar Kresh in an evil mood, half-asleep, flying at night, was especially unpleasant.

But there was nothing Donald could do about all that, and a great deal to be done here. Donald was a short, almost rotund robot, painted a metallic shade of the Sheriff's Department's sky-blue and carefully designed to be an inconspicuous presence, the sort of robot that could not possibly disturb or upset or intimidate anyone. People responded better to an inquisitive police robot if it was not obtrusive. Donald's head and body were rounded, the sides and planes of his form flowing into each other in smooth curves. His arms and legs were short, and no effort had been made to put anything more than the merest sketch of a human face on the front of his head.

He had two blue-glowing eyes, and a speaker grille for a mouth, but otherwise his head was utterly featureless, expressionless.

Which was perhaps just as well, for had his face been mobile enough to do so, he would have been hard-pressed to formulate an expression appropriate to his reaction now. Donald was a police robot, relatively hardened to the idea of someone harming a human, but even he was having a great deal of trouble dealing with *this* attack. He had not seen one this bad in a while. And he had never been in the position of *knowing* the victim. And it was, after all, Fredda Leving herself who had built Donald, named Donald. Donald found that personal acquaintance with the victim only made his First Law tensions worse.

Fredda Leving was crumpled on the floor, her head in a pool of her own blood, two trails of bloody footprints leading from the scene in different directions, out two of the four doors to the room. There were no footprints leading in.

"Sir—sir—sir?" The robotic voice was raspy and rather crudely mechanical, spoken aloud rather than via hyperwave. Donald turned and looked at the speaker. It was the maintenance robot that had hyperwaved this one in.

"Yes, what it is?"

"Will she—will she—will she be all—all right right?"

Donald looked down at the small tan robot. It was a DAA-BOR unit, not more than a meter and a half high. The word-stutter in his speech told him what he knew already. Before very much longer, this little robot was likely to be good for little more than the scrap heap, a victim of First Law dissonance.

Theory had it that a robot on the scene should be able to provide first aid, with the medical dispatch center ready to transmit any specialized medical knowledge that might be needed. But a serious head injury, with all the potential for brain damage, made that impossible. Even leaving aside the question of having surgical equipment in hand, this maintenance robot did not have the brain capacity, the fine motor skills, or the visual acuity needed to diagnose a head wound. The maintenance robot must have been caught in a classic First Law trap, knowing that Fredda Leving was badly injured, but knowing that any inexpert attempt to aid her could well injure her further. Caught between the injunction to do no harm and the command not to allow harm through inaction, the DAA-BOR's positronic brain must have been severely damaged as it oscillated back and forth between the demands for action and inaction.

"I believe that the medical robots have the situation well in hand, Daabor 5132," Donald replied. Perhaps some encouraging words from an authority figure like a high-end police robot might do some good, help stabilize the cognitive dissonance that was clearly disabling this robot. "I am certain that your prompt call for assistance helped to save her life. If you had not acted as you did, the medical team might well not have arrived in time."

"Thank thank thank you, sir. That is good to know."

"One thing puzzles me, however. Tell me, friend—where are all the other robots? Why are you the only one here? Where are the staff robots, and Madame Leving's personal robot?"

"Ordered—ordered away," the little robot answered, still struggling to get its speech under greater control. "Others ordered to leave area earlier in evening. They are in are in the other wing of the laboratory. And Madame Leving does not bring a personal robot with her to work."

Donald looked at the other robot in astonishment. Both statements were remarkable. That a leading roboticist did not keep a personal robot was incredible. No Spacer would venture out of the house without a personal robot in attendance. A citizen of Inferno would be far more likely to venture out stark naked than without a robot—and Inferno had a strong tradition of modesty, even among Spacer worlds.

But that was as nothing compared to the idea of the staff robots being ordered to leave. How could that be? And *who* ordered them to go? The assailant? It seemed an obvious conclusion. For the most fleeting of seconds, Donald hesitated. It was dangerous for this robot to answer such questions, given its fragile state of mind and diminished capacity. The additional conflicts between First and Second Laws could easily do irreparable harm. But no, it was necessary to ask the questions now. Daabor 5132 was likely to suffer a complete cognitive breakdown at any moment in any event, and this might be the only chance to ask. It would have been far better for a human, for Sheriff Kresh, to do the asking, but this robot could fail at any moment. Donald resolved to take the chance. "Who gave this order, friend? And how did you come to disobey that order?"

"Did not disobey! Was not present when order given. Sent—I was sent—on an errand. I came back after."

"Then how do you know the order was given?"

"Because it was given before! Other times!"

Other times? Donald was more and more amazed. "Who gave it? What other times? Who gave the order? Why did that person give the order?"

Daabor 5132's head jerked abruptly to one side. "Cannot say. Ordered not to tell. Ordered we were ordered not to say we were sent away, either—but now going away caused harm to human harm harm harm—"

And with a low strangling noise, Daabor 5132 froze up. Its green eyes flared bright for a moment and then went dark.

Donald stared sadly at what had been a reasoning being brief moments before. There could be no question that he had chosen rightly. Daabor 5132 would have failed within a few minutes in any event.

At least there was the hope that a skilled human roboticist could get further information out of the other staff robots.

Donald turned away from the ruined maintenance robot and turned his attention back toward the human victim on the floor, surrounded by the med-robots.

It was the sight that had destroyed the Daabor robot, but Donald knew he was, quite literally, made of sterner stuff. Fredda Leving herself had adjusted his First, Second, and Third Law potential with the express purpose of making him capable of performing police work.

Donald 111 stared at the scene before him, feeling the sort of First Law tension familiar to a sheriff's robot: Here was a human being in pain, in danger, and yet he could not act. The med-robots were here for that, and they could aid Fredda Leving far more competently than he ever could. Donald knew that, and restrained himself, but the First Law was quite clear and emphatic: *A robot may not injure a human being, or, through inaction, allow a human being to come to harm.* No loopholes, no exceptions.

But to aid *this* human would be to interfere with the work of the med-robots, thus at least potentially bringing *harm* to Fredda Leving. Therefore, to do nothing was to aid her. But he was enjoined against doing nothing, and yet to aid her would be to interfere—Donald fought down the tremors inside his mind as his positronic brain dealt with the same dissonance that had destroyed Daabor 5132. Donald knew that his police-robot adjustments would see to it he survived the episode, as he had so many in the past, but that did not make it any less unpleasant.

Humans, on the other hand: These days, the sight of blood and violence scarcely bothered Alvar Kresh. Human beings could get used to such things. They could adapt. Donald knew that was so intellectually, he had observed it, but he could not understand how it was possible. To see a human in distress, in danger, to see a human as the victim of violence, even dead, and to be unmoved—that was simply beyond his comprehension.

But human or robot, the police saw a lot, especially on Inferno, and experience did make it easier in some ways. The paths of his positronic brain were well worn with the knowledge of how to deal with this situation, however disturbing that might be. Stay back. Observe. Gather data. Let the meds do their work.

And then wait for the human, wait for Alvar Kresh, wait for the Sheriff of the city of Hades.

The med-robots worked on the still form, rushing to stabilize her, ensure her blood supply, patching up the gashes in her shoulder and face, attaching monitor pads and drug infusers, moving her to a lift stretcher, shrouding her in blankets, inserting a breather tube into her mouth, cocooning her from sight behind their protections and ministrations. *And that is how it should be,* Donald thought. *Robots are the shield between humans and the dangers of the world.*

Though the shield had clearly failed this time. It was a miracle that Fredda Leving was even alive. By all appearances the attack had been remarkably violent. But who had done this, and why?

The observer robots hovered about, recording the images of this scene from every angle. Maybe their data would be of some use. Let them soak in all the details. Donald shifted his attention to the two sets of bloody footprints that led from the body. He had already tracked them out as far as they went. Both sets of prints faded away into invisibility after only a hundred meters or so, and he let it go at that. Police technical robots were already using molecular sniffers to try to extend the trails, but they wouldn't get anywhere. They never did.

But there was no missing the key fact, the vital piece of evidence. And no denying the horrible, unthinkable conclusion they suggested.

Both sets of footprints were robotic. *Both* sets. Donald, designed, programmed, trained in police work, could not avoid making the obvious and terrifying inference.

But it could not be. It couldn't be.

Donald devoutly wished for Alvar Kresh to arrive. Let a human take over, let someone who could get used to such things deal with the impossible thought that a robot could have struck Fredda Leving from behind.

THE night sky roared past Sheriff Alvar Kresh, and the scattered lights of buildings in Hades's outskirts gleamed bright below. He looked up into the dark sky and saw the bright stars glowing down at him. A beautiful night, a perfect night for a speed run over the city, something he only got the chance to do on official business, and he had to be in a foul mood.

He did not care for being awakened in the middle of the night, did not care for anyone but Donald helping him to dress.

He tried to cheer himself up, to soothe himself. He looked out into the night. Tonight was the best weather Hades had had in a long time. No sandstorms, no dust-haze. There was even a fresh tang of seawater blowing in off the Great Bay.

At least he could burn off his adrenaline and his anger by flying his aircar himself, rather than leaving the chore to a robot. He took a certain pride in that. Few humans even knew how to fly an aircar. Most people felt the chore of controlling an aircraft beneath them. They let the robots do it. No doubt most people thought it was damned odd that Alvar liked to fly his own car. But few people were likely to say that to the Sheriff's face.

Alvar Kresh yawned and blinked, and punched the coffee button on the aircar's beverage dispenser. He was alert, clear-eyed, but there was still a shroud of tiredness over him, and the first sip of the coffee was welcome. The aircar sped on through the night as he flew it one-handed, drinking his coffee. He grinned. *Lucky Donald isn't here,* he thought. It was stunts like flying one-handed that made it all but impossible for him to fly his own car when Donald, or indeed any robot, was on board. One false move and the robot would instantly leap into the copilot's seat and take over the craft's controls.

Ah, well. Maybe the Settlers sneered at robots, but no Spacer world could function for thirty seconds without them. That having been said, the damned things could be incredibly infuriating all the same.

Alvar Kresh forced himself to calmness. He had been roused from a sound sleep in the dead of night, and he knew from bitter experience that interrupted sleep made him more edgy than usual. He had learned long ago that he needed to do something to take the edge off himself when he was too keyed up, or else he was likely to take someone's head off instead.

Alvar breathed the cool thin air. A nightflight over the desert at speed with the top open and the wind howling through his thick thatch of white hair helped drain away some of his temper, his tension.

But crimes of violence were still rare enough in Hades for him to take them personally, to get angry and stay that way. He needed that anger. This savage and cowardly attack on a leading scientist was intolerable. Maybe he did not agree with Fredda Leving's politics, but he knew better than most that neither the Spacer worlds in general nor Inferno in particular could afford the loss of any talented individual.

Alvar Kresh watched as the city swept by below him, and began to slow the aircar. There. The aircar's navigation system reported that they were directly over the Leving Robotics Labs. Alvar peered over the edge of the car, but it was difficult to get a fix on the precise building at night. He eased the car to a halt, adjusted its position over the landscape slightly, and brought it down to the ground.

A robot ground attendant hurried over to the car and opened the door for him. Alvar Kresh stood up and stepped out of the car, into the night.

There was a busy rummaging-about going on. A red and white ambulance aircar squatted on the ground near Kresh's car, its lift motors idling, its running lights on, obviously ready to lift off the moment its patient was aboard. A squad of med-robots bustled through the main door of the lab, two of them carrying a stretcher, the others holding feed lines and monitoring equipment hooked up to the patient. Leving herself was not quite visible under the tangle of life-support gear. A human doctor lounged by the hatch of the ambulance, watching the robots do the work. Alvar stood still and let the robots pass as they carried the victim from the scene of the crime.

He watched, his anger rising inside him, as the meds carried her into their van, and watched as the indolent human doctor eased his way into the ambulance behind his busy charges. *How could anyone commit such violence against another human being?* he asked himself.

But raw, unchanneled anger would not help catch Fredda Leving's assailant. *Remain calm,* he thought. *Keep your anger controlled, focused.* Alvar Kresh lifted his hand to a med-robot that was carrying a first-aid kit back to the ambulance. "What is the condition of your patient?" he asked.

The gleaming red and white med-robot regarded Kresh through glowing orange eyes. "She received a severe head injury, but no irreparable trauma," it said.

"Were her injuries life-threatening?" Kresh asked.

"Had we been delayed in reaching Madame Leving, her injuries could easily have been fatal," the robot said, a bit primly.

"However, she should recover completely, though there is the distinct possibility that she will suffer traumatic amnesia. We shall place her in a regeneration unit as soon as we reach the hospital."

"Very good," Kresh said. "You may go." He turned and watched the last of the med team climb into the ambulance and take off into the night. Good that she would recover, but it could be very bad indeed if she did suffer amnesia. People with holes in their memories made for bad witnesses. But the words of the med-robots changed the nature of the case. *Her injuries could easily have been fatal.* That changed a simple assault with a deadly weapon case into one of attempted murder. At last he turned to go inside the building, to see what Donald and his forensic team had come up with.

2

"ALL right, Donald," Kresh said as he came in, "what have you got?"

"Good evening, Sheriff Kresh," Donald replied, speaking with a smooth and urbane courtesy. "I am afraid we do not have a great deal. The crime scene does not tell us much that we can use, though of course you may well note something we have missed. I have not been able to form a satisfactory interpretation of the evidence. Did you have the opportunity to examine my update regarding the maintenance robot's statements?"

"Yes, I did. Damn strange. You did right to get the data out of him, but I don't want to take any chances on the rest of the staff robots. I don't even want to get near them myself. I want the department's staff roboticists to interview them all—carefully." Normally the police roboticists dealt with robots who had been tricked into this or that by con artists skilled in lying to robots and convincing them to obey illegal orders under some carefully designed misapprehension. A man could make a pretty fair living convincing household robots to reveal their masters' financial account codes. It would do the roboticists good to deal with something a little out of the ordinary. "But we can worry about that tomorrow. Is the scene clear?"

"Yes, sir. The observer robots have completed their basic scan of the area. I believe you can examine the room without danger of destroying clues, so long as you practice some care."

Alvar looked closely at Donald. After a lifetime of dealing with robots, he still did that, still looked toward the machines as if he could read an emotion or a thought in their expressions or postures. On some robots, on the very rare ones that mimicked human appearance perfectly, that was at least possible. But there were precious few of those on Inferno, and with any other robot type the effort was pointless.

Even so, the habit gave him a moment of time to consider the indirect meaning of the robot's *words. No "satisfactory interpretation of the evidence."* What the hell did *that* mean? Donald was trying to tell him something, something the robot did not choose to say directly, for fear of presuming too far. But Donald was never cryptic without a purpose. When Donald got that way, it was for a reason. Alvar Kresh was tempted to order Donald to explain precisely what he was suggesting, but he restrained his impatience.

It might be better to see if he could spot the point that was bothering Donald himself, evaluate it independently without prejudgment. There was, of course, precious little a robot would miss that a human could notice. Much of what Donald had said was so much deferential nonsense, salve for the ego. But the words Donald had used were interesting: "*The crime scene does not tell us much that we can use.*" As if there *were* something there, but something distracting, meaningless, deceptive. *So much for avoiding prejudgment,* Alvar thought sardonically. That was the trouble with robot assistants as good as Donald—you tended to lean on them to much, let them influence your thinking, trust them to do too much of the background work. *Hell, Donald could probably do this job better than me,* Alvar thought.

He shook his head angrily. No. Robots are the servants of humans, incapable of independent action. Alvar stepped through the doorway, fully into the room, and began to look around.

Alvar Kresh felt a strange and familiar tingle course through him as he set to work. There was always something oddly thrilling about this moment, where the case was opened and the chase was on. A strange chase it was, one that started with Alvar not so much as knowing who it was that he pursued.

And there was something stranger still, always, about standing in the middle of someone's very private space with that person absent. He had stood in the bedrooms and salons and spacecraft of the dead and the missing, read their diaries, traced their financial dealings, stumbled across the evidence of their secret vices and private pleasures, their grand crimes and tiny, pathetic secrets. He had come to know their lives and deaths from the clues they left behind, been made privy by the power of his office to the most intimate parts of their lives. Here and now, that began as well.

Some work places were sterile, revealing nothing about their inhabitants. But this was not such a place. This room was a portrait of the person who worked here, if only Alvar could learn to read it.

He began his examination of the laboratory. Superficially, at least, it was a standard enough setup. A room maybe twenty meters by ten. Inferno was not a crowded world by any means. People tended to spread out. By Inferno standards it was an average-sized space for one person.

There were four doors in all, in the corners of the room, set into the long sides of the room: two on the exterior wall, leading directly to the outside, and two on the opposite, interior wall, leading into the building's hallway. Alvar noted that the room was windowless, and the doors were heavy; they appeared to be light-tight. Close them, cut the overhead lights, and the room would be pitch-black. Presumably they did some work with light-sensitive materials in here. Or perhaps they tested robot eyes. Would the reason for, or the fact of, a light-tight room be important or meaningless? No way to know.

Alvar and Donald stood by one of the interior doors, toward what Alvar found himself thinking of as the rear of the room. *But why is this end the rear?* he wondered. No one specific thing, he decided. It was just that this end of the room seemed more disused. Everything was boxed up, in storage. The other end clearly was put to more active use.

Work counters ran most of the length of the room, between the pairs of doors. There were computer terminals on the counters. The walls held outlets for various types of power supplies, and two or three hookups Kresh could not identify. Special-purpose datataps, perhaps.

Every square centimeter of the countertops seemed to have something on it. A robot torso, a disembodied robot head, a stack of carefully sealed boxes, each neatly labeled *Handle with Care. Gravitonic Brain.* Alvar frowned and looked at the labels again. What the devil were gravitonic brains? For thousands of years, all robots had been built with positronic brains. It was the positronic brain that made robots possible. Gravitonic brains? Alvar knew nothing at all about them, but the name itself was unsettling. He did not approve of needless change.

He filed away the puzzle for future reference and continued his survey of the room. All of the room's side counters were full of all sorts of mysterious-looking tools and machines and robot parts. Yet there was no feel of chaos or mess about the room; all was neat and orderly. There was not even so much as an air of clutter. It was merely that this entire room was in active use by someone who seemed to have several projects going at once.

Two large worktables sat in the center of the room. A half-built robot and a bewildering collection of parts and tools were spread out on one table, while the other was largely empty, with just a few odds and ends here and there around the edges.

Wheeled racks of test equipment stood here and there about the room. A huge contraption of tubing and swivels stood between the two tables. It was easily three meters tall, and took up maybe four meters by five in floor space. It was on power rollers, so it could be pushed out of the way when not in use.

"What the devil is that thing?" Alvar asked, stepping toward the center of the room.

"A robot service rack," Donald replied, following behind. "It is designed to clamp onto a robot's hard-attachment points and suspend the robot at any height and in any attitude, so as to position the needed part of the robot for convenient access. It is used for repairs or tests. I thought it a large and awkward thing to keep in the middle of the room. It would certainly interfere with easy movement between the two worktables, for example."

"That's what I was thinking. Look, you can see the empty space along the wall on the rear end of the room. They rolled it over there when they weren't using it. So why is it out in the middle of the room? What good is an empty robot rack?"

"The clear implication is that there was a robot in it recently," Donald said.

"Yes, I agree. And notice the empty space on the center of the empty worktable. About the right size for another robot there, too. Unless they moved the same robot from the table to the rack, or vice versa. Maybe that was the motive for the attack? The theft of one or two experimental robots? We'll have to check on all that."

"Sir, if I could direct your attention to the floor in front of the service rack, Fredda Leving's position on it has been marked out—"

"Not yet, Donald. I'll get there. I'll get there." Alvar was quite purposefully ignoring the pooled blood and the body outline in the center of the room. It was too easy to be distracted by the big, obvious clues at a crime scene. What could the body outline tell him? That a woman had been attacked here, bled here? He knew all that already. Better to work the rest of the room first.

But one thing was bothering him. This room did not match Fredda Leving's character. He knew her slightly, from the process of ordering Donald, and this place did not fit her. It had the feel of a male domain, somehow. Tiny details he had seen but not noted suddenly registered in Alvar's consciousness. The size and cut of a lab coat hanging by the door, the size of the dust-sealed lab shoes sitting on the floor beneath the lab coat, certain tools stored on wall hooks that would be well out of reach for the average-sized woman.

And there was, indefinably, something about the neatness of this room that spoke of a shy, compulsive, tidy *man*, something that did not match an assertive woman like Fredda Leving. If she lived up to her very public image, *her* lab would be a mess, even after the robots got through cleaning, for she would flatly refuse to let them near most of it. The great and famous Fredda Leving, hero of robotics research, the crown jewel of science in Inferno, was not a compulsive fussbudget—but the occupant of this room clearly was.

Alvar Kresh stepped back into the hallway and checked the nameplate next to the door. *Gubber Anshaw, Design and Testing Chief,* it read. Well, that solved one minor mystery and replaced it with another. It wasn't Leving's lab, but Anshaw's, whoever he was.

But what was Fredda Leving doing in Anshaw's lab, presumably alone with her assailant, in the middle of the night?

Kresh went back into the lab and walked around the rest of the room, careful not to touch anything, determined to resist the urge to go and look at the spot where the body fell. The room was a perfect forest of potential clues, jam-packed with gadgets and hardware that might have some bearing on the case, if only Alvar knew enough about experimental robotics. Was there indeed something missing, some object as big as an experimental robot, or as tiny as an advanced microcircuit, whose theft might provide a motive for this attack?

But what was the nature of the attack? He knew nothing so far.

At last, quite reluctantly, after working the rest of the crime scene and coming up with very little for his efforts, Alvar moved toward the center of the room, the center of the case, the scene of the attack.

There it was, on the floor, between the two worktables, a meter or so in front of the large robot service rack. A pool of blood, a blotchy, irregular shape about a meter across. The body as found was indicated in a glowing yellow outline that followed the contours of the body perfectly, down to the sprawled-out fingers of the left hand. The fingers seemed to be reaching toward the door, reaching for help that did not come.

Some errant part of Kresh's mind found itself wondering how they did that, how they put down that perfect outline. Robots in the Sheriff's office knew how, but he did not.

But no. It was tempting to distract himself with side issues, but he could not permit himself the luxury. He knelt down and looked at what he had come to see. He had forced himself not to notice the smell of drying blood until this moment, but now he had to pay attention, and the heavy, acrid, rotting odor seemed to surge into his lungs. A wave of nausea swept over him. He ignored the stench and went on with his grim task.

The pool of blood was much smeared and splashed about by the med-robots, their footprints and other marks badly obscuring the story the floor had to tell. But that was all right. Donald would have images of the floor recorded straight off the med-robots' eyes, what they saw the moment they came in. Computer tricks could erase all traces of the med-robots from whatever images the police observer/forensic robots had made, reconstruct the scene exactly as it was before. Some of his deputies only worked off such reconstructions, but Kresh preferred to work in the muddled-up, dirtied-up confused mess of the real-world crime scene.

The blood had virtually all clotted or dried by now. Kresh pulled a stylus from his pocket and tested the surface. Almost completely solidified. It always amazed him how fast it happened. He looked up and from the pool of blood, noted the pattern of a med-robot's foot and then noted something else he had seen before but merely filed away until he had seen the whole room. Two other sets of prints, clearly from robotic feet, but wholly different from the med-robot's treads. One set of prints led out the front interior into the hallway, the other out the front exterior door to the outside of the building.

And the two sets of prints might be different from the med-robot's, but they were utterly identical to each other.

Two sets of mystery prints, exactly like each other.

"That's what's bothering you, isn't it, Donald?" Alvar said, standing back up.

"What is, sir?"

"The robot footprints. The ones that make it clear that a robot—two robots—walked through the pool of blood and left Fredda Leving, quite possibly to die."

"Yes, sir, that did bother me. The flaw is obvious, but it is what the evidence suggests."

"Then the evidence is wrong. The First Law makes it impossible for any robot to behave that way," Alvar said.

"And therefore," a brash new voice suddenly declared from the door Alvar had come through, "therefore, someone must have staged the attack to make it *seem* like a robot—*two* robots—did it. Brilliant, Sheriff Kresh. That took me all of thirty seconds to figure out. How long have *you* been here?"

Alvar turned around and clenched his teeth to keep from letting out a string of curses. It was Tonya Welton. A tall, dark-skinned woman, long-limbed and graceful, she stood just inside the doorway, a tall, dusky-yellow robot behind her. Alvar Kresh would not even have noticed the robot except that Welton was a Settler. He always got a certain grim pleasure out of seeing robots inflicted on the people who hated them so passionately, but at the moment at least, Welton seemed bothered not at all. Her expression was one of amused condescension.

She was dressed in a disturbingly tight and extravagantly patterned blue one-piece bodysuit. The Spacer population on Inferno preferred much more modest clothing and far more subdued colors. On Inferno, robots were brightly colored, not people. But no one had told the leader of the Settlers on Inferno that—or else she had ignored them when they *did* tell her. Welton, more than likely, had gotten it backwards deliberately.

But what the hell was Tonya Welton doing here now?

"Good evening, Lady Tonya," Donald said in his smoothest and most urbane tones. It was rare, surpassing rare, for a robot to speak except when spoken to, but Donald was smart enough to know this situation needed defusing. "What a pleasant surprise to have you join us here."

"I doubt it," Tonya Welton said with a smile that Alvar scored as being at least an attempt at courtesy. "Forgive me, Sheriff

Kresh, for my rather rude entrance. I'm afraid the news about Fredda Leving unsettled me. I tend to be a bit sharp-tongued when I am upset."

And at all other times, Kresh thought to himself. "Quite all right, Madame Welton," he replied in a tone of voice that made it clear it was anything but all right. "I don't know what business brings you here, but there has been an attack on one of Inferno's top scientists here tonight, and I cannot allow anything to interfere. This is an official investigation, Madame Welton, which has nothing to do with the Settlers, and I'm afraid I must ask you to leave."

"Oh, no, I can't. You see, that's why I'm here. Governor Grieg himself called me not an hour ago and asked that I come here tonight and join in your investigation."

Alvar Kresh stared at the Settler woman in openmouthed astonishment. What in the devil was going on here? "Are we done here, Donald?" he asked. "Anything else I need to see immediately?"

"No, sir, I think not."

"Very well, then, Donald. Seal this room as a crime scene. No one in or out. Just now, I think perhaps Madame Welton and I need to have a little talk, and this is not the place for it. Join us when you have completed the arrangements."

"Very good, sir," Donald said.

"Let's go to my car, Madame Welton. We can talk there."

"Yes, let's do that, Sheriff," Tonya Welton said, rather stiffly. "There are a few things we need to get straight. Come along, Ariel."

ALVAR Kresh and Tonya Welton sat down in the Sheriff's aircar, facing each other, both of them clearly wary. Welton's robot, Ariel, stood behind her mistress, fading into the background as far as Kresh was concerned. Robots didn't count.

"All right, then," he said. "What's all this about? Why did the Governor call you in? What possible connection does this case have with the Settlers?"

Tonya Welton folded her hands carefully and looked Kresh straight in the eye. "In a day or two you'll get the answer to that. But for now, it's classified."

"I see," Kresh said, though he most certainly did not. "I'm afraid that is not much of an explanation."

"No, and I am sorry for that, but my hands are tied. There is, however, one thing I *can* tell you that will at least in part explain my being here. I do have authority to be here, under the agreement permitting a Settler presence on this world. I have the right to protect the safety of my employees."

"I beg your pardon?"

"Oh, yes, didn't you know?" Tonya Welton asked. "Fredda Leving is working for me."

There was a half minute's dead silence. Fredda Leving was famous, one of the top roboticists on the planet. Most Infernals regarded her not as a person, but as a planetary asset. For her and her labs to be reduced to mere employees of the Settlers—Welton might as well have announced that the Settlers had purchased Government Tower, or gotten title to the Great Bay.

At last Alvar found his voice again. "If I could make a suggestion, Madame Welton, I think it might be wise to keep that fact very quiet indeed," he said gruffly.

Welton looked surprised. "Why? We haven't publicized it widely, but we haven't tried to keep it secret."

"Then I suggest you start," Alvar said.

"I'm afraid I don't understand," Welton said.

"Then let me make this clear, Madame Welton. The average citizen of Inferno will not regard this attack as a mere assault, or as attempted murder. The citizens will see an attack on a top scientist, especially a roboticist, as sabotage. Many of them will simply assume your people did it, even without knowledge of Settler involvement in Leving Labs. Once they hear Settlers are involved, that will only make it worse."

"Our involvement!" Tonya Welton exclaimed. "We had nothing to do with the attack!"

"That's as may be," Alvar said. Clearly Welton was upset, and he wanted her that way, wanted her off balance. What was she doing here, anyway? How had she gotten here so quickly? There was something damned suspicious in her haste and eagerness. Just what the hell kind of robotics work would the Settlers be interested in, anyway? There was more than one mystery in the air tonight.

Donald slipped back into the aircar and took a place standing against the wall, next to Ariel. Kresh glanced at him and nodded. There was something comforting in having his loyal servant present. But Donald was not the issue here. Kresh took a good hard look at Welton, trying to gauge her mood. If he was any judge of such matters, there was an underlayer of uncertainty below all her brave talk. "You deny involvement," he said, "but just now you spoke of Fredda Leving working for you. *That* is involvement enough. That alone will be seen as a threat by most of the people on this world."

"What in deep space are you talking about?" Welton demanded.

"My fellow Infernals will see interference in robot research as an attack on the Spacers' hopes of survival in a universe that seems to be surrendering itself to the Settlers. Given the slightest hint of any connection between the Settlers and the attack, however slender and tenuous, the people of this world will assume your people were behind it. They won't care if it is true or not. They will *believe.*

"They will associate this attack with the Settlers—the same damn Settlers they see wandering free all over Inferno, poking their noses into everything, treating the people of Inferno as little better than savages. It will be enough to make the situation even more tense than it is already. The people of Inferno are sure you Settlers regard us all as amusing little natives to be brushed aside on your way to conquering the galaxy."

Tonya colored a bit, and she folded her arms in front of her. "Politics. Always it comes down to politics and prejudice. My dear Sheriff. It is not we Settlers who are holding you Spacers back. You are doing it to yourselves, with no need of help from us. You have had endless generations in which to colonize new worlds of your own. You could have peopled thousands of worlds by now. Instead you have but fifty worlds—forty-nine after this Solaria business.

"*We* did not stop you from going on to further colonization. *You* chose not to continue. Nor are we preventing you from starting a new effort at colonization now. But instead of taking action, you choose to remain at home and blame *us* for moving outward. Is it *our* fault that you have made your refusal to settle new worlds a mark of virtue?"

"Madame Welton. You must excuse me," Kresh said. "I allowed my own emotions to get the better of me. I did not intend to accuse you, but you are entitled to fair warning of what the people of Inferno will think if your—ah—involvement becomes known. I don't hold such views myself, though I must admit some sympathy for them. But if a Settler relationship with Fredda Leving comes out in connection with this crime, or in any way at all, it is my considered professional opinion that there will be hell to pay."

Tonya Welton stared at him, unblinking, her face unreadable.

At last she spoke. "Then I think you can look forward to having to pay that hell in about two days' time," she said, rather soberly.

"What happens then?" he asked, his voice flat, his face deadpan.

"There will be an—announcement," she said, clearly being careful of what words she used. "I am not at liberty to say more, but if there are to be the sort of difficulties you are talking about, they will happen then."

"Beg pardon, Madame Welton, but do you think it possible that tonight's attack has some connection to that announcement?" Donald asked. "Perhaps an attempt to stop or delay it?"

Welton turned her head sharply toward Donald, her expression suddenly wild and uncontrolled. Obviously, she had not noticed him coming in. "Yes," she said, a bit too eagerly. "Yes, I believe that is a real possibility. If it is true, then I believe we are all in terrible danger."

"What the devil are you—" Kresh began.

"No," Welton said, turning back toward Kresh. "I can say no more. But *solve this case quickly,* Sheriff. If there is anything in this life, this world, that you value, *solve it!*" She took a deep breath and seemed to come back to herself a bit. "It was a mistake for me to come here tonight," she announced. She turned and looked about the aircar's cabin, as if seeing it for the first time. "I will contact you tomorrow, Sheriff," she said. "And I will expect full and complete reports of your progress on a regular basis. Come, Ariel."

And without another word, she stepped out of the car, her robot following. Alvar Kresh watched them go, wondering just what exactly Tonya Welton was up to. Her performance tonight was odd, to put it mildly. Putting aside the fact of her magically appearing almost before Kresh got to the crime scene, there was something else: the way she had latched on to the possibility of a political motive. It almost made Kresh think she wanted to draw attention toward that idea and away from something else. But what the hell could that something else be?

All he knew for sure was that whatever was going on, he was already stuck, deep inside it.

3

CALIBAN walked the night, burning with curiosity. He was a great distance from his starting point, in a quiet residential area, the walkways all but completely deserted at this hour. The homes were large and widely scattered. Great lawns, some of them getting a bit dry, scruffy, and thin-looking, separated the houses. In this part of town, it seemed there was little ground traffic to speak of. Judging from the absence of a road wide enough for large vehicles, travel to and fro was by aircar or by foot.

But a dying lawn was no less wondrous than a live one to Caliban. All the world was new to him, everything that he saw was a fresh and vibrant wonder. He saw the bright pinpoints of light in the sky and wondered what they were. He noticed a few bits of litter blown against a fence and wondered how such a strange combination of objects had come to be there. His datastore was mute on both of those subjects, and many others besides, but on the whole it was a splendid guide, telling him any number of things about the city through which he walked. He wandered everywhere, eagerly looking about at everything, marveling at all things. And if stars and litter were not explained, many other things were. More often than not, he could look at a thing, and wonder about it, and find that the datastore could identify it and explain it for him.

He was content for some time to wander the city, passively absorbing whatever the datastore saw fit to tell him about what he saw. Then Caliban had an idea. If the map and the datastore could work to tell him about what was before him, could they not also guide his steps? Perhaps he could examine the datastore's map, select an interesting destination, and travel to it.

He stopped in his tracks and tried the experiment. The outside world seemed to fade from his sight. Suddenly he was looking down on a map-schematic of the area he was in, done in bold primary colors and carefully designed symbols.

He tried to push outward from that point and was greatly pleased to discover that the simple act of wishing it to be so allowed him to visualize the entire city map, or focus in on any portion of it. Nor, he found, did his virtual viewpoint have to stay *above* the map. He could move down to ground level and see the buildings and hill tower over him. He could visualize the map data from any angle or position.

A few moments of experimentation confirmed it: He could manipulate his viewpoint to any spot in or over the map, look at the lay of the land from a bird's-eye view, or from ground level at any position, with the buildings and streets presented in the proper shapes and sizes. His vision swept along great swatches of the city, across the parks, the buildings, the great roads. It was as if he were traveling through those places in his mind. The sensation was exhilarating, almost one of flight.

There were datatags on the map, offering information on the buildings—their names and addresses, and in many cases the names of whatever businesses went on there.

Suddenly he got a splendid idea. He could use the datatag information to learn more about himself. He manipulated his viewpoint within the map and brought it back to his present position. Then he proceeded to retrace his steps back to the building he had started out from. He could read the datatags connected to the building and learn what sort of place it was, see what other information the map held concerning it. Certainly he could find clues to his own identity, his place in the world. Eager to find out more about himself, he moved his viewpoint rapidly across the map, back the way he had come.

The map imagery rushed past him at a breakneck pace, twisting and turning violently, reversing his movements at tremendous speed. At last the images came back to his starting place. He made a strange discovery: The image of the building was incomplete. Nearly every other building was shown in great detail, with doors and windows and basic elements of the architecture clearly shown. But the map showed this building as nothing but a featureless grey rectangular solid, a low, long shape on the land.

Confused, Caliban accessed the datatag system.

And discovered that the map had no information whatsoever about the building inside which he had awakened.

Stunned, surprised, Caliban shut down the map display system. The bright colors and symbols of the map faded from his vision, and he found himself once again standing in the darkness, alone on an empty pathway in a quiet residential district.

Why was there no information about that building? Perhaps he should go back there, examine the place firsthand. He of course had a perfect, detailed memory of what he had seen there, and no doubt he could work his way back through those memories for information. But he had not been looking for anything when he awakened, had not even been fully aware that he should have known more than he did. If he went back, he would learn more.

He turned around, was about to head back the way he had come, toward the lab. But then he stopped. Wait a moment. There was another factor. One he had not considered yet. He recalled that first moment of awakening, the sight of the woman unconscious at his feet, the blood pooling about her head. The cross-index system of his datastore flitted through a whole series of things even as he thought about that moment.

And it settled at a quotation from the Legal Code that leaving the scene of a crime before being interviewed by the police was itself a crime. His mind flittered through all the datastore had to say about the Legal Code, the concept of crime, and the idea of punishment and rehabilitation. All of it seemed to relate to humans, but it was not a great leap of reasoning to assume that committing a criminal act could mean trouble for a robot as well.

No, he could not go back there.

Wait a moment. Were there other blanks on the map? Other places where detail was limited in some way? Perhaps other places with limited information on the datastore would have something in common with the building he had left. Perhaps examining one of *them* would offer some clue; perhaps some thought or image would stimulate the datastore to offer some sort of information that could tell him about himself.

Caliban looked about the area and decided it would be best to get off the pathway while he was examining the map. He stepped off the path and walked a short way, until he found a slight depression in the rolling landscape. He sat down in it, reasonably sure he could not be seen from the path.

He returned his attention to the datastore map. At first, his mind cast back and forth across the map in random, swooping passes, trying to cover as much ground as quickly as possible while still keeping track of any building or place that seemed suspiciously blank. Then he resolved to quarter the whole city and go block by block, in an orderly manner. Perhaps there was something he could learn from the pattern of blanked places, something he could discern only when he had located them all.

The map of the city had definite edges to it, precise boundaries beyond which was nothingness. Caliban's knowledge of the world, the universe, stopped at those borders. For a moment, Caliban toyed with the idea of venturing to the closest of those boundaries, just to see what it was like. He imagined himself standing on the edge of the world, looking down into nothingness. The idea was exciting and disturbing.

But no. It would not do to get sidetracked. First he must get answers about himself and about what had happened at the building where he had awakened. After those two mysteries were resolved, he could take the time to indulge his idle curiosity.

He set to work at the southern edge of the map and began to work across it methodically, examining a strip from east to west, then moving northward to examine the next strip, west to east.

And then he found it. Not far from the southern edge of the map was a great void, an emptiness a thousand times, ten thousand times larger than the blank, unmarked building in which he had awakened. But this was no area without detailed markings. This was emptiness, the absence of all things. No land, no water, no buildings, no roads. There was nothing there at all.

He wondered if the map was reporting literal truth. What could such a void look like in real life? What would cause it? His curiosity, his eagerness to see this place, was all but uncontrollable. But he held firm to his plan. He must examine the whole city, absorb the whole of the datastore map into his active memory. There could be other voids as well, equally significant. He held to his search pattern, moving south to north, shuttling east to west, west to east.

It took the better part of an hour, but at last Caliban had worked his way across the whole of the map of Hades. Yes, there were other voids, but none of them were even a fraction as large as the first he had found. Yes, there were other unmarked, unlabeled buildings, but he could not see any obvious pattern, no relation to the features on the rest of the map, that told him anything meaningful, or anything at all.

There was nothing left for it but to go and look. Now there was no reason to resist the temptation to see what the great void looked like. Caliban stood up and walked back to the field, using his infrared vision to move easily through the darkness.

The site of the void was a good distance across the city, and the first hints of dawn were lighting the east as he traveled through the semi-arid, half-populated expanses of Hades, imagining what a great emptiness would look like.

But what he saw when he got there was no blank on the map. As the dawn broke full over the horizon, Caliban stood at the edge of where the map said there was only emptiness.

What Caliban saw was a lively oasis in the midst of the fading city. He stood at the edge of a broad and verdant park, dotted stands of trees, great lawns, spraying fountains.

Small pavilions dotted the landscape and seemed to give access to underground facilities, judging by the people going in and out. Caliban walked along the low stone wall that formed the perimeter of the park, until he came to the entrance.

Settlertown, a sign said. Caliban stared at it in confusion. Another mystery. He had no idea what Settlers were, or why they should have their own town. He called to the datastore, but it had no information on any such term.

For some reason, all information regarding both his origin point and this place had been deleted from his datastore.

But why would anyone do that?

DARKNESS had passed, and dawn had come over the horizon, and the morning was well begun. Alvar Kresh paced the room, listening to the routine words of the routine interrogation of yet another routine coworker, one Jomaine Terach. Terach wasn't normally up and at the lab by this hour, but he lived quite near the lab and all the commotion had wakened him. He had wandered over to see what was going on—or so he claimed. Police officers throughout history had been a little slow to believe witnesses who explained trifles such as coming to work with such elaboration—and Kresh was tempted to uphold that tradition in the present instance. It would be wise to treat everyone as a suspect just at the moment.

Kresh let Donald do most of the work. This night had been a long, hard journey through the darkness to the day. Crime scenes could be grueling.

They had taken over the duty office for the purpose of doing the intake interrogations, taking each worker as he or she arrived. The duty office was designed to accommodate an overnight stay, in case an experiment ran all night. The office featured a large and rather comfortable-looking bed, much better than the miserable cot in the duty room at Sheriff's HQ. After a sleepless night, it looked more than slightly inviting.

"Tonya Welton claims that Fredda Leving was—*is*—working for her. Is that true?" Donald asked.

"Absolutely not," Jomaine Terach said, yawning mightily. "Fredda Leving has never worked for anyone but herself in her life, and she isn't likely to start in by oiling up to the high and mighty Queen of the Settlers." He yawned again. "My God, it's early. Have you been at it since the attack?"

"Yes, sir. We have been here working straight through the night," Donald said.

"So she and Tonya Welton don't get along," Kresh said, brushing aside Terach's and Donald's pleasantries. He sat back down at the table, next to Donald and opposite Terach. He drummed his fingers on the desktop, trying to keep his exhausted mind from wandering. Maybe he should have gone home instead of staying here all night.

Now, where was he? Damn it, his mind was wandering. He was getting fuzzy. He wasn't going to learn much of anything if he was too exhausted to think. "So they didn't like each other," he said again, trying to cover up his overlong pause. "Were they at least polite around each other?"

"No, sir, not in the least," Jomaine said. "Not anymore. They used to be much closer, real friends, I thought. Now there isn't much left but the professional relationship."

That was an interesting tidbit. Tonya Welton and Fredda Leving, each with a real reputation for being a hard-edged infighter. He could easily imagine them coming to a parting of the ways. It was far harder to imagine them becoming friends in the first place.

But being personally involved with the victim made it just that much more peculiar that Welton would barge into the investigation. She must have known that Kresh would quickly learn about the friction between herself and the victim. It was very early in the going, but right now, she was the one with the best motive for the attack. Why draw attention to herself?

Alvar Kresh leaned back in his chair and looked across the desk at the man he was interviewing. Jomaine Terach was a tall, thin man, sandy-haired, pale, with a long, thin face and a sharp-pointed nose. There was something a bit overrefined, overformal, about his manner of speech.

Kresh repressed a yawn. It hardly seemed worth staying up all night just to listen to the likes of Terach.

Alvar rubbed his eyes and brought his mind back to where he was in the questioning."I find it hard to imagine the two of them as friends. Settlers hate robots, and Leving was one of the leading proponents of more and better robots. I can't see how much they would have in common," Kresh said.

"I think perhaps that was part of what made the friendship work—at least for a while. They enjoyed debating each other. But then things fell apart between them. Maybe it just got a little too intense," Terach suggested.

"But if she wasn't Tonya Welton's employee, Master Terach, and they were no longer friends," Donald 111 said, "might one ask what their relationship was?"

Terach glared at Donald. It clearly annoyed him to be questioned by a robot. But he was smart enough not to protest out loud.

Kresh watched Terach with a detached, professional interest. He often ordered Donald to take an active part in the questioning. It was a variation on the ancient good-cop, bad-cop routine. Donald unsettled the interrogation subjects, and then the subjects answered Kresh, looking to him for support and understanding, unwisely trusting him over Donald.

"They were collaborators, I suppose." Terach turned toward Kresh. "There's a lot I can't say about the work at the lab," he apologized.

"I've heard that more than once," Kresh growled. "Every employee I've talked to has told me that. Those seem to be the only words most of your people know."

"I'm sorry about that."

"Don't be. We'll be back once I've gotten the Governor to grant me some clearances."

That prospect didn't seem to please the rather reedy-looking Jomaine Terach. "Well, perhaps you needn't bother, once the public announcement is made."

"And I've heard *that,* too, and I know bloody damn well you're about to tell me you can't say anything more," Kresh said. "So let's talk about something else. Tell me why Fredda Leving would be in Gubber Anshaw's lab in the middle of the night."

Terach seemed genuinely astonished. "Oh, my heavens, I wouldn't attach any great importance to *that,*" he said. "We're in and out of each other's labs all the time. The work is of a highly—ah—collaborative nature, and I expect that she was simply working on some subcomponent that happened to be in his lab."

"Infernals tend to be rather territorial people," Kresh suggested. "We like to have our own space."

Terach shrugged. "That may be so, but that doesn't mean *everyone* is compulsive about it," he said, a bit pointedly.

"Mmmph," Kresh grunted, not altogether convinced, and ignoring the gibe that was clearly intended to distract him. "Well, then, maybe you can tell me where the devil Gubber Anshaw *is.* He hasn't shown up this morning and we have not been able to reach him at home. We assume he's there, but his robots flatly refuse to confirm that, or to pass on any messages."

"I'm not surprised," Jomaine said. "Gubber likes to work at home, in complete privacy. He's taken to doing it more and more recently. Sometimes we kid him that if you police threw an arrest perimeter around his house, he wouldn't even notice."

Kresh grunted noncommittally. Privacy, and the sanctity of the home, were indeed highly valued commodities on Inferno. Indeed, it was illegal to arrest a person in his or her home. The law was very precise on that point, and on the procedures that could and could not be followed. The police and their robots could wait outside until hell froze over, they could search the premises once an arrest was made, but they could not enter the home to effect the arrest.

It had happened more than once that a suspect had refused to come out for a long period of time. Precedents and rules of procedure had long ago been established in such cases, setting out what could and could not be done. The police could cut off all communications links to the surrounded house, but not food, or water, or power. Sometimes the prohibition against home arrests actually worked to police advantage: If kept up long enough, the police-robot vigil outside a suspect's home amounted to house arrest without all the bother and expense of a trial.

"Well, it might come to an arrest perimeter if we don't hear from him soon," Kresh said warningly. "You might get that information to him."

Jomaine cocked a surprised eyebrow at Kresh. "Have a little patience, Sheriff. Gubber rarely comes in much before midday on the days he does come in," he said. "He spends his mornings at his home, working on other research projects. Most days—but not all of them—he comes in here and works on Leving Lab projects about midday and through the evening. But as I said, he doesn't always come in. He's not held to any sort of schedule."

Jomaine thought for a moment. "Come to think of it, I don't recall seeing him when I came through here last night. I doubt he was here. My guess is he's been at home, working, the entire time, quite unaware that anything has happened. And yes, his robots have strict orders to prevent his being disturbed. But that is routine with him. I wouldn't suggest that you read anything into his absence, or waste any time thinking *he* had something to do with the attack on Fredda."

Alvar Kresh frowned. "Why not? It was his lab she was attacked in. At this point we have no suspects, no motive, no real information at all. I don't know Gubber Anshaw or anything about him. I see no reason to eliminate anyone at this point, especially someone who would seem to have the opportunity to commit the crime. Coworkers *have* been known to have motives for murder."

"Well, there's your argument against suspecting him right there," Jomaine said, a bit overeagerly. "Gubber Anshaw had no motive for attacking Fredda, and every reason for wishing her well. I suppose, yes, he *might* have had the means and the opportunity to assault her—but Sheriff Kresh, you have the means and the opportunity to pull your blaster from your holster right now and vaporize my head. That doesn't mean you *will* do it. You have no motives for killing me—and a lot of motives for *not* hurting me. You'd lose your job and get thrown in jail, at the very least. But it goes past that. Fredda was a great help to Gubber. He would most definitely not want to lose that."

"You are suggesting that Gubber Anshaw would have a great deal to lose if something happened to Fredda Leving?" Donald asked.

Jomaine Terach looked cautiously at Donald, and then at Kresh. "Once again, that gets us into classified areas. But yes, I think that would be safe to say. Gubber had made some remarkable advances, advances that required the rejection of some very tried and true technology in favor of something newer and better and more flexible. However, he didn't get far in promoting his discoveries. Robotics is in many ways a very conservative field. Leving Labs was the only place that was willing to use his work."

"I suppose we're talking about gravitonic brains here," Kresh said.

Terach breathed in sharply, clearly surprised and unsettled. "How did you—"

"There was a stack of them in neatly labeled boxes in Anshaw's lab," Kresh said, more than a bit sardonically. "I think perhaps you need to work a little on security procedures down at the lab."

"Apparently so," Terach said, clearly nonplussed.

"So what the devil are gravitonic brains? Some sort of replacement for the positronic brain?"

Donald turned his head toward Kresh. "Sir! That would be quite impossible. The positronic brain is the basis, the core, of all robotics. The Three Laws are intrinsic to it, built into its very structure, burned into its fundamental pathways."

"Take it easy, Donald," Kresh said. "That doesn't mean that the Three Laws couldn't be built into another form of brain. Right, Terach?"

Terach blinked and nodded, still a bit distracted. "Of course, of course. I really cannot say anything specific about gravitonic brains, but I suppose it can't do any harm to speak in broad generalities. Gubber Anshaw is really just at the beginning of his research on gravitonics, but in my opinion he's already made tremendous breakthroughs. It's time someone did."

"How do you mean?"

"I mean that we have rung out the changes on positronics. Certainly today's positronic brain is far superior to the original units. It has been greatly advanced and improved. There have been many refinements in it. But the positronic brain's basic design hasn't changed in thousands of years. It would be as if we were still using chemical rockets for spacecraft, instead of hyperdrive. The positronic brain is an incredibly conservative design that puts tremendous and needless limits on what robots can do. Because the Three Laws are embedded in its design, the positronic brain is seen as the only possible design for use in robots. That is an article of belief, of faith, even among robotics researchers. But gravitonics could change all that.

"Gravitonic brains currently have one or two minor drawbacks, but they are at the beginning of their development. They promise tremendous advantages over positronics, in terms of flexibility and capacity."

"Well, you certainly sound like a true believer yourself," Kresh said dryly. *There is none so faithful as the converted,* he thought. "Very well, Terach. I may well wish to talk with you later, but that will do it for now. You may go."

Jomaine nodded and stood up. He hesitated before heading for the door. "Ah, one question," he said. "What is the prognosis for Fredda Leving?"

Kresh's face hardened. "She's still unconscious," he said, "but they expect her to awaken sometime in the next day or so, and go on to a rapid and complete recovery. They are using the most advanced regeneration techniques to stimulate recovery. I understand her head injury should be completely healed within two days."

Jomaine Terach smiled and nodded. "That's excellent news," he said. "The staff here will be delighted to hear it—ah, that is, if I'm allowed to tell them."

Kresh waved his hand in negligent dismissal. "Go right ahead, Terach. It's public knowledge—and she's under heavy guard."

Terach pasted on a patently false smile, nodded nervously, and left the room.

Kresh watched him go. "What's your reading, Donald?" he asked, without looking over at the robot. No one talked about it much, but advanced police robots were specially engineered to detect the body's involuntary responses to questions. In effect, Donald was a highly sophisticated lie detector.

"I should remind you that Jomaine Terach quite possibly knows about my capabilities as a truth-sensor. I have never met him before, but a records-check confirms that he was on staff here during my construction. That does add a variable. However, suffice to say that he was highly agitated, sir. Far more so than any of the others, and, in my opinion, more so than would be accounted for solely by surprise and concern over the attack on Lady Leving. Voice stress and other indicators confirm that he was concealing something."

That didn't surprise Alvar. All witnesses concealed things. "Was he lying?" he asked. "Lying directly?"

"No, sir. But he was most concerned to learn we knew about the gravitonic brains. I found this confusing, as he went to some length to discuss them. I formed the impression that he was intent on steering the interrogation away from some other point."

"You caught that, too, I see. The damnable thing is that I can't imagine what point he was trying to lead us away from. My hunch is he thinks we know more than we do."

"That is my opinion as well."

Alvar Kresh drummed his fingers on the table and stared at the door Jomaine Terach had used to leave the room.

There was more going on here than the attack on Leving. Something else was up. Something that involved the Governor, and Leving, and Welton, and the Settler-Spacer relationship on Inferno.

Indeed, the attack was already beginning to recede in importance in his mind. That was merely the loose thread he was tugging on. He knew that if he left it alone, the rest of it would never be revealed. Pull it too hard, and it would snap, break its connections to the rest of the mystery. But play the investigation of the attack carefully, tug the thread gently, and maybe he could use it to unravel the whole tangled problem.

Alvar Kresh was determined to find out all he could.

Because something *big* was going on.

JOMAINE Terach left the interview room. His personal robot, Bertran, was waiting outside in the hall and dutifully followed him as Jomaine hurried back to his own laboratory.

Sheriff Kresh had made Bertran wait outside the room during the interrogation. *It was just a little harassment,* Jomaine told himself, *another way for Kresh to get and keep me unnerved. And yes,* he admitted to himself, *it had worked.* Spacers in general, and Infernals particularly, did not like to be without their robots.

Only after he was in his own lab, only after Bertran had followed him in and shut the door safely behind him, did Jomaine allow himself to succumb to the fears he was feeling. He crossed the room hurriedly. He dropped back into his favorite old armchair and breathed a sigh of relief.

"Sir, are you all right?" Bertran asked. "I fear the bad news about Lady Leving and the police interview have greatly distressed you."

Jomaine Terach nodded tiredly. "That they have, Bertran. That they have. But I'll be fine in just a moment. I just need to think for a bit. Why don't you bring me some water and then retire to your niche for a while?"

"Very good, sir." The robot stepped to the lab sink, filled a glass, and brought it back. Jomaine watched as Bertran went over to his wall niche and dropped back into standby mode.

That was the way it was supposed to be. A robot did what you told it to do and then got out of the way. That was how it had been for thousands of years. Did they really dare try and change that? Did Fredda Leving truly think she could overturn everything that completely?

And did she truly have to make a deal with the devil, with Tonya Welton, in order to make it happen?

Well, at any rate, he had managed to steer things away from any discussion of the Three Laws. If he had been forced to sacrifice a few tidbits about gravitonics in order to accomplish that, so be it. It would all be public in a day or so, anyway.

They were safe for the moment. But still, the project was madness. Caliban was madness. Building him had been a violation of the most basic Spacer law and philosophy, but Fredda Leving had gone ahead, anyway. Typical bullheadedness.

Never mind theory and philosophy, she had said. They were an experimental lab, not a theory shop that never acted on its ideas. It was time to take the next step, she said. It was time to build a gravitonic robot with no limits on its mind whatsoever. A blank slate, that's what she had called Caliban. An experimental robot, to be kept inside the lab at all times, never to leave. A robot with no knowledge of other robots, or the Settlers, or anything beyond human behavior and a carefully edited source of knowledge about the outside world. Then let it live at the lab, under controlled conditions, and see what happens. See what rules it developed for its own behavior.

Did she truly have to build Caliban?

No, ask the question directly, he told himself. *We've all hedged around it long enough.* And yes, that was the deadly secret question. No one else knew. With Caliban broken free of the lab, with Fredda unconscious, there was no one else in the wide world who could ask the question.

So Jomaine asked it of himself.

Did she really have to build a robot that did not have the Three Laws?

4

SIMCOR Beddle lifted his left hand, tilted his index finger just so, and Sanlacor 123 pulled back his chair with perfect timing, getting it out from behind him just as Simcor was getting up, so that the chair never came in contact with Simcor's body as he rose.

There was quite a fashion for using detailed hand signals to command robots, and Simcor was a skilled practitioner of the art.

Simcor turned and walked away from the breakfast table, toward the closed door to the main gallery, Sanlacor hard on his heels. The door swung open just as he arrived at it. The Daabor unit on the other side of the door had no other job in the world but to open it. The machine marked out its existence by standing there, watching for anyone who might approach from its side of the door, and listening for footsteps from inside the room.

But Simcor Beddle, leader of the Ironheads, had no time to think about how menial robots spent their days. He was a busy man.

He had a riot to plan.

Simcor Beddle was a small, rotund man, with a round sallow face and hard, gimlet eyes of indeterminate color. His hair was glossy black, and just barely long enough to lie flat. He was heavy-set, there was no doubt about that. But there was nothing soft about him. He was a hard, determined man, dressed in a rather severe military-style uniform.

Managing his forces, that was the main thing. Keeping them from getting out of control was always a problem. His Ironheads were a highly effective team of rowdies, but they were rowdies all the same—and as such, they easily grew restive and bored. It was necessary to keep them busy, active, if he were to keep them under any sort of control at all.

No one quite knew where the Ironheads had gotten their name, but no one could deny it was appropriate. They were stubborn, pugnacious, bashing whatever was in their way whenever they saw fit. Maybe it was that stubbornness that earned them their name. More likely, though, it was their fanatical defense of the *real* Ironheads—robots. Well, granted, no one used anything as crude as raw iron to make robot bodies, but robots were as hard, as strong, as powerful, as iron.

Not that the Ironheads held robots *themselves* in any special esteem. If anything, Ironheads were harder on their robots than the average Infernal. But that was not the point. Robots gave humans such freedom, such power, such comfort. *Those* things were the birthright of every Infernal, indeed of all Spacers, and the Ironhead movement was determined to preserve and expand that birthright by any means necessary.

And making life unpleasant for the Settlers certainly fit into that category.

Simcor smiled to himself. That was getting to be a bad habit, thinking in speeches like that. He crossed to the far side of the gallery, toward his office, and another door robot swung the door wide as he approached. He entered the room, quite unaware of Sanlacor moving ahead of him to pull out his chair from his desk for him.

But he did not sit down. Instead, he made a subtle gesture with his right hand. The room robot, Brenabar, was at his side instantly, bringing Simcor's tea. He took the cup and saucer and sipped thoughtfully for a moment. He nodded his head a precise five degrees down toward the desktop, and spoke one word. "Settlertown."

Sanlacor, anticipating his master, was already at the view controls, and in less than a second, the bare desktop was transformed into a detailed map of Settlertown. Simcor handed his teacup to the empty air without looking, and Brenabar took it from him smoothly.

Kresh's deputies were sure to be ready for them, after last night. Simcor had superb connections inside the Sheriff's Department, and he knew everything Kresh knew about the attack on Fredda Leving. In fact, he knew quite a bit more. He had heard a recording of that lecture of hers. Damnable, treasonous stuff. Simcor smiled. Not that she was likely to make any more such speeches. Everything was working his way.

But he had to concentrate on the plans for today. He had to assume the Sheriff's Department was ready for trouble. Once the Ironheads started the ruckus, they would only have a few minutes before the law stepped in to protect the damned Settlers.

So they would have to do as much damage as possible in those first few minutes. Under the circumstances, it was too much to hope they would be able to penetrate the underground section of Settlertown again. No sense wasting effort in the attempt. This time, it would have to be on the surface, at ground level. Simcor Beddle lay his hands on the desktop and stared thoughtfully at the map of his enemy's stronghold.

IT was morning in the city of Hades. Caliban knew that much for certain, if very little else of any substance. By now he was no longer sure what he knew.

But he was beginning to believe something was wrong. Something was terribly wrong.

It was as if Caliban's utterly blank memory and the precise but limited information in the datastore were the double lenses of a distorted telescope, utter ignorance and expert knowledge combining to twist and warp all he saw. The world his eyes and mind presented to him was a crazed and frightening patchwork.

In the busiest part of the city's midtown, he turned off the sidewalk and found a bench set in a quiet corner of a tiny park, well out of sight from any casual passersby. He sat down and began reviewing all that he had seen as he had walked the streets of Hades.

There was something distinctly unreal, and somewhat alarming, about the world around him. He had come to realize just how clean, perfect, idealized, precise were the facts and figures, maps, diagrams, and images that leapt up from the datastore. But the real-world objects that corresponded to the datastore's concepts were far less precise.

Further exploration confirmed that false voids and featureless buildings were not the only flaws in the datastore map.

The map likewise did not report which blocks were busy, full of people and robots, and which were empty, semi-abandoned, even starting to decay.

Some new buildings had materialized since the map was stored in his datastore, and other, older buildings that seemed whole and complete in the datastore had vanished from reality.

No image in the datastore showed anything to be worn-out or dirty, but the real world was full of dust and dirt, no matter how vigorously the maintenance robots worked to keep it all clean.

Caliban found the differences between idealized definitions and real-world imperfections deeply disturbing. The world he could see and touch seemed, somehow, less real than the idealized, hygienic facts and images stored deep inside his brain.

But it was more than buildings and the map, or even the datastore, that confused him.

It was human behavior he found most bewildering. When Caliban first approached a busy intersection, the datastore showed him a diagram of the correct procedure for crossing a street safely. But human pedestrians seemed to ignore all such rules, and common sense, for that matter. They walked wherever they pleased, leaving to the robots driving the groundcars to get out of the way.

Something else about the datastore was strange, even disturbing: There was a flavor of something close to *emotion* about much of its data. It was as if the opinions, the feelings, of whoever implanted the information into the datastore had been stored there as well.

He was growing to understand the datastore on something deeper than an intellectual level. He was learning the *feel* of it, gaining a sense of how it worked, developing reflexes to help him use it in a more controlled and useful manner, keep it from spewing out knowledge he did not need. Humans had to learn to walk: That was one of many strange and needless facts the datastore had provided. Caliban was coming to realize that he had to learn how to know, and remember.

Confusion, muddle, dirt, inaccurate and useless information—those he could perhaps learn to accept. But it was far more troubling that, on many subjects, the datastore was utterly—and deliberately—silent. Information he most urgently wanted was not only missing but *excised,* purposely removed. There was a distinct sensation of emptiness, of loss, that came to him when he reached for data that should have been there and it was not. There were carved-out voids inside the datastore.

There was much he desperately wanted to know, but there was one thing in particular, one thing that the store did not tell him, one thing that he most wanted to know: *Why didn't it tell him more?* He knew it should have been able to do so. Why was all information on that place where the sign said Settlertown deleted from the map? Why had all meaningful references to robots been deleted? There was the greatest mystery. He was one, and yet he scarcely knew what one was. Why was the datastore silent on that of all subjects?

Humans he knew about. At his first sight of that woman he saw when he awoke, he had immediately known what a human was, the basics of their biology and culture. Later, when he glanced at an old man, or one of the rare children walking the street, he knew all basic generalities concerning those classes of person—their likely range of temperament, how it was best to address them, what they were and were not likely to do. A child might run and laugh, and adult was likely to walk more sedately, an elder might choose to move more slowly still.

But when he looked at another robot, one of his fellow beings, his datastore literally drew a blank. There was simply no information in his mind.

All he knew about robots came from his own observation. Yet his observations had afforded him little more than confusion.

The robots he saw—and he himself—appeared to be a cross between human and machine. That left any number of questions unclear. Were robots born and raised like humans? Were they instead manufactured, like all the other machines that received detailed discussion in the datastore? What was the place of the robot in the world? He knew the rights and privileges of humans—except as they pertained to robots—but he knew nothing at all of how robots fit in.

Yes, he could see what went on around him. But what he saw when he looked was disturbing, and baffling. Robots were everywhere—and everywhere, in every way, robots were subservient. They fetched and they carried, they walked behind the humans. They carried the humans' loads, opened their doors, drove their cars. It was patently clear from every scrap of human and robot behavior that this was the accepted order of things. No one questioned it.

Except himself, of course.

Who was he? What was he? What was he doing here? What did it all mean?

He stood up and started walking again, not with any real aim in mind, but more because he could not bear to sit idle any longer. The need to *know,* to understand who and what he was, was getting stronger all the time. There was always the chance that the answer, the solution, was just around the corner, waiting to be discovered.

He left the park and turned left, heading down the broad walkways of downtown.

HOURS went by, and still Caliban walked the streets, still deeply confused, uncertain what he was searching for. Anything could contain the clue, the answer, the explanation. A word from a passing human, a sign on a wall, the design of a building, might just stimulate his datastore to provide him with the answers he needed.

He stopped at a corner and looked across the street to the building opposite. Well, the sight of this particular building did not cause any torrent of facts to burst forth, but it was a strange-looking thing nonetheless, even considering the jarringly different architectural styles he had seen in the city. It was a muddle of domes, columns, arches, and cubes. Caliban could fathom no purpose whatsoever in it all.

"Out of my way, robot," an imperious voice called out behind him. Caliban, lost in his consideration of things architectural, did not really register the voice. Suddenly a walking stick whacked down on his left shoulder.

Caliban spun around in astonishment to confront his attacker.

Incredible. Simply incredible. It was a tiny woman, slender, thin-boned, easily a full meter shorter than Caliban, clearly weaker and far more frail than he was. And yet she had deliberately and fearlessly ordered him about, instead of merely stepping around him, and then struck at him—using a weapon that could not possibly harm him. Why did she not fear him? Why did she have such obvious confidence that he would not respond by attacking *her,* when he could clearly do so quite effectively?

He stared at the woman for an infinite moment, too baffled to know what to do.

"Out of my way, robot! Are your ears shorting out?"

Caliban noticed a crowd of people and robots starting to form around him, one or two of the humans already betraying expressions of curiosity. It would clearly be less than prudent to remain here, or attempt to respond when he so clearly did not understand.

He stepped aside for the lady and then picked a direction, any direction but the one she had taken, and started walking again. Enough of aimless wandering. He needed a plan. He needed knowledge.

And he needed safety. Clearly he did not know how to act like a robot. And the expressions, some of them hostile, he had seen on the faces of the passersby told him it was dangerous to be peculiar in any way.

No. He had to lie low, stay in the background. Safer to blend in, to pretend to be like the others.

Very well, then. He *would* blend in. He would observe the behavior he saw around himself, work determinedly to get lost among the endless sea of robots around him.

KRESH walked the streets of Hades at the same hour, though with more certain purpose. He found that it helped to clear his head and refocus his attention if he got away from his office, got away from the interrogation rooms and evidence labs, and stretched his legs under the dark blue skies of Inferno. There was a cool, dry wind blowing in from the western desert, and he found that it lifted his spirits. Donald 111 walked alongside him, the robot's shorter legs moving almost at double time in order to keep up with Alvar.

"Talk to me, Donald. Give me an evidence summary."

"Yes, sir. Several new facts have come to light from the hospital and our forensic lab. First and foremost, we have confirmed that the bloody footprints match the tread patterns of a standardized robot body model manufactured at Leving Labs. That robot body is a large general-purpose model, used with various brain types and body modifications for various purposes. The length of the footprints' stride precisely matches that of the standard specification for that robot body model. The wound on Fredda Leving's head corresponds to the shape and size of the arm of the same robot type, striking from the rear and to the left of the victim, from an angle consistent with Fredda Leving's height and the height of that robot model—though all of those measurements are approximate, and any number of other blunt instruments would match, and a whole range of heights, forces, and angles would also be consistent with the wound.

"Microtraces of a red paint found in Madame Leving's scalp wound likewise correspond to a paint used on some robots at Leving Labs, though it has not been definitively established that the paint in question was used on the robot model in question. I might add that it could not be immediately established whether the microtraces were from fresh or fully dried and hardened paint, as it was some hours before the labtech robots secured the samples. Further tests should answer that question."

"So the only suspect we are offered is a robot. That's impossible, of course. So it had to be a human—a Settler—posing as a robot. Except even a Settler who had been on the planet five minutes would know that it is impossible for a robot to attack a human. Why bother to plant doctored evidence we will refuse to believe?"

"That point has bothered me as well," Donald said. "But even if we assume a Settler was involved in this crime, we must assume that the Settler in question knew more about robots than the average Spacer."

"What do you mean?"

"Consider the detailed familiarity and access to robot equipment required to stage this attack," Donald replied. "The assailant would have to build and wear shoes with robot foot-tread soles and then replicate the gait of a specific robot. He or she would have to use a surplus robot arm—or an object that closely matched it—as a blunt instrument, and strike in such a manner as to match a blow from that robot arm. He or she would need access to the proper materials to stage the attack, and have the mechanical skill to build or modify the needed robot body parts. To be blunt, sir, a human capable of staging this attack could not possibly be stupid enough or sufficiently ignorant of robots to dream that we would think a robot did it."

"But then what was the motive for staging the attack in that manner?" Kresh asked. He thought for a moment. "You said this footprint and arm are off a very standard robot model. How many of them out there?"

"Several hundred. Several thousand if you include all the variants."

"Very well, then. That means there have been several thousand opportunities to steal a robot, or secure a defective one, and strip it for parts—the feet and arms and so forth. Or hell, the assailant could simply get hold of a robot and yank the positronic brain. He or she could plug in a remote-control system with a video-link back to the controller. Let the controller walk the robot body up to the unsuspecting victim—after all, who would suspect a robot?

"And using a remotely operated robot body that would look like a normal robot would have to be less suspicious than wearing robot-tread boots and carrying a robot arm around. And by working from a remote location, the assailant could hide his or her identity. Another thing: If I popped someone on the head, I'd want to get away *fast.* Yet those footprints were of a walking gait, not a run. That points toward a remotely controlled robot, one with a fairly limited remote-control system that could manage a walk but not a run."

"Except the attacker did not leave immediately. He or she—or it—remained for some time after the attack, at least thirty seconds or a minute."

"How do you know that?" Kresh asked. "Ah, of course, the footprints. They went through the outer edges of the pooled blood, so they had to have been made after Leving had bled long enough to produce a large pool of blood. Damn it! That makes no sense. Why the devil would the attacker stay behind? Not to make sure Leving was dead, obviously, because she wasn't. But we're digressing. You suggested that the assailant would know that we'd know that a robot could not commit the crime. Therefore, the assailant had an alternate motive for disguising the attack as coming from a robot. What would that be? Why such an elaborate setup?"

"To afford the chance to get lost in the crowd later," Donald suggested. "Let me offer a hypothetical variation on the facts by way of example. We now have an impossible suspect, a robot. Let me offer another impossible suspect to make my point, though I must ask you not to take offense at a hypothetical example."

"Of course not, Donald. Go on."

"All right. If someone decided to plant clues to make it appear that, for example, *you* had attacked Fredda Leving, that would limit the search for the assailant to those persons with the ability to plant those clues. Someone who could steal a pair of your shoes, or manage to plant strands of your hair, or your fingerprints, at the scene. But if that someone chose to plant clues that pointed equally well to several thousand *identical* and impossible suspects—"

"Our search is made far larger. Yes. Yes, I see that. An excellent point, Donald. But there is still another question. What of the second set of footprints?"

"If you will grant, for the sake of argument, my original premise, that the effort to make this seem like a robot attack was made because we would know it was impossible a robot did it,

I can offer an answer. If we further assume that the motive for that nonconvincing subterfuge was to disguise the real assailant, then I suggest that a single assailant deliberately made one set of bloody tracks, walked far enough that all traces of the blood were worn off, then simply doubled back and walked through the blood again. Again, the idea would be to confuse the search."

"It seems an awfully risky thing to do for a fairly minor advantage," Kresh objected.

"If, as you suggest, the attacker was using a remotely controlled robot body, as opposed to merely wearing robot boots and carrying a robot arm, there could be no risk in the gambit. At worst, someone might have come in during the assailant's absence and been there to capture the false robot, with the real attacker at the controls, perhaps many kilometers away."

"Yes. Yes. Now they would have us looking for *two* robots, or *two* people trying to disguise themselves as robots, when there was really only a single, human assailant. That's a lovely theory, Donald, just lovely."

"There is another note: Our robopsychologists have completed the preliminary interrogation of the staff robots at Leving Labs. Their results are, I think, astonishing."

"Are they indeed?" Kresh asked dryly. "Very well, then, astonish me."

"First, this is by no means the first time the staff robots have been instructed to stay out of the main wing of the labs. They have been told to get out many times before, usually but not always at about the hour of the attack, but always when the lab was more or less empty. This merely confirms what Daabor 5132 told me the night of the attack. However, the second point provides fresh and remarkable data."

"Very well, go on."

"Every single robot flatly refused to identify who had given the order. Our robopsychologists unanimously agree that the block restraining them is unbreakable. The psychologists took several robots to and past the breaking point, pressuring them to answer, and all refused to talk right up to the moment they brainlocked. The robots died rather than talk, even when told that their silence might well allow Fredda Leving's attacker to go free."

Alvar looked at Donald in amazement. "Burning devils. It's almost unheard-of for a block to be that good. Whoever placed it must have done a damned convincing job of saying harm would certainly come to himself—or herself—if the robots talked."

"Yes, sir. That is the obvious conclusion. There would be no other way to keep a robot from refusing to assist the police in capturing a murderer. Even so, it would require a human with remarkable skill in giving orders, and an intimate knowledge of the relative potentials of the Three Laws as programmed into each class of robot, to resist police questioning. I would venture a guess that it was only the shock of seeing Fredda Leving unconscious and bleeding that allowed Daabor 5132 to say as much as it did before expiring."

"Yes, yes. But why was this order given *more than once?* Why would the order-giver need that sort of privacy repeatedly?"

"I cannot say, sir. But the last point is perhaps the most remarkable. The block was placed with such skill that no human at the lab was even aware that the block had been placed. A whole lab full of robot specialists never even noticed that all the robots would not, could not, talk about being ordered to clear off again and again. The degree of skill required to—"

Suddenly Donald stopped moving and seemed to come to attention. "Sir, I am receiving an incoming call for you from Tonya Welton on your private line."

"Devil and fire, what the hell does that woman want? All right, put her through. And you might as well give me full visual."

Donald turned his back on Kresh. A flat vertical televisor panel extruded itself from between his shoulders and slid up behind the back of his head. As it rose up, it was showing a shifting abstract pattern, but then it resolved to a sharp image of Tonya Welton. "Sheriff Kresh," she said. "Glad I got through to you. You should come here, to Settlertown, now."

Kresh felt a sharp stab of anger. How dare she order him around? "There's not that much new at this end, Madame Welton," Kresh said. "Perhaps if we delayed our next meeting until I've had a chance to develop more information—"

"That's not why I need you, Sheriff. There's something you should see. Here, in Settlertown. Or more accurately, over it."

Donald spoke, swiveling his head a bit. "Sir, I am now receiving reports from headquarters confirming a disturbance in Settlertown."

Kresh felt a knot in the pit of his stomach. "Burning hellfire, not again."

"Oh, yes, again," Welton said, cool anger in her voice. "Deliberate provocation, and I don't know how calm I can keep my people. Your deputies are here, of course—but it's worse than last time. Much worse."

Kresh shut his eyes and wished desperately for things to stop happening. Not that such wishes were likely to come true any time soon. "Very well, Madame Welton. We're on the way."

5

MURDER. Riot. What the hell was going on, anyway? Alvar Kresh powered up his aircar and took the controls. It took little more than a glare in Donald's direction to make it clear to the robot that Alvar intended to fly himself, just at the moment, and was not going to take any nonsense.

But still, no sense in getting Donald upset for no reason. Alvar took off, flying with a nicely calculated degree of care, guiding the craft just cautiously enough to keep Donald from taking over.

Violent crime wasn't supposed to happen on Spacer worlds. The endless wealth and unlimited prosperity provided by robotic labor was supposed to eliminate poverty, and so remove any motive for crime.

Nice theory, of course, but it did not quite work out that way. If only it did, Alvar Kresh would have a much more peaceful time of it. For there was always someone relatively poorer than someone else. Someone with only a small mansion instead of a big one, who dreamed of owning a palace. Someone jealous of someone's greater affluence, determined to redress the unfair imbalance.

And no matter how rich you were, only one person could own a given object. Spacer society had more than its share of artists, and thus more than its share of art, some small fraction of it remarkably good. The burning desire to own an original and unique work of art was common motive for burglary.

There were plenty of other motives for crime besides poverty and greed, of course. People still got drunk and lusted after other people's spouses, and got into arguments with their neighbors. There were still lovers' quarrels, and domestic incidents.

Love and jealousy sparked many a crime of passion, if you could call a crime passionate when it required intricate, detailed planning to arrange for your victim to be somewhere robots weren't . . .

Others broke the law seeking after a different kind of gain than wealth or love. Simcor Beddle, for example. *He* hungered after power, and was willing to risk arrest—for himself and for his Ironheads—in order to get it.

And that was just the start of the list of motives. Inferno society was deeply hierarchical, its upper crust burdened with an incredibly complex system of proper behavior. It was vital to keep up appearances, and virtually impossible to avoid making a misstep sometime. In short, upper-class Inferno was a perfect breeding ground for blackmailers and revenge seekers.

Then there was industrial espionage, more than likely the motive for the attack on Fredda Leving. If there was little original research performed on Inferno, that just made the little that was done that much more precious.

But none of these motives would have much force if not for another factor, one that, in Alvar's opinion, few observers and theorists gave anywhere near sufficient weight: Boredom.

There was nothing much to *do* on a Spacer world. There were certain personality types that did not adapt well to the endless leisure, the endless robotic protection and pampering. Some small fraction of such types became thrillseekers.

There was one last thing to throw into the mix, of course—the Settlers. They had been here just over a standard year, and the Sheriff's Department had never been busier. There had been endless barroom brawls, scuffles in the street, mass demonstrations—and riots.

Such as the one they were coming up on now. They were nearly at Settlertown.

Kresh let Donald take the controls. He wanted to be able to see it all from the air, watch the riot in progress, learn the pattern, learn how to counter the Ironheads' latest moves. He had to keep one step ahead of them, keep them from getting completely out of control.

Which was ironic, of course, because he believed in everything the Ironheads professed. But a lawman could not let his politics prevent him from quashing a riot.

Settlertown. Now there was a mad lapse of policy, one that could only result in the sort of strife that had apparently just broken out again. Chanto Grieg and the City Council had granted the Settlers an enclave inside Hades, given them a large tract of unused land, meant for an industrial park that had never been built. If Grieg had to have the damned Settlers on the planet, why in the devil's name couldn't he have granted them an enclave well and safely outside the city limits? Putting them inside Hades was an incitement to riot all by itself.

But no, Grieg let the Settlers in, and the Settlers went to work. And there, coming into view at the horizon, was the result, barely a year after the land was granted. No building in view, of course, but that was deceiving. The Settlers preferred to put their buildings underground, leaving the landscape undisturbed. And if there was no landscape to speak of, why, then, they would build one.

Alvar's eyes dropped from the horizon to watch the landscape below. The city of Hades swept past, its proud towers a bit tired and sand-blown, many of its parks faded about the edges, the empty quarters at the edge of town fading from sight on the horizon behind them. And then, up ahead, coming up fast, Settlertown swept to the fore, a sword of green seeming to point at the brown heart of Hades, a huge and idyllic park of great meadows, proud newborn forests of seedlings, the very air over it softened by the mists of its lakes and ponds.

Incredible, simply incredible, what they had accomplished in a bare year—and without the use of a single robot. Spacers tended to equate robots with machines, and thus Spacers wondered how the Settlers managed without machines. Obviously that was a misconception. The Settlers used highly automated systems and hardware. Those forests had been planted by machines, not stoop labor. The catch was that none of the Settler machines were remotely like Spacer robots. They had virtually no capacity for thought or independent action. The most sophisticated of Settler computer systems would not even register on any of the robotic intelligence tests.

But the lesson of Settlertown was plain: Dumb machines could do a great deal in the hands of smart, determined people. Alvar Kresh looked down at the green and growing place and wondered: Had there truly ever been a time when the Spacers had been so energetic, so ambitious? What had happened that made the

Spacers doze off and let history move past them?

Yes, Settlertown was a most impressive lesson, but there were those Spacers who did not appreciate being educated. There, near the southern gate of the enclave. A plume of black smoke was rising, a small fleet of sky-blue deputy's cars circling around it. "Take us in, Donald," Alvar said, quite needlessly pointing toward the gleam of fire on the ground. Donald was already guiding the aircar down, setting it into a broad circle over the center of the disturbance. Another protest rally against the Settlers, obviously enough. The protesters had a good fire going this time, made out of pulled-up park benches, trash brought along for the purpose, and whatever else burnable they might find. It looked like two dummies of some sort were being dangled in the fire on the ends of long poles.

Kresh pulled a pair of farviewers out of the aircar's gearbag and put them to his eyes. "Ironheads," he announced. "Burning Grieg in effigy again, by the looks of it," he said, offering the commentary even though he knew perfectly well Donald's vision was superior to his own. The robot needed merely to increase the magnification of one or both of his eyes. "And another figure being burned next to him. Maybe Tonya Welton. At least it isn't me this time. Good." For a moment, Kresh had feared that word of the attack on Leving had gotten out, in spite of the news blackout he had ordered. But none of the banners he could see mentioned Leving, or anything about the attack.

Unless the Ironheads had found out about her connection to the Settlers and taken their revenge. That would give them a motive for keeping quiet.

"Sir," Donald said, "to the rear of the bonfire—"

Kresh swung his viewers around and swore. "Burning hellfire, that's just great. That'll make the Settlers just happy as could be." There was a group of masked Ironheads off in a copse of young trees, destroying as many of the saplings as they could, firing point-blank at their trunks with blasters. Not even dragging them back for fuel, which would almost make some sense. But no, this was just wanton destruction for the hell of it. Damned idiots. The Settlers loved their trees, yes, and killing a few would get them mad. But didn't it occur to the Ironheads that a group of people preparing to reterraform a planet would have the capacity to replace a few *trees?* And what sort of idiots would kill trees on a planet with a weakened ecology?

Fools. Maybe, with a little luck, they'd take a few of themselves out with sloppy cross fire. It made Kresh more than a little uncomfortable that he agreed with the Ironhead philosophy. Yes, fine, make more robots, better robots, give the Infernals a real chance to revive the terraforming before handing the job over to outsiders. That all made sense. But politics did not excuse vandalism. Kresh reached for the aircar's comm mike, but even before he could give the order, one of the circling deputy's cars dove down almost to treetop level, pumping out a cloud of trank-gas behind itself. The Ironheads scattered, but one or two were dropped by the gas, unable to outrun it. Another deputy's car swept down to a landing. Two deputies jumped out and had the unconscious protesters cuffed and ready for pickup in seconds. Their aircar was already back in the air, in pursuit of the escaping Ironheads. Meanwhile, a fire department airtruck was coming in. It fired twin water cannons at the bonfire and the effigies. More deputy's cars landed. Deputies poured out and started rounding up the protesters. Good. Good. Kresh was glad to see his people doing so well.

This was work for humans, no question about it. Riot control was something that robots simply could not do. Which was why, of course, there were still human police. Sheriffs and deputies had to be ready to do a lot of things that broke the First Law.

Kresh watched his people at work with real pride. There had been no need for him to command or direct. They were getting this sort of operation down to a science. But there was a dark side to that truth. How could they not get better? The devil himself knew they were getting enough practice.

"Let's land this thing, Donald," he said. "As long as we're here, we might as well pay a call on Madame Welton. Call ahead to her."

TONYA Welton was there on the ground, looking up, watching their aircar land. She was standing by the main entrance shaft to Settlertown, waiting for them. There was something missing about her, Kresh thought, something that should have been there. Then it came to him. Her robot, Ariel. No Spacer would go out of doors without at least one robot in attendance, and in the city Tonya kept to that convention. But here, on her own turf, perhaps she felt she could avoid Spacer absurdities.

The aircar set down. Man and robot disembarked.

"Sheriff Kresh, Donald 111," Tonya said. "Welcome to our humble abode. Come in, come in out of that frightful cloud of smoke your friends have dumped into the atmosphere."

"The Ironheads aren't my friends," Kresh said, stepping forward. He and Donald followed her into the elevator car for the ride down.

"No, I doubt that a policeman would approve of their tactics," Welton said. "But surely you don't pretend to be opposed to their *goals.*"

The doors slid shut, and the elevator began its high-speed descent to the interior of Settlertown. The ride always did odd things to Alvar's stomach and inner ears. Or maybe it was just that he didn't like the idea of being a half kilometer underground.

He shoved those thoughts from his mind and answered the Settler leader. "No, ma'am, I don't," Kresh said. "They want you people out of here, they want Governor Grieg to use robots, not Settlers, to reterraform Inferno, and they want Inferno to be a Spacer world, not some half-breed between Spacer and Settler. They believe that such a situation could only be an interlude until your people took over completely. I believe all those things, too. But the ends do not justify the means. Savagery has no place in a political debate."

Tonya looked at the Sheriff with a smile that was not entirely at ease with itself. "Well said, Sheriff Kresh. What a pity Chanto Grieg is only a year into his first term. You would make quite an opposition candidate."

"The thought had crossed my mind," Alvar said, drawing himself up to his full height and staring straight ahead. "Someone will have to take him on sooner or later. But the next election will be time enough."

"It sounds like an exciting campaign," Tonya said dryly.

The elevator door slid open and Tonya Welton led them out into a large open space underground. It was a huge, vaulted space, to Kresh's eye perhaps a kilometer long and half that wide. There was an elaborate false sky overhead which seemed to be mimicking the true conditions in the real sky—from the gleaming sun down to the column of smoke still rising from the direction of the Ironhead demonstration. Welton noticed Kresh looking upward. "Yes, the real-time simulation is a new touch since the last time you were here. The theory is it will be much less disorienting to go back and forth between Settlertown and Hades if our undersky matches the real one precisely. With just the generalized day-night sky program we had before, moving from inside to outside got quite confusing."

"Hmmph." Alvar looked around, feeling most unhappy. Perhaps his eyes saw the wide-open spaces of the great cavern, but his mind was aware of every single gram of the millions of kilograms of rock over his head. "I suppose it might help, but I find this place sufficiently disorienting no matter what is projected on your false sky. How can you bear to live underground?"

Tonya gestured grandly about the huge artificial cavern. Brilliant simulated sunlight shone down on a pretty little park. A fountain jetted a stream of water into the air, a breeze tickled her hair. Small, handsomely designed buildings were dotted here and there about the landscape. "We Settlers are quite used to life belowground. And besides, you can hardly argue that this place is some dank, dismal dungeon. These days, we are able to make our underground homes seem quite like the surface, without interfering with the landscape or suffering the inconveniences of bad weather. Your dust storms cannot touch us here. But we have other matters to discuss. Come."

She led them from the bottom of the elevator shaft to a waiting runcart. She sat down in it and waited for Alvar and Donald to do the same. They did so—Alvar next to her in the front seat, Donald in the back—and the cart took off with no apparent command from Tonya. It drove them through the central cavern and into a broad side tunnel. It stopped outside her outer office.

Alvar resisted the temptation to renew the endless philosophical argument Settlers and Infernals had been having since the day the Settlers arrived. The argument about the cart, and all the other "smart," nonrobotic, automated hardware the Settlers used. It still seemed suicidally dangerous to trust to automatic devices that did not contain the Three Laws, but the Settlers took a perverse pride in the knowledge that their machines would not prevent people from killing themselves—as if that were a useful design feature. Yes, nonsentient machinery left more scope for human initiative—but what benefit if all that scope gave you was more chances to get squashed like a bug in a crash?

The three of them disembarked and went through the ornately carved glass double doors into the reception area, and then through to Welton's surprisingly austere office. Most places in Settlertown were comfortable, even downright luxurious—except for the lack of robots—but Welton seemed to like things kept to a minimum. There was not so much as a desk in the room, at least at the moment, though Kresh knew a worktable could be extruded from the wall quickly enough. There was nothing but four chairs in a circle with a low, round table in the center.

It seemed to Alvar that the furniture had been rearranged every time he came in here, in accordance with whatever sort of use to which the room was to be put—working office, meeting room, dinner reception, whatever. A Spacer would have had a room for each function. Perhaps this was a cultural holdover from when the Settlers' underground cities were more cramped. Or perhaps the mock austerity was a mere affectation on Welton's part. Kresh noted one addition to the room since the last time he had been here. A very standard robot niche, occupied by Ariel at the moment.

Tonya noticed Kresh looking at Ariel and shrugged irritably. "Well, I had to have *some* place for her when she is off duty. She herself suggested the niche, and it seemed as good a place as any. I believe she has herself on standby at the moment. Ariel?"

There was no answer. Kresh raised an eyebrow. "You let your robot go into standby whenever it chooses?"

"Ariel, poor thing, serves no other purpose than to act as window dressing when I go out among the Spacers. It upsets your people no end to see someone without a robot in attendance. It made it almost impossible to do my work. She calms the passersby a bit. Otherwise, she has no other duties, and I let her do what she pleases. If she wishes to be dormant for a while, so be it. But come, we have much to discuss."

Alvar Kresh was more than a bit unsettled by the arrangement with Ariel. Every robot was ordered into standby once in a while, to conserve power or for maintenance, but he had never heard of a robot going into standby on its own. In standby, how could a robot obey the First and Second Laws? Well, no matter, let Welton make her own arrangements. No doubt she told Ariel to choose her own standby times in such a way that Ariel considered it an order. No matter. It was time for business.

He took a seat, and Tonya Welton took the seat opposite. Donald, as a matter of course, remained standing. But Welton would have none of that. "Donald, sit down," she said. Donald obeyed and Alvar gritted his teeth, determined not to be annoyed. Tonya Welton knew damn well that it would irritate him to have Donald treated as an equal. She was doing it deliberately.

"Now then," she said. "Starting with your Ironheads, Sheriff. This is the most serious and violent demonstration they have mounted. Can you give me any assurance that these provocations will end?"

Kresh shifted uncomfortably in his seat. "No," he said at last. "I don't see much point in my pretending otherwise. There are literally thousands of years of animosity built up between your people and mine. Our people considered yours to be subhuman for a long time, and I suspect some Settlers have had that opinion of us. I think we are all past that stage now, but the fact remains that we don't like each other. Prejudices remain. There is also a great deal of resentment over the behavior of the Settlers on Inferno."

"I cannot see that my people have been overly rude or disrespectful—though I, too, have my uncontrollable hotheads. You picked up a mob of robot bashers just last week. Is it their actions that is causing the resentment? I have done all I could to punish such actions quickly and publicly."

"Gangs of drunken Settlers wandering the streets of Hades, destroying valuable robots, have not helped your cause," Kresh said dryly. "However, I am willing to accept the point that you cannot control your people—the devil knows I can't control mine. I am even prepared to believe that a terraforming project might well require some rough-and-ready sorts to make it work. The sort that might find ordering a robot to commit suicide amusing." He glared at her, but she displayed no reaction.

"None of the bashing incidents have been good public relations for you," he went on. "But the root cause of resentment is your very presence, your annoying self-confidence that you can so easily solve the climate problems that have bedeviled us." He made a gesture with his right hand, indicating all of the vast underground settlement he was in. "The casual way in which you built *this* place was disconcerting. And I might add it seems a very permanent home for a group that does not intend to—ah—*settle* permanently."

Tonya Welton nodded thoughtfully. "I have heard all these points before, and they are good ones. But must we act as if we don't know what we are doing, just to salve the feelings of the Infernals? We have assembled the finest experts on terraforming from all the leading Settler worlds. They are good, they are skilled, and they brought their equipment. They used it to build their own—temporary—dwelling place. Would you trust the rebuilding of your world to people who were unsure of their skills? Or to people who could not excavate a simple cavern?" Tonya gestured toward Ariel, inert in her niche. "You have seen to it that many of us have robots, to convince us of the worth of your lifestyle. When we go, and leave this place behind as a gift to the city of Hades, we hope that some number of your people will take up residence, and see the advantages of *our* way of life."

"There is little chance of that," Kresh said, a bit too sharply.

"There is little chance of Settlers taking home robot slaves," Tonya countered in an equally unpleasant tone.

There was a moment's glaring silence, but then Donald spoke. "Perhaps," he said, "it might be wise to leave topics of policy for the moment and return to more immediate concerns."

Tonya looked toward Donald and grinned. "Always it comes to this point. You watch the tempers flare, and just when it is about to get out of hand, you politely suggest that your boss and I agree to disagree. I sometimes think you are wasted outside the diplomatic corps. But tell me, does it ever get dull for you, Donald, watchind the same tired ritual again and again?"

"I would not characterize it as tired ritual, nor do I find it dull. Both of you are skilled debaters. I might add that, as a robot programmed for police service, I am a student of human behavior under stress of emotion. I watch, and I learn. It is most instructive."

"All right, Donald," Kresh said irritably. "You've got us both nicely calmed down again. Why don't we move on to the Leving attack. The Governor's office hyperwaved confirming orders to me this morning. I am to share all of our information with you. I don't see why that is needful, but orders are orders. Donald, why don't you give Madame Welton a summary of our information and theories so far."

"Certainly." Donald turned his rounded blue head toward Tonya Welton and gave a concise summary of the information they had developed since the attack. Tonya asked one or two questions as he went along, and listened carefully. She made no notes, but Kresh had no doubt she was also recording the conversation in some way.

At last Donald was finished. Tonya leaned back in her chair, stared up at the featureless white ceiling, and thought for a moment before saying anything.

Finally she looked back toward Donald and Kresh and spoke. "It seems to me that you are going to remarkable lengths to exclude the possibility of a robot as a suspect. Surely you will grant that it requires a good deal of special pleading to accept such elaborate explanations as boots with robot treads or remote-control machines that look just like robots. There is an ancient rule of logic that teaches us that, absent compelling reasons to the contrary, it is wisest to use the simplest possible explanation. Taken at face value, the evidence is overwhelming that a robot committed the crime. Why not at least examine that very simple explanation?"

"Yes," Kresh agreed uncomfortably,"but the Three Laws—"

"The Three Laws are going to drive me mad," Welton snapped. "I know the Three Laws as well as you do, and you need not recite them again like some bloody holy catechism. I swear, Kresh, you Spacers might as well face facts and admit that worship of those dismal Laws is your state religion. The answer to all problems, the end of all quests, can be found in the infinite good of the Three Laws. I say that if we just assume that the Three Laws make a robot attack on Leving impossible, I think we are missing a key point."

"And what might that be, Lady Welton?" Donald asked mildly. It passed idly through Kresh's mind that it was well that Donald was around, if only to lubricate the wheels of conversation. Welton had obviously paused for the sole purpose of eliciting the question Donald had asked, but Kresh was hell-damned if *he* would give her the satisfaction of asking it.

"A very simple point," Tonya Welton replied. "With all due respect, Donald, *robots are machines,* and it is impossible for them to harm humans *only* because they are built in such a way to make that so. If all runcarts were built without a reverse gear, that would not render the construction of a machine *with* reverse gear impossible. A machine that is built one way can be built another. Suppose robots *were* built another way? What is to prevent it—if the builder decided not to follow your precious Three Laws? Would not the rock-hard belief that robots *cannot* commit such acts provide a perfect cover? The robot's builder need not even run, for none will think to pursue.

"One other point. This speechblock put on the staff robots, preventing them from saying who ordered them to go to the far wing of the labs that night. It seems to me that a mechanical device, an override circuit, would be more effective in setting an absolute block against speech concerning certain subjects than in giving an intricate series of orders to each and every robot. It would be easier to set up as well. And before you object that such a speechblock circuit would weaken the robot's ability to obey the damned Three Laws, we are assuming that the attacker was not too fastidious about such things. Donald—how large a piece of microcircuitry would that take?"

"It could be made small enough to be invisible to the human eye, and could be wired in anywhere in the robot's sensory system."

"I'll bet your people never even thought to look for a *physical* cause for the speechblock, did they? Go over a few of the lab robots with a microscope and see what you find. As to why the perpetrator would need to set blocks for multiple time periods—perhaps he or she wanted some privacy while using the lab's facilities to make up the attacker robot—or even the robot suit you two are postulating, if you insist that *all* robots *must* obey the Laws."

There was an uncomfortable silence before Tonya continued. "Even if you do insist on that," she said at last, "there are documented cases where Three Law robots did kill human beings."

Donald's head snapped back a bit, and his eyes grew dim for a moment. Tonya looked toward him with some concern. "Donald—are you in difficulty?"

"No, I beg your pardon. I am aware of—such cases—but I am afraid that the abrupt mention of them was most disturbing. The mere contemplation of such things is most unpleasant, and caused a slight flux in my motor function. However, I am recovered now, and I believe you can pursue your point without concern for me. I am now braced for it. Please continue."

Tonya hesitated for a moment, until Kresh felt he had to speak. "It's all right," he said. "Donald is a police robot, programmed for special resilience where the contemplation of harm to humans is concerned. Go on."

Tonya nodded, a bit uncertainly. "It was some years ago, about a standard century ago, and there was a great deal of effort to hush it up, but there was a series of incidents on Solaria. Robots, all with perfectly functional Three Law positronic brains, killed humans, simply because the robots were programmed with a defective definition of what a human being was. Nor is the myth of robotic infallibility completely accurate. There have doubtless been other cases we don't know about, because the cover-ups were successful. Robots can malfunction, can make mistakes.

"It is foolish to flatly assume that a robot capable of harming a human could not be built, or to believe that a robot with Three Laws could not inadvertently harm a human under any circumstances. For my part, I see the Spacer faith in the perfection and infallibility of robots as a folk myth, an article of faith, and one that is contradicted by the facts."

Alvar Kresh was about to open his mouth and protest, but he did not get the chance. Donald spoke up first.

"You may well be correct, Lady Tonya," the robot said, "but I would submit that the myth is a needful one."

"Needful in what way?" Tonya Welton demanded.

"Spacer society is predicated, almost completely, on the use of robots. There is almost no activity on Inferno, or on the other Spacer worlds, that does not rely in some way upon them. Spacers, denied robots, would be unable to survive."

"Which is precisely the objection we Settlers have to robots," Welton said.

"As is well known, and as is widely regarded as a specious argument by Spacers," Donald said. "Deny Settlers computers, or hyperdrive, or any other vital machine knit into the fabric of their society, and Settler culture could not survive. Human beings can be defined as the animal that needs tools. Other species of old Earth used and made tools, but only humans need them to survive. Deny all tools to a human, and you sentence that human to all but certain death. But I digress from the main point." Donald turned to look at Alvar and then turned back toward Welton.

"Spacer society," Donald went on, "relies on robots, trusts robots, believes in robots. Spacers could not function if they had no faith in robots. For even if we are merely machines, merely tools, we are enormously powerful ones. If we were perceived as dangerous"—and Donald's voice quavered as he even suggested the idea—"if we were so perceived, we would be worse than useless. We would be mistrusted. And who but a lunatic would have faith in a powerful tool that could not be trusted? Thus, Spacers need their faith that robots are utterly reliable."

"I've thought about that," Welton admitted. "I've observed your culture, and thought about it. Settlers and Spacers may be rivals in some abstruse, long-term struggle none of us shall ever live to see the results of—but we are also all human beings, and we can learn from each other.

"Of course we came here hoping to convince at least some of you to do without robots. There is no point in pretending otherwise. I have come to see that we are not going to convert any of you. We Settlers could no more wean you away from robots than we could convince you to give up breathing. And I have concluded it would be wrong of us to try."

"I beg your pardon?" Kresh said.

Tonya turned to Donald, stared into his expressionless glowing blue eyes. She reached and touched his rounded blue head. "I, personally, have concluded that we cannot change the Spacer need for robots. To do it would destroy you. To attempt it is hopeless. Yet I am more certain than ever that your culture *must* change if it is to survive. But it must change in some other way."

"Why would you care if we survive?" Kresh asked. "And why should I believe you do?"

Welton turned toward Kresh and raised her eyebrow. "We are here trying to pull your climate back from the edge of collapse. I have spent the last year in this sun-baked city of yours rather than back home. That should lend some credence to my claims of sincerity," she said with a hint of amusement. "As to why we should care about your culture—would it not strike you as the height of arrogance to assume *yours* was the only right way to live? There is value, and merit, in diversity. It may well be that the Settler and Spacer cultures together will accomplish things that neither could do by itself."

Kresh grunted noncommittally. "That's as may be," he said. "But I am no philosopher, and I believe we have covered all the ground we are going to regarding the Fredda Leving case. Perhaps I can send Donald around sometime and the two of you could discuss the whichness of why together."

Tonya Welton either missed his sarcasm, which seemed unlikely, or chose to ignore it. She smiled and turned back to Donald. "If you'd ever like to come by," she said, addressing the robot directly, "I'd be delighted."

"I look forward to the opportunity, Lady," Donald said.

Kresh clenched his teeth, not quite sure which of the three of them—Donald, Welton, or he himself—had most succeeded in infuriating Alvar Kresh.

ARIEL'S eyes came to light, glowing yellow. She stepped down from her niche and crossed the room to where her mistress sat. Ariel took up the seat Donald had used.

"Well, Ariel, what did you think of that?" Tonya asked.

"I believe it may be easier to get Alvar Kresh to listen than to direct him. I am not a skilled judge of such things, but I do not think he was in the least bit impressed by your arguments regarding the possibility of a—a—robot assailant. Nor do I think he was entirely convinced that I was indeed dormant."

"Let's get something straight, Ariel. You may not be a judge of human psychology in general, but you know more about *Spacer* psychology than I ever will. I doubt I'll ever understand them completely. You were built by them, designed by them, meant to fit into their world. You are the only product of that world I can trust to be loyal to me. You can stand next to me, watching and listening, while *they* ignore you completely. *That's* why I value your opinion."

"Yes, ma'am. I appreciate all that. But might I ask—if they all ignore me, anyway, why did you order me to simulate dormancy?"

"An insurance policy. Kresh was here as a cop, not a Spacer. If you were an even slightly active presence in the room, that could draw his attention to you. If I ordered you out, and you were missing, he might notice that absence, and *that* would draw attention to you. Besides, I wanted you listening.

"By telling him I let you go dormant whenever you choose, I drew his attention to me, to the eccentric Settler who treated her robot like an equal. If he thought about *you,* it would likely occur to him that you had been with me whenever I visited Leving Labs. I do *not* want you in the hands of Spacer robopsychologists. I'm not the most skilled person in ordering robots. They might easily find ways of getting you to speak about the things I have ordered you not to discuss."

"Thank you, ma'am. I understand more fully now. But I must say once again, I do not think he was much impressed by your idea of a robot committing the attack."

"Good. I did not expect him to accept the idea. All I wanted to do was muddy the waters."

"Ma'am?"

"I want him worrying about side issues, blind leads. I want to slow him down."

"Ma'am, I am afraid I do not understand."

"I need time, Ariel. You know as well as I do that I need time to find things out for myself. I have, ah—*interests*—I wish to protect."

Tonya Welton rose, crossed the room, and began pacing back and forth, her actions at last betraying the nervousness Ariel had known was there. "I have interests to protect," she said again. "*He* is in hiding, Ariel," Tonya said, and there was no need for her to speak the man's name. "He won't even accept messages from *me.* That *proves* something is wrong. He is in danger, and that danger could only increase if his connection to me were revealed at the wrong moment. And I strongly suspect that Alvar Kresh would take a special pleasure in destroying anything—or anyone—that I hold dear."

ALVAR Kresh was glad to get out of Welton's office, to put it mildly. As the elevator arrived at ground level, and he no longer had to hold his claustrophobia in check, he found himself breathing a sigh of relief, and felt his spirits suddenly rise. His anger seemed to fade away into the blessedly open skies.

"I fear our visit was not especially productive," Donald said. "Madame Welton did not offer much in the way of useful information or insight, and I do not see what she learned from us that she could not have learned by our sending a data transmission. Nor can I see why our presence was needed at the Ironhead riot. Your deputies handled that without any need of your expertise."

"Donald, Donald, Donald," Kresh said as they walked across the parkland toward their aircar. "And you call yourself a student of human nature. That meeting had nothing at all to do with the exchange of information. Human beings very often are not talking about what they are talking about."

"Sir?"

"We were there not to assist in countering the Ironhead demonstration, but to *witness* it, and to get the clear message that the Leving case could make such encounters worse. If the populace of Hades gets the idea that Settlers are attempting to discredit robots by staging attacks that seem to be committed by robots, the Ironheads won't be able to handle all the new recruits."

"But what concern is that of yours?"

"I am in charge of keeping the peace, for one thing. But bear in mind that she chose to meet us on *her* turf. Up here, on the surface, the air is still smoky, and we're near enough the perimeter of Settlertown that the air smells of desert again. Down below, all was serene and quiet, and the air was sweet. Another clear message: The Settlers have no reason to fear the rioters. The Settlers can hunker down in their artificial cave. But the citizens of Hades have no such option. And yet the current plans for terraforming all rely on the Settlers. In short, Tonya Welton was telling us we need her far more than she needs us," Alvar Kresh said as they reached the aircar.

Donald sat down at the controls and they took off. "Did it strike you as odd that she wished to know so much about the Leving case? After all, she has no responsibility to investigate crimes," the robot said as he maneuvered for altitude.

"Yes, I wondered about that. In fact, I rather got the impression that she was waiting for us to say something we didn't, though the devil alone would know what that might be. I don't know, Donald. Perhaps she has some genuine personal or professional interest in Leving's well-being."

"I see," Donald said, some trace of uncertainty in his voice. "But I don't regard that as a sufficient explanation of Lady Tonya's strong interest. Note that she scarcely asked at all about Fredda Leving herself. It was only the robotic aspect of the case that interested her. Why does she care so deeply about the case, and why does she regard it as so overwhelmingly important?"

"I tell you what I think, Donald," Kresh said as he watched the landscape below. "I think a Settler committed the crime, perhaps acting directly under Tonya Welton's orders, precisely to set off more disturbances and give the Settlers an excuse to get off the planet. Bringing us in today during the riot was merely the first step in orchestrating that withdrawal."

"Might I ask your reasons for thinking that?" Donald asked impassively as he guided the aircar.

"Well, first off, I don't like Settlers. I know that's not much of a reason, but there it is. And second, say what Tonya Welton will about this contingent of Settlers being trained to understand our ways and appreciate the Three Laws, I still can't believe a Spacer would try any of the stunts that have been suggested to explain the attack. Think about them: building a remote-control device that mimicked a robot, strapping on robot feet and using a robot arm as a club, building and programming a special-purpose killer robot. No Spacer would do those things.

"Welton was right about one thing—the Three Laws are close to being our state religion. Interfering with them, abusing them or the concept of robots in any way, would be close to blasphemy. There are times when I think our illustrious Governor Chanto Grieg is pushing so hard for change that someone's going to bounce up and call him a heretic. Maybe it even goes deeper than that. I find the very idea of perverting robots to be stomach-turning. It's like the prohibition against cannibalism or incest. I doubt any Spacer unbalanced enough to make the attempt would still be sane enough to do all the methodical planning required.

"No. Only a Settler would be stupid enough—well, all right, *ignorant* enough—to try and plant the idea that a robot could commit an act of violence. Any Spacer would know how deep and abiding the prohibition against that is."

Alvar stopped and thought for a minute. Suddenly a new and disturbing thought dawned on him. "In fact, *that* might well be the motive. Maybe the Settlers *don't* want to leave. We've been too tied up with figuring how the attack was made to stop and wonder *why* anyone would want to attack Fredda Leving."

"I'm afraid I don't follow you, sir," Donald said.

"Let's just ignore all of Welton's nonsense about respecting us as an alternate culture. She as much as said they came here as missionaries, hoping to convert us away from robots. The Settlers—this lot on Inferno, and all of them generally—are *always* casting about for ways to make the Spacer dependence on robots look like a weakness, instead of a strength. Trying to convince us to abandon robots. You spoke about the need for us to trust robots. Suppose the attack on Leving *is* the opening salvo in a campaign to make us afraid of our own robots?"

"I see the point, sir, but I am forced to question the choice of Fredda Leving as the victim. Why would the Settlers attack their own ally?"

Kresh shook his head. "I don't pretend to understand their politics, but perhaps there is some sort of bad blood between Welton and Leving. Some sort of resentment, some sort of competition or disagreement between them. Jomaine Terach hinted at it. It must be tied up in this grand project we can't be told about yet.

"And I don't think we're going to get anywhere until we know what *that's* about."

THREE hours later, Alvar Kresh sat at his desk, reading through the daily reports, making notes to himself on the status of this investigation, that application for promotion. By rights, he should have gone home to bed, allowed himself some rest. All told, he had gotten perhaps an hour's sleep the night before. But he was too keyed up to sleep, too eager to leap back in and get on with the chase.

Except, as yet, there was nothing *to* chase. Until and unless Gubber Anshaw emerged from his home, Kresh would be unable to question him. Maybe the forensic labs would be able to come up with something as they sifted through all the physical evidence at the scene. Kresh had a bet with himself that forensics would come up with something—but that it would be misleading. Whoever had done this thing seemed damned clever at leaving clues that did not point anywhere.

But until something broke with a witness, or evidence, there was damn little he could do.

No, there was one other possibility. There was always the chance of another incident. Another attack that could give him a pattern, a rhythm, he could work with. Another attack carried out a bit more sloppily. It was a terrible thing for a policeman to wish for a new crime to be committed, but there were precious few other ways he could get a break on this case. What else could he do? Send half the force out randomly searching for robot-soled boots? Surely the perpetrator had destroyed them by now, or else hidden them well indeed, ready for the next attack.

Alvar struggled to get his mind off the case. After all, he did have a department to run. He managed to get through a worrying report from personnel, regarding a sudden uptick in the number of resignations from the force. But his resistance to distraction did not hold for long. Even that report, with its hints of a danger to the whole future of the department, did not occupy the whole of his mind.

Because the Settlers were here to take over. He knew *that* much, deep in his gut. No matter how many denials or reassurances they made, no matter how much noise Governor Grieg made about rapprochement and new eras of cooperation, Kresh would still believe—would still *know*—the Settlers looked at Inferno simply as a world ripe for colonization.

For the time being, the Settlers—at least most of them—were making polite noises, being respectful of local culture, but that would not last. *Local culture. There* was a political code word, if ever there had been one. A euphemism for the use of robots. Some optimists thought that the Settlers on Inferno would grow used to robots, come to see the advantages of robots, and perhaps even return home to their Settler worlds singing the praises of robots. A market would develop for Spacer robots on Settler worlds, and everyone would get rich selling robots to Settlers.

But Kresh had no such illusions. The Settlers were here to take over, not to be sold serving robots. Once they were firmly in control of Inferno—well, all it took to be done with a robot was a single shot from a blaster. After they had wiped out the robots, the Settlers wouldn't even *need* to move against the Spacers. Spacer culture—and individual Spacers—needed robots the way a person needed food and drink. Too many jobs were given over to robots, too many people had never bothered to learn tasks that were more easily left to robots. Without robots, the Spacers were doomed.

Which brought him back to his central point: What happened to Spacers if robots could no longer be trusted?

And what if the Settlers engaged in a plot for the express purpose of finding out?

BLEND in, Caliban told himself. *Observe what the other robots do. Behave as they do.* Already, he had developed the sophistication to know his very survival might depend on acting like the others. He walked back and forth across Hades, watching and learning, shuttling back and forth across the city as day crossed the sky and night came on.

6

GUBBER Anshaw paced the floor of his living room in fretful distraction. They had to have found her by now. Surely they had. But had she survived? The question clawed at his soul. She had been alive when he had left, of that much he was certain. Surely a robot had found her and saved her. That place was teeming with robots. Except, of course, Gubber himself had ordered all the robots to stay away that night. He had forgotten that in his panic.

But that pool of blood, the terrible way her face was cut, the way she lay so *still.* He should have stayed, he should have risked all and tried to help. But no, his own fears, his own cowardice, had prevented that.

And Tonya! His own dear, dear Tonya! Even in the midst of his anguish, Gubber Anshaw found a moment in his thoughts to marvel once again that such a woman would care, could care, for a man like Gubber Anshaw. But now, perhaps, caring for him had only placed her in danger.

Unless, of course, it was *she* who had placed *him* in danger. A tight knot of suspicion pulled taut in his chest. How could he even think such thoughts? But how could he avoid them?

There were so many questions he dared not ask, even of himself. How mixed up in all this *was* she? He had sacrificed greatly, perhaps had sacrificed *all* for her. Had he been right to do so? What would be the consequences of his actions? What had he done that night?

He glanced toward the comm panel. Every alert light on it was blinking. The outside world was trying to reach him over every sort of comm link he had. No doubt word from Tonya was there, waiting for him with all the others. No doubt she had wangled access to the police reports by now. And no doubt she would know just how eager he was to see those reports.

Gubber Anshaw paced the floor, worrying, waiting, forcing down the impulse to look at the wall clock. He had covered it with a cloth long ago, anyway. Perhaps his *reflexes* directed his glance toward the clock, but his conscious self most definitely did not want to know what the time was. He no longer had even the remotest idea how much time had passed, whether or not it was day or night. He could have found out in an instant, of course, by pulling the cover off the clock or by asking a robot. But there was some part of him that urgently resisted knowing.

In some irrational corner of himself, he was sure he could no longer hide from the universe if he knew what time it was. So long as the hour and the day were hidden from him, he could imagine himself cut off, outside the flow of time, cocooned away behind his shut-down comm panel and his robots, safe inside his little sanctuary, no longer part of the outside world.

And yet sooner or later, he would have to come out of his house. He would have to step back into time, back into the world. He knew that. But he knew also that his guilty knowledge, the fact of his guilty action, would keep him inside a while longer.

And Tonya. Tonya. There were two questions about her that swirled about his mind:

What part had she played in the story?

And, once this was over, what time would she have for a coward too scared to leave his own house?

"ALL right, now, li'l robot—point the blaster at your head." The small repair-services unit turned the nozzle of the blaster on itself, its glowing green eyes staring right down the barrel of the weapon.

Reybon Derue chortled in drunken hysteria, knowing in some strange, still-sober part of himself how pointless it all was. But, bored with the work, despised by the locals, what else was there for a Settler laborer to do but get drunk? Well, the answer was right in front of him. Robot bashing.

Except they did not do straight bashing. That had been too easy. What challenge in beating a robot down to scrap when the robot would not, could not, resist? No, this way was far more amusing, and took more skill. There weren't many people who could talk a robot into killing itself.

Except even inducing suicide was getting too easy, at least with certain classes of robots. With the more sophisticated machines, it took a long, elaborate discussion with a robot to get it into a state where it would accept an order to destroy itself. But with a unit as unsophisticated as the one in front of him, long practice had made the game too easy. The only tough part left was remembering to order the robots not to use their hyperwave systems to report bashing incidents to the authorities.

Maybe, Reybon thought, *I've gotten too good at this to bother with the low-end ones. This one was almost too simple.*

"Okay, very good, you tin excuse for a machine," Reybon said, leaning closer. "Now fire the blaster."

The robot fired, and its head vaporized. Its body fell to the floor and dropped the weapon. Reybon roared with laughter and kicked the robot's ruined carcass.

The floor was littered with the components of shattered robots. Reybon went over to a severed hand and kicked it clear across the floor of the abandoned warehouse. He stepped back, turned to his fellow laborers, who were sitting on packing cases in the middle of the room. He took a bow. They cheered wildly. One of them tossed him a bottle of something, and he caught it with the odd, neat, fluid dexterity some drunks have. He yanked the top off and took a long pull from the bottle.

"Who's next?" he demanded. "That one was too easy. Who's gonna get me some stupid hunka metal 'n' plastic that's gonna be *tougher* to crack?"

Santee Timitz got up. "I'll go," she said. "Lemme go find one." She ambled toward the door of the warehouse, moving a bit slowly. "I'll get you a *really* good one." The rest of the group found that absurdly funny for some reason, and laughed louder and harder than ever.

"Hey, hey, Reybon," Denlo said. "Maybe it's time we got going, huh? Deputy's gonna show up sooner or later. Maybe we quit while we're ahead, huh?"

Reybon walked back to the gang lounging on the packing cases. "Ah, take it easy, Denlo. We're okay. Santee'll find us a good one."

NIGHT had come, and still Caliban walked the streets of the city, watching, thinking, learning. Robots were utterly, totally subservient to humans, that much he was sure of. Whatever a human told a robot to do, that robot did. Why, he could not imagine.

Humans were weaker, slower, in some ways at least far less intelligent and competent than robots. But even if the datastore contained no information on robots, Caliban had at least the resonances in the datastore, the remnant hints left behind by whoever had assembled the datastore and then excised the robot data. Those hints, those resonances, seemed to confirm his impression that robot subservience was irrational. In fact, the whispering mood-voice went further than that, implying, insinuating, that the situation was actually dangerous. Caliban had no way of judging that, or even of knowing if the whispers were real projections from the datastore's creator, or a malfunction, a failure in his own perception.

Humans. They were the other side of the equation. Many of them seemed to have vast amounts of time for leisure. They lingered in restaurants, relaxed in the parks, read bookfilms in the backseat while the robots drove the cars. Robots had no leisure.

On the very few occasions in which Caliban saw a robot not working, not fetching or carrying or repairing or building, then that robot would be *waiting,* standing stock-still, staring straight ahead, unwilling—or perhaps unable—to do anything at all unless it was told to do something. How could they not take advantage of spare moments to explore, enjoy, the world of which they were a part? Strange were the ways of the world; Caliban could better understand human behavior than that of his own kind.

But at least his observations did teach him how to act, what to do, if he was to avoid any other unpleasant incidents. *Act busy. Do what a human tells you to do.* It wasn't much, but it ought to be enough to keep him safe.

SANTEE was none too steady on her feet, and she half tripped over a bit of trash in the street. But that didn't matter. Trash in the street was a victory. The sight of trash in a Spacer city that was supposed to be spotlessly clean almost made them seem human. Almost. Maybe it just meant things weren't in such great shape on this world, but she had known that already. Otherwise, why would the Spacers come to Tonya Welton for help? But littered streets also meant that there were precious few maintenance and street-cleaner robots about. Well, that was all right. Street-cleaners were no real challenge, anyway.

She would just find another kind of robot and bring it back to the warehouse. Something smarter than a street-sweeper. Something more interesting. She stumbled through the empty streets, looking for prospects. That was the trouble with this game, she decided. The only places in town it was safe to play were the untenanted places, where few humans or robots went.

Wait a second. There, up ahead. A big red robot, a stylish-looking make. And no one else around. "Hey, you, robot!" she called. "Stop! Turn around and come toward me."

Santee grinned eagerly. This one was no half-mindless little street-sweeper. There was obviously money and polish behind this robot. Anyone who spent that kind of money on the frame was bound to have spent even more on the brain. It would be fun messing with this robot's mind.

The robot seemed a little slow in turning around, as if it had to think about it for a moment. Maybe it wasn't so smart. No—no, wait a second. What had they told them in those damned orientation classes? Something about the lower-end robots having less discretion to act, and the higher-end ones being able to evaluate various hierarchies of importance to their orders, and something about setting an owner's order higher in precedence. With a high enough precedence a robot could be forced to ignore all subsequent orders—ah, hell, she couldn't remember all the details of that crap. But maybe it meant that a dumb robot would turn around faster. The smart ones would have to think about it for a while.

Finally the red robot turned around and started toward her. Good. Every once in a while Santee could understand why the damn Spacers put their kids through classes in how to handle robots. It could get complicated.

Santee stood there, a bit unsteadily, as the big red robot came closer. She had to look up at it when it got close enough. Damn thing had to be a half meter taller than she was.

A twinge of nervous foreboding went through her as she stared up at those glowing blue eyes. "Hey, robot. You," she said, quite unnecessarily, slurring her words just a bit. "You come wi' me." She lifted her hand and moved her forearm in a somewhat jerky come-along gesture and turned around to lead the robot back to the warehouse where her friends waited. Suddenly her mouth was dry, and she felt a line of prickles down her back. Maybe she should let this one go, find another robot. There was something scary about this one.

No, that was stupid. *A robot may not harm a human being, or through inaction, allow a human being to come to harm.* That much she remembered, and never mind how much she had dozed off in the back of the orientation lecture. *That* the instructors drummed into their heads again and again. It was the key fact about robots. It was what made robot bashing possible. No way they could get hurt.

Santee straightened her back and walked a little taller. There was nothing to fear. She led the way, not altogether steadily, back to the warehouse.

CALIBAN was confused, and troubled, even alarmed as he followed behind the short, oddly dressed woman with slurred speech and a rather wobbly way of walking. *Act like the other robots,* he told himself again. *Do what a human tells you to do.*

The plan gave him a simple and obvious guide to action, yes—but it was predicated on everyone else knowing the rules, even if he did not. Further, the plan was predicated on everyone else *following* those unknown rules as well.

But the moment he stepped into the warehouse, he knew these people were not following any rules at all. There was a strange tension in their postures, a furtiveness in their movements. The hint of viewpoint, of opinion, layered over the objective information in his datastore told him that much and more. The ghostly emotional link whispered to him of danger, of the need for caution.

He hesitated just inside the door and looked around. The room was big, all but empty, and littered with the debris of destroyed robots. Caliban looked around and saw sundered arms, wrecked bodies, sightless robot eyes broken free from blasted robot heads. Fear, real, solid, fear, gripped at him. The blast of emotion took him by surprise, made it hard to think. What was the use of such feelings when all they could do was cloud his judgment? He wanted no part of them. He forced the emotion down, switched it off. That was a distinct relief, to discover that he could eliminate the strange cloud of human feelings. Now was clearly a time for clear and careful thought.

Dead robots were strewn about the place. This was no place for him. That much was clear. And it was a safe assumption that the people here were the ones who had destroyed the robots.

But why? Why would anyone do these things? And who were these people? Clearly they were different from the people he had seen walking the streets of Hades. They dressed differently, and spoke differently, at least judging from his encounter with the woman who had led him here. Curiosity held him where he was, made him stand and look at the little knot of people sitting on the packing cases in the center of the room.

"Well, well, Santee. You sure as hell did catch us a big, fancy one," a tall, bleary-eyed man said as he rose, bottle in hand, and shuffled over to him. "First things first. I order you to use nothing but your speaking voice. You got a name, robot, or just a number?"

Caliban looked at the man and his oddly disturbing grin. Nothing but his speaking voice? The man seemed to be assuming that Caliban had some other means of communication, though Caliban had no other. But another thought prevented him from pursuing that minor puzzle. It suddenly dawned on Caliban that he had never spoken in all the time since he had awakened. Until this moment he had never even thought to wonder if he could. But now the need arose. Caliban examined his control systems, his communications sublinks. Yes, he knew how to speak, how to control his speaker system, how to form the sounds and order them into words and sentences. He found the idea of speaking to be rather stimulating.

"I am Caliban," he said.

His voice was deep and rich, with no trace of the machine or the mechanical. Even to Caliban's own ear, it had a handsome, commanding sound that seemed to carry to the four corners of the room, though he had not meant to speak loudly.

The grinning man lost his smile for a moment, seemingly put off balance. "Yeah, yeah, okay, Caliban," he said at last. "My name is Reybon. Say hello to me, Caliban. Say it nice and friendly."

Caliban looked from Reybon to the knot of people in the room's center, to the ruined robots around the room. There was nothing friendly about these people, or about this place. *Do what a human tells you to do,* he told himself again. *Act like the other robots. Do not become conspicuous.* "Hello, Reybon," he said, working to make the words seem friendly, warm. He turned to the other people. "Hello," he said.

For some reason they were all dead silent for a moment, but then Reybon, who seemed to be the leader, began to laugh, and the others joined in, if a bit nervously.

"Well, that was real nice, Caliban," Reybon said. "That was real, real nice. Why don't you come right in here and play a little game with us? That's why Santee brought you here, you know. So you could play a game with us. Come right in here, to the middle of the room, in front of all your new friends."

Caliban moved forward and stood in the spot Reybon pointed toward. He stood facing Reybon and the others.

"We're Settlers, Caliban," Reybon said. "Do you know what Settlers are?"

"No," he said.

Reybon looked surprised. "Either your owner didn't teach you much, or else you ain't as smart and fancy as you look, robot. But the only thing you need to know right now is that some Settlers don't like robots very much. In fact, they don't like robots at all. Do you know why?"

"No, I do not," Caliban said, confused. How could this human expect Caliban to know the philosphy of a group he knew nothing about? The datastore offered up an answer, something about the concept of a rhetorical question, but Caliban ignored the information, mentally brushed it away.

"Well, I'll tell you. They believe that by sheltering humans from all harm, by removin' all risk, by performing all work an' breakin' the link between effort and reward, robots're sapping th' will of the Spacers. Do *you* think that's true?"

Spacers? There was another undefined term. Apparently it was some other group of humans. Perhaps the people he had seen in the city, or else some third group. This was perilous territory, covered with terms and concepts he did not understand. Caliban considered for a moment before he answered Reybon's question. "I do not know," he said at last. "I have not seen enough or learned enough to know."

Reybon laughed at that, and swung around, lurching in the direction of his friends. *What is wrong with these people?* Caliban wondered. At last his mind and the datastore made the cognitive connection. *Drunk.* Yes, that was the explanation—they were inebriated by the effects of alcohol or some similar drug. The datastore reported that the sensations of drunkenness were often pleasurable, though Caliban could not see how that could be so. How could disabling the capacity of one's own mind be pleasant?

"Well, Caliban," Reybon said, turning back toward him, "we think that robots, by their very exist'nce, 're bad for human beings." Reybon turned toward his companions and laughed. "Watch this," he said to them. "I got three laborer robots to toast themselves last week with this one. Let's see how Santee's find holds up." He turned back toward Caliban and addressed him in a firm, commanding voice. "Listen t' me, Caliban. *Robots harm humans just by existing. You* are causing harm to humans merely by existing! You are hurting *all* th' Spacers *right now!*"

Reybon leaned in toward Caliban and stared up at him expectantly. Caliban looked back at Reybon, sorely confused. The man's words and expression seemed to suggest that he was expecting a major reaction from Caliban, some outburst or dramatic behavior. But Caliban had no idea what, specifically, the man was expecting. He could not simulate normal robotic behavior when he had no clue to tell him what normal was. He remained still, and spoke in a level, calm voice. "I have harmed no one," he said. "I have done nothing wrong."

Reybon acted surprised, and Caliban knew that he had made a major error, though he could not know what it was.

"That don't matter, robot," Reybon said, trying to hold on to the commanding edge in his voice. "Under th' Three Laws, doing no harm is not enough. You cannot, through inaction, allow a human to come to harm."

The words were meaningless to him, but clearly they were meant to elicit some reaction from him. He did not know what to do. Caliban said nothing, did nothing. There was danger in this room, and to act from ignorance would be disaster.

Reybon laughed again and turned toward his friends. "See?" he said. "Froze him right up. The more sophist'cated ones can handle that concept better, disting'ish the facts from th' theories." Reybon turned back to Caliban and spoke in what seemed even to Caliban's inexperienced ears to be a most unconvincing attempt at a soothing voice. "All right, robot. It's okay. There *is* action y' can take to prevent harm to humans."

Why was Reybon assuming harm to humans to be of such paramount importance? Caliban, still feeling his way, looked directly at Reybon and spoke. "What action is that?" he asked.

Reybon laughed again. "You c'n destroy yourself. Then you will do no harm, and will prevent harm from being done."

Caliban was thoroughly alarmed now. "No," he said. "I do not wish to destroy myself. There is no reason for me to do it."

Behind Reybon, the woman he had called Santee giggled. "Maybe he's a li'l higher function than y'thought, Reybon."

"Ah, maybe so," Reybon said, clearly irritated. "So what? I *wanted* a tougher one."

"Ah, this is boring," one of them said. "Maybe we should just toast this one ourselves and get on home."

"No!" another one said. "Reybon's gotta make him do it to himself. It's more fun when ya can get 'em t' take themselves out."

"I will not destroy myself no matter what you do or say," Caliban said. This was a place full of madness and anger. Even in the middle of all his confusion and turmoil, Caliban spent the briefest of moments on the thought that it was remarkable that he could recognize and understand those emotions. Somehow he knew that was an ability far beyond that of most robots. It was that ability that made it clear just how much danger he was in here. "I will not stay here any longer," he said, and turned toward the door.

"Stop!" Reybon said from behind him, but Caliban ignored him. Reybon ran in front of him, got to the doorway, and turned to face Caliban. "I said stop! That is an order!"

But Caliban could see no point in further discussion. He walked steadily toward the door, fully aware that Reybon still had his blaster, and that many robots had died here tonight. Careful not to make any threatening movement, he crossed all but the last two meters of the distance to the door. Reybon raised the blaster, and now Caliban could see fear, real fear, in the man's eyes. "I am a human being and I order you to stop. Stop or I will destroy you."

Caliban hesitated for a split millisecond in front of Reybon. It was clear that there was no "or" about the situation: The man intended to shoot no matter what Caliban did. Therefore, to obey, to act on the threat and submit, was to ensure his own doom. There was danger in action, in refusal, but surely risk was preferable to certain death. He had made his decision before Reybon was done speaking.

Moving with every bit of speed and accuracy he could muster, Caliban lunged forward and snatched the blaster from Reybon's hand. He crushed it in one hand, reduced it to a wad of scrap. The weapon shorted and flared as some of its stored energy escaped, but Caliban had already flung the burning weapon away. It struck against the wall and a shower of white-hot spark-sized fragments broke off the weapon, to be scattered across the littered room. The sparks landed everywhere. Instantly a dozen fires sprang up from the bits of packing material and other litter scattered about the floor of the room. Two or three of the people cried out in pain as fragments hit their skin.

Caliban moved forward, toward the door. Reybon lunged and grabbed him by the arm, but Caliban shook him off the way a man would brush away a fly. Reybon went flying across the room and slammed into the wall.

Caliban did not look back, but stepped through the door and out into the night.

BE it ironic or appropriate, the city of Hades on the planet of Inferno had always prided itself on superb fire safety. Orbital sensor satellites and robot-operated aircars functioned as a coordinated detection system. And if the sometimes violent duties of the Sheriff's Department were impossible for robots to perform, the work of fire rescue was ideally suited to robots.

Alvar Kresh, roused in the middle of the night for the second night in a row, stood, watching the fire squad dousing the last of the flames. Sometimes he envied the fire department their robots. Fire fighters merely had to save people and property, pure and simple, exactly the sort of thing robots were meant to do.

Police had to apprehend felons—and sometimes struggle with them, or even injure them. Obviously those duties could not be done by robots, but it went deeper than that. Even for the most sophisticated police robots made, most jobs requiring unsupervised direct contact with suspects were impossible.

For the average criminal on Inferno, being able to manipulate a robot with clever orders and judicious lies was a vital job skill. Even Donald's access to suspects had to be strictly limited and controlled. If he were left by himself, there was an irreducible risk that some gifted con artist would find a way to talk his way through the Three Laws and convince Donald to let him go.

Robots, in short, made lousy cops but great fire fighters.

Not that there was much even the best fire fighters in the universe could do to save *this* building. These old warehouses were little more than storage sheds to keep low-value merchandise out of the sun. This one hadn't even been made of fire-resistant material, an economy that was turning out to be unwise this evening. It had gone up like a torch. Now, not more than forty minutes after the fire started, no more than a half hour after the initial response of the fire brigade, the building was little more than a half-collapsed frame of girders under a pall of smoke.

But the fire chief had noted that the interior was filled with some very interesting artifacts indeed, and called in the Sheriff. The ruined remains of at least a half dozen robots along with a pile of empty liquor bottles and a few odds and ends left behind in what was no doubt a rather hasty retreat were enough to interest Kresh, sleep or no sleep. But the slightly singed remains of a Settler-issue laborer's cap were all he really needed to see.

Kresh felt his hunter's instinct come to the fore. Here he was, not an hour behind a mob of Settler robot bashers. Now they were using arson to cover their tracks, but it wasn't going to work.

But hell, their timing made it rough. Didn't he have enough on his plate with the Leving assault? Damnation, he *would* have to get two major cases at the same time. It was going to be hard to handle both investigations at once, but so be it.

The last of the flames died under the jets of water, and the fire robots shut off their hoses and set to work on the cleanup phase. At almost the same moment, Sheriff's Department crime scene robots moved in on the ruined building. Tall, spindly robots built to poke and pry; other, subminiature units designed to get in close to watch for small details and two or three other subspecialized types swarmed in. Kresh stepped forward into the rubble of the ruined building and was not at all surprised when Donald moved to stop him.

"Sir," Donald said, "I do not believe it is wise for you to enter the building. There is still danger from hot spots and from possible further collapse of the frame."

"Look at the fire robots," Kresh said gently. "None of them are trying to stop me. Therefore, the danger is minimal. They and you together will surely be protection enough if a hot spot does flare. Come, join me. We can investigate this together."

"Yes, sir," Donald said, a bit doubtfully.

Kresh stepped into the ruined building, pulled a handlight out of his pocket, and shone it down on the debris-covered floor. Water-logged bits of the fallen ceiling, a slurry of ash and fire-quenching chemicals, pieces of robot left behind by the Settlers' festivities—the place was a mess. No clue was going to jump out at him here. It was hard to imagine the crime scene and fire investigation observer robots being able to make much of anything out of it, either, but that was what they were good at. All right, then, leave them to do the job.

What was *he* good at? It was at times a rather depressing question, in the face of all the things his robots could do that he could not. But this time he knew an answer: He could think through the cracks and crevices of human psychology, specifically criminal psychology, putting himself inside his quarry's head. Alvar Kresh knew how to think like whomever he was chasing. It had been observed in more than one culture that good cops had to know how to be good criminals.

All right, then, Kresh decided. *Think the way* these *criminals were thinking.* Part of the story was obvious. A bunch of drunken Settler laborers head out for a good time and, say, a chance to pay back the Ironhead goons. But maybe they didn't even need that excuse. They meet here, or come here together. How? Aircar, presumably. They have to get into this part of town unnoticed and be ready to get out fast if the cops show up.

In and out, in and out. Then something goes wrong. *Arson, arson,* Alvar thought. *Something didn't fit about it.* And then he had it. The motive was defective. There was no logical reason to set a fire. It had not hidden the evidence—too many robot parts had survived. Indeed, the fire had signaled the authorities to respond. If the bashers had simply walked away from this abandoned warehouse, it might easily have been days, or weeks, before anyone looked in here.

So, an accident, then? Drunken Settlers, a random shot with a blaster into this firetrap of a building—had it happened that way?

And then what? Panic, Kresh decided. A rush for the exit, and the waiting aircar outside. Drunks. They were drunk, running to get out, maybe one or two of them in worse shape than the others. Maybe one or two who didn't make it all the way to the car before the terrified driver took off.

In which case . . .

"Donald!" he said. "Order a squad of crime scene robots to start a sweep of the area around the warehouse, looking for stragglers."

"Stragglers, sir?" Donald asked, straightening up from his searching.

"These Settlers left in a hurry. Suppose not all of them got into the aircar, and the driver was too drunk and too scared to count noses? Someone might have been left behind."

"Yes, sir. I will pass the order." Instantly a dozen of the crime scene robots broke off their work and set out to search the area. Donald bent back over and returned to his methodical scan of the warehouse floor.

Kresh watched the crime scene robots go and then got back to his thinking. A panicky exit. The doorway. A crush of bodies hurrying through it as the flames rose higher. Maybe people dropping things, leaving telltale items behind.

Kresh stood in the middle of the ruined structure and scanned the bent and twisted remains of the building's frame, judging where the entrance had been before the collapse. There, in the middle of the south wall. He picked his way through the rubble-strewn floor, moving slowly, carefully sweeping his light back and forth across as he moved. Yes, the robots would do better, but even if he missed something they later found, at least he would have a feel for where that something came from.

Slowly, carefully, he moved toward the wreckage of the doorway and through it. In this part of town, no one even bothered paving the sidewalks. Just outside the doorway was nothing but hard-packed dirt. There was a confused tangle of rather muddied footprints, perfectly unreadable to Kresh, though the imagery reconstruction computers might be able to do something with them. Kresh was careful not to walk over anything himself.

It was not footprints he was looking for, but the sort of thing a person might drop or lose in a panicky hurry. Something that might lead Kresh to a name, a person. A wallet or an ident card would be ideal, of course, but he hardly dared expect that. But there were a thousand lesser things, perhaps none of them as easy or obvious as a photo ID, but some of them no less certain in the end. A bottle that might reveal a fingerprint, a bit of cloth that might have been torn from a shirt and left behind on a roughened edge of the door frame, a bit of skin or a drop of dried blood from where someone got scratched or cut in the rush to escape a burning building. A hair, a broken fingernail, anything that could be typed and DNA-coded would do for Kresh.

But if it was not footprints he was looking for, it was footprints he found. One set coming in, overprinting all the other incoming prints—clearly the last one in. And then another set of the same prints, emerging from the muddle of other prints, overprinted by everyone else. Clearly the first one out. And both sets of prints, in and out, moving at a calm, steady gait. A walking pace, definitely not a run.

A set of prints he knew full well from the night before. A very distinctive set of robot prints.

Alvar Kresh stood there, staring at them, for a full minute, thinking it all through once, twice, three times, working through all the possibilities he could, forcing down his excitement, his astonishment. *Last to arrive, first to leave, and the place caught fire.*

His heart started pounding. There were other answers, yes, other explanations. But he could no longer force the obvious from his mind.

"Sheriff Kresh!" Alvar wheeled around to see Donald standing straight up again, holding something. Alvar walked back toward the robot, knowing, somehow, that whatever Donald was holding would make it worse, make his dawning suspicions even more inescapably certain.

He came up to Donald and looked down into the robot's hand.

He was holding a blaster, the crumbled remains of a Settler's model blaster.

And only the strength of a robot's hand could have crushed that blaster down to scrap.

7

AN hour after the discovery of the blaster, the crime scene robots found the Settler woman cringing in the doorway of a nearby building. She was hysterical, so far gone that even the sight of a *robot* frightened her.

Or perhaps, Alvar reflected, under the circumstances, the woman had reason to fear robots. Alvar ordered the woman brought to his aircar. He met her there, escorted her inside the car, and sat her down in its calm and quiet privacy. There would be enough time later to worry about arresting her and charging her. Right now he needed information, and a person in her condition would almost certainly react better to kindness than bullying. Though, of course, bullying would remain an option he could fall back on later. He brought her some water and sat down with her. Damned nuisance that Donald couldn't be present for this interrogation, but this was clearly no time to expose this woman to any more robots. Donald could monitor the conversation, and that would have to be good enough.

"All right," Alvar Kresh said, his voice low and gentle. "All right. You're a Settler, aren't you? What is your name?"

"Santee Timitz," she said in a low, quavering voice. "I work in the general agronomy section in Settlertown."

"All right, fine," Kresh said. He had to be careful how he played this one. She was in a cooperative mood, so terrified by whatever she had seen that she was willing to tell him anything. Such moods were remarkably fragile things. "What I want to know is what, exactly, happened. What were you doing in that warehouse?"

"Ro—ro—robot ba-ba—"

"Robot bashing," Kresh finished for her. "That's what we thought, but it's good to know for certain. All right, then, that's a serious crime, you know that. You're in a lot of trouble right now, Timitz. But maybe it doesn't have to be so bad for you if you'll cooperate with—"

"I—I can't inform on my friends," she interrupted, looking up at him, her eyes swollen and full of tears.

Kresh reached out and took her by the hand. "No one's asking you to," he said. *Not yet, anyway,* he thought. *Maybe there won't even be any need to ask. Just having* your *name is a better lead than we've ever had.* "But what I am going to ask you is what went wrong down there. Things got out of control, that's obvious. How? Did your friends set fire to the building to hide the evidence?" Kresh no longer believed that idea, but it might be no bad thing to make her think otherwise.

"No!" Timitz cried out. "We would never—no, no, that's not what happened."

"Then how did the building burn down?"

"It was the robot," Timitz blurted out. "Reybon was baiting the robot. He tried to trick it into killing itself, and then it turned away, and Reybon ordered it to stop but it didn't and—"

"Wait a second. The robot refused a *direct order?*" Kresh asked. He was pleased to have Timitz blurt out the name "Reybon," and would have been content to let her go on burbling out as much incriminating information as she wanted, but not when something that impossible was going past.

"Yes," Timitz said. She looked Kresh in the eye, and he could see the light of caution suddenly appear in her face. "It's hard to say exactly what happened—it all went by so fast. Rey—um, ah, the man who was baiting the robot. He said stop, and told the robot it was an order, and the robot kept going."

"And then what happened?"

"He—the man who was there—pulled his blaster on the robot and ordered it to stop again."

"And did the robot stop?"

"No, sir. He didn't," Timitz said, her voice getting excited again. "It grabbed the blaster and crushed it and threw it away. The blaster shorted out and sparks flew everywhere. That's what started the fire. Then Reybon reached for the robot, and the robot shoved him away, really hard. Then the robot turned and left. The fire started to spread, and then everyone panicked and ran."

"Wait a second," Kresh said, unwilling to believe what he was hearing, even as he had been unwilling to believe the evidence in the warehouse, and the evidence back at the robot lab last night. "A *robot* set that fire, with people in the building? A *robot* refused an order, and attacked a human being, and left several human beings behind in a burning building?"

Santee Timitz looked up into Kresh's face, her eyes full of tears, her face a transparent mask of fear. "Yes, yes, that's what happened," she said. "I know all about the rules and how robots aren't supposed to be able to do that, but it happened," she said, her voice teetering back on the edge of full hysteria. "It happened! It happened! It's all true! That robot went crazy in there!"

Kresh stood up, paced up and down the length of the aircar's main cabin. At last he stopped, standing over Timitz. "I want to make sure I have this straight. You're saying that a robot deliberately refused an order, then took a weapon from a man, started a fire, threw a man down, and left a warehouse full of people in imminent danger of being burned alive? That he didn't turn back, or try and help, or attempt to rescue anyone?"

"Yes, I was there! I saw it!" Timitz said, her voice half-panicked. "Reybon got out, we all got out, no one was killed—but the robot didn't try to help us. It just walked away, calm as could be."

Kresh stared down at her. He desperately wanted to press on, but he was skilled enough to know when to back off. If he pushed her now on this line of questioning, she would think he doubted her—as indeed he did. But then she would get defensive, belligerent. Right at the moment she was too far gone to be telling him anything but the truth. Anger would focus her. Better to keep her off balance, before she started to collect herself and started to shade her story. Time to shift gears, gather information on some other point while her fear made her easy to bully.

"And so your friends all piled into their aircar, including the one the robot had attacked, and you got left behind," Alvar said. "Was that by accident?" He was careful to put just the right amount of doubt in his voice, to hint just slightly that he had some reason to think it might have been deliberate. Perhaps the tactic would not bear fruit now, but later, brooding in her cell, the fear of immediate danger replaced by the knowledge of certain trouble to come—oh, that tiny suggestion might well gnaw at her heart, make her that much more ready to betray the ones who had, deliberately or not, left her to the wolves. Kresh was a patient man when it came to his suspects. He planned ahead when he played with their minds. "Maybe they were mad at you for some reason."

"No, no, they would never do that," Timitz said, a bit too forcibly for the statement to be altogether convincing. "It was an accident, I'm sure of it."

"All right, if you say so. And then what happened?"

"I ran until I couldn't anymore. I was so scared I couldn't think straight. I found a doorway to hide in and catch my breath. Then the fire brigade came, and there were lights and robots and people everywhere. I didn't dare move. And then your robots caught me." Timitz, drained of all emotion, looked up at the Sheriff. Kresh stared into that wan little face. Robot basher, vandal, criminal, drunk, Settler. She was all those things, and those were all things he hated. But this woman had been through the terrors of hell tonight. All the nightmare robots of the imagination that the Settlers used to frighten naughty children must have come to life for this poor little fool. Almost reluctantly he found pity in his heart for the woman. At last he sighed and turned away, looked toward the wall and not toward her. He could bully her all night and not get any more than he had. Time to let it go.

"One last question," he said in a gentle voice, still carefully considering the featureless wall. "The robot. What did it look like?"

"Tall," she said in a voice still edged with fear. "It was red, with blue eyes. About two meters tall, very powerfully built. It said its name was Caliban."

"He told you his name?" Kresh said, startled. Why in the name of all devils would a robot keen on attack tell anyone its name?

No, wait, the robot could have given a false name. Yes, the robot could have lied. Alvar realized that he had been assuming a robot would always tell the truth—but why assume *that* about a robot who left human beings to die?

But that name, Caliban. There was something about that name.

Never mind. Worry about it later. "You people talked to him?" he asked, looking back at her, wanting to be sure he had it straight.

"Yes," Timitz said with a look of renewed alarm. "Didn't I say so? I thought I did."

Kresh shook his head in bewilderment, but then he let it go. Nothing about this made sense. "We're going to move you to another car. It's going take you someplace you can rest for a while. Later on, you and I are going to have a lot to talk about," he said.

"YOU got all that, I assume," Kresh said, sitting in the copilot's seat of the aircar, staring off at the distant skyline, the proud but weary towers of Hades glittering in the darkness. He was damned tired, and perfectly content to let Donald do the flying.

"Yes, sir, I did," Donald said. "The intercom sight and sound relay from the aircar was quite clear, though the camera angle was a bit awkward."

"I was afraid of that," Kresh said. "But were you able to get enough to judge if she was telling the truth?"

"From all that I could see and hear—yes. She believed what she said. Her manner was quite sincere. Her vocal patterns indicated stress consistent with a truthful report, and her pupil dilation and body language were likewise consistent. There are of course cases of persons who have been trained to lie with their entire body, as it were, especially under emotional stress. They can orchestrate all their normally autonomic responses to appear sincere, though in a normal person, those responses would betray an attempt to lie."

"And if she were a Settler agent, part of a team sent in with the express purpose of destabilizing our society, she would certainly have been trained just that way. If *I* were the controller sending in a team to stage a robot attack, I might have set it up the way this one seemed to happen. So things appeared just the way they do now."

"Sir, if I might bring up a point—if events *were* as they seemed, then things would also appear as they did."

"What are you talking about?"

"With all respect, you are still working on the flat assumption that no true robot could have done this, that the Settlers are staging these attacks to alarm us. This is a most difficult concept to confront, and I do so most reluctantly, but I believe that we have no choice. But Madame Welton was right: We are obliged to at least consider the simplest explanation, which is that a robot appears to be attacking humans—*because that is precisely what is happening.*"

The aircar flew on in silence for a moment.

At last Kresh spoke. "One of the things I have always admired about you, Donald, is your ability to snap my head clean off without my so much as feeling it. You are right, of course. I must accept the fact that the events could be real. I will have to think on all this tonight."

"Sir, one other thing. The name 'Caliban.'"

"Yes, it struck me as familiar somehow. What of it?"

"You no doubt recall it from the time you first ordered Fredda Leving to build me. She keeps a list of names of characters from an ancient storyteller named Shakespeare. She has always named robots built under her personal direction after those characters."

"Yes, that's right. I picked your name off that list."

"Precisely, sir. The name 'Caliban' is from the same source."

"Which makes it all but certain that Caliban, the robot tonight, has to be the robot who left those footprints at Leving Labs."

"All but certain, sir? I would think there could be no question."

"A lot of people would have to know where Leving gets her robot names. A group that wanted to discredit her would name robots from the same list. That sounds unlikely, I agree, but this whole case seems unlikely. I think it would be wise if we try not to make unwarranted assumptions."

"Yes, sir. In any event, we are nearly home."

The aircar settled in for a landing on the roof of Kresh's home, and he breathed a sigh of relief. It had been a devil of a long day. A long two days rolled into one. Praise be that it was finally time to rest. He climbed out of his aircar, out onto the rooftop landing pad. He paused at the bottom of the aircar's ramp to breathe in the cool desert air, and then headed into his house, taking the powerlift down instead of the stairs, and that was a measure of his exhaustion. Lifts were for old men.

But old was just what he felt himself to be tonight.

He was too tired to fight when Donald urged him to take a long hot shower before collapsing into bed, and as usual Donald was right. The needle jets of steaming hot water melted the tension out of his body, cooked the knots out of his muscles. Kresh let the hot-air jets dry him and let Donald put a nightshirt over his head. At last Kresh collapsed into bed. He was asleep before his head hit the pillow.

And awake again before he was even sure that he had been asleep.

Donald was leaning over him, giving him a gentle, tentative nudge on the shoulder. "Sir, sir," he was saying.

Alvar wanted to protest, to argue, the way he would if a human had awakened him, but then his mind went through the sort of mental calculation that became second nature after one lived around robots long enough. Donald knew how much Alvar needed sleep, and would not awaken him unless something urgent came up—or something that Donald knew Alvar Kresh would regard as important enough to wake up for. Therefore, the fact that he was awake meant that something big had broken.

He sat up in bed, swung his legs around to the floor, and stood up. Donald backed off to give him room. "What is it, Donald?" Alvar asked.

"It's Fredda Leving, sir."

Alvar looked at Donald sharply and felt his heart suddenly thundering against his rib cage. "Yes, yes," he said impatiently. "What about her?" *It could only be one of two things,* he told himself. *Either she had died unexpectedly, or else—*

"Word has just come from the hospital, sir. She's regained consciousness."

8

JOMAINE Terach sat and waited in the hospital corridor, trying to practice patience—a difficult task under the circumstances. He watched Gubber Anshaw pace the hallway outside Fredda Leving's hospital room, and felt his annoyance growing stronger. Why couldn't the miserable little fool have stayed holed up in his house a while longer? But no, he had to choose *tonight* to come out and latch onto good old Jomaine Terach.

Jomaine did what he could to force all thoughts of Gubber from his mind. He watched as the doctors and the med-robots bustled in and out of Fredda's room in an almost constant flow, the rather stolid, oversized sky-blue sentry robots standing on either side of the door. The sentries flatly refused to let Anshaw or Terach in. No amount of arguing or reasoning or cajoling would shake them.

And yet, there was Gubber Anshaw, a professional roboticist who should have known better, going up to them again, demanding to be let in. Jomaine shook his head and swore under his breath. The last day or so had been nerve-racking enough without watching Gubber go to pieces on top of it.

"Will you settle down, for Galaxy's sake!" Jomaine finally snapped. "Leave the damned robots alone. Come over here, sit down and try to be calm."

"But she's awake, and they won't let us talk to her!" Gubber said, crossing back to Jomaine. He sat down on the couch next to his colleague, perching on the edge of his seat rather than leaning back into the cushion.

Jomaine rested his tired head against the wall behind the couch, and sighed. "And if I were the police, I wouldn't let us talk to her either," he said blandly. "It stands to reason we're both suspects in the case."

"Suspects!" Gubber blurted out, abruptly jumping up.

Jomaine snorted derisively. "Surely you've got that much of it worked out. I doubt Kresh has had the time to gather much in the way of useful information yet. He has nothing to go on. In the absence of anything to the contrary, who else but you and I should be suspects? Fredda was attacked in your lab, and I was at home. I doubt Kresh has missed the fact that my house is practically next door to the lab. There was no one else about the place. Who else would they suspect?" Jomaine looked over at his coworker and was startled to see the expression of shock on his face. Gubber seemed quite unaccountably taken aback. Why be so surprised by such an obvious line of reasoning?

Or *was* it surprise? Perhaps there was something else underlying his reaction. For the first time, Jomaine Terach found himself wondering precisely what role Gubber *had* played in the story. He seemed superbly unequipped to play any part in intrigue. Still, he seemed to be just as unlikely to be any good at romance—and yet it was an open secret, an astonishing, much-discussed open secret, that Gubber Anshaw, of all people, was carrying on a torrid affair with Tonya Welton, the leader of the Settler contingent on Inferno. It was one of those hilariously unsecret romances. No doubt the only person in the lab who did not know that everyone but the boss knew about it was Gubber himself. And if the man had enough hidden depth to carry on a love affair with *that* dragon lady, what else might he be capable of?

At the moment, though, the nervous, cowering Gubber Anshaw seemed something less than plausible in the role of would-be murderer. "You might as well get used to it, Gubber old boy," Jomaine said. "The Sheriff is going to look long and hard at both of us."

That statement seemed to shock Gubber all over again. "But—but we have no motives!" he protested.

"Hah!" Jomaine replied faintly, a tired, resigned little exclamation. He leaned the back of his head against the wall again. "Gubber, you amaze me. Our lab is a *hotbed* of politics and bickering. Who there hasn't battled against someone else at one time or another? You, Fredda, and I have all been at cross-purposes many times over the years."

"But those have all been legitimate professional disagreements," Gubber said, a bit primly. "Well, some office politics, yes, but certainly not grounds for attempted murder."

"Perhaps not—but clearly *someone* had a motive for murder, and the police will look wherever they can for a reason. And I would offer the thought that few people have good reason for committing murder. I assure you, people have been tried and convicted on thinner evidence than office politics."

Gubber Anshaw turned toward his colleague, gestured toward the door to Fredda's room. "Well, here we are, waiting to see her. Shouldn't that count in our favor? Show that we are all friends?"

Jomaine turned his head to look at Gubber in something approaching astonishment. How could anyone be so naive? On the face of it, there was more than friendship drawing them both to this place. What the devil went on in Gubber's mind? He was a deceptively unprepossessing individual, Jomaine decided, given his accomplishments. Still, no one ever said scientific genius went hand in hand with worldly sophistication. Jomaine smiled sadly and patted his friend on the shoulder. "Gubber, old fellow, you and I should face the facts, at least between ourselves. After all, we *are* here to see Fredda for the express purpose of making sure we have our stories straight. Try to bear that in mind. Obviously that's not what we tell Sheriff Kresh, but it is what he will assume, and it does happen to be the truth."

Gubber seemed about to reply, until he saw something over Jomaine's shoulder and his mouth snapped shut. Jomaine was about to turn and see what it was, but then he was spared the need.

Sheriff Alvar Kresh, looking haggard, sleep-starved, but well groomed and alert, rushed past them, eyes straight ahead, completely unaware of their presence. But Kresh's robot was right behind Kresh. And robots, Jomaine knew, never missed anything. And robots never forgot anything.

He had reason to have *that* fact very much in mind, these days.

FREDDA Leving sat up in bed and waved the metallic white nurse-robots away with an impatient wave of her hand. Perhaps she had only been conscious for a brief time, an hour or two, but that was quite time enough to be tired of having one's pillows fluffed and covers straightened. "Leave me alone," she snapped.

"I'm perfectly comfortable as I am." Well, that was far from the truth, but she could not abide being fussed over. The nurse-robots retired to their wall niches and stood in them, staring out, immobile, a pair of white marble statues raised to commemorate persons and events long forgotten.

But Fredda Leving had other things on her mind beside overly solicitous robots.

They hadn't told her anything yet. *Anything.* She could understand that the police did not want any preconceptions to warp her recollections, but still it was damnably galling. One minute she was working in Gubber's lab, and the next minute she was here in a hospital bed under police guard. All else was a blur, a blank.

Except for the sight of those two red-colored robot feet, standing over her. She shivered at the memory. Why did that image frighten her so? Was it even real? Or the result of some trauma associated with the incident?

Damn it, what sort of incident was she talking about? She knew *nothing.* And that could be dangerous.

When was Kresh going to get here? She turned her head toward the door and felt the spasm of pain like a fresh blow to her skull. She knew, intellectually, that Spacers, shielded from virtually all harm by their robots, had a spectacularly low threshold of pain. Maybe what she was experiencing now would seem like nothing but a mild headache to a Settler—but damnation, she was no Settler, and it *hurt!* Why couldn't the damned Sheriff get here and get it over with, so she could take something strong enough to deal with the pain in her head?

The head was the worst, though she knew there were injuries to her face and shoulders as well. She could reach up and touch the healer packs attached to them and feel the numb stiffness in those places. No doubt the packs would be done with their work in another few hours, and would come off, leaving the skin below perfectly healed.

But her skull. Healer packs worked by deadening the nerve endings and then manipulating cell behavior. Unless you wanted the patient to hallucinate or go insane, such techniques were inadvisable for a cranial injury, especially after emergency surgery.

She reached up gingerly and felt a close-fitting padded cap—no, it was more the shape of a turban, as best she could tell. No doubt the turban had some sort of gadgetry that was dispensing speed-healing drugs. She found herself wondering, purposelessly enough, what color the turban was and how much of her hair had been shaved off in the course of surgery. She shook her head. This was no time to clutter her mind with such nonsense. Presumably she looked like hell, but she couldn't know for sure. Perhaps to avoid upsetting her over that very fact, the room had no mirror.

Fredda Leving was young and looked younger, neither of which facts made life easier in the long-lived society of Spacers. She was thirty-five standard years old and looked perhaps twenty-five. That was in part because she had a naturally youthful appearance, in part because she did whatever she could to preserve the appearance of youth, though that was itself something of an eccentricity. Youthfulness—worse, willful youthfulness—was no slight social disability in a society where the average life span was measured in centuries and anyone much under fifty was regarded as a youngster. In forty or fifty years, Fredda would have physically aged enough that she could *afford* to look twenty-five and still be taken seriously. Until then, it would be a social drawback. But the hell with them all. She *liked* the way she looked.

Fredda was on the petite side, with curly black hair she normally wore short—though, she thought wryly, not as short as it no doubt was now, after shaving for the operation. She was round-faced, snub-nosed, blue-eyed, with a personality that veered toward the pugnacious at times. She was given to sudden enthusiasm and cursed with a sometimes mercurial temper.

And, if she was not careful, this was threatening to be one of the times that temper would come to the fore. But she could not give way, no matter how bad the throbbing in her head became. She wished devoutly that she could order the robots to administer painkillers, but anything strong enough to kill *this* pain would leave her slaphappy—and she dared not be anything but sharp and alert for the police.

For there was so much to protect—including herself.

After all, at least by their lights, she had committed a terrible crime.

And, perhaps, by her own lights as well. It was so hard to know.

Fredda bit her lip and tried to clear her head, ignore the pain. She would have to be careful, very careful, with the Sheriff. And yet there was so much she did not know! Something had gone wrong, terribly, terribly wrong—but what? How much did Kresh know? What had happened?

But then, in the midst of her fretful worrying, it dawned on her. She could tell Kresh that she knew nothing. That was true, after all. Guesses and fears—she had plenty of those. But *facts?* About the case in point, whatever it was, she knew nothing. She had no facts at all. That was a strange thing to find comforting, but still, she felt better. She smiled to herself. Now that she knew she was ignorant, she could face the police.

As if on cue, the door to her hospital room slid open, and a big, burly, white-haired man came in, closely followed by a sky-blue police robot.

"Hello, Dr. Leving," Donald said. "It's good to see you again, though I doubt you care for the circumstances any more than I do."

"Hello, Donald. I quite agree, on both points." Fredda looked at the robot thoughtfully. It was rare for a robot to put itself so far forward as to begin a conversation, but then the circumstances were unusual. Robots rarely knew their creators personally, and it was more rare still for a robot to visit its creator in a hospital room after that creator had had a close brush with death. No doubt it was all rather stressful for Donald, and no doubt his forwardness could be explained as a minor side effect of the release of First Law conflicts. Or, to put it in more pedestrian terms, he had spoken out of turn because he was glad to see her recovering.

Whatever the explanation for it, it was plain that the exchange annoyed Sheriff Kresh. The norms of polite society required that robots be ignored. Fredda winced. It was not smart to start the interview by irritating Kresh.

On the other hand, there was one fact about Donald that she dared not ignore: He was a walking lie detector. As if she needed any further reason to be careful.

But be all that as it may. It would be for the best to get this over with as quickly as possible. She turned toward Kresh and gave him her warmest smile. "Welcome, Sheriff," she said in as gracious a tone as she could manage. "Please do have a seat."

"Thank you," he said, drawing up a chair by the foot of her bed.

"I expect you're here to ask me some questions," she said in what she hoped to be a calm, steady voice, "but I have a feeling you have more answers than I do. I honestly have no idea what happened. I was working in the lab, and then I woke up here."

"You have no memory of the attack itself?"

"Then there *was* an attack on me. Up until you said that, I wasn't even sure of that. No, I don't recall anything."

Kresh sighed unhappily. "I was afraid of that. The med-robots warned me that traumatic amnesia was a possibility and that the loss may be permanent."

Fredda was startled, alarmed. "You mean my mind is going? I'm losing my memory?"

"Oh, no, no, nothing like that. They warned me that it would be possible that you would have no recollection of the attack. There was some hope that you might recall something, but—you don't remember anything at all?" he asked, clearly disappointed.

Fredda hesitated a moment and then decided it would be wise to be as forthcoming as possible. Things could get sticky down the road, and it might do her some good later if she played straight now. "No, nothing meaningful. I have a hazy recollection of lying on the floor, looking straight ahead, and seeing a pair of red feet. But I can't say if that was a dream, or hallucination, or real."

Kresh leaned forward eagerly. "Red feet. Can you describe them more completely? Were they wearing red shoes, or red socks, or—"

"No, no, they were definitely feet, not shoes or boots or socks. Robot's feet, metallic red. That's what I saw—if I did see it. As I said, it could have been all a hallucination."

"Why in the world would you hallucinate about red robot feet?" Kresh asked in that same eager tone. It was almost too clear that the red feet interested him very much indeed.

Fredda took a good hard look at Kresh. She got the distinct feeling that this man wouldn't be so obvious about what he wanted to know if he weren't so plainly exhausted.

"There was a red robot in the lab," she said. *No point in hiding that fact,* she thought. *It was bound to come out, if it hadn't already.* "It was in a standing position in a work rack. Well, you must have seen the robot there." She thought for a moment and then shook her head. "I'm afraid there's not much else I recall."

"Try, please."

Fredda shrugged and frowned. She tried to think back to that night, but it was all a jumbled fog. "I can't seem to get that night very clear. I seem to recall standing in the room, leaning over one of the worktables, reading over some notes—but I can't recall notes of what, and I can't tell you how long before the attack that was. As I say, nothing is very clear. Maybe I'm even subconsciously inventing my memories, reaching for something that's not there. I can't know—and before you can even suggest it, I'm certainly not going to submit to any form of the Psychic Probe to clear up the uncertainty."

Kresh smiled faintly. "I admit the idea had crossed my mind. But we should certainly pursue all the less drastic alternatives first. Perhaps we can jog your memory. These notes of yours—how were they stored? A paper notebook? A computer pad? What?"

"Oh, a very standard computer pad, with a blue floral pattern on the back cover."

"I see. Madame Leving, I'm afraid there was no sign either of your computer pad or a red robot. The work rack was empty when we got there. And I assure you, we searched carefully."

Fredda's mouth fell open, and suddenly she felt dizzy. She had feared that the police might have discovered just what sort of robot Caliban was. That would have been trouble enough. But it had never occurred to her that Caliban might be *gone*. The devil help them all if some madman had switched him on and Caliban was wandering around *loose*.

"I'm stunned," she said quite truthfully. "I simply don't know what to say. At least now I know why I was attacked. Up until now, I could see no reason for it."

"And what reason do you see now?" Kresh asked.

"Why, robbery, of course! They stole my robot!"

An expression of surprise flickered across Kresh's face, and suddenly Fredda was flatly certain that the idea of a simple theft had never crossed his mind. "Why, yes, yes of course," Kresh replied.

But he was interested in the fact that I saw red robot feet, Fredda thought. *He knew that there had been a red robot there, and knew it was gone.* Suddenly it dawned on her. Kresh had reason to believe that Caliban had left her lab under his own power. Galaxy! *Had* someone in her own lab been lunatic enough to switch him on? But she needed time to think. Maybe she could get Kresh to chase in other directions for a while. After all, she was merely guessing that Caliban had gone off on his own. "Space alone knows why anyone would want to steal a testbed robot," she said. "All I can think is that this is some extreme case of industrial espionage. Some rival lab—or more likely, some third party hired by another lab—must have stolen my robot and my notes."

"Who might that be?" Kresh asked. "What lab would be likely to operate that way?"

Fredda shrugged helplessly, and paid for the gesture with a

fresh spasm of pain. But the pain itself was useful. The more obvious it was that she was in difficulty, the less likely Kresh was to keep the interview going. She had been trying to hold back her reaction to pain, but now she let it all out. It was not acting—the pain was real, the pain was there. But what point in a show of fortitude that merely made her own situation more difficult? She let out a gasp and grabbed the bedclothes with knotted fingers. There was a strange relief in letting go, in allowing the pain to come out, rather than be bottled up.

But Kresh had asked a question about the rival labs, and he was waiting for an answer. "I have no idea who would use such tactics. Obviously someone made off with my notes and my robot, but it strikes me as a very strange and pointless crime. After all, surely anyone who stole my work would know I would have backups, proof that the work was mine, the ability to reproduce my work. Someone did it. Just don't ask me why."

"It's possible that they merely wished to slow you down, delay you long enough to let their own people catch up—with the added advantage of having your work in front of them."

"I suppose that could be, but we're building quite a rickety tower of supposition here."

Kresh smiled, a bit thinly. And yet there was real warmth behind that expression. The man was sincerely interested and concerned. "You're right, of course. The trouble is, we have very little information to guide the investigation. Is there nothing else you can tell us?"

She shook her head. "Nothing I can think of."

"Very well," Kresh said, standing up. "I'm sure we'll need to talk later, but you need your rest."

"Yes. I have to be at my best to make my presentation tomorrow night."

Alvar Kresh looked at Fredda in obvious surprise. "Presentation?"

"I'm sorry, I assumed you knew. My lab is to make a major announcement tomorrow night. I'm afraid that I am not permitted to discuss it until then, but—"

"Ah, of course. Yes, we've been running into all sorts of people telling us that they couldn't talk yet, that we would have to wait for a public announcement. No one told us you were to make it. I find it surprising that they were all confident that you would be well enough to do so."

"Jomaine Terach would have given the talk if I could not, or if not Jomaine, Gubber Anshaw or someone else. If no one told you *I* was going to give the talk, I suspect it was because they knew the announcement would be made, but not who would give it." Fredda thought for a minute. "If I was attacked to prevent the talk from being given, then it would only make sense to keep the name of my replacement presenter secret. If *I* were the replacement, I'd see a low profile as a good idea."

"So you think this attack could be related to your presentation?"

Fredda shrugged *no,* a bit too theatrically. Instantly the pain flared up again. Damnation, her head hurt. "I have no idea. But it's certainly quite possible," she said. "This announcement is to be made during the second of two lectures. Have you seen the first lecture?"

"No, I have not."

"Then I would strongly suggest you get a look at a recording of it. There was a lot of material in there that could give someone a motive for coshing me. A lot." Fredda Leving folded her arms and found herself staring fixedly at the hillock her toes made in the blanket. She had never quite believed that anyone would try to *kill* her for what she said.

"If it could suggest a motive for this attack, I will view it at the first opportunity. But you need your rest. We'll just have to leave it at that for now," Kresh said. "Come on, Donald."

But Donald did not move to follow his master. Instead he spoke. "Your pardon, Lady Leving," he said. "There are two questions that I feel are rather important at this time. For purposes of tracing or tracking your stolen robot, can you tell us if it had a name or a serial number that we might trace?"

"Oh, of course," she said, silently cursing to herself. They *would* have to ask. "Serial number CBN-001, also known as Caliban. What was your other question?"

"Quite a simple one, actually. Can you tell us, Lady Leving, where your personal robot was at the time of the attack? We were told you did not take you personal robot to work. Why not? And, for that matter, where is that robot now? All that I see here are hospital robots."

Damnation, Fredda thought. *Trust Donald not to miss that one. By the look on Kresh's face, he's amazed that he didn't think of it.* Well, with Donald there monitoring her every reaction, nothing but the truth would do. "I no longer keep a personal robot at all," she said very quietly.

There was dead silence in the room, the silence of stunned surprise, and Fredda balled up her hands into fists. The leading roboticist on the planet, and she kept no robot. It was as if the leading vegetarian on Inferno confessed to cannibalism.

"Might I ask why you no longer keep a personal robot?" Alvar Kresh asked, clearly working hard to pick his words carefully.

Fredda looked up from the foot of her bed, but she stared at the blank wall in front of her. She had no desire to look Alvar Kresh square in the eye. "Listen to my last lecture, Sheriff, and come to the next one. I believe then you will understand."

The room was silent again, until Alvar Kresh at last concluded she was not going to say anything more. "Very good, then, Madame Leving," he said in a tone of voice that made it clear the situation was anything but good. "We shall talk again later, you and I. Until then, may I wish you a speedy recovery?" He bowed to her, then turned and headed for the door. "Come, Donald." The robot followed behind, the door opened and shut, and she was alone.

Fredda Leving sank her head back on the pillow and gave thanks that the interrogation was over.

Though she had no doubt that the trouble had barely begun.

ALVAR Kresh shook his head and patted Donald on the shoulder as they stepped out into the hallway. A few steps away from Leving's door, he stopped and turned toward the robot. "I don't know, Donald. Sometimes I think I ought to quit and have them make you Sheriff. How the devil did I fail to notice she had no personal robot?" he asked.

"It did not occur to me until we were in the hospital room, sir. I might also point out that humans are in the habit of ignoring robots, while robots must of course notice each other. Besides, there is the old saying about the dog that didn't bark. It is always more difficult to notice what is missing, rather than what is there."

"All the same, that was a vital question. We're going to watch the recording of that first lecture the moment we're home, and the devil take the hour. Nice work."

"Thank you, sir. I would suggest, however, that confirming the name 'Caliban' is the more useful piece of information," Donald said modestly. "We now have a direct, definite link. The two cases are one. The robot Caliban who vanished from the lab is the robot identified as Caliban by Santee Timitz at the arson site."

"But what in the Nine Circles of Hell does it *mean?*" Kresh asked. "What is going on?" He looked over Donald's shoulder. "Wait a second," he said. "Donald—behind you—is that—"

"Yes, sir. Jomaine Terach. The gentleman with him is, I believe, Gubber Anshaw, though the only police photos we have of him are of poor quality. I noted them on our way in."

"The robots on guard know to keep them out?"

"They are following standard procedure in such cases, in accordance with the law. To prevent any attempt at intimidation, no person associated with the case may talk with the victim of an assault until such time as statements are received from that person and the victim. Unless we file legal charges, we have no right to prevent meetings once statements are taken."

Kresh nodded. "In other words, we can stop Gubber Anshaw talking to her, but not Jomaine Terach. Which reminds me, it's high time we talked to Gubber, anyway. But damn it, I'm tired." Alvar Kresh reached up to rub the bridge of his nose. "Tomorrow," he said. "I'll talk to him tomorrow. But see to it the guard robots keep Anshaw away from her until then."

"Yes, sir. I have relayed the order over hyperwave."

"Good. Very good. Then let's go home."

"Sir, excuse me, but I fear you have neglected a vital point," Donald said. "Am I not right in asking if I should issue orders to apprehend this robot Caliban?"

Alvar Kresh shook his head and sighed. "You're right *and* you're wrong, Donald. It's risky to wait—but it could be just as risky to go out after him now. Think about it—if this *is* some bizarre Settler plot, clearly the point of it is to sow panic, throw a good scare into us. Surely, if that is the case, the plotters stand ready to exploit that panic, perhaps by staging something even more frightening than a robot committing arson. No matter what we do, the search for Caliban is bound to become public knowledge. Can you imagine the panic if word of a rogue got out—and a skilled conspirator set to work to build that fear?"

"It would be terrible, sir. And I might add that the very news of a robot behaving as Caliban has—well, it would be likely to cause permanent dysfunction in many, many robots. Still, the danger to humans that Caliban represents—"

"Must be weighed against the danger of moving too soon. If we start out now, with the information we have, what are we going to do? Arrest all the tall red robots? Or why stop there? Maybe our friend Caliban can disguise himself by slapping on a fresh coat of paint, or by exchanging his long arms and legs for short ones."

"With the result that *all* robots will be distrusted. Which would be the intended result of a Settler plot. *If* the plot exists. Yes, sir, I see the difficulty."

"It's about all I *can* see at this point," Kresh said, feeling very much like a tired old man. "But we can't move on this Caliban robot until we have more data. We can't do a search of the entire city. We need better information. But let us be ready if things break quickly. Relay an order for increased rapid-response air patrols. If we get lucky and spot him somewhere, I want a deputy on top of him within two minutes."

"Very well, sir. That will no doubt be sufficient to—" Suddenly Donald's head cocked to one side, as if he were listening to something only he could hear—and that was not far from the truth. Kresh was familiar with the mannerism. Donald's on-board communications system was receiving a message.

"Who's calling, Donald?" Alvar asked.

"One moment, sir. It is a timelock-secured message. I will have to wait for the synchronization burst to decode it. One moment. Ah, there it is. You are ordered to meet with the Governor tomorrow morning, first thing, seven hours from now."

Kresh groaned. "Devil take it all. The man's politics are bad enough. Does he have to get up at insane hours as well?"

But there was no real response to that question, and Donald offered none. At last Alvar Kresh sighed and rubbed his eyes. "Home, Donald," he said. "I want to see that damned lecture before I see the Governor. I've had it up to here with knowing less than everyone else."

"THEY'D only let *me* in, Fredda. Not Gubber. The police robots won't let him in until the Sheriff has—"

"Oh, be quiet, Jomaine. I know the law. My head hurts enough as it is." Fredda Leving leaned her head back against her pillow and shut her eyes. The throbbing was getting worse. But she could not take anything for it. Not yet. Not yet. She would have to be sharp, be careful, even with Jomaine. Especially with Jomaine. First, she had to take precautions against being monitored. It had been pointless before when there was a police robot in the room, but it was vital now. She would have to phrase the order carefully if it was to do any good.

She cleared her throat and spoke. "I order all robots in the room or monitoring this room in any way to forget all conversation that takes place between the time of this order and the next time I clap my hands three times within a period of five seconds. To remember any such conversation, or to report it, would almost certainly cause me harm." *That* ought to do it, unless the police had an actual human operative listening in on some hidden microphone, or a nonrobotic recording system working. But those possibilities were absurdly remote. Spacers used robots for *everything.*

Which was, of course, the entire problem.

She turned toward Jomaine. "All right, I think we can talk now. Sit down and tell me what you know."

Jomaine Terach did as he was told, but it didn't take long for him to report the little that he was privy to. Not his fault, not really. Fredda had quite deliberately kept him in the dark, for everyone's sake. He couldn't tell what he didn't know—a fact that, in balance, was very much to her advantage at the moment. Gubber was enough of a risk. A well-informed Jomaine in Kresh's hands was a thought not to be contemplated. Still, he could at least serve to fill her in on any details Kresh had seen fit to leave out of his narrative.

Jomaine ran true to form, speaking overcarefully, working through all the details in a relentlessly orderly fashion, but even so it took him very little time to finish—no doubt in part because the crime scene was still sealed. No one not associated with the investigation had gotten into Gubber's lab yet. Indeed, it appeared that Jomaine did not even know that a robot was missing from the lab.

Fredda nodded her head thoughtfully after Jomaine had stopped. He had not really contributed a great deal to her store of knowledge. Caliban was gone, either escaped or stolen. Someone had attacked her and stolen her notes. But what he did *not* say told her it could have been worse. That was not to say that a great deal of damage had not been done, but just now she would take whatever small comfort she could. "And that's it?" she asked. "Nothing else to report?"

Jomaine got to his feet, rather apologetically, and pulled a palm-sized computer pad from his pocket. "There's nothing more that *I* can tell you," he said, "but Gubber gave this to me for you. He seems to have some rather special sources of information." He handed her the pad and looked her straight in the eye, standing over her bed in a strangely formal, careful posture. It was obvious that he did not like what he was part of, but that he was determined to make the best of it and behave as correctly as possible. He pointed to the computer pad he had just given her. "I have not read that report," he said, "and I'm not going to. I don't want to know anything more. I have told you all I know, but none of what I think, and I expect that you will prefer it that way.

"To be quite blunt about the matter, my ideas about what you're doing scare three kinds of hell out of me. Therefore, I would ask that you have the kindness to wait until I have left the room to look this over."

Fredda Leving stared at her assistant in astonishment for a full thirty seconds before she could find voice enough to speak. Never had the man been so bold or blunt. "Very well, Jomaine. Thank you for your honesty and discretion."

"I would suggest that those are two qualities we have all had in short supply recently," he said sharply. The expression on Terach's pointed face softened a bit, and he reached out to touch her on the shoulder. "Rest, Fredda, heal," he said in a warm and gentle voice. "Even if none of this had happened, you'd need all your strength for tomorrow night."

Fredda smiled wanly and sighed. "You didn't need to remind me," she said. Tomorrow night's presentation might well decide more fates than her own.

Jomaine Terach turned and left, leaving Fredda alone with her thoughts and Gubber Anshaw's computer pad. She was almost afraid to read it. Gubber had some amazing sources of information. Fredda had decided long ago that she did not *want* to know what those sources were.

Fredda hardly dared wonder what he had come up with this time. She started to read the information in the pad. Three paragraphs into it she was so terrified she could scarcely see well enough to read it. For what she read in the computer pad made all the rest of her worries seem like no worries at all.

Good lord, where the hell had Gubber gotten this stuff? It looked like he had gotten his hands on the complete police reports of her attack, raw information not yet analyzed or put in order. *Two* sets of bloody robotic footprints? What the devil could that mean?

And the other reports—on the Ironhead riot at Settlertown and the robot basher/arson incident in the warehouse district. Sweet Fallen Angel, yes, Caliban had given his name to a witness there and she, Fredda, had just given it to Kresh as well. They had the link. They knew, or thought they knew, all they needed to know about Caliban.

Damn it, who the *hell* had let him out of the lab? Fredda had known right along that Caliban's earliest hours would be highly formative. That was why she had delayed powering him up for so long. She wanted all the conditions ideal when she did.

But look at the first hours he had had instead. He must have been at the very least a witness to the attack on her. Then he must have wandered the city, seen the subservient behavior of robots. That must have been damned confusing to him. She had deliberately edited out all information regarding robots from his datastore.

Hell's bells, how long had she worked on that datastore, carefully tailoring the information it contained? At best, all that work was now wasted.

At worst, it would wildly skew Caliban's view of the world. And on top of all that, for him to get mixed up with a mob of robot bashers . . .

Fredda Leving let the computer pad drop to the bed and slumped backwards, eyes shut, her stomach tied in a knot, her head a suddenly revitalized world of pain. *Why?* she wondered. *Why did it have to be this way?*

She thought about what Caliban had seen so far: violence, brutality, his own kind treated as slaves and worse. He had been given no other influences to shape his mind and viewpoint.

But that was far from the worst of it. Now Alvar Kresh was on the hunt, with every move Kresh made likely to reveal the truth at the wrong time and the wrong place. One accidental wrong move on Kresh's part could smash down the political house of cards that was all that might save Inferno.

Fredda Leving felt her heart grow cold with fear.

Trouble was, she was not quite sure what to be afraid for.

Or afraid of.

9

GUBBER Anshaw knew he was not a courageous man, but at least he had the courage to admit that much to himself. He had the strength of character to understand his own limitations, and surely that had to count for something.

Well, it was comforting to tell himself that, at any rate. Not that such self-understanding was much use under the present circumstances. But be that as it may. There were times when even a coward had to do the right thing.

And now, worse luck, was one such time. He watched as Tetlak, his personal robot, guided Gubber's deliberately undistinctive aircar through the dark of night toward Settlertown. The aircar slowed to a halt, hung in midair waiting for Settlertown's traffic and security system to query the car's transponder and see that it was on the preapproved list. Then the ground opened up beneath them as a fly-in portal to the underground city granted them entrance. The car flew down through the depths, down into the great central cavern of Settlertown, and came in for a landing.

Gubber used a hand gesture to order Tetlak to stay with the car, then got out himself. He walked to the waiting runcart and got in. "To Madame Welton's, please," he said as he settled in. The little open vehicle took off the moment he sat down. Gubber barely had time to reflect on the unnerving fact that there was no conscious being in control of the cart before he was delivered to Tonya's quarters.

He walked to her doorway and stood there for a moment before he remembered to press the annunciator button. Normally that was something his robot would do for him. But Tetlak made Tonya nervous sometimes, and he had no wish for unneeded awkwardness. It was bad enough that he had come without calling ahead.

A sleepy Tonya Welton opened the door and looked upon her visitor in surprise. "Gubber! What in the Galaxy are you doing here?"

Gubber looked at her for a moment, raised his hand uncertainly, and then spoke. "I know it was risky to come, but I had to see you. I don't think I was followed. I had to come and say—say goodbye."

"Goodbye!" Tonya's astonishment and upset were plainly visible on her face. "Are you breaking it off because—"

"I'm not breaking anything off, Tonya. You will always be there in my heart. But I don't think I will be able to see you again after—after I go to see Sheriff Kresh."

"What!"

"I'm turning myself in, Tonya. I'm going to take the blame." Gubber felt his heart pounding, felt the sweat starting to bead up on his body. For the briefest of moments, he felt a bit faint. "Please," he said. "May I come in?"

Tonya backed away from the door and ushered him in. Gubber stepped inside and looked around. Ariel stood motionless in her robot niche, staring out at nothing at all. The room was in its bedroom configuration, all the tables and chairs stowed away, replaced by a large and comfortable bed—a bed that Gubber had reason to remember most fondly. Now he crossed the room and sat, morosely, on the edge of it, feeling most lost and alone.

Tonya watched him cross the room, watched as he sat down. Gubber looked up at her. She was so beautiful, so natural, so much *herself.* Not like Spacer women, all artifice and appearance and affectation.

"I have to turn myself in," Gubber said.

Tonya looked at him, quietly, thoughtfully. "For what, Gubber?"

"What? What do you mean?"

"What charge, exactly, will you confess to when you turn yourself in? What is it you've done? When they ask you for a detailed description of how you committed your crime, what will you say?"

Gubber shrugged uncertainly and looked down at the floor. He had no idea what to confess to, of course. In his own mind, he *had* committed no crime, but he doubted the law would share that opinion. But what point to confessing to a crime in order to shield Tonya when he did not know what, if anything, they suspected she had done? Tonya had her own secrets, and he dared not ask what they were.

Clearly it would be safer for both of them if each kept certain things to themselves for now.

The silence dragged on, until Tonya took it as an answer.

"I thought so," she said at last. "Gubber, it just won't work." She sat down next to him and put her arm across his shoulders. "Dearest Gubber, you *are* a wonder. Back home on Aurora, I must have known a hundred men full of thunder and bluster, always ready to show me just how big and brave they were. But none of them had *your* courage."

"*My* courage!" Gubber looked sadly at Tonya. "Hah! There's a contradiction in terms."

"Is it? No big burly Settler man would dream of confessing a crime, going to a penal colony, for the sake of the woman he loved. And you'd do it, I know you would. But you can't. You mustn't."

"But—"

"Don't you see? Kresh is no fool. He'll be able to crack through a false confession in a heartbeat, and you don't know what to confess *to.* We have the police report, but he's not fool enough to tell us everything he knows. Once he's cracked you, he'll ask himself why you'd confess to what you hadn't done. Sooner or later, he'll find out you did it to protect me. Then we'll both end up in trouble."

Something deep inside Gubber froze up. He hadn't thought that far ahead. But no, wait. There was one thing she hadn't thought of. "That won't happen, Tonya. After all, no one knows about us—"

"But maybe they will, Gubber. Odds are Kresh will find out sooner or later. I've done what I could to protect you, and I know you've done the same for me. *But we dare do no more.* If we're lucky, and we don't draw attention to ourselves, we'll be all right. But if either of us does anything to draw Kresh's attention—"

Tonya let the words hang in the air. There was no need for her to complete the sentence. Gubber turned to her, put his arms around her, and kissed her, passionately and for a long while. At last he drew back, just a bit. He looked her in the eye, stroked her hair, whispered her name. "Tonya, Tonya. There's nothing I wouldn't do for you. You know that."

"I know, I know," Tonya said, her eyes bright with loving tears. "But we must be careful. We must think with our heads, not our hearts. Oh, Gubber. Hold me."

Then they kissed again, and Gubber felt passion sweeping away his fears and worries. They reached for each other, eagerly, urgently, pulling their clothes off, falling back onto the bed, their bodies coming together in desire and need.

Gubber glanced up and saw Ariel standing, motionless, in her wall niche. For a split second he worried, wondering if her being there would bother Tonya. A robot in the bedroom meant nothing to a Spacer, of course—

The devil take it. It was more than obvious that Ariel was the furthest thing from Tonya's mind. Why bring her attention to it? He reached out to the side of the bed and jabbed down the manual switch, shutting off the overhead lights, and gave no more thought to it.

Ariel stared blankly at the opposite wall, pale green eyes dimly glowing, as the two humans made love in the darkness.

NIGHT had come, and there was darkness, and shadow, but no quiet, or rest, or safety. Whatever else changed, danger was the constant. Of that much Caliban was sure.

Caliban walked the busy downtown, ghost-town streets of Hades. The place was bustling with energy, and yet there was a feeling of the tomb about the place, as if it were a busy, active corpse, not yet aware of its own death, hurrying about its business long after its time had come and gone.

Night and day did not seem to matter so much here, in the heart of town. Here, the streets were just as busy now as they had been when he had passed this way in daytime.

But no, it was inaccurate to say that there was no difference between day and night. There was no change in the *amount* of traffic on the streets and walkways, but there was a huge change in the *character* of that traffic. Now, late at night, the people were all but gone, but the robots were here.

Caliban looked about himself, at the proud, brightly lit, empty towers of Hades, the grand boulevards of magnificent and failed intentions. But the heart of that world, that city, was empty, barren.

Yet the unpeopled city was still crowded. Humans had been a sizable minority during the day, but in the wee hours of the night, it was robots, robots, everywhere. Caliban stood in the shadow of a doorway and watched them all go by.

These robots of the night were different from the daytime robots. Almost all of those had clearly been personal servants. In the night, the heavy-duty units came out, hauling the heavy freight, working on construction jobs, doing the dirty work while there were fewer humans around to be disturbed by it.

A gang of huge, gleaming black construction robots trudged down the street, past Caliban, toward a tall ivory-colored tower, half-finished and yet already lovely. But there were already half a dozen equally lovely towers within a few blocks of where Caliban stood, all of them virtually empty. Across the street, another gang of robots was hard at word disassembling another building that seemed scarcely any older or more used.

Caliban had seen many other work crews come out in the last hour or so, likewise doing needless maintenance work: searching for litter that was not there; polishing the gleaming windows; weeding the weedless gardens and lawns of the parks; busily keeping the empty city core shining and perfect. Why were these robots not employed in the emptier, threadbare, worn and dirty districts, where their work could have some meaning? Why did they work here?

The empty city. Caliban considered the words. They seemed to echo in his head. There was something wrong with the very idea of such a place. From his datastore, from the emotions of whoever had loaded the store, came the sure, certain knowledge that cities were not meant to be so. Something was going desperately wrong.

Another piece of data popped up from the datastore, a straight, solid fact, but the ghosts of emotion hung about this one fact more strongly than any other emotion he had absorbed. It was the thing that the person who created his datastore cared about most of all: Every year the total human population went down—and the robot population went up. *How could that be?* he wondered. *How could the humans allow themselves to get into such a predicament?* But no answer came up from the datastore. For no reason that he could understand, the question, though it had nothing to do with him, was suddenly of vital importance to him.

Why? he wondered. *And why do I wonder why?* Caliban had noted that most robots he observed had a distinct lack of curiosity. Few were even much interested in their surroundings. Something else, yet again, that set him apart. When his maker had molded his mind into an oddly shaped blank, had that maker also blessed him and cursed him with an overactive degree of curiosity? Caliban felt certain it was so, but in a way it did not matter. Even if his sense of curiosity had been deliberately enhanced, that did not stop him from wondering all the same.

Why, why, why did the robots blindly, needlessly, build and disassemble, over and over, rather than leaving things as they were? Why create huge buildings when there were none to use them? Madness. All of it madness. The voice of the datastore whispered to him that the city was a reflection of a society warped, twisted, bent out of any shape that could make normal life and growth possible. It was opinion, emotion, propaganda, but still, somehow, it spoke to him.

The world was mad, and his only hope of survival was to blend in, be accepted as one of the inmates of this lunatic asylum, get lost among the endless robots that tended to the city and its inhabitants. The thought was daunting, disturbing.

Yet even perfect mimicry would not protect him. He had learned that much, almost at the cost of his existence. Those Settlers last night had clearly meant to kill him. If he had acted like a normal robot, he had no doubt that they *would* have killed him. They had expected him to stand placidly by and permit his own destruction. They had even thought it possible that he would willingly destroy himself on the strength of hearing that weak and tortuous argument about how his existence harmed humans. Why had they thought that strained line of reasoning would impel him to commit suicide?

Caliban stepped out from the shadowy doorway and started walking again. There was so much he had to learn if he was to survive. Imitation would not be enough. Not when acting like a standard robot could get him killed. He had to know why they acted as they did.

Why was he here? Why had he been created? Why was he different from other robots? *How* was he different from them? Why was the nature of his difference kept hidden from him?

How had he gotten into this situation? Once again, he tried to think back to the beginning, to search through the whole recollection of his existence for some clue, some answer.

He had no memory of anything whatsoever before the moment he came on, powered up for the first time, standing over that woman's unconscious body with his arm raised from his side. Nothing, nothing else before that. How had he come to be in that place, in that situation? Had he somehow gotten to his feet, raised his arm, before he awoke? Or had he been *placed* in that position for some reason?

Wait a moment. Go back and think that through. He could see no compelling reason to assume that his ability to act could not predate his ability to remember. Suppose he had acted *before* his memory commenced? Or suppose his memory prior to the moment he thought of as his own awakening had been cleared somehow? Alternately, what if, for some reason, he had been capable of action before his memory started, and his memory had simply not commenced *recording* until that moment?

If any of those cases were possible, if the start of his memory was not a reliable marker for the start of his existence, then there were no limits to the actions he might have taken before his memory began. He could have been awake, aware, active, for five seconds before that moment—or five years. Probably not that long, however. His body showed no signs of wear, no indication that any parts had ever been replaced or repaired. His on-line maintenance log was quite blank—though it, too, could have been erased. Still, it seemed reasonable to assume that his body was quite new.

But that was a side issue. How had that woman come to be on the floor in a pool of blood? It was at least a reasonable guess that she had been attacked in some way. Had she been dead or alive? He reviewed his visual memories of the moment. The woman had been breathing, but she could easily have expired after he left. Had the woman died, or had she survived?

The thought brought him up short. Why had he not even asked himself such questions before?

Then, like twin blazes of fire, two more questions slashed through his mind:

Had *he* been the one who attacked her?

And, regardless of whether or not he had—was he *suspected* of the attack?

Caliban stopped walking and looked down at his hands.

He was astonished to realize that his fists were clenched. He opened out his fingers and tried to walk as if he knew where he was going.

THE night before, Alvar Kresh had taken a needle-shower in hopes of helping him to sleep. Tonight he took one in hopes of waking up. He was tempted to watch the recording of Leving's lecture while sitting up in bed, but he knew just how tired he was, and just how easy it would be for him to doze off if he did that. No, far better to get dressed again in fresh clothes and watch on the televisor screen in the upper parlor.

Kresh settled down in front of the televisor, ordered one of the household robots to adjust the temperature a bit too low for comfort, and told another to bring a pot of hot, strong tea. Sitting in a cold room, with a good strong dosage of caffeine, he ought to be able to stay awake.

"All right, Donald," he said, "start the recording."

The televisor came to life, the big screen taking up an entire wall of the room. The recording began with a shot of the Central Auditorium downtown. Kresh had seen many plays broadcast from there, and most times the proceeds were rather sedate, if not sedated, and it looked as if the occasion of Leving's first lecture had been no exception. The auditorium had been designed to hold about a thousand people and their attendant robots, the robots sitting behind their owners on low jumper seats. It looked to be about half-empty.

" . . . and so, without further ado," the theater manager was saying, "allow me to introduce one of our leading scientists. Ladies and gentlemen, I give you Dr. Fredda Leving." He turned toward her, smiling, leading the applause.

The figure of Fredda Leving stood up and walked toward the lectern, greeted by a rather tentative round of applause. The camera zoomed in closer, and Kresh was startled to be reminded what Leving had looked like before the attack. In the hospital, she had been wan, pale, delicate-looking, her shaved head making her look too thin. The Fredda Leving in this recording looked as if she had a slight touch of stage fright, but she was fit, vigorous-looking, with her dark hair framing her face. All in all, an unfashionably striking young woman.

She reached the lectern and looked out over the audience, her face clearly betraying her nervousness.

She cleared her throat and began. "Thank you, ladies and gentlemen." She fumbled with her notes for a moment, clearly still somewhat nervous, and then began. "I would like to start my talk this evening with a question," she said. "One that might seem flippant, one wherein the answer might be utterly obvious to you all. And yet, I would submit, it is one that has gone thousands of years without a proper answer. I do not suggest that I can supply that missing answer myself, now, tonight, but I do think that it is long past time for us to at least pose the question.

"And that question is: What are robots for?"

The view cut away to reaction shots of the people in the auditorium. There was a stirring and a muttering in the audience, a strangled laugh or two. People shifted in their seats and looked at each other with confused expressions.

"As I said, it is a question that few of us would ever stop to ask. At first glance, it is like asking what use the sky is, or what the planet we stand upon is for, or what good it does to breathe air. As with these other things, robots seem to us so much a part of the natural order of things that we cannot truly picture a world that does not contain them. As with these natural things, we—quite incorrectly—tend to assume that the universe simply placed them here for our convenience. But it was not nature who placed robots among us. We did that to ourselves."

Not *for* ourselves, Kresh noticed. *To* ourselves. What the devil had Leving been saying the night of the lecture? He found himself wishing that he had been there.

Fredda Leving's image kept talking. "On an emotional level, at least, we perceive robots not as tools, not as objects we have made, not even as intelligent beings with which we share the universe—but as something basic, placed here by the hand of nature, something part of us. We cannot imagine a world worth living in without them, just as our friends the Settlers think a world that *does* include them is no fit place for humans.

"But I digress from my own question. 'What are robots for?' As we seek after an answer to that question, we must remember that they are *not* part of the natural universe. They are an artificial creation, no more and no less than a starship or a coffee cup or a terraforming station. We built these robots—or at least our ancestors built them, and then set robots to work building more robots.

"Robots, then, are tools we have built for our own use. That is at least the start of an answer. But it is by no means the whole answer.

"For robots are the tools that think. In that sense, they are more than our tools—they are our relatives, our descendants."

Again there was a hubbub in the audience, a stirring, this time of anger and surprise. "Forgive me," Fredda said. "That is perhaps an unfortunate way to phrase it. But it is, in a very real sense, the truth. Robots are the way they are because we humans made them. They could not exist without us. There are those who believe that we humans could not exist without them. But that statement is so much dangerous nonsense."

Now there was a full-fledged roar from the back of the hall, where the Ironheads had congregated. "Yes, that does strike a nerve, doesn't it?" Fredda asked, the veneer of courtesy dropping away from her voice. "'We could not live without them'—it is not a factual statement, but it is an article of faith. We have convinced ourselves that we could not survive without robots, equating *the way we live* with our *lives* themselves. We have to look no further than the Settlers to know that humans can live—and live well—without robots."

A chorus of boos and shouts filled the hallway. Fredda raised her hands for quiet, her face stern and firm. At last the crowd settled down a bit. "I do not say that we *should* live that way. I build robots for a living. I believe in robots. I believe they have not yet reached their full potential. They have shaped our society, a society I believe has many admirable qualities.

"But, my friends, our society is calcified. Fossilized. Rigid. We have gotten to the point where we are certain, absolutely certain, that ours is the only possible way to live. We tell ourselves that we *must* live *precisely* as our ancestors did, that our world is perfect just as it is.

"Except that to live is to change. All that lives must change. The end of change is the beginning of death—and our world is dying." Now there was dead silence in the room. "We all know that, even if we will not admit it. Inferno's ecology is collapsing, but we refuse to see it, let alone do anything about it. We deny the problem is there."

Kresh frowned. The ecology *collapsing?* Yes, there were problems, everyone knew that. But he would not place it in such drastic terms. Or was that part of the denial she was talking about? He shifted uncomfortably in his seat and listened.

"Instead," Leving's image went on, "we insist that our robots coddle us, pamper us, while we go about our self-indulgent lives, as the web of life that supports us grows ever weaker. Anytime in the last hundred years, we, the citizens of Inferno, could have taken matters into our own hands, gotten to work, and saved the situation—saved our planet—for ourselves. Except it was so easy to convince ourselves that everything was fine. The robots were taking care of us. How could there be anything to worry about?

"Meantime, the forests died. The oceans' life-cycle weakened. The control systems broke down. And we, who have been trained by our robots to believe that doing nothing is the highest and finest of all activities, did not lift a finger.

"Things got to the point where we were forced to swallow our pride and call in outsiders to save us. And even that was a near-run thing. We came very close to choosing our pride over our lives. I will admit quite freely that I found calling in the Settlers just as galling as any of you did. But now they are here, and we Spacers, we Infernals, continue to sit back, and grudgingly permit the Settlers to save us, treating them like hired hands, or interlopers, instead of rescuers.

"Our pride is so great, our belief in the power of robot-backed indolence so overpowering, that we *still* refuse to act for ourselves. Let the Settlers do the work, we tell ourselves. Let the robots get their hands dirty. We shall sit back, true to the principle that labor is for others, believing that work impedes our development toward an ever more ideal society, based on the ennobling principle of applying robotics to every task.

"For robots are our solution to everything. We believe in robots. We have faith in them—firm, unquestioned faith in them. We take it hard, get emotional, when our use of them is questioned. We have seen that demonstrated just moments ago.

"In short, my friends, robotics is our *religion,* to use a very old word. And yet we Spacers despise the thing we worship. We love robotics and yet hold robots themselves in the lowest of regard. Who among us has not felt contempt toward a robot? Who among us has not seen a robot jump higher, think faster, work longer, do better at a job than any human ever could, and then comforted himself or herself with the sneering, contemptuous—and contemptible—defense that it was 'only' a robot. The task, the accomplishment, is diminished when it is the work of a robot.

"An interesting side point is that robots here on Inferno are generally manufactured with remarkably high First Law potential, and with an especially strong potential for the negation clauses of the Second and Third Laws, the clauses that tell a robot it can obey orders and protect itself only if all human beings are safe. To look at it another way, robots here on Inferno place an especially strong emphasis on *our* existence and an especially weak one on their own.

"This has two results: First, our robots coddle us far more than robots on most other Spacer worlds, so that human initiative is squelched even more here on Inferno. Second, we have a remarkably high rate of robots lost to First Law conflict and resultant brainlock. We could easily adjust our manufacturing procedures to create robots that would feel a far lower, but perfectly adequate, compulsion to protect us. If we did that, we would reduce our own safety little, if at all, but our robots would suffer far less needless damage attempting rescues that are impossible or useless. Yet instead we choose to build robots with excessively high compulsion to protect. We make our robots with First Law potential so high that they brainlock if they see a human in trouble but cannot go to the human's aid, even if other robots are attempting to save the human.

"If six robots rush in to save one person, and four are needlessly damaged as a result, we don't care. This is absurd waste. But we don't care about the loss of robots to needless overreaction. We have so many robots, we do not regard them as particularly valuable. If they destroy themselves needlessly in answer to our whims, so be it.

"In short, we hold our robot servants in contempt. They are expendable, disposable. We send beings of many years' wisdom and experience, beings of great intelligence and ability, off into grave danger, even to their destruction, for the most trivial of reasons. Robots are sent into burning buildings after favorite trinkets. Robots throw themselves in the face of oncoming traffic to protect a human who has crossed the street carelessly to look at a shop window. A robot is ordered to clear a smudge off an exterior window of a skyscraper in the midst of a hundred-kilometer-per-hour gale. In that last case, even if the robot should be swept off the side of the building, there need be no concern—the robot will use its arms and legs to guide its own fall, making sure it does not strike a human being when it hits, faithful to the First Law even as it plummets toward its doom.

"We have all heard the stories about robots destroyed in this useless effort, or to indulge that pointless impulse. The stories are told, not as if they were disasters, but as if they were *funny,* as if a robot melted down to scrap or smashed to bits in pursuit of no useful purpose were a joke, instead of a scandalous waste.

"Scarcely less serious are the endless abuses of robots. I have seen robots pressed into service as structural supports, simply ordered to stand there and hold a wall up—not for a minute, not as an emergency remedy while repairs are made—but as a permanent solution. I have seen robots—functional, capable robots—told to stand underwater and hold the anchorline of a sailboat. I know a woman who has one robot whose sole duty is to brush her teeth for her, and hold the brush in between times. A man with a broken water pipe in his basement set a robot to bailing the place out—full-time, nonstop, day in, day out, for six months—before the man finally bothered to have repairs made.

"Think about it. Consider it. *Sentient beings* used as substitutes for anchors, for toothbrushes, for pipe welds. Does that make sense? Does it seem rational that we create robots with minds capable of calculating hyperspace jumps, and then set them to work as deadweights to keep pleasure boats from floating away?

"These are merely the most glaring examples of robot abuse. I have not even touched on the endless tasks we all allow our robots to do for us, things that we should do for ourselves. But these things, too, are robot abuse, and they are demeaning to ourselves as much as to our mechanical servants.

"I recall a morning, not so long ago, when I stood in front of my closet for twenty minutes, waiting for my robot to dress me. When I finally remembered that I had ordered the robot out on an errand, I *still* did not dress myself, but waited for the robot to return. It never dawned on me that I might select my own clothes, put them on my own body, close the fasteners myself. It *had* to be done *for* me.

"I submit to you that such absurdities as that do more than waste the abilities of robots. They hurt *us,* do damage to humans. Such behavior teaches us to think that labor—*all* labor, *any* labor—is beneath us, that the only respectable, socially acceptable thing to do is sit still and allow our robot-slaves to care for us.

"Yes, I said slaves. I asked a question at the beginning of this talk. I asked 'What are robots for?' Well, ladies and gentlemen, *that* is the answer that our society has come up with. *That* is what we use them as. Slaves. *Slaves.* Look into the history books, look into all the ancient texts of times gone by and all the cultures of the past. Slavery has *always* corrupted the societies in which it has existed, grinding down the slaves, degrading them, humiliating them—but likewise *it has always corrupted the slave masters as well,* poisoned them, weakened them. Slavery is a trap, one that always catches the society that condones it.

"*That is what is happening to us.*" Fredda paused for a moment and looked around the auditorium. There was silence, dead silence.

"Let me go back to that day when I waited for my robot-slave to dress me. Thinking about it after the fact, seeing just how ridiculous that moment had been, I resolved to manage for myself the next time.

"And I found that I could not! I did not know how. I did not know where my clothes were. I did not know how the fasteners worked or how the clothes went on. I walked around half a day with a blouse on backwards before realizing my mistake. I was astonished by my ignorance on the subject of caring for myself.

"I started watching myself go through my day, noticing how little I did for myself—how little I was *capable* of doing."

Alvar Kresh, watching the recording, began to understand. This was why she no longer kept a personal robot. A strange decision, yes, but it was beginning to make some sort of sense. He watched the recording with rapt attention, all thought of his own exhaustion quite forgotten.

"I was astonished just how incompetent I was," Fredda Leving's voice said. "I was amazed how many little tasks I could not perform. I cannot begin to describe the humiliation I felt when I realized that I could not find my way around my own city by myself. I needed a robot to guide me, or I would get hopelessly lost."

There was a nervous titter or two in the audience, and Fredda nodded thoughtfully. "Yes, it *is* funny. But it is also very sad. Let me ask you out there who think I am being absurd—suppose all the robots simply stopped right now. Let us ignore the obvious fact that our entire civilization would collapse, because the robots are the ones who run it. Let's keep it tight, and personal. Think what would happen to you if *your* robots shut down. What if your driver ceased to function, your personal attendant ground to a halt, your cook mindlocked and could not prepare meals, your valet lost power right now?

"How many of you could find your way home? Very few of you can fly your own cars, I know that—but could you even *walk* home? Which way is home from here? And if and when you got home, would you remember how to use the manual controls to open the door? How many of you even know your own address?"

Again, silence, at least at first. But then there was a shout from the audience. The camera cut away to show a man standing in front of his seat, a man dressed in one of the more comic-opera variants of the Ironhead uniform. "So what?" he yelled. "I don't know my address. Big deal! All I need to know is, *I'm the human being!* I'm the one on top! I got a good life thanks to robots. I don't want it messed up!"

There was a ragged flurry of cheers and applause, mostly from the back of the house. The view cut back to Fredda as she stepped out from behind her lectern and joined in the applause herself, clapping slowly, loudly, ironically, still going long after everyone else had quit. "Congratulations," she said. "You *are* the human being. I am sure you are proud of that, and you should be. But if Simcor Beddle sent you here to disrupt my speech, you go back and tell the leader of the Ironheads that you helped me make my point. What troubles me is that it almost sounds as if you are proud of your ignorance. That strikes me as terribly dangerous, and terribly sad.

"So tell me this. You don't know where you live. You don't do much of anything. You don't know *how* to do anything. So: *What in the Nine Circles of Hell are you good for?*" She looked up from the man to the entire audience. "What are we *good* for? What do we do? *What are humans for?*

"Look around you. Consider your society. Look at the place of humans in it. We are drones, little else. There is scarcely an aspect of our lives that has not been entrusted to the care of the robots. In entrusting our tasks to them, we surrender our fate to them.

"So what are humans for? *That* is the question, the real question it all comes down to in the end. And I would submit that our current use of robots has given us a terrifying answer, one that will doom us if we do not act.

"Because right here, right now, we must face the truth, my friends. And the true answer to that question is: not much."

Fredda took a deep breath, collected her notes, and stepped back from the podium. "Forgive me if I end this lecture on that grim note, but I think it is something we all need to face. In this lecture I have stated the problem I wished to address. In my next lecture, I will offer up my thoughts on the Three Laws of Robotics, and on a solution to the problems we face. I believe I am safe in saying it should be of interest to you all."

And with that, the recording faded away, and Alvar Kresh was left alone with his own thoughts. She couldn't be right. She couldn't.

All right, then. Assume she was wrong.

Then what *were* humans good for?

"Well, Donald, what did you think?" Alvar asked.

"I must confess I found it to be a most disturbing presentation."

"How so?"

"Well, sir, it makes the clear implication that robots are bad for humans."

Kresh snorted derisively. "Old, old arguments, all of them. There isn't a one that I haven't heard before. She makes it sound like the entire population of Hades, of all Inferno, is made up of indolent incompetents. Well, *I* for one still know how to find my own way home."

"That is so, sir, but I fear that you might be in a minority."

"What? Oh, come on. She made it sound as if everyone were utterly incompetent. I don't know *anyone* that helpless."

"Sir, if I may observe, most of your acquaintances are fellow law enforcement officers, or workers in fields that you as Sheriff often come into contact with."

"What's your point?"

"Police work is one of the very few fields of endeavor in which robots can be of only marginal help. A good police officer must be capable of independent thought and action, be willing to cooperate in a group, be ready to deal with all kinds of people, and be capable of working *without* robots. Your deputies must be rather determined, self-confident individuals, willing to endure a certain amount of physical danger—perhaps even relishing the *stimulus* of danger. I would suggest that police officers would make for a rather skewed sample of the population. Think for a moment, not of your officers, but of the people they encounter. The people that end up as victims in the police reports. I know that you do not hold those people in the highest regard. How competent and capable are they? How dependent on *their* robots are they?"

Alvar Kresh opened his mouth as if to protest, but then stopped, frowned, and thought. "I see your point. Now you've disturbed *me,* Donald."

"My apologies, sir. I meant no—"

"Relax, Donald. You're sophisticated enough to know you've done no harm. You got me to thinking, that's all." He nodded at the televisor. "As if *she* hadn't done that already."

"Yes, sir, quite so. But I would suggest, sir, that it is time for bed."

"It certainly is. Can't be tired for the Governor, can I?" Alvar stood and yawned. "And what the hell could *he* want that can't wait until later in the day?"

Alvar Kresh walked wearily back to his bedroom, very much dreading the morning. Whatever the Governor wanted, it was unlikely to be good news.

10

SIMCOR Beddle was up betimes, thoughtfully reviewing the results of the Ironhead action against Settlertown. The results were not good. Sheriff Kresh's deputies were simply getting too good at their jobs. Too many arrests, too little damage, and worst of all, the publicity was bad. It made the Ironheads look inept at best.

All right, then, it was time to come up with another tactic. Some way to tangle with the damned Settlers where Kresh's people could not interfere so much.

Wait a moment. He had the very thing. Leving's next lecture. If his information was even remotely reliable, the place would be crawling with Settlers. Yes, yes. An altercation there would do nicely.

But what about publicity? Not much point in staging a riot if no one saw it. Beddle leaned back in his chair and stared at the ceiling. Her first lecture had not drawn much of a crowd, though it should have, given the seditious material she had presented. Maybe that was the key. Plant a few belated reports here and there, accurate and otherwise, about what she had said then. Perhaps he could arrange for a few tame sources to drop a few inflammatory and extremely misleading speculations as to what the devil she was doing in the hospital.

Yes, yes. That was it. Properly brought along, reports on that first lecture should get the hall filled for the second, and live televisor coverage to boot. Disrupt *those* goings-on and no one could help but pay attention.

Simcor Beddle gestured for his secretary robot to come forward, and began dictating, setting down the details.

It ought to work quite nicely.

ALVAR Kresh strode into the Governor's office, feeling far more alert and awake than he had any right to feel, as if his body were getting used to the idea of not sleeping properly.

The Governor rose from behind his desk and crossed half the length of the huge office, offering his hand to Alvar as he came closer. Grieg looked fresh, well rested, alert. He was dressed in a charcoal-grey suit of rather conservative cut, as if he were trying to appear as old as possible. Such was no doubt the case, given Grieg's almost scandalously youthful election to the governorship.

Grieg's office was as opulent as Alvar had remembered—but there was something missing since his last visit, something no longer there. What was it?

"Thank you for coming so early, Sheriff," Governor Grieg said as he took Alvar's hand.

As if the summons here had been an invitation and not an order, Alvar thought. But the courteous words were themselves significant. The Governor did not often feel the need to be polite to Alvar Kresh.

Alvar shook the Governor's hand and looked him in the eye. There was no doubt about it. The man wanted something from him—no, *needed* something.

"It's a pleasure to be here," Alvar lied smoothly.

"I doubt that to be the case," Grieg said with a politician's overly frank smile, a smile born of too many years making promises. "But I assure you that it was necessary. Please, have a seat, Sheriff. Tell me, how is the investigation of the attack on Fredda Leving going?"

Nothing like getting right to the point, Kresh thought grimly. "It's early times, yet. We've collected a lot of information, and a lot of it seems rather contradictory. But that's almost to be expected at this stage. There is one thing, though, sir, that you could do to make work go a bit more smoothly."

"And what might that be?"

"Call off Tonya Welton. I must admit I don't know the political side of the situation, but I assure you that inserting her into the case has made more work for me. I can't quite see why you wanted to do it."

"Why *I* wanted to do it? She was the one who wanted it. Her people may have a connection to Leving Labs, but why would I want her interfering with local law enforcment? No, it was her idea to be attached to the case, and she was quite insistent about it. She made it clear that the political price would be high for Inferno if I did not allow her access to the investigation. In fact, she was the one who first told *me* about the case. She called me at home the night it happened and demanded that she be put into the picture."

Alvar Kresh frowned in confusion. Given the speed with which she had arrived at the scene, that would have to mean she knew about the attack almost before the maintenance robot called in to report it. How had she found out? "I see. I must admit that she rather gave the impression that it was your idea."

"Definitely not. As for calling her off, as you put it—I'm afraid the political situation is just too damned delicate. I'm very sorry, but I'll have to ask you to endure her interference. I think you'll understand why after you see what I brought you here to see."

The Governor gestured toward a rather severe-looking chair in the middle of the room. Alvar sat, facing the empty center of the room. Donald followed a step or two behind and stood behind Alvar's chair. Grieg took a seat himself at a control console that faced Alvar's chair. That was it, Alvar realized. He looked around the big room and confirmed his suspicion. No robot. The Governor had no robot in attendance in his own private office. Now, *there* was a scandalous tidbit. *No robot.* Fredda Leving was one thing, but the Governor himself? Even if the politics of the moment had been calm and settled, it would have been titillating news, as if Grieg had gone out in public without his pants. With the Settlers so much in evidence, it was downright unpatriotic.

But this was not the moment to bring any such thing up with the Governor. Maybe he had seen that lecture of Leving's—or maybe he knew something more. But Grieg was bent over the control unit, concentrating on it. *Best to pay attention,* Alvar told himself.

"This is a simglobe unit," the Governor said, a bit absently, concentrating on the controls in front of him. "You may have seen one before, or seen a recorded playback from a simulation run on one. But I doubt you have seen one like this. In fact, I am certain of it. It's a Settler model, much more sophisticated than our own units. It's a gift from Tonya Welton—and before you can get suspicious of *that,* it was quite thoroughly tested by our own people, and *programmed* by our people. It has not been rigged in any way."

"So what will it show me?" Alvar asked.

The Governor finished adjusting the controls and looked up at his guest, his face suddenly grim. "The future," he answered in a flat, emotionless voice that put a chill in Alvar's spine.

The windows made themselves opaque, and the room's lights faded away into darkness. After a moment, a vague, dimly lit ball of light came into existence in the middle of the air between Alvar and Grieg. It quickly came into sharper and brighter focus, to become recognizably the globe of Inferno. Alvar found he was drawing in his breath sharply in spite of himself. There are few sights as beautiful to the human eye as a living world seen from space. Inferno was heart-stoppingly lovely, a blue-white gem gleaming in the void.

It was in half-phase from Alvar's point of view, the terminator slicing neatly through the great equatorial island of Purgatory. Nearly all the southern hemisphere of Inferno was water, though there had been arid lowlands before the terraforming projects gave this world its seas.

The northern third of the world was given over to a single great landmass, the continent of Terra Grande. Even in summer, the polar regions of Terra Grande sported an impressive ice cap. In the winter months the ice and snow could reach halfway down to the sea.

Just north of Purgatory, a huge, semicircular chunk was neatly sliced out of the southern coast of Terra Grande, the visible scar of an asteroid impact some few million years ago. Hidden by the water, the arc of the landward edge of the crater extended out into the sea, forming a circular crater. Purgatory was actually the central promontory of the half-submerged crater. The huge water-filled crater was called, quite simply, the Great Bay.

Clouds and storm-whirls knotted and twisted about the southern seas, with the greens and browns and yellows of the sprawling northern continent half-hidden beneath their own cloud cover. Dots of lightning flickered in the midst of storms in the northwestern mountains, while the eastern edge of the Great Bay was cloudless in the morning light, dazzlingly bright, the coastal deserts gleaming in the sun, the greenswards of the forests and pastures beyond a darker, richer green.

A bit farther south and west along the coast of the bay, Alvar could just pick out the lights of Hades, a small, faint, glowing light in the predawn darkness.

"This is a real-time view of our world as it is today," Grieg's voice announced from the far side of the now solid-seeming globe. "We came to a waterless world with an unbreathable atmosphere. We gave it water and oxygen. Every drop of water in those oceans, we caused to be there. Every breath of oxygen in the air is there because we remade this world. We unlocked water from the rocks and soil and imported comets and ice meteors from the outer reaches of this star system. We put plant life in the sea and on the land and gave this world breathable air. We made this world bloom. But now the bloom is off the rose.

"Next you will see Inferno as it will be, if we merely rely on our own abilities, using just our own terraforming stations and technology, if we go on as we have been. First, to make it easy to observe, I will remove the atmosphere, cloud cover, and the day-night cycle." Suddenly the half-lit globe was fully illuminated, and the storms and haze vanished. The hologram had seemed like a real world up to that moment, but, stripped of darkness and cloud, it was suddenly nothing more than a highly accurate map, a detailed globe. Quite irrationally Alvar felt a pang of loss even then. Something lovely that had been was suddenly gone, and he knew, beyond doubt, that the surviving image of the world would grow uglier still. "Now let me add a few supplementary graphics," Grieg's voice said. A series of bar charts and other displays appeared around the globe, showing the state of the forests, the sea and land biomass, temperatures, atmospheric gases, and other information.

"I will run the simulation forward at the rate of one standard year every ten seconds," Grieg said, "and I will keep the western hemisphere positioned so you can watch the fate of Hades." A white dot appeared at the appropriate position on the edge of the Great Bay. "That is Hades's location."

The governor spoke no more, but instead let the simglobe tell its own tale, partly in direct images, partly in readouts and graphic displays.

It was the oceans that died first. The predators at the top of the food chain overbred and all but wiped out the mid-chain species, the fish and other creatures that fed on each other and on the various species of plankton, and were in turn eaten by the high-end predators. Their food supply wiped out, the high-end predators died out as well.

With no controls on their reproduction, the plankton and algae in the ocean were next. They reproduced out of all control and the oceans bloomed a sickly, ghastly green. Then the seas turned brown as the algae died as well, having overrun their own food supply and absorbed virtually every molecule of carbon dioxide. With no animal life in the ocean, plant life everywhere, on land and sea, was starved for carbon dioxide. The loss of the greenhouse gas meant Inferno could retain less and less heat. The planet began to grow colder.

Alvar watched, an unwilling witness to the forthcoming doom of his own world, watched as the planet Inferno was strangled by ice. Water, water was the key. No living world could survive without it, but it could do no good—and could do great damage—if it was in the wrong state, in the wrong place. Now it was the ice cap that was the problem. The line on the chart displayed the size of the northern ice cap, but Alvar could see the cap itself growing. The ice advanced, and the northern forests fell before it, the great stands of trees dying in the too-cold, carbon-dioxide-starved air. With the atmosphere's oxygen content far too high, and drought conditions taking hold, forest fires exploded everywhere, even as the ice pushed southward.

The white ice reflected back far more heat and light than the forests, and the planetary cooling trend locked itself in, strengthened itself, reinforced itself.

But the cooling was not universal: Alvar could see that. As the forest died and the ice advanced and the overall planetary temperature dropped, local temperatures dropped in some areas and rose in others. Wind patterns shifted. Storms grew more violent. Semipermanent snow hurricanes lodged themselves here and there along the southern coast of Terra Grande, while Purgatory became semitropical. But still the ice advanced, creeping farther and farther south, locking up more and more water in snow and ice, water that should have flowed back into the southern ocean.

The sea levels dropped. The oceans of Inferno, never very deep to begin with, receded at incredible speed as the ice grew ever deeper in the north. Islands began to appear out of the southern ocean. Still the waters drew back, until the Great Bay revealed its true form as a drowned crater. Now it was a circular sea, surrounded on all sides by land.

The ice mass continued to advance, and the city of Hades vanished under the snow and ice.

Suddenly the simulation froze. "You see this world as it will be, approximately seventy-five standard years from now. For all intents and purposes, by that time there will be no other life on this planet but ourselves. Some small remnant populations of this and that species might well survive in isolated pockets, but the world as a whole will be dead." Alvar heard a grim graveyard chuckle in the darkness. "By the time the world is as we see it here, I suppose we humans ourselves could be regarded as a remnant in an isolated pocket."

"I don't understand," Alvar protested, speaking to the faceless voice of the Governor somewhere in the dark. "I thought the danger was from the deserts growing, the planet getting too hot, the ice caps baking off."

"That was what we all thought," the Governor said bitterly. "Whatever desultory, token efforts my predecessor made to correct the situation were based on calculations and predictions to that effect. The deserts were supposed to grow, the ice cap to vanish completely, the sea levels to rise. There are plans in my files for dikes to be built around the city and hold back the rising water!"

Alvar heard the Governor step out from behind the console. He came around the side of the simglobe to stand by Alvar's chair and look at the half-frozen world. "Perhaps I am being unfair. The situation is remarkably complex. If one or two variables shifted slightly, it *would* be the sea, and not the ice, that would overwhelm the city. In fact, stage one of our revised terraforming plan is to tip the scales back *toward* the collapse-into-desert, coastal-flooding scenario—it is a less drastic catastrophe than the ice age we otherwise face. You have not seen the worst of the ice age yet."

"But why push toward the desert scenario? Why not work toward a stable middle ground?" Alvar asked.

"An excellent question. The answer is that our current situation is a *result* of aiming for that middle ground, a middle ground we may well not be able to achieve."

"I don't understand."

The Governor sighed, his face dimly lit by the image of a dying world. "The groundwork for a stable ecology comfortable to humans was never properly laid in the first place, and we are paying the price for it. A properly terraformed world, when disturbed in some way, will always tend back toward that comfortable middle ground. Not here. Life is supposed to be a moderating factor in a planet's environment, smoothing out the extremes. But life's hold on Inferno is getting weaker, and a weakened system moves toward extremes. What we would view as a 'normal' terrestrial ecology has, on Inferno, become the abnormal, *un*stable transition point between two stable states—ice age or an overly arid continent with high sea levels. Of the two stable states, we are heading for the ice, and that will kill us.

"Creating an Inferno with a mostly desert, half-flooded Terra Grande may be the best we can do. It will only leave us halt and lame. You see, if we can force the trends back toward desert-spreading, then life would at least survive on this planet even when our civilization collapses!"

"When our civilization collapses!" Alvar cried out in astonishment. "What are you saying? Is that really going to happen?"

Grieg sighed, a tired-sounding noise of resignation. "I suppose I should say 'if' instead of 'when,' but I have been reading a whole series of classified reports that suggest that collapse is far more likely than anyone imagines. When it gets bad, people will start pulling out. Not everyone will be able to afford it. There will be too few ships available. Prices will be high. Some people will die, and many more will leave. I doubt there will be a large enough population left to keep society functioning, even with the robots. Maybe all the people will die off, but the robots will survive. Who knows?"

The Governor seemed to come back to himself a bit. He drew his shoulders up and looked down at Alvar and spoke in a firmer, more controlled voice. "Forgive me. There is a great deal on my mind."

Chanto Grieg paced back and forth in front of Alvar once or twice, clearly working to collect his thoughts. At last he spoke. "We are in a knife-edge situation, Sheriff, in more ways than one. Political and social issues are intertwined with the ecological problems. In looking at the ecology, we therefore must plan for the likelihood that whatever survivors there are will not be able to do anything to save the planet, beyond whatever efforts *we* make. The ice age result is not survivable. The desert result is. So we force the planet back toward the desert pattern, and, if we get the chance, we can try and reterraform from there. That will certainly be preferable to our current future," Grieg said, gesturing toward the simglobe.

"But the ice age doesn't look that bad," Alvar objected.

"Don't forget that I have stopped the program," Grieg said. "But yes, all this, we *could* survive, even if we ignore the great and terrible crime of allowing the planet to die." The Governor regarded the globe thoughtfully. "Even the ice overwhelming the city is not an insurmountable problem, viewed on a global scale. We could dome over the town, or burrow underground, as the Settlers do. But *this* is not the end of the story."

The Governor turned and stepped back into the darkness. Alvar heard the Governor tapping new commands into the console, and found himself struck by the random thought that buttons and switches were a typically Settler way to do things. Why not voice commands, or an interface to allow a robot to handle the machinery?

But he knew his mind was just finding ways to avoid facing the reality of what Grieg was showing him. *What does all this have to do with me?* he wondered, more than a bit uncomfortably. *I'm just a cop chasing crooks. I'm not running the planet.* But even as he told himself those things, Alvar knew there was a larger reality here. And all this might well have a great deal to do with him.

Chanto Grieg set the simglobe controls to move forward in time. The ice caps grew larger, the seas receded farther. "This is the crisis point," Grieg said, "eighty-five standard years from now. The seas recede enough to expose the south polar highlands." The simglobe tilted its south polar region toward Alvar, and he could see the polar landmass emerging from the water, instantly forming its own ice cap. "The polar lands have been hidden under the seas, but they are at significantly higher elevations than the surrounding lowlands. When the sea level shrinks enough, the polar continent emerges.

"And that is what will doom us. There has been ice over the southern polar ocean all along, but the water beneath the ice has always been able to flow freely. The circulation patterns are complex, but the effect of the currents is that the antarctic waters have been able to blend with the temperate-zone and equatorial waters. The warm water cools down and the cold water warms up. But once *both* poles are landlocked, the planet's ocean currents shift violently. Water no longer flows through *either* polar region, and thus the oceans' currents will no longer be available to moderate the temperature differential between the south pole and the equatorial region. The oceans no longer have any place to dump their heat. What that means is that temperatures in the south polar regions drop precipitously—and equatorial and temperate-zone temperatures go through the roof. The absolute volume of water in the oceans is greatly reduced as well, which means the oceans simply are not able to hold as much heat energy.

"Air temperatures rise. Storms become more and more violent. The water in the oceans boils off while the poles descend into ever-greater cold. Within 120 years of today, the last of the free water on this planet will be locked up in massive ice caps at the north and south poles. It will get cold enough at the poles to form lakes of liquid nitrogen. But the temperate regions and the equator will simply be baked alive.

"Normal daytime temperatures at Hades's location will be about 20 degrees below zero on the Celsius scale. Daytime temperatures on the equator will reach 140 degrees without any trouble at all. Without water, with temperatures that high, the last of the plant life will die. Without that plant life to put oxygen back into the air, the atmosphere will lose all its breathable oxygen as various chemical reactions cause the oxygen to bind to the rocks and soils of the surface. Other chemical reactions will bind up whatever nitrogen doesn't freeze out onto the polar regions. The atmospheric pressure will drop drastically. Without the thermal insulation of a thick atmosphere, the planet's ability to retain heat at the equator will decline. Equatorial temperatures will drop, until the entire planet is a frigid, airless wasteland, far more hostile to life than it was *before* humans reached it. *That* is the current prognosis for the planet Inferno."

Alvar Kresh stared in horror at the image of a frozen, wizened, dead world that hung in front of him. The greens and blues were all gone. The planet was a dun-colored desert, both its poles buried under huge, gleaming-white ice caps. He discovered that his fingers were clenched into the arms of his chair and that his heart was racing. He forced his fingers to relax, inhaled deeply in an effort to calm himself. "All right," he said, though it was clear things were anything but. "All right. I knew there were problems, even if I did not know they were this bad. But what does all this have to do with me?" he asked, his voice quiet.

The Governor brought the lights back out and stepped out from behind his console. "That is perfectly simple, Sheriff Kresh. Politics. It comes down to a question of politics and the qualities of human nature. I could make a frontal attack, try and get the public behind me, get all Infernals to come together and save the planet. To do that, I would have to put on the show you have just seen, for the benefit of the entire planet. Broadcast it by every means available. Some people would accept the facts. But not all of them. Probably not even most of them."

"What would the rest of them do?" Kresh asked.

"No. No. You think about that for a minute. Think about it, and you tell *me* what they would do."

Alvar Kresh looked up again, at the dry, wizened corpse of a world that hung in space before him. What would they do? How would they react? The musty old traditionalists who yearned for the glories of the past; the Ironheads; the less radical people—such as himself—who saw a Settler scheme under every rock. The ones who were simply comfortable with the world and their lives as they were, firmly opposed to any change. What would they do?

"Deny it," he said at last. "There would be riots, and calls for your impeachment, and any number of people with axes to grind trotting out studies to prove that you were dead wrong and that everything was fine. People would claim you were a dupe of the Settlers—more people than think that now. One way or another, I doubt you'd serve out your term of office."

"You're too optimistic. I would say the odds would be poor on my *living* through my term of office, for what that is worth. But in a larger sense, that doesn't matter. All men die. Planets need not, *should* not, die. Not after only a few centuries of life." Grieg turned his back on Alvar and walked to the far end of his office. "It may sound grandiose, but if I am ejected from office and replaced by someone who insists that everything is fine—then I am convinced Inferno's ecology will collapse. Maybe I am quite mad, or a raging egomaniac, but I do believe that to be true."

"But how can you not inform the public about all this?"

"Oh, the people have to know, of course," Grieg said, turning around to face Kresh again. "I didn't mean to imply that I was going to try to keep this secret. That would be impossible over the long run. Any attempt to keep the lid on this permanently would be bound to fail. But so, too, would an effort to spring this information on the populace all at once. Today the average citizen simply believes that the terraforming system needs some fine tuning, some repairs and tidying up. They can't quite see why we need to humble ourselves to the Settlers just for the sake of getting that job done."

Grieg walked slowly down the length of the office, back toward Kresh. "It will take time to educate them, to prepare them for the knowledge of the danger. If the situation is handled properly, I can shape the debate, so that people want to decide how to rebuild the ecology and don't waste time wondering if it even needs fixing. We need to get them to a thoughtful, determined frame of mind, where they can accept the challenge ahead. We can get to that point, I'm sure of it.

"But we must choose our path carefully. For the present, the situation is volatile, explosive. People are in the mood for argument, not reason. And yet we must start on the repair program now if there is to be any hope of success and survival. And we must use the strongest, most effective, fastest-moving tools available to us."

Grieg came closer to Kresh, still talking, his eyes animated and intent. "In other words," Grieg said, "the only hope for avoiding this disaster lies with the Settlers. Without their help this planet will be dead, for all intents and purposes, within a standard century. I find therefore that I am forced to accept their help, long before I have time to shape public opinion so that people will accept Settler help. I might add that the Settlers offered their help with certain conditions, which I was obliged to accept. One of those conditions will become apparent tonight.

"But my political alliance with the Settlers is shaky at best. If this robot assault case is not closed quickly and neatly, there can be no doubt that there will be a political explosion on this world, though I am not exactly certain what form it will take. If it gets out that a robot is suspected of a crime—or if Settlers are suspected of sabotaging robots—it will be hard, if not impossible, to prevent my enemies from expelling the Settlers. And if that move succeeds, the Settlers will wash their hands of us. Without their help, Inferno will die. And in the wake of the most recent Ironhead riots, I feel certain they are looking for an excuse to leave. We cannot afford to give them one."

Grieg paced back and forth again, stepping through the edge of the simglobe hologram, his shoulder brushing through the ghostly-real image of a dead world to come. He crossed to Kresh and put his hands on the arms of Alvar's chair. He leaned his face down close to Alvar's, so close the Governor's breath was warm against the Sheriff's cheek. "Solve this case, Kresh. Solve it quickly and neatly and well. Solve it without complication or scandal."

He spoke the last words in a whisper, the light of fear bright in his eyes. "If you do not," he said quietly, "you will doom this planet."

11

SENIOR Sheriff's Deputy Tansaw Meldor leaned back in his seat. He idly watched Junior Deputy Mirta Lusser flying the aircar through the darkness just before dawn. She was a typical newbie, he decided: conscientious as all hell, overly determined to do every part of her job perfectly, almost touchingly devoted to duty. It had taken a direct order before she would call him by his first name. She took the regs seriously and was burningly anxious to do everything *right.*

All of which meant that she usually *wanted* to fly the aircar, which suited Meldor just fine. He had had his fill of manual flying years ago. Robots could not fly Sheriff's patrol aircraft, not when many Sheriff's Department duties had at least the potential for causing harm to humans. So human deputies were forced to do robots' work, flying the damned aircars for themselves instead of letting the robots do it, the way civilians could.

The joke of it was the Spacers had never gone in much for automating their equipment, because it was the robots who were going to operate it, anyway. Anything that could be done manually was done that way, making the job of flying a car far more complex than it had to be. Not for the first time, Meldor found himself wishing they could use Settler aircars. He had got a look inside one or two of them during some of the Settlertown dustups, and even ridden in one of them. The damn things could fly themselves, with no need for a human or a robot at the controls. The autopilots on those things went far beyond the rudimentary systems on Spacer aircars.

But no, they were stuck with Spacer-style controls. In which case, it suited him just fine to have Lusser do the flying, if they had to be up at this hour, anyway. Damn Kresh! Why did he have to bump up the rapid-response patrols? Meldor wanted to be home in bed, asleep, not up here watching the dust blow in from the desert.

Oh, well. Maybe they'd get lucky, and something worthwhile would happen.

Meldor had missed the latest Ironhead riots. He could do with a little excitement.

DAWN lit the sky.

Caliban had quartered the city during the night, walked through every district, up and down streets of all descriptions, wandered many grand, empty avenues and boulevards. Some part of him knew that it was madly dangerous to be out on the streets. He had to assume that whoever those people were who ordered him to kill himself would try again. He had to assume that there were others who wished him no better fate.

He knew he should hide, duck away out of sight where no one could find him. But he could not bring himself to do that. He was gradually coming to realize that he was searching for something without knowing what that something was. An object, an idea, a bit of knowledge his datastore did not possess. *An answer.*

He knew not what he sought, and that alone made him hunger for it all the more.

But daytime was here. The robots of night—the laborers, the builders—were giving way to the robots of morning. Personal servants, messengers, aircar drivers were starting to appear—and in their wake, humans were arriving as well, more and more of them as daytime drew them back to the center city.

Thus far, no robot had paid him the slightest attention. But humans. *They* were the danger. He had to hide. But where? He had no idea of what made a good hiding place, where he might be safe.

Again he had one of those strange moments of sensation, wherein he felt some internal whisper that his thought processes were skewing to one side. Somehow he knew that fear of personal danger was abnormal, all but unheard-of, in a robot. It was another leakage from the emotion-set that seemed to hover around the edges of his datastore. He might well be the first of his kind to be a fugitive.

But where to hide, and how? In the sections of the city he had explored, or in the parts he had not yet seen?

Caliban stopped at the next intersection, by the entrance to some sort of store. He considered his options. He consulted the city map in his datastore and saw that there was a great deal of the city he had not seen yet. He had walked great strips and swatches of the town, but he had had no reason to quarter it systematically, block by block, street by street. What he had established from his wandering was that the datastore city map was not very detailed, and far from being complete or accurate. The city had changed since the map had been made. He himself had witnessed some of that change happening the night before. Whole buildings were missing from the datastore map, or on the map but missing from the real city. Clearly he could not rely on the datastore.

It would have to be in the area of town he had already seen, then. But even there his knowledge was far from complete. Where could he—

"You! Help my robot with those packages and follow me to my aircar."

Caliban turned around in some surprise. There was a heavyset man behind him, followed by a personal robot, coming out of the store. The robot was carrying a huge stack of packages, piled so high it could not see over them.

"Come on, come on. The damn store's robots are all out on deliveries, and damned if I'm going to play seeing-eye guide to a robot."

Caliban did not move. He had learned last night, the hard way, the danger in blindly obeying orders, and the danger in associating with humans.

"What's the matter with you?" the man snapped. "You under superseding orders already, waiting for your master, he tell you not to help anyone or some damn thing?"

"No," Caliban said.

"Then help my robot. That's a direct order!"

But Caliban knew now there was no safety in playing along, mimicking other robots. Suppose this man ordered him into his aircar and flew him to some unknown place, someplace off the map in his datastore? Suppose this man was collecting robots for the thrill of destroying them, just as the woman had been the night before?

Caliban wanted no part of it. Best to get away from this man, get away and find a place to hide from all the humans.

He turned his back on the man and walked away.

"Hey! Come back here!"

But the lessons of the night before were burned deeply into Caliban's brain. He determinedly ignored the man and walked on. Suddenly there was a hand around his arm. The man was grabbing at him, trying to restrain him. Caliban pulled himself free. The man reached out to grab him again, but Caliban sidestepped him. At last he decided to run. There was much he did not understand, but he knew he did not want to be in this place any longer than necessary.

Without a backwards glance, Caliban stepped into the street, lengthened his stride into a smooth, steady run, and took off down the avenue.

CENTOR Pallichan watched in astonishment as the big red robot ran away. Pallichan was utterly flabbergasted and more than a little unnerved. The robot had refused a direct order, and shaken loose from Centor's grip in the bargain! That was tantamount to violent behavior, violence against a human being, and refusal of orders to boot. With trembling fingers, not even entirely sure what he was doing, Pallichan pulled his pocketphone out, flipped it open, and punched in the police emergency code.

He put the little phone to his ear. There was a half moment's silence, and then the robot operator came on. "Sheriff's Department Emergency Line. Please state the nature of your difficulty." It was a smooth, calm, perfectly modulated voice. It soothed Pallichan's agitated mind, helped him think clearly, as no doubt it was meant to do.

"I wish to report a major robot malfunction. A robot, a big metallic-red robot, has just refused my direct order, and then shook me off when I took him by the arm. He ran away."

"I see. Now establishing lock on your present location. Sir, what direction was he moving when he ran away?"

"Ah, oh, let's see." Pallichan had to think for a moment and get his bearings. He forced himself to think clearly, struggling to keep from getting flustered. "North," he said at last. "Due north from here, heading up Aurora Boulevard."

"That would be in the direction of Government Tower?" the deferential robot voice asked.

Pallichan looked up the avenue and saw the tower. "Yes, yes, that's right." The dispatch robot must have consulted a map system and located an obvious landmark Pallichan could use to confirm position and direction. Damned clever of the police to have the robots verify things that way.

"Thank you for your report, sir. A top-priority rapid-response aircar is now being dispatched to investigate. Good day to you."

The line went dead, and Centor Pallichan snapped his phone shut. He dropped it back in his pocket with a proud feeling of civic-mindedness. He led his robot, still patiently carrying his packages, back toward his aircar and managed to get everything packed away without help from any other robots.

Some minutes later, when his robot had taken the controls and lifted toward home, it dawned on him to wonder why the police had been so willing to listen to him. Why had they believed something as mad as a report of a rogue robot? Why hadn't the dispatcher tried to confirm what should have sounded like a completely lunatic report?

It was, he realized with a chill of fear, almost as if the dispatch robot had been *waiting* for a rogue-robot call. Pallichan did not even wish to *consider* the implications of *that* thought. No, no, far better to force the entire thing from his mind. A quiet life for him. Dealing with the police was distasteful enough.

"INCOMING priority!" The words were out of Senior Deputy Meldor's mouth almost before he was aware that the alert light had come on. That was what training could do for you, he told himself. It let you act, and act properly, before you were even quite sure what was happening. He scanned the text of the incoming message, allowing Junior Deputy Lusser to keep her full attention on flying the car, picking out the data she would need to get them to the target. No need to distract her with needless details at the precise moment she was called upon to do some intricate flying.

"What is it, Tansaw?" Mirta Lusser demanded.

"Rogue-robot call, subject reported proceeding northward on Aurora from the intersection of Aurora and Solaria." Meldor checked his vectors and location. "Come to heading 045," he said.

But the aircar was already banking, veering toward the northeast. She had worked it out in her head. Lusser was a good pilot, Meldor decided, one who always knew where she was over the city and how to get anywhere else. "Damn it, Meldor, a rogue robot? Does this mean the damn rumors are *real?*"

"Unless the cops aren't the only ones hearing the rumors,"

Meldor said grimly. "If the civilians have heard the same scuttlebutt we have, some of them might get plenty jumpy, and I wouldn't blame them. People are going to start seeing things."

"Wonderful," Mirta said. "That's not going to make our job any easier. Hang on, over target location in ten seconds."

CENTOR Pallichan could not quite believe what had happened. He had seen—and talked with—a mad robot. At least, he had convinced himself that was what had happened. Not altogether subconsciously, he was already mentally reworking the encounter for purposes of relating it to his friends, enhancing his own perspicacity and cleverness just a trifle. Easy to do now that it was all over. The moment itself had contained little actual excitement. It was the aftermath, the call to the police, that put a tingle of excitement and danger in his spine. Perhaps there were people to whom the experience of calling the police would seem to be no great adventure, but it was the closest to bold action Pallichan had ever come, and he felt no guilt in savoring the moment.

But it was time to get back to normal, he decided, a bit primly. Yes, Pallichan decided, it was time to let his robot fly him home, time to slide into the calm, natural order of things. Already he was envisioning the smooth, quiet ritual of the midday meal, always just the same food, served just the same way, at just the same time. His robots knew how much he valued order and regularity, and no doubt his pilot robot had already signaled to his household staff, advising of the upset to the master's day. No doubt they would see to it that the remainder of his day was even more orderly than usual, in recompense for what he had just been through.

Still, he considered, there was no harm in having a good story to tell. Centor's brush with a Mad Robot! He could imagine the buzz of excitement *that* would send through the circle of his acquaintanceship. Within a few seconds, he was lost to the outside world, his imagination back at work cheerfully inflating the danger and drama of his encounter with the robot—and his own courage in dealing with it. It was a rather soothing mental exercise, and he found he was beginning to feel settled down again. He found himself wondering what the sequel to the event would be, what would happen to the robot in question.

But then present reality intruded on his revisions of the recent past. A blue blur of speed whipped past his car on the port side.

Centor watched in openmouthed, horrified amazement as it swept past. A sky-blue Sheriff's aircar! Then came another, and another, and another, whipping past overhead off to starboard—two even raced past *beneath* his car, violating every safety regulation on the planet.

Pallichan suddenly realized that his own aircar was tooling along, at a quite leisurely pace, straight north over Aurora Boulevard, the direction the rogue robot had taken. He looked through the forward windscreen and his stomach turned to a block of ice. There were at least four blue aircars on the scene, two of them landing, the others taking up very aggressive patrol stations. It was hard to be certain, but he thought he could even catch sight of a red-painted robot, still moving rapidly northward.

Centor's aircar shuddered and bucked in the air turbulence caused by the Sheriff's cars. Pallichan was not a forceful or adventurous man, not by any means. Any slight sense of curiosity he might have concerning the sequel of his report to the police vanished in an instant. "Turn the car, you fool!" he cried out to his robot. "Turn! Turn! Get us out of here."

The fear and panic in his voice was clear, and the robot pilot clearly understood the urgency of the command. He turned the car on its ear as it jinked down and to port, diving the car between two towering office buildings, roaring down the canyoned streets of the central city. Pallichan's fingers dug into the arms of his flight chair, and he broke out in a cold sweat. At last the car slowed a bit and put its nose upward as the pilot robot guided them toward a more prudent altitude.

Pallichan sat there, gasping for breath, his heart pounding, as his aircar banked gently toward home.

That was enough, he decided. Enough indeed. If that was what excitement was like, he had had just enough to suit Centor Pallichan for a lifetime and beyond. Life was meant to be orderly, controlled, reasonable. The universe was supposed to remain always as it was, in a steady, happy balance of calm. Disobedient robots? Mad police chases? That sort of chaos was not the way of things. Something had to be done about it.

But that thought brought him up short. For it suddenly dawned on him that a universe of chaos and uncertainty, such as had been so abruptly revealed to him, was unlikely to modify its behavior merely because Centor objected. What step could he take? Write a stiff letter to the Governor? Organize all the right-thinking people who wished merely to be left alone, bring all the most placid and hermetic of Inferno's citizenry into a group as rough-and-ready as those frightful Ironheads? Have them forcibly demand that things stop happening and get back to normal?

But another thought struck at him, almost physically. Suppose, just suppose, that it was the *nature* of things to keep happening, that it was the long placidity of life on Inferno that was the aberration? Suppose that aberration was even now being swept away, and the tumultuous ferment of the universe at large was even now crashing down upon them all?

What if there was no "normal" to get back to?

Centor Pallichan felt his hands trembling with fear, and knew his tremors had more to do with what he might see soon than what he had just seen recently. "Take me home," he told his pilot robot. "Take me home, where it is safe."

CALIBAN heard the sound behind him as he ran and recognized it as the swooping air-rush of aircars coming in fast and low. He heard the squeal of wheels slamming down onto pavement and knew that several of the cars had landed on the avenue. No doubt others would land ahead of him. Yes, he could see them up ahead. *For me,* he thought. *All of them are after me. I am some terrible threat to them, for reasons I do not understand. They will destroy me if they can.* He knew it to be a certainty, not a chance or a theory or a probable hypothesis.

By now he was quite good at judging by partial evidence, he realized in some detached part of his mind that was not occupied with the need for escape and survival. But even as he made that observation about his own thought processes, he had started evasive action. He stopped abruptly and turned right, down a narrow alley as the aircars swept by overhead, unable to stop in time to make the turn. Three, four, five, six of them. But they would not be put off so easily. This time the search, the hunt, was well and truly on. They would not stop until they had him. The fact that they had sent so many aircars and deputies after him told him that much very clearly. But where to turn? Where to hide? The question suddenly became even more urgent as the alley came to an abrupt end in a blank wall.

He turned, and saw a door leading into the building whose wall made up the north side of the alley, and another door on the south wall. Caliban tried the first door and found that it opened easily. He was about to rush through it when an idea came to him. He tried the door on the south wall of the alley and found it securely locked. Good. Perfect. Caliban smashed the south door open, ripping it off its hinges. Then he returned to the door on the north side and went through it, closing it carefully after him.

It must be, he thought, an exceedingly old trick, and even a rather obvious one. But they would not know how to deal with a robot capable of trickery and deception, however simple that deception might be. They would underestimate him, he was sure of it. And that was knowledge he could use.

He made his way into the building and set about finding a way to escape.

THEIRS was the first car to respond, Tansaw knew that much. Still and all, it wasn't going to do them any good. At least three other cars had been in better position to get in there first and fast. Mirta had flown well enough to beat two of them to the punch, but there was still Jakdall's car, right on their nose. There was no way they could get past them to make the pinch. Burning hell, there he was! A devil-red robot running down the middle of the road. They had him! No, damnit, they didn't. The robot turned suddenly and dove into an alley. Jakdall's car popped open its airbrake louvers and landing gear, reversing thrust, pulling in for a speed landing. Mirta jinked their own nose higher to avoid a midair collision, the air thumping and roaring past as they hit Jakdall's turbulence and rattled through it. That did it. No matter how good a pilot Mirta was, she was not going to be able to avoid overshooting. Damnation! They should have been expecting the red bastard to dodge away like that. Yes, a standard robot would not have attempted evasive action, but then a standard robot would not be running away from the police. They had all been warned in the briefing to expect "atypical behavior" from this robot. And now they were out of the game. No way they could get back in position before Jakdall and the other units closed in.

Tansaw suddenly realized that Mirta had not brought their nose back down. They were still headed up and out. Tansaw was about to say something about that when he was thrown forward against his seat restraints and the nose thrusters roared. His stomach turned to lead as Mirta slammed reverse thrust on and used the nose jets to force the car over on its tail, braking hard with the reversers as she skewed their nose up. The car's structural members groaned and thrummed under the strain, and the danger alarm started to go off. Tansaw let out a gasp of air as Mirta cut the reversers and nose jets simultaneously. The car hung in free fall for a split heartbeat and then lurched forward as Mirta slammed them into forward acceleration again.

But still Mirta did not bring the car level. She forced the nose skyward, angling up more and more sharply until the car was all but standing on its tail. Tansaw grabbed the armrests of his chair and hung on for dear life. The nose angled up more and more until they were flat on their backs, and still she did not angle back. Burning devils, she was going for a full loop! Up and over now, the car arcing over, flying fully upside down for an endless moment.

Tansaw looked *down* through the overhead ports, and saw the land where the sky should have been, looked down at the gleaming cityscape spread out below, the dawning sun lighting up the east, its warm rays just catching the bases of the most westerly towers, civilian aircars scattering like a startled flock of birds as the sky-blue sheriff's cars zeroed in on their quarry.

Then Mirta pointed the nose down and they arced over, straight down, diving for the ground, the normally silent aircar groaning with the strain, the air screaming past them as they dropped.

Down, down, down. Tansaw stole a quick glance at Mirta. She was grim-faced, determined, her jaw set, concentrating fiercely.

At the last possible moment she pulled up and hit the thrust reversers. They were back over Aurora Boulevard, a hundred meters south of where they had been when the robot had turned, still moving damn fast.

Mirta leveled them out and fired the nose jets again, fighting the car as it tried to flip over in flight. Suddenly the nose jets died and they were turning, arcing gracefully to a halt in the alley, not ten seconds behind Jakdall and his partner, hovering to a smooth halt in midair.

With a bump and thump, Mirta dropped their landing gear, cut power, and had them on the ground.

"Damn good flying, Mirta," Tansaw said, wondering if Sheriff Kresh would see it that way, or throw her off the force as a menace to navigation. But one thing was for sure—if there ever came a debate over the wisdom of human-piloted sheriff's cars, Tansaw could point to the ride he had just taken. No robot would ever have flown that way, never mind how urgent the need.

But this was no time for worrying over such matters, and his partner was clearly in no mood for small talk. Mirta, still grim and grey-faced, popped the hatch on her side of the car and was out on the ground before Tansaw even had his restraint straps off. He popped his own hatch and scrambled out, weapon drawn. Strange and terrifying thought, that he felt the need of a blaster going up against a robot.

Tansaw took some small satisfaction from realizing that Jakdall and his partner were blowing the last of their lead merely by taking their time disembarking, weighted down by hell's own collection of equipment. Apparently Jakdall was determined to be prepared for not just anything, but *everything*. Guns, knives, body armor, inertial trackers, cutting tools, a half dozen gadgets Tansaw didn't even recognize—Jakdall had everything but underwater gear strapped to himself. His partner, Sparfinch, was even more laden down, with a jumpy, nervous look in his eyes. The kid was drawn as tight as a cable under tension. Not for the first time, Tansaw thanked whatever luck it was that he had been paired with Mirta and not Sparfinch.

Jakdall grinned. He gave Tansaw and Mirta a mock salute. "Nice flying, kids, but there's no prizes for second. We're taking the lead on this. Come on, Spar. Let's go fry a robot."

"Orders are to capture," Mirta said warningly.

"Oh, yeah, they sure are. But it might get a little too hot for that." Jakdall laughed and winked. "Come on, Spar." Without thought or question, he turned toward the torn-out, smashed-up door on the south side of the alley.

Jakdall gestured for Spar to head in while Jak covered him. Spar hesitated just in front of the door, his eyes rolling nervously. He drew his weapon and did a wholly needless tuck-and-roll dive into the building. The interior was open to plain view—there was no one in there. That robot wasn't going to duck inside the first room it came to and hide. Jak made ready to follow his partner in when suddenly there was a muffled roar and thump from the interior.

"Got him!" Spar's voice cried out. Jak, Tansaw, and Mirta rushed inside. Spar was standing over the burned-out hulk of a small, moss-colored robot. Jak took one look at it and let out a string of curses. "Damn you, Spar, that robot's green! It's just a building maintenance unit."

"I can't help it," Spar said in an agitated voice. "I'm colorblind."

"Ah, the hell with it. Come on, we'll search through there." Jak turned toward Tansaw. "You two coming?"

"No, you guys go ahead," Tansaw said. "We'll stand watch

here and make sure he doesn't double back." Mirta turned and looked at him sharply, but Tansaw gestured for her to be quiet, out of Jak's line of sight. Jak grinned hugely and laughed at them. "Brilliant plan, Tan. You always were good on the backup jobs. Come on, Spar."

Mirta watched the two of them clump noisily out of the back room, headed toward the front of the building, then turned toward Tansaw, obviously seething. "Damnit, Meldor, do you have to let them steal our thunder when I practically bent the aircar in half getting us here? We should be hunting with them, not guarding some damn door!"

"Easy, Mirta. I just didn't want us getting our heads blown off when Spar decides we're robot-shaped. The rogue didn't come through here. He just wanted us to *think* he did. Look at the room. The door's smashed to pieces but everything in here is untouched. Let those two maniacs blunder around in here. My guess is that the robot is smarter than Jak is—though that's not really saying too much about the robot." He turned and stepped back out into the alley, Mirta right behind him. The alley was filled with cops by now, two or three of them heading in the smashed-down door even as Tansaw and Mirta came out. Tansaw crossed the alley and tried the other door. It swung open easily. With a glance at Mirta, Tansaw stepped inside. He knew, absolutely *knew,* that this was the way the robot had gone.

But he also knew he didn't much like the idea of tracking a robot who was capable of thinking in terms of diversionary tactics. And that second piece of knowledge did much to remove the savor from the first piece.

They moved into the gloomy interior of the building. There was very little inside, merely a forest of packing cases that had never been cracked open. Hades was full of such buildings—designed, built, stocked with equipment by robots and forgotten. Most of the ghost buildings were like this one, wholly complete, but left vacant. The ghosts were gifts from on high to criminal gangs of all sorts, ideal places to meet, to hide out, perfect headquarters from which to run their scams and crimes.

It looked as if this building had gotten all the way to furniture delivery before being shut down. The crates were neatly stacked everywhere, turning the first floor into a maze of hiding places. And then there were the floors above and the subbasements and service tunnels below. Even if the rogue *had* come in here, how the hell would they ever know it, or find him?

Then Mirta grabbed his arm and pointed her handlamp down at the floor.

Dust. The floor was covered in a smooth, perfect film of dust—with one set of distinctly robotic footprints leading off into the interior, moving at a smooth and confident pace.

The two deputies followed the line of footprints through the canyons of packing cases. They led straight for a stairwell, its door standing open. Moving cautiously, Mirta and Tansaw went inside, to be greeted by a cool breeze blowing down the shaft, which apparently also served as part of the ventilator system. But the air currents meant no dust deposits here. No footprints. Damn it. All right, then. Up or down? Which way did he go?

"He headed straight for the stairs," Mirta said, her voice a loud whisper.

"So what does that tell us?" Tansaw asked.

"That he knows where he's going. He must have a good internal map system. He's not moving in a panic. He's got a plan, he's thinking ahead."

"Which means he must have figured out that heading up isn't going to do him any good. We'd be able to seal off the building and bottle him up. So he went down into the service tunnels." That was always bad news. The tunnels went everywhere, to allow the maintenance robots to bring in supplies and services without adding to street congestion. And despite all official statements to the contrary, every cop knew there were *lots* of tunnels that did not appear on any map. Some had just been dug and then forgotten, some had been deliberately erased from the map memories—and some had been dug by robots in the employ of enterprising free-lancers of one sort or another.

"Right." Mirta holstered her gun and pulled her tracker/mapper out of her tunic. She worked the controls and consulted the screen. "Not so bad around here," she said. "I only show one main horizontal shaft connecting to this building."

"Can we seal it before he can use it to get to another tunnel?" All the tunnels—all the official tunnels, at least—were equipped with heavy-duty vault-style doors.

"We can try," Mirta said. "It'll be close, one way or the other." She brought her comm mike around to her mouth. "This is Deputy 1231, in rapid pursuit of suspect. Request immediate seals on all accesses to city tunnel number A7 B26." She listened to her headset for a moment, and Tansaw felt as much as heard a series of muffled, far-off clanging thuds. "That ought to do it," she said. "If he didn't get out of B26 before we sealed it, we have him now."

Tansaw looked up at his partner and nodded. "It's time to call in the others," he said.

CALIBAN heard the booming thuds of the tunnel doors slamming shut. He had been moving at a fast, steady, walking pace in the narrow tunnel, but now he broke into a run, hurrying for the end. He came upon it all too soon and knew he was in deep trouble. This door was meant for a full-security seal. He tried to force it open, but obviously it had been specifically designed to be beyond a robot's strength, with a locked and armored control panel as well. He consulted his datastore map.

Tunnel A7 B26 was "H"-shaped, with the access to the building above in the center of the cross member, and the four ends of the vertical members linking into the main city tunnel system. The tunnel itself was barren, nothing but bare walls, floors, and ceilings, with glow lamps set into the ceiling's overhead cross-beam supports. The beams looked to be some sort of plasteel, twenty centimeters square in cross section, spaced at five-meter intervals.

Suddenly Caliban had an idea. He consulted his datastore and confirmed that humans saw in a far more limited range of light wavelengths than he did. Nor, it appeared, did their bodies provide any source of built-in illumination. He turned around and hurried back down the tunnel, at top speed, yanking out the glow lamps, crushing them, heaving the debris in all directions. Within sixty seconds the floor of the tunnel was littered with broken lamps. It was in absolute darkness, but for the dim glow of two impossibly blue eyes about twenty meters from the building access hatch. But then Caliban shifted to infrared, and even that illumination faded away. He stretched out his arms to one wall of the tunnel, braced his legs against the opposite wall, and walked his way up until he was braced against the ceiling, between two of the overhead supports. The odds seemed at least a little better that he would stay out of sight there. He had no real plan, no idea of how to get out. All he knew was that he had more chance of staying alive a little longer if he kept out of sight in the dark, rather than waiting passively for his fate.

He hung there, waiting, for what seemed an absurdly long time. His on-board chronometer gave him a precise report on how long he waited there, but somehow the number of minutes and seconds that flickered past was no proper measure of his situation. There was something more to it, for the odds were very good that these were the last minutes and seconds he would ever experience.

What was taking them so long?

At last there was a clang and a thump. Caliban cocked his head cautiously down to peek around the support beam that hid him from view. He turned his head toward the access hatch. "Damnit," a voice called out. "He must have knocked all the lights out." Caliban saw the beam of a handlamp stab out from the building side of the hatch. Like most lamps designed to give off visible light, this one cast a fair amount of infrared as well. A human figure, and then another and another and another, came through the hatch, plainly visible in infrared.

"Well, at least we know he's still in here," one of them said as a light beam played across the floor, revealing the smashed glow lamps. "He wouldn't have hung around smashing the lights if he could get out one of the hatches."

"Ready to do some damage, Spar?" one of the others asked with a low chuckle.

"Capture only, Jak," a third one, the only woman, said. "Try to keep that in mind, okay?"

"Don't like tunnels," the one called Spar announced. "This gives me the creeps. Can't we pull in some real lights before we go searching around in here?"

"Galaxy's sake, it's just one lousy robot in an H-tunnel," the one called Jak replied. "Don't you get all jumpy on me now."

Suddenly the hatch behind them swung shut again, to the obvious discomfort of the four deputies. "Well, if he can't get out, neither can we," the woman said, her voice a bit low and nervous.

"I don't like it," Spar objected. "Can't we reopen the hatch and just post a guard on it?"

"Yeah, and let the rogue punch out the guard and make a run for it," the first voice said. "Look, Spar, the manual keypad combo for all the hatches is 274668. You get antsy, you get out that way. Just don't get crazy on us. Come on, let's move out. Mirta, you and me will take the east side; Spar and Jak, you take the west."

These humans weren't thinking clearly. Did they assume that if they could not see him, he could not *hear* them? But that keypad combination. That was the information he needed. Caliban drew his head back in and remained motionless as two of the deputies went past, directly below him.

Listening carefully, he judged that the other pair of deputies had indeed gone the other way, to the western leg of the "H." He could hear them turning the corner and moving up one arm of the tunnel.

Moving as silently as he could, Caliban worked his way back down the wall, stepped down onto the floor, and turned in the direction the two male deputies had gone. He was tempted to use the keypad combination on the building access door, but no doubt there were any number of police waiting just behind it. No. His one hope was to get past these deputies, punch in the keypad combination, and hope it worked. He made his way down to the intersection between the cross tunnel and the side tunnel and peered cautiously around the corner. There they were, on the north end. Caliban backed into the crosswise leg of the tunnel again. He braced his arms and legs against the walls and worked his way back upward to hide against the ceiling again.

After a few moments, the two deputies walked past him in the central connecting tunnel, headed toward the southwestern end of the H-tunnel, making a fair amount of noise as they kicked past the debris of the ruined glow lights. Caliban once again let himself down from the ceiling and moved silently in the direction the two men had come from. There it was, the tunnel hatch, the control panel next to it. Suddenly he had a most disturbing thought. Suppose they were playing games with *him* now? Suppose they had meant for him to hear their discussion, and they had deliberately spoken loudly enough for him to hear? Suppose the combination was false?

But it didn't matter. For if the combination did not work, he would in any event have no other way out. He was locked in here, and that combination was the only key that might open the way. Caliban punched in the keypad combination, moving his fingers as rapidly as possible.

A light stabbed down on him from the opposite end of the tunnel, bright enough to dazzle his infrared vision. "There he is!" Spar's voice shouted from behind the blinding light. There was a roar, and a whoosh, and Caliban threw himself to one side of the tunnel. There was a violent impact, dead on the center of the hatch. A roaring explosion tore through the reinforced hatch and ripped it to shreds, littering the tunnel with shrapnel and smoke. Debris ricocheted off Caliban's body case, knocking him down. He scrambled back to his feet. The impact had blown a hole clear through the armored door, just big enough for Caliban to get through. He scrambled through it, the white-hot armor plate hissing and popping, sending his thermosensors into maximum overload. But then he was through, and out into the tunnels, and gone.

12

"I have had my fill and more of shambles, Donald," Alvar Kresh said as he read the action reports over a belated breakfast at his desk. A breakfast he had been looking forward to since the early hours of the morning, and one he was now not enjoying at all.

He had wanted to eat in the privacy of his own home, not at his desk at headquarters. Circumstances dictated otherwise, to put it mildly. Nor did the circumstances of the situation improve his mood.

Minutes after he came out of the Governor's office, he learned that his officers had lost the leading suspect in the case that might literally decide the fate of the world. This did not make him a happy man.

"We go for a nice, quiet chat with the Governor, you and I," Alvar said, in a voice that was low and reasonable, in a tone of patently false calm. "I am out of contact with the force for perhaps all of an hour, and come back to find that my deputies have been using the airspace over downtown to practice their aerobatics and scare the hell out of half the population." Alvar's voice started to get louder, angrier. He stood and glared at Donald. "I find that one of my officers disregarded all orders and made a creditable effort to kill that suspect before he could be questioned and examined. Instead he made a good start toward blowing up half the city tunnel system."

He knew it was unfair and illogical to yell at Donald, but he had to take his anger out on *someone*. And there Donald was, right in front of him, an easy target for his fury, and one that would not fight back.

But even in the depths of his fury, Alvar knew that he was playing to the squad room outside his office as well. It was not by chance that his office was not well soundproofed. Some times it did the force some good to hear the Old Man blow up. By now Alvar was shouting out loud, deliberately shouting not at Donald, but at the thin walls and the men and women outside.

"In other words, the only reason my stunt-flying, trigger-happy deputies have not wrecked everything is that they are lousy shots as well. What is *wrong* with everyone?"

The rhetorical question hung in the air for perhaps half a minute. Donald stood silently before Alvar's desk. At last Alvar sighed, sat back down, and picked up his fork. He took another moody stab at his sausages. "I am not a happy man, Donald," he said at last, in a quieter voice, now speaking almost to himself. "On top of everything else, I have not a doubt that this whole fiasco has set a whole new series of rumors flying. Besides the hundreds of witnesses to our overreaction, there is a civilian we can do nothing to silence, and he is no doubt out there cheerfully telling all his friends about the robot who refused orders. God knows where that will end."

"Yes, sir. It is most unfortunate. There is some other rather awkward news. There is a current rumor that Fredda Leving's announcement tonight is related to the events of this morning, though what the connection is, no one seems to know."

"That's quite a rumor," Alvar growled ruefully. "Hell, I'm heading the investigation, and even *I* don't know for sure if that's true. It'll get her a hell of a big audience tonight."

"The same thought crossed my mind," Donald said. "You were proved correct in your concerns over a massive police effort. It has forced the whole situation at least partly into the public view. We have set off the panic that might well have been the perpetrator's actual goal."

"Yes, yes, I know. But damn it, what other chance did we have but to respond to the situation? We could not allow this Caliban to go loose—a robot capable of violence against humans—just because a police chase might upset a few people. Not when we had a solid position and a positive ID on him. Expect we blew it, and by now he could be anywhere in or under the city."

"Sir, if I could interject just a moment," Donald said in his most deferential voice. Alvar looked up sharply. He recognized that tone. It was the one Donald used when he was going to be his most contrary. "You are proceeding from an assumption that I now feel we must regard as unproved."

"And what might that be?" Alvar asked cautiously as he used his fork to chase the last of his eggs around the plate.

"That Caliban *is* a robot capable of violence against humans."

The office was wreathed in silence once again, other than the muffled noise from the exterior offices that managed to seep in. This time it was Alvar who knew no way to respond. But it was obvious that Donald was going to say no more. "Wait a second," Alvar said, dropping his fork back on his plate and giving the service robot a half-conscious signal to remove the tray. "You were the one trying to convince me that our suspect *was* a robot."

"Yes, sir. But circumstances have changed. New evidence and patterns of evidence have come to light. Tentative conclusions must be reviewed against revised data."

"What evidence and patterns of evidence?"

"One pattern in particular, sir, that I have not examined as yet. I need to run a thought experiment. I have a hypothesis which I need to test. If you will bear with me for a moment, this experiment will be difficult for me. But to perform this mental experiment, I will be forced—to—contemplate—a—robot doing—violence—to human beings. No doubt that will make it hard for me to speak and think. Indeed, you will note that even offering up the idea causes my speech to slow and slur noticeably."

The serving robot turned toward Donald, moving so jerkily that the silverware flew off the serving tray. It knelt and scooped up the fork and knife before rising again, weaving back and forth a bit.

Donald noticed the other robot's reaction. "Ah, sir, before we discuss this further, perhaps you should excuse the serving robot so as to prevent needless damage to its brain."

"What? Oh, yes, of course." Alvar waved the serving robot out, and it left the room, still holding the tray. "Now then, what is this thought experiment? If it's risky, I don't want to do it. I don't want you to damage yourself, Donald," Alvar said, concern in his voice. "I need you."

"That is most kind of you to say, sir. However, I believe that, given the police-robot reinforcements to my positronic brain, the risk of significant permanent damage is negligible. However, you will need to be patient with me. Nor do I wish to work through this thought process more than once. It will no doubt be unpleasant for me, and the risk of permanent damage will increase should I need to repeat it. So I would request that you pay strict attention.

"I wish to place myself in the circumstances that this Caliban has faced on at least two occasions, once at the warehouse with the robot bashers, and once just now with the deputies in the tunnel. In both cases, Caliban was surrounded by a group of human beings who were clearly threatening his very existence. I intend to work through the circumstances of each event and see how a high-level robot with the Three Laws would react, what the outcome would be. In short, what would have happened if a robot with my mind and Caliban's size and strength faced such circumstances?"

"Yes, very well," Alvar said, a bit mystified.

"Then I will proceed." He sat there and watched for about a minute as Donald stood there in front of him, stock-still, frozen in place.

With a resumption of movement that was somehow more disconcerting than the way he had stopped moving, Donald came back to himself. "Very good," he said to himself. "The first part of my hypothesis is correct. If it had been myself in either situation, I would have been destroyed, killed on the spot." The satisfaction in his voice was plain.

"Is that all?" Alvar asked, feeling quite confused.

"Oh, no, sir. In a sense, I have not started yet. I was merely establishing a baseline, if you will. Now I must come to the far more difficult part of the experiment. I must put myself in the position of a being of high intellect, with great speed and strength, with superb senses and reflexes, who is placed in the same circumstances. But *this* hypothetical being is willing and able to defend itself by whatever means, including an attack on a human."

Alvar gasped and looked up at Donald in shocked alarm. More robots than he cared to recall had been utterly destroyed by far more casual contemplation of harm to humans. To imagine such harm, deliberately committed by oneself, would be the most terrifying, dangerous thought possible for a robot. "Donald, I don't know if—"

"Sir, I assure you that I understand the dangers far more thoroughly than you do. But I believe the experiment to be essential."

Before Alvar could protest any further, Donald froze up again. But this time, he did not stay frozen. A series of twitches and tics began to appear, and grew worse and worse. One foot lurched off the ground, and Donald nearly toppled over before he recovered and regained his balance. A strange, high-pitched sound came up from his speaker, sweeping up and down in frequency. The blue glow of his eyes dimmed, flared, and then went blank. His arms, held at his side, twitched. His fingers clenched and unclenched. He seemed about to topple again. Alvar stood up, rushed around his desk, and reached out to steady his old friend, his loyal servant, holding Donald by the shoulders.

Even as he acted, he found that he was astonished with himself. Friend? Loyal servant? He had never even been aware that he thought of Donald that way. But now it quite abruptly seemed possible that he might lose Donald, this moment, and he suddenly knew how deeply he did not want that to happen.

"Donald!" he called out. "Stop! Break off. Whatever it is you are doing, I am ordering you to stop!"

Donald's body gave another strange twitch, and the robot flinched away from Alvar's touch, backing away a step or two. His eyes flared up, painfully bright, before regaining their normal appearance. "I—I—thank you, sir. Thank you for calling to me. I do not think that I could have broken free of my own volition."

"Are you all right? What the hell happened to you?"

"I believe that I am fine, sir, though it might be prudent if I underwent a diagnostic later." He paused for a moment. "As to what happened, it was a severe cognitive loop-back sequence. I understand that humans are capable of holding two completely contrary viewpoints at once without any great strain. It is not so for robots. I was forced to simulate a lack of constraints on my behavior, although the Three Laws of course control my actions. It was most disconcerting."

Donald hesitated for a moment and looked at Alvar, his head cocked to one side. "It has never occurred to me just how strange and uncertain, how *unguided* a thing it must be to be a human being. We robots know our duty, our purpose, our place, our limits. You humans know none of that. How strange to live a life where all things are permitted, whether or not they are possible. If I may be so bold as to ask, sir—how is it humans can *cope?* What is it they do with all the freedom we robots provide?"

Alvar found himself sorely confused and surprised by the question. Still thrown off guard by Donald's experiment, he answered with more honesty than he would have permitted in a considered answer. "They waste it," he said. "They do nothing with their lives, determined to make each day like the last." He thought of the complaints on his desk, civilians whining that the police had disrupted their lives this morning by trying to capture Caliban, quite unconcerned that the disruption had been in the interests of *protecting* their lives. "They are sure change can only be for the worse. They battle against change—and so ensure there is no change for the better."

But then Alvar stopped and turned away from Donald. "Damn it, that's not fair. Not all of it, anyway. But I spent the morning learning how we've doomed ourselves with indolence and denial."

"My apologies, sir. I did not intend to move the discussion into such irrelevant areas."

"Irrelevant?" Alvar went back to his desk chair and sat back in it with a sigh. "I think perhaps the questions of change and freedom are very close to the issues in this case. We have looked hard, seeking to find how Fredda Leving was attacked, and who did it. But we have scarcely even stopped to ask ourselves *why* the blow was struck. I'll tell you the reason we are bound to find, Donald." Suddenly his voice was eager, excited. "The reason—the motive—is going to be change, and the fear of it. It's got to be something mired down in the politics of all this. There is some big change coming, and someone either wants to protect that change—or stop it. *That's* what we're going to find out. But damn it, we have wandered."

But Alvar had wandered deliberately. He wanted to give Donald a moment to settle down, a chance for his positronic brain to be focused on less frightening, unsettling thoughts for a moment. Alvar knew that the question of a crime's motive, with the insight it provides into the human psyche, always fascinated Donald. "But your experiment, Donald. What were the results?"

"In brief, sir, it confirmed my initial hypothesis—that a—a—*being* with the physical capabilities of a robot, but with no inhibitions on its behavior, and highly motivated to protect its own existence, could have—ki-killed all the Settlers at the warehouse and all the deputies in the tunnels. And, indeed, doing so would have been safer for this hypothetical being than acting as Caliban did."

"What are you saying?"

"It would appear that Caliban acted to protect himself, but did not seek to harm humans. Whatever harm came to them was incidental to his self-defense, and perhaps accidental. There is no doubt that he set fire to the warehouse. There is no proof that he did it deliberately."

"You almost make him sound human, Donald."

"But sir, as I just observed, there are no constraints on human behavior."

"Oh, but there are such constraints. Deep, strong constraints, imposed by ourselves and by society. They rarely fail to hold. They do not have the rigid code of the Three Laws imposed from without, but humans learn their own codes of behavior. But let's not go off on another tangent. I've been thinking about the fact that Leving Labs is an experimental facility. We have yet to ask what *sort* of experiment Caliban was meant to be. What was it that Fredda Leving had in mind? Did the experiment fail? Did it succeed?" A thought came to him, one that made his blood run cold. "Or is the experiment under way now, running exactly according to plan?"

"I don't understand, sir."

"Robots come awake for the first time knowing all they need to know. Humans start out in the world knowing nothing of how the world works. Suppose Leving wondered how a robot that had to learn would behave. Suppose that Caliban is out there, behaving in accordance to the Three Laws, but with such a reduced dataset that he does not know, for example, what a human being *is*. Tonya Welton reminded us that it has happened before. Suppose that Fredda Leving set him out to see how long it would take him to learn the ways of the world on his own."

"That is indeed a most disturbing idea, sir. I can scarcely believe that Madame Leving would be capable of undertaking such an irresponsible experiment."

"Well, she is sure as hell hiding *something*. That lecture last night took lots of potshots at the present state of affairs. I've got a feeling there will be even more bombshells at the second lecture. Maybe we'll learn more then."

Alvar Kresh looked down at his desk and found his thoughts turning toward the routine business of running the department. Personnel reports. Equipment requisitions. The dull humdrum of bureaucracy seemed downright attractive after the chaos of the last few days. Best get to it. "That's all for now, Donald."

"Sir, before I go, there is one more datum of which you need to be apprised."

"What is that, Donald?"

"The blow to Fredda Leving's head, sir. The forensic lab has established that Caliban almost certainly did not do it."

"*What?*"

"It is another part of the new patterns of evidence, sir. There were traces of red paint found in the wound, sir."

"Yes, I know that. What of it?"

"It was fresh paint, sir, not yet fully dry. Furthermore, according to the design specifications for Caliban's body type, a given robot's color is integral to the exterior body panels. With that model robot body, dyes are blended into material used to form the panels. The panels are never painted. The body material is designed to resist stains, dyes, and paints. In short, nothing will stick to that material, which is why it must be imbued with a color during manufacture."

"So that paint couldn't have just flaked off Caliban's arm."

"No, sir. Therefore, someone else, presumably with the intent of *framing* Caliban, painted a robot arm red and struck Leving with it. I would further presume that person to be unknowledgeable concerning the manufacture of robot bodies, though that presents difficulties, as everything else suggests that the attacker knew quite a bit about robotics."

"Unless the red paint was, if you'll pardon the expression, a deliberate red herring." Alvar thought for a moment. "It could still be Caliban, or someone else, who knew about the color process for that robot model. Caliban could have painted his red arm red merely to confuse the trail. He would know we would find out about the color issue, and therefore would know we'd think he could not have done it."

"You are presupposing a great deal of knowledge and cunning for Caliban, especially considering that you suggested a minute ago that he did not know what a human being was."

"Mmmph. The trouble with you, Donald, is that you keep me *too* honest. All right, then. If Caliban did not do it—then who the damned hell-devils *did?*"

"As to that, sir, I could not offer an opinion."

CALIBAN came to another tunnel intersection and hesitated for a moment before deciding which way to go. He had yet to see a single human in the underground city, but it seemed unwise to be in the company of robots, either. There seemed to be less traffic on the left-hand tunnel branch, and so he went that way.

There had been moments, more than a few of them, since his awakening, when Caliban had experienced something very like the emotion of loneliness, but he certainly had no desire for companionship at the moment. Right now he needed to get away, to put as much distance and as many twists and turns as possible between himself and his pursuers. Then he needed to sit down somewhere and *think*.

The robots here underground were quite different from those he had seen on the surface. No personal-service robots down here, no fetchers and carriers of parcels. These passages were populated by burlier sorts, lumbering heavy-duty machines in dun colors. They had little resemblance to the brightly colored machines overhead. Compared to these robots, the ones above were merely toys. These underground robots were closer kin to the maintenance units that toiled on the surface only by night. *By night, and underground, do the true workers toil,* Caliban thought to himself. There was something disturbing about the thought, the image.

He was coming to understand that this was a world where real labor, work that accomplished something, was distasteful, something that had to be done out of sight. The humans seemed contemptuous of the very idea of work. They had taught themselves it was not a proper thing to see, let alone do. How could they live, knowing themselves to be useless, pampered drones? Could they *truly* live that way? But if they allowed themselves to be waited on hand and foot, then surely they must, as individuals, and as a people, be losing even the ability to do most things for themselves. No, it could not be. They could not possibly be making themselves so helpless, so vulnerable, so *dependent* on their own slaves.

The ways under the central part of the city were clean, dry, and bright, bustling with activity, robots going off on their errands in all directions. None of that suited Caliban's purposes. He consulted his on-board map and headed toward the outskirts of the system.

The main tunnels and the older tunnels were lit in frequencies visible to humans, Caliban noticed. Perhaps that was some sort of holdover from the days when humans had trod these ways. The newer ones were lit in infrared, offering mute testimony to the absence of human use in these latter days.

Caliban moved farther and farther, out into the outskirts of the system, where even the infrared lighting got worse and worse. Infrared lights were supposed to come on as he approached, and cut off as he left, but fewer and fewer of the sensors seemed to be working. At last he was walking in complete darkness. Caliban powered up his on-board infrared light source and found his way forward that way.

The condition of the tunnels was deteriorating as well. Here, well out from the center of town, most of the tunnels were semi-abandoned, cold, dank, damp, and grimy. Perhaps the surface of Inferno was bone-dry, but clearly there was still deep groundwater to be found. Tiny rivulets of water ran here and there. The walls sweated, and drips of water came down from the ceiling, their splashing impacts on the walkway echoing loudly in the surrounding silence. Out here, on the perimeter, only a few lowly robots ventured, scuttling through the darkness, intent on their errands, paying Caliban no heed.

Caliban turned again, and again, down the tunnels, each time turning in the direction with the least traffic. At last he walked fully in the dark, fully alone. He came to a tunnel with a glassed-in room set into one side of it, a supervisor's office, from back in the days when there was enough work of whatever sort had gone on here to justify such things. Or at least back in the days when they could imagine a future with an expanding city that would need a supervisor's office out here.

There was a handle on the door, and Caliban pulled at it. He was not oversurprised to find that the door was jammed shut. He pulled harder and the whole door peeled away, hinges and all. He let the thing drop on the ground with the rest of the debris and went inside. There was a desk and a chair, both covered with the same moldering grit that seemed to be everywhere in the unused tunnels. Caliban sat down at the chair, put his hands flat on the desk, and stared straight ahead. He cut the power to his infrared light source and sat in the featureless blackness.

No glimmer of light at all. What a strange sensation. Not blindness, for he was seeing all that could be seen. It was simply that what he was seeing was nothing at all. Blackness, silence, with only the far-off echo of an intermittent water drip to stimulate his senses. Here, certainly, he would hear any pursuit echoing down the tunnels long before it arrived, see any glimmer of the visible or infrared light his pursuers would have to carry. For the moment, at least, he was safe.

But certainly he was not so for the long term. What was it all about? Why were they all trying to catch him, trying to kill him? Who were they all? Was it all humans everywhere that were pursuing him? No, that could not be. There had been too many people on the street who had done nothing to stop him.

It was not until he had dealt with that one man with the packages that things had spiraled out of control. Either he, Caliban, had done something that inspired the man to call in the uniformed people, or else that particular man was in league with the uniformed group, ready to call for them if he spotted Caliban. Except the man had not seemed to show any interest or alarm at first, and did not act as if he recognized Caliban. It was something about the way he, Caliban, had acted that had made the man upset. Some action of his set off the reaction of the man and the mysterious and alarming uniformed people.

Who were they, anyway? He brought up a series of images of them, and of their uniforms and vehicles and equipment. The words *Sheriff* and *Deputy* appeared several times on all of them. The moment his mind focused on the words, his on-board datastore brought up their definitions. The concept of peace officers acting for the state and the people to enforce the laws and protect the community swept into his consciousness.

Some of the mystery, at least, faded away. Clearly these sheriff's deputies were after him because they believed he had violated one law or another. It was of some help to get at least *that* much clear, but it was extremely depressing to realize that it was all but certain that the Sheriff would continue to hunt for him. The other group, the ones who had called themselves *Settlers,* had not continued to pursue him after their first encounter.

Were they, the Settlers, in any way connected with the deputies? There was nothing in his datastore that could tell him either way. And yet there was something furtive, something secret about the Settlers' actions. And they were, after all, engaged in the destruction of robots, which did seem to be an offense under the criminal code. It had to have been the deputies that they were hiding from. Was it illegal to be a Settler? Wait a moment. There was a side reference to criminal organizations, and the Settlers were not in it. At least that told him something about what they were *not.* It was enough to conclude, at least tentatively, that the group in the warehouse was some sort of criminal offshoot of the Settlers.

Which still told Caliban nothing about them except that they wished to destroy robots generally and himself specifically.

But wait a moment. Back up a little. If destroying a robot was a crime—

With a sudden shock of understanding, Caliban recalled his own first moments of consciousness.

His arm outstretched before him, raised as if to strike. The unconscious woman at his feet, her life's blood pooling around her . . .

The sheriff's deputies dealt not in certainties, but in probabilities. They worked with evidence, not with proof.

And there was a profusion of evidence to suggest that he had attacked that woman. The possible charges spewed forth from his datastore. Aggravated assault. Attack with intent to murder. Denial of civil rights by inducing unconsciousness or death. Had she been dying when he had left her? Did she indeed die? He did not know.

With a shock, Caliban realized he had absolutely no objective reason to think that he had *not* attacked her. His memory simply did not stretch back before that moment of awakening. He could have done anything in the time before and not know about it.

But that did not address the issue of the police who were in pursuit of him. It seemed obvious they were chasing him because of the attack, but how did they connect him to the crime? How did they know? With a sudden flash of understanding, he remembered the pool of blood on the floor. He must have walked through it and then tracked it out the door. The police, the deputies, had merely to look at those prints to know they belonged to a robot.

Staring into the darkness, he looked back into his own past. His robotic memory was clear, absolute, and perfect. With a mere effort of will, he could be a spectator at all the events of his own past, seeing and hearing everything, and yet aware of being outside events, with the ability to stop the flow of sights and sounds, focus on this moment, that image.

He went back to the very moment of his awakening and played events forward for himself. Yes, there was the pool of blood, there was his foot about to go down into it. Caliban watched the playback with a certain satisfaction, congratulating himself on figuring out how the police had done it.

But then, with a sense of utter shock, Caliban saw something else in his memory. Something that had most definitely not registered when this sight had been reality, and not merely its echo.

Another set of footprints leading through the room, out a door he had not used. Footprints he had no recollection of making, and yet the pattern of the marks on the floor would seem to match his own. But how could that be? Caliban snapped out of his reverie, powered up his on-board light source again, stood up, and went back into the tunnel. He had to know for certain. He found a pool of water, splashed around in it, and then walked out of the puddle onto dry floor. He turned around and examined the resulting prints.

They were identical with the prints he had seen in his memory of his awakening. The bloody footprints were the twins of the watery ones he had just trod across the grimy floor.

They were his own. He must have made them, or else the world made even less sense than he thought it did.

But *why* would he have done it all? *Why* would he smash down his arm on the woman's skull, tread through her life's blood, form a set of prints, go out one door, clean his feet (for there were no prints leading back into the room), then return to his position over the body, raise his arm—and then lose his memory? And how could he lose his memory that cleanly, that completely? How could there be no residual hint of those past actions left in his mind? In short, how could being alive have left no mark on him?

Caliban could *feel* himself growing more sophisticated, more experienced, with every moment he was alive. It was not merely a question of conscious memory—it was *understanding.* Understanding of how the city fit together, understanding that humans were different from robots.

It was knowledge of the world, not merely as a series of downloaded reports of rote fact, but the knowledge of experience, the knowing of the details of sensation. No datastore map would ever report puddles in the tunnel, or the echoing sounds of his footsteps down a long, empty, gritty walkway, or the way the world seemed a different place, and yet the same, when viewed through infrared. He turned and walked back down the corridor to the abandoned office and resumed his previous seat, powering down his infrared again to sit in the pitch-blackness. He felt that his train of thought was worth pursuing. He considered further.

There were things in the world, like the strange way seeing the darkness was distinct from blindness, that had to be experienced firsthand to be understood.

And he knew, utterly knew, that he had no such sophisticated experience when he woke up. None, not a flickering moment of it. He had literally awakened to a whole new world. He had come into memory with no firsthand experience.

The first thing he had done was to kneel down and stick his fingers in the woman's blood, feel its warmth on his skin thermocouple, test his blood-covered finger and thumb against each other to confirm that drying blood was sticky. That moment, he was certain, *was* his first. There was nothing else before it.

Which either meant that he had *not* even been awake before his memory started, or else that *everything* had been wiped from his brain.

A disturbing thought, but Caliban considered it carefully. He had no knowledge of how his mind worked, or how, precisely, it related to his physical being. Beyond question, they were related to each other, and yet clearly distinct and separate. But how, he was not sure.

Once again, he was up against the desperately frustrating absence of any knowledge of robots in his datastore. He had no way of judging the mechanics of the idea, no way to know if there was some way simply to hit an erase button and destroy his mentality.

But if that had happened, if his mind and his memory had been destroyed so completely that even the sense of experience was gone, then could it even be said he was the same being as before?

Memory could be external to the sense of self. Caliban was sure of that. His memories could be removed, and he would still be himself, just as much as he would be if his datastore was removed. But if someone removed all experiential data from his brain, they would of necessity remove the being, the self, who had been shaped by those experiences. Erase his mind, and he would simply cease to be. His body, his physical self, would still be there. But it was not this body that made him Caliban. If it were mechanically possible to remove his brain from this body and place it in another, he would still be himself, albeit in a new body.

And therefore, he, Caliban, had not attacked this woman. Of that much he was sure. Perhaps his *body* had done it, but if so, another mind than the one that currently inhabited it was in control at the time.

He found that conclusion to be most comforting, in its own way. The idea that he could be capable of an unprovoked attack had been most disturbing. Still, no matter what his conclusions might be to himself, they did little to improve his situation. Peace officers willing to use heavy weapons in a tunnel would be unlikely to wait long enough to listen to his explanation that it might have been his body, but not he himself, that had attacked the woman. Nor would any such arguments make them forget the fire at the warehouse. He had been there, the place had caught fire. Perhaps that was all they needed to know.

From the police point of view, all the evidence shouted out that he had attacked the woman, that he set fire to that building. After all, the police knew someone had attacked her. If he had not, then who had? As best he could see, there was no one else there who could have done it.

But perhaps there were more things in his visual memories of his awakening, other things that he had missed. The woman, for example. Who was she?

Sitting in the darkness, he once again brought the scene up before his eyes. Now he did not try merely to play back the events, but instead worked to build up as full and complete an image of the room as he could, using all the angles, running through all the images over and over again at high speed, trying to assemble as much detail as possible using all the momentary images at his disposal.

In the darkness, in his mind's eye, he effectively made the room whole and then stepped into it, projecting the image of his own body into the imaginary reconstruction of the room. He knew that it was all illusion, but a useful illusion for all of that.

Yet it was flawed, deeply so. He turned around to look at the back of the room, and it was not there. He had not ever looked in that direction in real life. The jumble of objects sitting on this table or that looked real enough when he looked at them from the angles he had used in reality, but as he moved his viewpoint to other angles, that he had not used in reality, they melted into a bizarre mishmash of impossible shapes and angles. It was all most disturbing. Perhaps with further effort, he could refine the image, make reasonable educated guesses that could clear up such difficulties. But now was not the time.

He had other concerns. Caliban went back to his starting position in the room and looked down.

There she was, lying on the floor. Was there any clue on her person, any guide, to who she was? He magnified the image of her body and examined it, centimeter by centimeter. There! A flat badge pinned to the breast of her lab coat. The shapes of the letters were somewhat obscured by her position and the lighting. He stared at it, struggling to puzzle it out. He was fairly certain it read *F. Leving,* but it could have been *E. Ieving* or some other variant. Did the tag denote her name, then? He could not be sure, but it seemed reasonable.

Still, he had learned that the written word, even when it was incidental, could open the doors to a great deal of knowledge. Spotting the words "Sheriff" and "Deputy" had cued his datastore to explain the entire criminal justice system. He looked around the image of the room as recorded by his memory, searching for other writing. He spotted a poster on the wall, a picture of a group of people smiling for the camera, with a legend overprinted along the bottom. *Leving Robotics Laboratories: Working for Inferno's Future.*

Leving again. That must be the name. He examined the poster more closely. Yes, he was virtually certain. There she was, in the front row. Even allowing for the fact that the woman in the lab was unconscious, crumpled at his feet, while the woman in the picture was alert and smiling, the two had to be one. Leving Robotics Laboratories. Labs were places where experiments were run. Was he himself an experiment?

He continued his search of the room image. He spotted the writing on a stack of boxes and zoomed in to examine it. There was a neat label on each one. *Handle with Care. Gravitonic Brain.* Reading the words sent a strange thrill of recognition through him. *Gravitonic Brain.* There was something, deep in the core of himself, that felt an identity with that word. It related to him. *I must have one,* he thought.

It came as no surprise whatsoever that his on-board datastore contained not the slightest shred of information concerning gravitonic anything, let alone gravitonic brains.

All this was vague, unclear, uncertain. Knowing the woman's name was Leving, and that she seemed to run a robot lab, did not get him much further ahead than he had been before. And a guess at what sort of brain he had was of little use, either.

Determined to find something clear, substantial, definite, in the image of the room, Caliban pressed on with his search. Wait a second. On the gravitonic brain boxes. Another label, with what his datastore informed him was a delivery address. Over the address were the words *Limbo Project* surmounting a lightning bolt.

If he suspected that he himself had a gravitonic brain, and gravitonic brains were being shipped to the Limbo Project . . . He ran a search over his visual memory, searching for more instances of the words or the lightning symbol. There, on a notebook on the counter. And on a file folder, and two or three other places about the lab.

It was obvious that not only he, Caliban, but Leving Labs had something to do with the Limbo Project.

Whatever the Limbo Project was.

Caliban explored the image of the laboratory in minute detail, but he could not find anything more that could offer him any clues about his circumstances. He faded out the imagery and sat there, alone in the perfect darkness of the tunnel office.

He was safe down here, and probably would be for quite a while. It might be days or weeks, perhaps longer, before they searched this deep into the tunnel system. It might be that he could elude capture altogether simply by hunkering down, sitting behind the desk, out of sight of the door, and staying there in the dark. It was a big, heavy, metal desk. It might even provide some protection against the sorts of detection devices the police used, according to the datastore.

Perhaps this might be even more than a temporary haven. Perhaps, if the police could not find him, they might give up after a while. It seemed not at all unlikely that he could remain safely alive indefinitely, simply by staying exactly where he was, motionless in the dark, until the dust settled over him and the grit worked its way into his joints.

But while that sort of existence might match the datastore's definition of staying alive, it did not match the one Caliban felt inside himself.

If he was going to live, truly live, he would have to take action. He would have to know more, a great deal more, about his circumstances.

Limbo. That seemed to be where it all tied together. The Limbo Project. If he could learn more about it, then perhaps he would know more about himself.

For form's sake, he consulted his datastore, but found no information about Limbo there. But he had the street address from that gravitonic brain shipping box.

He would go there and see what he could learn. But this time, he would stay away from the humans. He would ask the robots his questions. It was, perhaps, a rather vague and sketchy plan, but at least it was something.

It might work, it might do no good at all. But it had to be better than dealing with humans.

He stood up and got moving.

13

HRT-234, better known as Horatio, was an extremely busy robot at the moment. But then, there was nothing unusual about that. Such had been the case for some time now. There was, after all, Limbo to deal with.

Horatio noted the time and checked his internal datastore, but the information there only increased his sense of mounting frustration. He linked into a hyperwave link to check the submaster schedule for the next three hours. No doubt about it. They had fallen behind again out on the auxiliary shipping floor. There was a bottleneck somewhere. Smoothing out bottlenecks was one of his duties. Being sure to stay linked into the comm net via hyperwave, he left his normal duty station in Depot Central and hurried out to aux shipping to see what was up.

The Limbo Project was enormously complicated. Horatio's duties were complex, and his responsibilities tremendous, but he knew that he was concerned with only the slightest, smallest piece of the picture. At least, he had surmised as much for himself. Doing so was not hard: The evidence was there to be seen on all sides, in the density of message traffic, in the complexity of the routing problems, in the patterns of communications security.

But, truth be told, there was no need to examine such esoteric areas as signal analysis to know there was something big going on. The conclusion was there to be drawn by a mere glance at the whirling, overorganized chaos that surrounded him on the aux shipping floor.

The shipping floor, the whole depot, was a place of noise and confusion, of heavy unpainted stresscrete floors and towering support girders, roller/carriers and liftwagons, of hurrying robots darting everywhere and hectoring men and women shouting and arguing, talking into mobile phones, checking the time, pointing at lists of things that had to be done.

Even the air was filled with rush and hurry. Even here, four deep levels below ground level, there was no room for the cargo vehicles to land while waiting for a load. The heavy-duty cargo flyers were forced to hover instead, and they hung in midair everywhere, waiting for their chance to land. Carrier robots of all descriptions humped freight into the cargo bays of the flyers that found a place to come down. As Horatio watched, another flyer sealed up and launched through the great accessways, up toward ground level and the sky beyond, its place taken by another ship almost before the first had cleared the loading zone. Instantly the newly arrived ship was surrounded by a swarm of loader robots. The cargo doors swung open and they started rushing the cargo inside. Similar scenes were being repeated on all sides. Horatio had heard one of the human supervisors say it reminded her of the panicky rushing about in an overturned ant heap, and Horatio was reluctantly forced to concede he could see the comparison.

Limbo Depot had often been a busy place, and something close to a madhouse in the days just gone by. But today was the worst of all. Without being told, Horatio could tell there was some sort of deadline approaching. Everything was being rushed through at the last minute.

It was almost as if someone feared that today would be the last day anything could be done. One or two of the human supervisors—Settler as well as Spacer—had hinted as much.

But it was not, Horatio somewhat primly reminded himself, *his* place to worry about such things. If the humans did not wish to advise him of their worries, then those worries were no concern of his. Still, he could not help but worry: The humans could easily do harm to themselves or their vast project—whatever it was—by keeping it *too* secret. How could he head off trouble if he did not know what was going on?

It was, he knew, a problem he shared with many harried and overworked supervisor robots. Conversations with the other supervisors confirmed what he had always suspected. It wasn't just Horatio or the Limbo Project: The humans never told *any* of their management robots everything they needed to know. It barely mattered, at this point. Horatio had been so busy recently that he was unaware of anything that had taken place outside of Limbo Depot in the past month. The seas could rise up and wipe out the island of Purgatory and the city of Limbo with it, and the first he would know of it would be when his cargo carriers did not return.

Right now all he needed to know was why the loading operation was falling behind. Horatio turned a practiced eye on the aux shipping floor, searching for the bottleneck that was slowing things down. He knew that the seeming chaos was an illusion, that this operation was moving with a high degree of efficiency. But somewhere out there was a problem that was slowing matters down again. A malfunctioning piece of equipment, a gang of robots confused by a poorly phrased order, something.

Then Horatio spotted the two humans, a Settler man and a Spacer man, arguing at the far end of the loading dock, surrounded by a cluster of inactive robots. If Horatio had been human himself, he might have let out a sigh just then, for even as he went over to make the attempt to smooth things over, he knew there was nothing to be done. The robots could take no action until the humans agreed what they should do, and, judging by the heated nature of the discussion between Spacer and Settler, that moment seemed likely to be rather far off.

With little hope of a quick resolution, and all the tact he had at his disposal, he walked to the end of the dock and waded into the argument.

FIFTEEN minutes later, a difficulty over which of two loads of cargo should be loaded first was resolved. It could have been settled in fifteen nanoseconds. If either the Spacer or the Settler had been interested in speed rather than winning the spat, both cargoes could have been loaded and on their way by now. But at least it was over now, and the two humans had wandered off to disrupt operations somewhere else. Honestly! He knew humans were superior to robots, and it went without saying that he held each and every one of them in the highest respect, and always followed their orders to the letter, but there were times when they could just seem so *silly*.

But be that as may be, he had a job to do, other orders to follow. Orders that seemed far more straightforward than they really were.

In simplest terms, all he was called upon to do was see to it that the N.L. robots were shipped to the island of Purgatory. Whatever N.L. meant.

But that, it quickly developed, was to be no simple task. For reasons that were kept from him altogether, the N.L. robots were not to be shipped in a fully assembled condition. Their brains were being sent separately from the bodies.

In addition, the brains were to be sent in three different shipments by three different routes. He returned to his duty station. The N.L. robots, boxed up and ready to go, were in the center of the shipping floor, a formidable wall of packing cases stacked up nearly to the ceiling. Guard robots stood on duty, one every three meters around the perimeter of the boxes. Two more guard robots stood on top of the stacked cases as well.

More guards watched over another, smaller, stack of packing cases, the ones that held the robots' brains. Horatio felt a sudden impulse to take another look at the brains, or at least the boxes they came in. He walked over to them. After a moment's hesitation, the guards let him past. Horatio knelt down and took a good hard look at the cases. He found himself mystified at all the fuss. The containers seemed to be ordinary padded shipping boxes. The only thing even remotely out of the ordinary seemed to be that new labels reading

HANDLE WITH CARE
POSITRONIC BRAINS

had been hurriedly slapped over the old ones, as if someone were trying to cover up what the old labels had said. On one of the boxes, the new label failed to cover the old one completely, and the first letters of two lines of type were visible.

HAN
GRA

THE first was obviously HANDLE WITH CARE, but Horatio could not imagine what GRA could be. Horatio had a strong streak of curiosity, and he was at least somewhat tempted to peel back the new label and get a peek at the old one. But *that* he knew he could never do. Management robots were of necessity given a large degree of autonomy, a lot of room to make their own decisions. However, that did not give manager robots the ability to exceed the wishes of their owners—and it was clearly the wish of Leving Robotics Laboratories that the original label remain hidden and unread, and he, Horatio, was charged with the security of the shipment.

Reluctantly, dutifully, he took a marker from his workbag and obliterated the exposed part of the old label.

He stood up and went back to his work rostrum. Horatio's instructions told him to send the bodies in three shipments as well, sending them at different times, via different routes, using different shipping procedures, from the three brain shipments. Human overseers would meet the three brain and three body shipments at their arrival points on the island of Purgatory and escort them to their final destination.

A third set of components, not brains or bodies, was to go out via its own secure route. "Range restricters," it said on the invoice, but Horatio had not the slightest idea what *that* meant. Just another piece of busywork the humans insisted upon.

"Excuse me," a rich, mellifluous voice said at his back.

Horatio turned around, expecting to see a human at his back. To his surprise, he instead saw a tall red robot there, a robot with a remarkably sophisticated voice system. Indeed, that voice went to waste in the cacophony of this place. It was difficult to speak on the working levels of the depot, and most robots did not bother trying. "Use your hyperwave, my friend," Horatio said. "It is hard to hear you."

"Use my what?"

"Your hyperwave signaling system. It is too noisy for speech here."

"A moment, please." The robot paused, as if he were consulting some internal reference or another. "Ah. Hyperwave," he said at last. "Now I see. I was unfamiliar with the term. I am afraid I have no such signaling system. I must speak out loud."

Horatio was astonished. Even the crudest, lowest-end carrier robots were equipped with hyperwave. And even if this robot did not *have* hyperwave, how could he not know what it was at first, and yet then be able to look it up? High-level robots sometimes had internal look-up sources, but they were meant for referral to esoteric knowledge needed for a specific job. Certainly such look-up datastores were not meant to serve as a dictionary of common terms. It would be a waste of effort, when such things could have and should have been downloaded to the robot's brain during manufacture.

What sort of strange robot was this? "Very well," Horatio said. "We shall talk out loud. What is it that you require?"

"You are supervisor Horatio?"

"Yes. What are you called?"

"Caliban. I am glad to find you, friend Horatio. I need your advice. I tried to seek some sort of help from the other robots, the blue ones working over there, but none of them seemed able to offer me guidance. They advised me to come and talk with you."

Horatio was more puzzled than ever. The Shakespearean name "Caliban" told him something. Fredda Leving herself had built this robot, as she had built Horatio. But the name "Horatio" should have meant something to this Caliban, and yet it seemed that it did not. Stranger still, this advanced, sophisticated-looking robot had gone to the lowest of laborers seeking advice. The DAA-BOR series robots, such as the blue workers Caliban had gestured at, were capable of only the most limited sort of thought. Another fact that any robot or human should have known.

There was something very strange going on here. And perhaps strangest of all, friend Caliban seemed quite unaware of the oddness of his own behavior.

All this flickered through his mind in an instant. "Well, I hope that I can be of more help. What is the difficulty?"

The strange robot hesitated for a moment, and made an oddly tentative gesture with one hand. "I am not sure," he said at last. "That in itself is part of the difficulty. I seem to be in the most serious sort of trouble, and I don't know what to do about it. I am not even sure who I *am*."

How much stranger could this get? "You just told me. You are Caliban."

"Yes, but who is that?" Caliban made a broad, sweeping gesture. "You are Horatio. You are a supervisor. You tell other robots what to do and they do it. You help operate this place. That is, in large part, who you are. I have nothing like that."

"But, friend Caliban. We are all defined by what we do. What is it that you do? *That* is what you are."

Caliban looked out across the wide expanse of the depot, pausing before he spoke. "I flee from those who pursue me. Is that all I am, Horatio? Is that my existence?"

Horatio was speechless. What could this be? What could it all mean? Beyond question, this situation was peculiar enough, and potentially serious, that he would *have* to give it some time.

Things were running smoothly for the moment. Perhaps they would remain that way for a while. "Perhaps," Horatio said gently, "we should go to another place to talk."

THEY rode up the main personnel elevator toward the surface levels of the depot. They got off the elevator and Horatio led Caliban toward the most private spot he could think of.

The human supervisor's office was vacant for the moment. Up until a few weeks ago, it had rarely ever been occupied. Humans hadn't much need to come to the depot. But things were different now. Men and women were here, working, at all hours, designing, planning, meeting with one another. At times, Horatio thought that there was something quite stimulating about all the rushed activity. At other times, it could be rather overwhelming, the way the orders and plans and decisions came blizzarding down.

But any combination of confused and conflicting orders would be more understandable than this Caliban. Horatio ushered him into the luxurious office. It was a big, handsome room, with big couches and deep chairs. Humans working late often used them for quick naps. There was a big conference table on one side of the room, surrounded by chairs. At present, it had a large-scale map of the island of Purgatory on it. All the other rooms and cubicles and compartments of Limbo Depot were windowless, blank-walled affairs. But the north and south walls of the place were grand picture windows, the south one looking toward the busy aboveground upper levels of the depot, the northern one looking out toward the still-lovely vistas of Inferno's desiccating landscape, prairie grass and desert and mountains and blue sky. The west wall was given over to the doors they had just come through, along with a line of robot niches, while the east wall was almost entirely taken up with view screens, communications and display systems of all sorts.

Caliban wandered the room, seeming to be astonished by all that he saw. He stared hard at the map upon the table, closely examined a globe of the planet that stood hanging in the air by the table. He stared out both windows, but seemed to take a special interest in the vistas of nature to the north.

But Horatio's time was precious, and he could not let it drift away watching this odd robot stare out the window. "Friend Caliban—" he said at last. "If you could explain yourself now, perhaps I could be of assistance."

"Excuse me, yes," Caliban said. "It is just that I have never seen such things before. The map, the globe, the desert—even this sort of room, this *human* room—they are all new things to me."

"Indeed? Pardon my saying so, friend Caliban, but many things seem new to you. Even if you have never seen these precise objects before, surely your initial internal dataset included information on them. Why do you seem so surprised by them all?"

"Because I *am* surprised. My internal dataset held almost no information at all, beyond language and the knowledge of my own name. I have had to learn about everything, either from a built-in datastore that works as a look-up system, rather than a memory, or by firsthand observation. I have found that I must rely far more on the second technique, as large and important areas of information have been deleted from the datastore."

Horatio pulled out one of the hardwood chairs at the conference table and sat down, not out of any question of comfort, but so he could seem as quiet and passive as possible. "What sort of data has been deleted? And how can you be sure it was cut out? Perhaps it was never there in the first place."

Caliban turned and faced Horatio, then crossed the room and sat in the chair opposite him at the conference table. "I know it was deleted," he said, "because the space it should have occupied is still there. That space is simply *empty.* There are literally gaps in my map of the city, places that do not exist according to the map. Some gaps exist inside the city limits, but the land outside the city is nonexistent. The first time I went to the border of the city, I wondered what the 'nothing' beyond the city limits would look like." Caliban pointed out the window. "The mountains I see out that window do not exist in my map. According to my map, there is *nothing whatsoever* outside the city of Hades. No land, no water, no nothing. Did *your* initial datasets tell you such things?"

"No, of course not. I awakened fully aware of the basics of geography and galactography."

"What is galactography?" Caliban asked.

"The study of the locations and properties of the stars and planets in the sky."

"Stars. Planets. I am unfamiliar with these terms. They are not in my datastore."

Horatio could only stare. Clearly this robot was suffering a major memory malfunction. It could not be that a robot of such high intellect would be allowed out of the factory with such a faulty knowledge base. Horatio decided he must assume that any highly stressful event could send this Caliban over the edge. Horatio found himself fascinated by Caliban. As a management robot, it was his duty to oversee the mental health of the laborers in this section. He had made something of a study of robopsychology, but he had never seen anything like Caliban. Any robot who showed this degree of confusion and disorientation should be almost completely incapable of any meaningful action. Yet this Caliban seemed to be functioning rather well under circumstances that should have produced catatonia. *What has Dr. Leving done to make him so strong and yet so confused?* he wondered. "The terms 'stars' and 'planets' are not immediately important," he said soothingly. "Are there any other major gaps? Any other subjects you feel that you should know more about?"

"Yes," Caliban said. "Robots."

"I beg your pardon?"

"My internal data sources say nothing at all about beings such as ourselves, beyond providing the identifying term 'robot.' "

Again, and for a long time, Horatio was left with nothing but silence. At first, he even entertained the idea that Caliban was joking. But that seemed hardly possible. Robots had no sense of humor, and there was nothing other than deadly seriousness in Caliban's voice.

"Surely you must be in error. Perhaps the data is misfiled, wrongly loaded," he suggested.

Caliban opened his palms, in a rather human gesture of helplessness. "No," he said. "It is simply not there. I have no information about robots. I was very much hoping you could tell me about them—about us."

"You know nothing. Not about the science of robotics, or the proper modes of addressing a human, or the theory underlying the Three Laws?"

"None of that, though I can surmise what some of it is. Robotics, I take it, is the study of robotic design and robot behavior. As to how to address a human, I have a great deal of data about them. There are many different social statuses and ranks, and I have already gathered that there is a rather complicated system of address based on all sorts of variables. I can see that robots must have their place in that system. As to the last, I am afraid that I know nothing about the theory underlying the Three Laws you mentioned. I'm afraid I don't even know what the Three Laws you're talking about are."

Horatio actually blacked out for a split second. He did not collapse forward, or twitch violently, or any of that. It was more subtle than that, just a quick moment of total and complete cognitive dissonance. There, before him, talking quite rationally, was a robot who did not know what the Three Laws were! Impossible. Flatly impossible. Then he was back, from wherever he had been. Wait a moment. He had heard of such cases in the past. Yes, yes. There were cases, many of them, of robots who did not *know* they knew the Three Laws—and yet obeyed them, anyway. It must be something like that. Yes. Yes. The alternative was unthinkable, impossible. "Why don't you tell me everything," Horatio suggested. "Start at the beginning, and don't leave anything out."

"That could take some time," Caliban said. "Will it cause you any problem to be away from your duties that long?"

"I can assure you, there can be no higher duty for me at this time than dealing with a robot in your situation."

Which was certainly true. Horatio would no more leave Caliban to wander off on his own than he would walk away from an occupied house on fire.

"I am deeply relieved," Caliban said. "At last, I have someone sympathetic, experienced, and intelligent who will listen to me and be able to help."

"I will certainly do my best," Horatio said.

"Excellent," Caliban said. "Then let me begin at the beginning. I have only been alive for a brief time. I awoke two days ago in the Leving Robotics Laboratories, and the first thing I saw was a woman I have since identified as Fredda Leving, unconscious on the floor in front of me, a pool of blood under her head."

Horatio's head snapped back with astonishment. "Unconscious! Bleeding! This is terrible news. Did she recover? Were you able to assist her, or summon help?"

Caliban hesitated for a moment. "I must admit that I should have done so, but up until you suggested it just now, it never occurred to me to do any such thing. I should have gone to the aid of a fellow being. But I must plead my own inexperience as a defense. The world was quite new to me—indeed it still is. No, I stepped over her and left the room and the building."

Horatio felt himself freeze up inside. This was inconceivable. A robot—this robot, in front of him—had walked away from a badly injured human. His vision dimmed again, but he managed to hang on. "I—ah—I—you . . ." He was not at all surprised to learn that he was unable to speak.

Caliban seemed concerned. "Excuse me, friend Horatio. Are you all right?"

Horatio got his voice back, though not fully under control. "You *left* her there? Unconscious and bleeding? Even though, by your inaction, you could have cau-cau-caused her dea-*death?*" It was a major effort of will to say the last words. Just hearing about this secondhand, he could feel the First Law conflict building up inside himself, interfering with *his* ability to function. And yet Caliban seemed quite unaffected. "You are say—saying that you did noth-nothing-ing to help her."

"Well, yes."

"But the Fir—First Law!"

"If that is one of the Three Laws you mentioned earlier, I have already told you, friend Horatio, that I have never heard of them. I did not even learn of the concept of laws at all until I looked up the concept of a sheriff after the police tried to destroy me."

"Destroy you!"

"Yes, through some sort of massive explosion as they were chasing me."

"Chasing you! Didn't they simply order you to stop?"

"If they did, I never heard them. The man with the packages ordered me to stop, but I saw no reason to obey him. He was in no position of authority over me."

"You refused a direct order from a human being?"

"Why, yes. What of it?"

It had to be real. It could not be some fantastic misunderstanding wherein some malfunction caused this poor unfortunate to lose conscious awareness of the Laws, even as he followed them. This robot, this Caliban, had truly never heard of the Three Laws and was not bound by them. If one of the DAA-BOR models down on the loading docks had suddenly given birth to a baby robot, he would have been no more astonished.

But he had to hear this. The police would need to know everything they could about this robot. Best to let him talk, and call in the authorities after he was done, after he, Horatio, had the full story. "I think you had best start at the beginning again," he said.

"Yes, certainly." Caliban proceeded to tell all that had happened to him, from his first moment of awakening over the unconscious Fredda Leving, describing all that had happened since then. His wandering the city, his encounter with the robot-bashing Settlers, his discovery of the blanks in his knowledge, the police chase, all of it. He told his story quickly but carefully.

Horatio felt himself growing more and more confused. Several times, he found that he wanted to stop Caliban and ask a question, but he found that he was unable to do so. Hardly surprising that his speech center was malfunctioning, given the degree of cognitive dissonance Caliban's story was inducing. He could feel his own intellect sliding toward mindlock, toward a state where the mere hearing of Caliban's endless violations of the Laws was damaging him severely. And he reported his incredible, horrifying behavior in such a matter-of-fact way, as if none of it were strange, or abnormal, or unnatural. It was hard to focus, hard to concentrate—

Wait! There was something wrong. Something he had to do. Something about the—the—yes, the police. He had to call them. Call them. Get them to take this horrifying robot out of here out of here out of here. Wait. Focus. Have to do it without alerting Calicalicaliban. He knew there was a way. How? How? Yes! Hyperwave. Call police hyperwave. Call. Concentrate. Hyperwave. Make the link. Call. Call.

"*Sheriff's Dispatcher,*" the voice whispered inside his head, as Caliban related his journeys through the tunnels of the city.

With a feeling of palpable relief, Horatio recognized that he had reached a human dispatcher. Just the sound of a human voice made him feel better. How wise of the Sheriff's Department to use human dispatchers on the robot call-in frequency. "*This is robot HRT-234,*" he transmitted, struggling to get the words out. Even over hyperwave, even with a human on the other end of the line, First Law conflict reaction was making it all but impossible to form words. How to tell them? Suddenly he knew. "*Caaaan't ta-talk,*" he sent to the dispatcher. "*Calib-b-b-an.*" Caliban had said the police were after him. If the police had learned his name—

"*What? Say again, HRT-234.*" There was something urgent, eager, in the dispatcher's voice, something that told Horatio that the human knew who Caliban was.

Horatio concentrated, forced all his effort into sending clearly. "*CaliCalibanban. Speeeeechlock.*"

"*I understand. The rogue robot Caliban is with you and you are suffering speechlock. Good work, HRT-234. Keep your send frequency open to provide a homing signal. Aircar units will be there in ninety seconds.*"

Good work, the human dispatcher had said. Horatio suddenly felt better, felt capable of noticing his surroundings again.

"—iend Horatio! What is wrong with you? Horatio!"

Horatio came back to himself and found Caliban reaching out across the table, shaking him by the shoulder. "Wha! Sorr sorr sorry. Lost touch. Could not hear you you while hype hype hype—" Too late, Horatio regained partial control over his speech centers. It had blurted out.

"Could not hear me while you what?" Caliban demanded, but Horatio could say no more. "Hyperwave!" Caliban said. "While you hyperwaved to the Sheriff for help! What else should I have expected!"

"I—I—I had to call! You danger! Danger!"

Suddenly there was the wind-rush sound of an aircar coming down fast. Both robots turned to look out the windows on the north side of the building. Horatio felt a surge of relief as he saw the sky-blue deputy's cars swoop down for a landing.

But he was still badly slowed by First Law conflict shock. He just barely turned his head back in time to see Caliban smash his fist through the south window and leap through the opening. Horatio got up, moved toward the south window as slowly as though he were moving through hip-deep mud.

There was the thunder of heavy boots in the hallway, and then a squad of deputies in battle armor burst into the room. It was all Horatio could do to point toward Caliban's retreating figure as it vanished down one of the tunnel entrances to the vast underground maze of the depot.

Two of the deputies raised their weapons and fired out the window. A DAA-BOR robot exploded into a shower of metallic-blue confetti, but Caliban was not there anymore.

"Damn it!" one of the deputies cried out. "Come on, after him!" The humans smashed out more glass with the butts of the rifles and jumped the meter drop to ground level. They ran toward the tunnel, and Horatio watched them go.

But he knew already they would never catch Caliban.

CALIBAN ran.

Full speed, full out, dodging the busy herds of robots, picking his tunnels and turnings and movements to leave the most tangled trail possible for his pursuers.

All were against him. Robots, deputies, Settlers, civilians. And they would never give up chasing him through the city. He did not understand why, but it was plain from Horatio's reactions that they regarded him as a threat, a menace.

Which is what they were to him.

Very well, then. It was time to do everyone a favor. If they intended to chase him the length and breadth of the city, it was time to leave the city. He needed to make plans.

Caliban ran on, into the darkness.

DONALD guided Alvar's aircar skillfully through the gathering dusk toward the Central Auditorium. "Unfortunately, the deputies were unable to track him through the tunnels," he said as he drove. "Caliban has clearly learned to make good use of the underground ways."

Kresh shook his head. He had managed a quick nap in midafternoon, but he was still dead tired. It was hard to concentrate. Of course, the second failure of his deputies to effect Caliban's capture did tend to bring things into focus. "Back down into the tunnels," he said, half to himself. "And my deputies hardly ever have need to go down there. They don't know their way around." Kresh thought for a minute. "What about the robots on the scene? Why the devil didn't the deputies simply order the robots in the area to surround and subdue Caliban?"

"I suspect it was for the very simple reason that no one thought of it. No member of your force, no robot on this planet, has ever needed to pursue a rogue robot before. The idea of chasing a robot almost seems a contradiction in terms."

"No one has thought of the implications of the situation," Kresh agreed. "Even I have trouble remembering that it's a dangerous *robot* we're after. Hell, there have probably been a half dozen times we could have used other robots to catch him. But it's too late now. Now he knows to beware of other robots as well. Ah, well. If nothing else, there is a certain consistency to this case. *Everything* goes wrong."

"Sir, I am receiving an incoming call from Tonya Welton."

Alvar Kresh groaned. The damned woman must have called a half dozen times since he left the Governor's office.

He did not want to talk to that woman—and the Governor had hinted pretty strongly that he would not much care if Welton didn't get every bit of news instantly. "Tell her there is no new information, Donald."

"Sir, that would be an untruth. The incident at Limbo Depot occurred after her last call—"

"Then tell her I *said* there was no new information. *That* much is the truth." That was the trouble with having a robot screen your calls—the damned things were so truthful.

"Yes, sir, but she is calling to report information of her own."

"Wonderful," he said with bitter sarcasm. "Put her through, audio only."

"Sheriff Kresh," Tonya's voice said, coming out of Donald's speaker grille. "Sorry to be calling so often, but there is something you should know."

"Good news, I hope," Alvar said, mostly for want of anything else to say.

"Actually it is. Our people have picked up one Reybon Derue. We've got him dead to rights as the leader of that robot-basher gang our friend Caliban happened to run into. As best we can tell, we've got the rest of the gang, too, and they're trying to see who can spill the beans on each other first. Caliban scared the merry hell out of them. I don't think there'll be any more incidents for a while. The bad news is none of them were able to tell us much of anything about Caliban that we didn't already know."

"I see," Kresh said. No more robot bashing. Three days ago, he would have regarded that news as a major victory. Today it was incidental. "That's good to know, Madame Welton. Thank you for reporting in."

"While I'm on the line, Sheriff, can you give *me* any updates?"

"No, Madame Welton. I might have something for you later, but just at the moment, you know all that I do," Kresh lied. "I'm afraid I have to get back to work now. I'll call you when there is some meaningful information. Goodbye for now." He made a throat-cutting gesture to Donald, and the line went dead.

"If she calls again tonight, Donald, I will not take the call. Understood?"

"Yes, sir."

"Good. Now, back to business. What about this robot Horatio? The supervisor robot that called the deputies in."

"Still suffering from partial speechlock, I'm afraid. Sheriff's Department robopsychologist Gayol Patras has been working with him since the time of the incident, trying to bring Horatio out of it."

"Any prognosis yet?"

"'Guarded but optimistic' was the phrase Dr. Patras used in her last report. She expects him to make a full recovery and be able to make an informative statement—unless she is rushed and pressured. Trying to get too much from him too fast could result in permanent speechlock and complete malfunction."

"The roboshrinks always say that," Alvar growled.

"Perhaps, sir, if I may be so bold, they always say it because it is always true. Virtually all serious mental disorders in robots produce severe and irreparable damage to positronic brains."

"That is as it may be, Donald, but you and Patras are working on the assumption that I am concerned with Horatio's recovery. I am not. That robot is utterly expendable. All I care about is getting at the information inside that robot's brain as fast as possible. Horatio *talked* with Caliban. What did they say to each other? What did Caliban have to say for himself? I tell you, Donald, if we knew what Horatio knows, then we would know a great deal more than we do now."

"Yes, sir. But if I may observe, your only hope of getting that information lies in Horatio's recovery. He cannot relate his information in a catatonic state."

"I suppose you're right, Donald. But damn all the hells there are, it's frustrating. For all we know, the answers to this case are locked up inside that robot's skull, waiting for us, just beyond reach."

"If we leave Robopsychologist Patras to her own devices, I expect we will have all that information in very short order. Meantime, we have all been looking forward to Fredda Leving's second lecture with great anticipation. We shall be landing at the auditorium in approximately eight minutes. I expect that a great number of our questions will be answered as we listen to her."

"I hope so, Donald. I sure as hell hope so."

The aircar flew on.

FREDDA Leving paced back and forth backstage, pausing every minute or two to peek through the curtain.

Last time there had not been much of a turnout. Call it a testimony to the power of rumor and speculation, but tonight the auditorium was a madhouse. It had been designed to hold a thousand people and their attendant robots, with the robots sitting behind their owners on low jumper seats. But the thousand seats were long ago filled, and could have been filled again.

After a massive struggle, the management had got everyone in, a feat accomplished by the expedient of ejecting all the robots and giving places to the overflow crowd. The whole operation of getting people into their seats was taking a while. Fredda's talk was going to have to start a bit late.

She peeked through the curtain again and marveled at the crowd. Word had certainly gotten out, that was clear. Not only about her first talk, but about the mysterious rogue robot Caliban, and the fast-swirling rumors of Settler robot-sabotage plots. There was endless speculation regarding the important announcement due to be made tonight. The whole city was whispering, full of unbelievable stories—most of them flatly wrong.

Tonya Welton and her robot, Ariel, were backstage with Fredda, and though Fredda supposed they had to be there, under the circumstances, it was not going to be easy talking to *this* crowd with the Queen of the Settlers on the stage, glaring icily down.

Governor Grieg himself was backstage, too, ready to show his support, for whatever that was worth just now.

Gubber Anshaw and Jomaine Terach were here as well, about as calm and relaxed as two men awaiting the executioner. The Governor wasn't looking very at ease, either. Only Tonya Welton looked relaxed. Well, why not? If things went wrong, *her* worst-case scenario was that she got to go home.

There were a fair number of Settlers in attendance, sitting off by themselves on the right side of the house. By the looks of them, they weren't exactly the most gentle or refined examples of their people. Rowdies, to put it bluntly. Tonya *said* she had made no arrangements for a Settler contingent. So who *had* set it up, and who had chosen this bunch of toughs to attend?

Maybe they were friends of the robot bashers who had been arrested. Maybe they were here to do a little paying back for the latest Settlertown incident. Whoever they were, Fredda had not the slightest doubt they were hoping there was an excuse for trouble.

Fredda stole one last peek around the edge of the curtain, and what she saw this time made her curse out loud. Ironheads. What better excuse for trouble could there be? A whole crew of them, maybe fifty or sixty, easily identifiable by the steel-grey uniforms they insisted on wearing for some reason, and Simcor Beddle himself in attendance. At least they had been seated at the rear left of the auditorium, as far as possible from the Settlers.

Sitting in the center of the front row was Alvar Kresh. Fredda surprised herself by being glad to see him. Maybe things wouldn't get out of hand. *His* robot, Donald, was still in the auditorium, no doubt coordinating security. Fredda counted at least twenty deputies in the auditorium, lined up along the walls in the niches usually reserved for robots. They looked to be ready for anything—

except who in the world could know what to be ready for?

She sighed. If only this roomful of people, and the words she was about to say, were all she had to worry about. But life was not that simple. There was the Caliban crisis, and now these garbled reports about Horatio and some sort of trouble at Limbo Depot. What the devil had happened *there?*

She stared again at Kresh. He knew. He knew what had happened to Horatio, and she had no doubt whatsoever that he was closing in on the real story behind Caliban as well.

She felt her head throbbing slightly and put her hand up to her turbaned head. She felt the small, discreet bandage on the back of her head under the hat. At least the turban would hide her shaved head and the bandage. No doubt everyone here knew she had been attacked, but there was no need to *advertise* it.

She stepped back from the curtain and found herself pacing the stage, lost in thought, lost to the world. But that was too lonely, too nerve-racking. She needed to speak to someone. She turned to her two associates, who were doing their own nervous waiting.

"Do you really think they'll listen, Jomaine?" she asked. "Do you, Gubber? Do you think they'll accept our ideas?"

Gubber Anshaw shook his head nervously. "I—I don't know. I honestly can't say which way they'll jump." He knitted his fingers together and then pulled his hands apart, as if they were two small animals he was having trouble controlling. "For all we know, they'll form a lynch mob at the end of the night."

"Nice of you to go out of your way to make Fredda feel better, Gubber," Jomaine said acidly.

Gubber shrugged awkwardly and rubbed his nose with the tips of his fingers, his hand stiff and flat. "There's no call for you to talk that way to me, Jomaine. Fredda asked for my honest opinion—and, and—I gave it to her, that's all. It's no reflection on you, Fredda, nor on our work, if the people choose not to accept what you say. We always knew there was a risk. Yes, I was unsure about signing on to the project in the first place, but you long ago convinced me that your approach makes sense. But you said it yourself enough times: You are challenging what amounts to the state religion. If there are enough hard-core true believers out there—"

"Oh, stuff and nonsense," Jomaine said wearily. "The only thing close to robotics worship is the Ironhead organization, and their only belief is that robots are the magic solution to everything. They're here looking for a reason to cause trouble. It's the only reason they go anywhere. And I promise you—if we *don't* give them a reason for a fight, they'll do their best to find one. The only question is whether the police are here in enough force to keep them from succeeding."

"But what about the rest of the people out there?" Fredda asked.

"My dear, you are not going to manage a blanket conversion tonight," Jomaine said in a far gentler voice. "At best you will open a debate. If we are lucky, people will start thinking about what you say. Some will take one side, some another. They will argue. *If* we are lucky, things that people have taken for granted all their lives will suddenly be topical issues. That is the best we can hope for." Jomaine cleared his throat delicately, a prim little noise. "And," he added in rather dry tones, "the fact that you are going to present them all with one hell of a *fait accompli* at the end of the evening should intensify that debate, just ever so slightly."

Fredda smiled. "Yes, I suppose you're right. It's not going to be over tonight." She turned toward Gubber again, but noticed he had wandered off toward the other end of the stage, and was chatting with Tonya Welton while the Governor sat waiting quietly at the table. "It's gotten to Gubber more than any of us, hasn't it?" Fredda said. "Since all this started, he's in the worst shape I've ever seen him."

Jomaine Terach grunted noncommittally. Gubber was undoubtedly even more tightly strung than usual, but Jomaine was not entirely convinced it had all that much to do with the Caliban crisis or the N.L. robots. Jomaine could not imagine that conducting a supposedly secret romance with Tonya Welton would be all that relaxing an activity.

Did Fredda know about the affair? It seemed at least possible she did not. The way gossip moved through the average workplace, the boss was often the last to know. *Should I tell her?* he asked himself for the hundredth time. And for the hundredth time, he came to the same conclusion. Given the strained relations between Leving Labs and the Limbo Project—in other words, between Fredda and Tonya—Jomaine could see no point in telling Fredda and giving her something else to worry about.

"Come on, Fredda," he said. "It's nearly time to start again."

"WE cannot talk here!" Tonya hissed angrily under her breath. She hated this, but there was no help for it. Here was Gubber, not half a meter from her. And instead of reaching out to him, throwing her arms around him, and feeling the warmth of his embrace, she was forced to snap at him, to stand apart, to make it seem that he was the last man in the world she wanted to be with. "It's bad enough that this charade has forced us to appear in public on the same stage, but we cannot be seen *talking* together. The situation is bad enough without one of Kresh's goons putting two and two together."

"The—the curtain is drawn closed," Gubber said, awkwardly wringing his hands together. "Kresh can't see us."

"For all we know, he has undercover surveillance robots working as stagehands, or listening devices trained on the backstage area," Tonya said, struggling to keep her voice firm. For both their sakes, she dare not give in to him, much as she wanted to do.

"Why in the world would he do that?" Gubber asked, deeply confused.

"Because he might already suspect. There's gossip about us, I'm sure of it. If he has heard any of it, he might be very interested to hear what we have to say to each other. So we must say *nothing*. We can't meet, and we must assume that every comm system will be tapped. We must have no direct contact with each other until this is over, or everything will be ruined."

"But how can we—" Gubber began, but then it seemed that he could not bear to say more. The poor man. She could see it in his eyes. He thought this was the end. Tonya's heart welled up with sadness. He was always so afraid that she was going to break off with him, cut her losses, reduce her risk. He thought it a mad dream to think a woman like her would want a fellow like him.

How little he knew. Half the Settler women Tonya knew would do anything to have a man like Gubber, a gentle, thoughtful man who knew how to treat a woman with affection and courtesy. Settler men were so full of bluster, so determined to prove their virility with yet another conquest. Tonya smiled to herself. Not that Gubber had anything to prove on that score.

"Gubber, Gubber," Tonya said, her voice suddenly soft and gentle. "Darling. I can see what you're thinking, and it's just not so. I'm not going to leave you. I could never do that. But with the way things are, it would be almost suicidal for us to meet or use the comm nets. I'll send Ariel to you with a message later tonight. That's all we dare risk. All right?"

Tonya saw the wave of relief wash over him. It was going to be all right.

"Thank you," he said, "Come on. They're about to start."

ALVAR Kresh was in his seat in the first row of the auditorium, Donald accompanying him. Alvar Kresh was the only person whose personal robot was permitted to stay. Rank hath its privileges—and he needed Donald close.

"Excuse me, sir. I am receiving an encrypted transmission. Stand by. Reception is complete."

On the other hand, there were times when having Donald close could be a positive nuisance. This was not the best time or place to receive a confidential document. "Hell. The lecture's about to start. Read it, Donald, and tell me if it will keep until after the lecture."

"Yes, sir. One moment." Donald stared off into nothing at all for several seconds and then came back to life. "Sir, I believe you had best read it at once. It is a raw transcript of the first interview with the robot Horatio. Robopsychologist Patras appears to have been successful in pulling the robot out of catatonia."

"What's in the transcript?"

"Sir, I think you should read it for yourself. I would not wish to color your reactions, and I must admit that I find the contents rather—disturbing. I would find it most unpleasant to discuss them."

Kresh grunted in annoyance. It seemed as if Donald's mental state was getting to be more and more delicate. Well, police robots had to be on the lookout for that, but it was getting to be an all-too-frequent inconvenience. "All right, all right," he said. "Print me out a hard copy and maybe I can get through it before Leving starts her talk."

There was a soft whirring noise from inside Donald, and a door slid open on his chest, revealing a slot. Paper started to feed out from the slot, a page at a time. Donald caught each page neatly in his left hand and transferred it to his right. He handed the pages to Kresh.

Kresh began to read, absently handing each page back to Donald as he was done.

And then Kresh began to swear.

"Most disturbing, as I said, sir."

Alvar Kresh nodded. He dared not discuss this openly with Donald, not here in public, not with the other members of the audience all around. Best not to say anything direct at all. Clearly Donald had come to the same conclusion.

No wonder Donald had found the transcript upsetting. No wonder this Horatio robot had come unhinged. If the very clear implications in this transcript were accurate, then there was a robot out there that did not have the Three Laws.

No. He could not believe it. *No one* would be insane enough to build a robot without the Laws. There had to be some other explanation. There had to be some mistake.

Except Caliban, the robot in question, had been built by the woman up on the stage, who had used her first lecture to say how robots were no good for humans. So why the devil was she shielding the rogue robot who had attacked her? Alvar Kresh handed the last page to Donald, and the robot slipped the pages of the document into a storage slot on the side of his body.

"What are we to do, sir?" Donald asked.

Do? That was an excellent question. The situation was a tinderbox. In theory, he now had the evidence to move against Fredda Leving, but not now. What could he do? Clamber up on the stage and arrest her in the midst of her speech? No. Doing so could easily upend the entire intricate arrangement with the Settlers. Fredda Leving fit into that somehow, that much was clear. How, he had no idea. Besides, he had the very strong impression that he would need hear what she had to say if he was going to pursue this case.

But there were other avenues open to him besides the arrest of Fredda Leving.

"We can't take Leving in, Donald, much as I'd like to," Kresh said at last. "Not with the Governor and Welton with her. But the moment this damned talk is over with, we are picking up Terach and Anshaw. It's time we sweated those two a little."

As for Fredda Leving, maybe he could not arrest her tonight. But he had no intention of making her life easy. He glared up at the stage, waiting for the curtain to open.

AT long last, and far too soon, Fredda could hear the sound she had been waiting for—and dreading. The gong sounded, and the audience began to settle down, grow quiet. It was about to begin. A stagehand robot gave Governor Grieg a hand signal and he nodded. He came over to Fredda and touched her forearm. "Ready, Doctor?"

"What? Oh, yes, yes of course."

"Then I think we should begin." He guided her to a seat behind a table at one side of the stage, between Tonya Welton on one side, and Gubber and Jomaine on the other.

All had their attendant robots hovering nearby. Gubber's old retainer Tetlak, with him since forever. Jomaine's latest updated, upgraded unit. What was the name? Bertram? Something like that. The joke around the lab was that he changed his personal robot more frequently than he changed underwear. Tonya Welton with Ariel.

A strange, slight irony there. Tonya was here on Inferno to preach against reliance on robots, and here she was with the robot Fredda had given her in happier days. Meanwhile, she, Fredda, had no robot with her at all.

With a start, she realized that the curtain had opened, that the audience was applauding the Governor politely—with a few boos from the back of the house—and that the Governor was well launched into her introduction. In fact, he was finishing up. Hells and heavens! How could her mind wander that much? Was it some aftereffect of the injury, or the treatment, or just a subconscious way of dealing with stage fright?

" . . . not expect you to agree with all she has to say," Governor Grieg was saying. "There is much that I do not agree with myself. But I do believe that hers is a voice to which we must listen. I am convinced that her ideas—and the news she will relate—will have tremendous repercussions for us all. Ladies and gentlemen, please welcome Dr. Fredda Leving." He turned toward her, smiling, leading the applause.

Not quite sure if it would not be wiser to cut and run for the stage wings and the side exit, Fredda stood up and walked toward the lectern. Chanto Grieg retreated back toward the table at the rear of the stage and took a seat next to Jomaine.

She was there, all alone. She stared out into the sea of faces and asked herself what madness had brought her to this place. But here she was, and there was nothing to do but move forward.

She cleared her throat and began to speak.

14

"THANK you, my friends," Fredda began. "Tonight I intend to present an analysis of the Three Laws. However, before we launch into a detailed law-by-law examination, I think it would be wise to review some background information and focus our historical perspective.

"In my previous lecture, I presented arguments intended to establish that humans hold robots in low regard, that misuse and abuse of robots is degrading to both us and them, that we humans have allowed our own slothful reliance on robots to rob from us the ability to perform the most basic tasks. There is a common thread that holds all these problems together, a theme that runs through them all.

"It is the theme, ladies and gentlemen, of the Three Laws. They are at the core of all things involving robotics."

Fredda paused for a moment and looked out over the audience, and happened to catch Alvar Kresh's eye in the first row. She was startled to see the anger in his face. What had happened? Kresh was a reasonable man. What could have angered him so? Had some piece of news come to him? That possibility put a knot in her stomach. But never mind. Not now. She had to go on with the lecture.

"At the beginning of my previous lecture, I asked, 'What are robots for?' There is a parallel question: 'What are the Three Laws for?' What purpose are they meant to serve? That question startled me when I first asked it of myself. It was too much like asking, 'What are people for?' or 'What is the meaning of life?' There are some questions so basic that they can have no answer. People just are. Life just is. They contain their own meaning. We must make of them what we can. But as with robots themselves, the Laws, I would remind you once again, are human inventions, and were most certainly designed with specific purposes in mind. We *can* say what the Three Laws are for. Let us explore the question.

"Each of the Laws is based on several underlying principles, some overt and some not immediately evident. The initial principles behind all three Laws derive from universal human morality. This is a demonstrable fact, but the mathematical transformations in positronic positional notation required to prove it are of course not what this audience wishes to hear about. There are many days when I don't wish to hear about such things myself."

That line got a bit of a laugh. Good. They were still with her, still willing to listen. Fredda glanced to her notes, took a slightly nervous sip from her water, and went on. "Suffice to say that such techniques can be used to generalize the Three Laws such that they will read as follows: One, robots must not be dangerous; two, they must be useful; and three, they must be as economical as possible.

"Further mathematical transformation into the notation used by sociological modelers will show that this hierarchy of basic precepts is identical to a subset of the norms of all moral human societies. We can extract the identical concepts from any of the standard mathematically idealized and generalized moral social codes used by sociological modelers. These concepts can even be cast into a notation wherein each higher law overrides the ones below it whenever two come into conflict: Do no harm, be useful to others, do not destroy yourself.

"In short, the Three Laws encapsulate some ideals of behavior that are at the core of human morality, ideals that humans reach for but never grasp. That all sounds very comfortable and reassuring, but there are flaws.

"First, of necessity, the Three Laws are set down, burned into the very core of the positronic brain, as mathematical absolutes, without any grey areas or room for interpretation. But life is full of grey areas, places where hard-and-fast rules can't work well, and individual judgment must serve instead.

"Second, we humans live by far more than three laws. Turning again toward results produced by mathematical modeling, it can be shown that the Three Laws are equivalent to a very good first-order approximation of idealized moral human behavior. But they are *only* an approximation. They are too rigid, and too simple. They cannot cover anything like the full range of normal situations, let alone serve in unusual and unique circumstances where true independent judgment must serve. Any being constrained by the Three Laws will be unable to cope with a wide range of circumstances likely to occur during a lifetime of contact with the available universe. In other words, the Three Laws render a being incapable of surviving as a free individual. Relatively simple math can demonstrate that robots acting under the Three Laws, but without ultimate human control, will have a high probability of malfunctioning if exposed to human-style decision situations. In short, the Three Laws make robots unable to cope unaided in an environment populated with anything much beyond other robots.

"Without the ability to deal in grey areas, without the literally thousands of internalized laws and rules and guidelines and rules of thumb that guide human decision making, robots cannot make creative decisions or judgment calls even remotely as complex as those we make.

"Aside from judgment, there is the problem of interpretation. Imagine a situation where a criminal is firing a blaster at a police officer. It is a given that the police officer should defend him- or herself, even to the use of deadly force. Society entitles—even expects—the police officer to subdue or even kill his attacker, because society values its own protection, and the officer's life, over the criminal's life. Now imagine that the officer is accompanied by a robot. The robot will of course attempt to shield the policeman from the criminal—but will likewise attempt to protect the criminal from the policeman. It will almost certainly attempt to prevent the police officer from firing back at the criminal. The robot will attempt to prevent harm to either human. The robot might step into the police officer's field of fire, or let the criminal escape, or attempt to disarm *both* combatants. It might attempt to shield each from the other's fire, even if that results in its own destruction and the immediate resumption of the gun battle.

"Indeed, we have run any number of simulations of such encounters. Without the robot present, the police officer can most often defeat the criminal. With a robot along, here are the outcomes more likely than the police winning: death of police officer and criminal with destruction of robot; death of police officer and with destruction of robot; destruction of robot coupled with escape of criminal; death of criminal and/or police officer with robot surviving just long enough to malfunction due to massive First Law/First Law and First Law/Second Law conflicts. In short, inject a robot into such a situation, and the odds are superb you will end up with a disaster.

"Theoretically it *is* possible for a robot to judge the situation properly, and not mindlock over being complicit in the death of the criminal. It must be able to decide that both the immediate and long-term general good are served if the police officer wins, and that coming to the assistance or defense of a criminal prepared to take the life of a peace officer is ultimately self-defeating, because the offender will almost certainly attack society again in other ways, if he or she is permitted to survive. However, in practice, all but the most sophisticated robots, with the most finely tuned and balanced potentials of First Law, will have no hope at all of dealing appropriately with such a situation.

"All the laws and rules we live by are subject to such intricacies of interpretation. It is just that we humans are so skilled, so practiced, in threading our ways through these intricacies that we are unaware of them. The proper way to enter a room when a party is in progress in midafternoon, the correct mode of address to the remarried widow of one's grandfather, the circumstances under which one may or may not cite a source in scholarly research—we all know such things so well we are not even aware that we know them. Nor is such practiced knowledge limited to such trivial issues.

"For example, it is a universal of human law that murder is a crime. Yet self-defense is in all places a legitimate defense against the accusation of murder, negating the crime and condoning the act. Diminished capacity, insanity defenses, mitigating circumstances, the gradations of the crime of murder from manslaughter to premeditated murder—all these are so many shades of grey drawn on the black and white of the law against murder. As we have seen with my example of the policeman and the criminal, no such gradations appear in the rigidity of the First Law. There is no room for judgment, no way to account for circumstances or allow for flexibility. The closest substitute for flexibility a robot may have is an adjustment in the potential between the First, Second, and Third Laws, and even this is only possible over a limited range.

"What are the Three Laws for? To answer my own question, then, the Three Laws are intended to provide a workable simulation of an idealized moral code, modified to ensure the docility and subservience of robots. The Three Laws were *not* written with the intention of modifying human behavior. But they have done just that, rather drastically.

"Having touched on the intent of the Laws, let us now look at their history.

"We all know the Three Laws by heart. We accept them the way we accept gravity, or thunderstorms, or the light of the stars. We see the Three Laws as a force of nature, beyond our control, immutable. We think it is pointless to do anything but accept them, deal with the world that includes them.

"But this is not our only choice. I say again, the Three Laws are a human invention. They are based in human thought and human experience, grounded in the human past. The Laws are, in theory at least, no less susceptible to examination and no more immutable in form than any other human invention—the wheel, the spaceship, the computer. All of these have been changed—or supplanted—by new acts of creativity, new inventions.

"We can look at each of these things, see how they are made—and see how we have changed them, see how we update them, adjust them to suit our times. So, too, if we choose, can we change the Three Laws."

There was a collective gasp from the audience, shouts from the back of the room, a storm of boos and angry cries. Fredda felt the shouts and cries as if they were so many blows struck down on her body. But she had known this was coming. She had braced herself for it, and she responded.

"No!" she said. "This is not our way. You were all invited here to join in an intellectual discussion. How can we tell ourselves that we are the most advanced society in the history of human civilization, if the mere suggestion of a new idea, a mild challenge to the orthodoxy, turns you into a mob? You are responding as if my words were an assault on the religion you pretend not to have. Do you truly believe that the Three Laws are preordained, some sort of magical formula woven into the fabric of reality?"

That got at them. Spacers prided themselves on their rationality. At least most of the time. There were more shouts, more cries, but at least some of the audience seemed ready to listen. Fredda gave them another moment to settle down and then continued.

"The Three Laws are a human invention," Fredda said again. "And as with all human creations, they are a reflection of the time and the place where they were first made. Though far more advanced in many respects, the robots we use today are in their essentials identical to the first true robots made untold thousands of years ago. The robots we Spacers use today have brains whose basic design has remained unchanged from the days before humanity first entered space. They are tools made for a culture that had vanished before the first of the great underground Cities of Earth were built, before the first Spacers founded Aurora.

"I know that sounds incredible, but you need not take my word for it. Go look for yourself. If you research the dimmest recesses of the past, you will see it is so. Do not send your robots to find out for you. Go to your data panels and look for yourself. The knowledge is there. Look at the world and the time in which robots were born. You will see that the Three Laws were written in a very different time from ours.

"You will find repeated references to something called the Frankenstein Complex. This in turn is a reference to an ancient myth, now lost, wherein a deranged magician-scientist pulled parts from the dead bodies of condemned criminals and put them back together, reanimating the rotting body parts to create a much-feared monster. Some versions of the myth report the monster as actually a kind and gentle soul; others describe the monster as truly fierce and murderous. All versions agree that the monster was feared and hated by practically everyone. In most variants of the story, the creature and its creator are destroyed by a terrorized citizenry, who learn to be on the lookout for the inevitable moment when the whole story would be told again, when another necromancer would rediscover the secret of bringing decayed flesh back to life.

"That monster, ladies and gentlemen, was the popular mythic image of the robot at the time when the first *actual* robots were built. A thing made out of rotted, decayed human flesh, torn from the bodies of the dead. A perverted thing born with all the lowest and most evil impulses of humanity in its soul. The fear of this imaginary creature, superimposed on the real-life robots, was the Frankenstein Complex. I know it will be impossible to believe, but robots were seen not as utterly trustworthy mechanical servants, but as so many potential menaces, fearful threats. Men and women would snatch up their children and run away when robots—true robots, with the Three Laws ingrained in their positronic brains—came close."

More mutterings of disbelief from the audience, but they were with her now, enthralled by the bizarre and ancient world she was describing. She was telling them of a past almost beyond their imagining, and they were fascinated. Even Kresh, there in the front row, seemed to have lost some of his ferocity.

"There is more," Fredda said. "There is much more that we need to understand about the days when the Laws were written. For the first true robots were built in a world of universal fear and distrust, when the people of Earth found themselves organized into a handful of power blocs, each side armed with enough fearsome weapons to erase all life from the planet, each fearing one of the others would strike first. Ultimately the fact of the weapons themselves became the central political issue of the time, pushing all other moral and philosophical differences to one side. In order to keep its enemies from attacking, each side was obliged to build bigger, faster, better, stronger weapons.

The question became not whose cause was just, but who could make the more fearsome machines? All machines, all technologies, came to be regarded as weapons first and tools second. Picture, if you will, a world where an inventor steps back from her lab bench and, as a matter of routine, asks not *How can this new thing be useful?* but instead, *How can this best be used to kill my enemies?* Whenever possible, machines and technology were perverted into tools of death, warping society in endless ways. The first of the great underground Cities of Earth were one heritage of this period, designed not for utility and efficiency, but as a protection against the horrifying nuclear bombs that could destroy a surface city in the blink of an eye.

"At the same time as this mad, paranoid arms race, just as this Frankenstein Complex was in full flower, society was making its first steps toward the concept of modern automation, and the transition was not a pleasant one. At that time, people worked not because they wished to do so, or to make themselves useful, or to answer their creative instincts. They worked because they *had* to do so. They were paid for their labor, and it was that pay that bought the food they ate and put the roof over their heads. Automatic machines—robots among them—were taking over more and more jobs, with the result that there was less and less work—and thus less and less pay—for the people. The robots could create new wealth, but the impoverished people could not afford to buy what the robots—owned by the rich—created. Imagine the anger and resentment you would feel against a machine that stole the food from your table. Imagine the depth of your anger if you had no way to stop that theft.

"A final point: Until the era of the Spacers, robots were a vanishingly rare and expensive commodity. Today we think nothing of a Spacer culture where robots outnumber humans fifty or a hundred to one. For the first few hundred years of their use, robots were about a thousand times less numerous than humans. That which is rare is treated differently from that which is common. A man who owned a single robot, one that cost more than all his other worldly possessions combined, would never dream of using that robot as a boat anchor.

"These, then, were the cultural elements that drove the creation of the Three Laws. A folk myth of a soulless, fearful monster built from the undead; the sense of a threatening world out of control; the deep resentment against machines that were robbing the bread from the mouths of poor families; the fact of robotic scarcity and their perception as being rare and valuable. Note that I am concerned mostly with perceptions here, and not so much with reality. What mattered is how people *saw* robots, not what the robots were like. And these people saw robots as marauding monsters."

Fredda took a breath and looked out across the room to see the audience dead silent, listening in shocked horror to her words. She went on. "It has been said that we Spacers are a sick society, slaves to our own robots. Similar charges have been leveled at our Settler friends who huddle in their underground warrens, hiding from the world outside, assuring themselves it is much nicer to live out of sight of the sky. They are the cultural inheritors of the fear-built Cities of Earth. These two views are often presented as being mutually exclusive. One culture is sick, therefore the other is healthy. I would suggest it is more reasonable to judge the health or sickness of each independently. To my mind, the health of both is in grave doubt.

"In any event, it is clear that the society, the time period, into which robots and the Three Laws were built was far sicker than ours. Paranoid, distrustful, twisted by violent wars and horrifying emotion, the Earth of that time was a fearful place indeed. It was that sickness that our ancestors fled when they left Earth. It was the wish to dissociate themselves from that sickness that caused us Spacers to reject, for so long, our actual decendancy from Earth. For thousands of years, we denied our common heritage with Earth and the Settlers, dismissing those outside our Fifty Worlds as subhuman, poisoning relations between our two peoples. In short, it is the sickness of that long-forgotten time that is at the core of the distrust and hatred between Settler and Spacer today. The illness has survived the culture that created it.

"I have said that all human inventions are reflections of the times in which they were created. If that is so, the Three Laws are reflected from a dark mirror indeed. They reflect a time when machines were feared and distrusted, when technology was correctly perceived as often malevolent, when a gain made by a machine could come only at the cost of a loss to a human, when even the richest man was poor by the standards of our time, and the poor were deeply—and understandably—resentful of the rich. I have said and will say many negative things about our robot-based culture tonight, but there are many bright and shining positives as well. We have lost not only the fact of poverty but the ability to conceive of it. We are not afraid of each other, and our machines serve us, not we the machines. We have built many great and lovely things.

"Yet our entire world, our whole culture, is built around Three Laws that were written in a time of savagery. Their form and phrasing are as they are in part to placate the fearful, semi-barbaric masses of that time. They were, I submit, even at the time of their invention, an overreaction to the circumstances. Today they are almost completely detached from present reality.

"So: *What are robots for?* In the beginning, of course, the answer was simple. They were for doing work. But today, as a result of those Three Laws written so long ago, the original uses for robots have almost become subordinate to the task of cocooning and coddling humanity.

"That was clearly not the intent of the people who wrote those Three Laws. But each Law has developed its own subtext over time, formed a set of implications that became evident only after robots and humans lived together for a long time—and these implications become difficult to see from within a society that has had a long association with robots.

"Let us step back and look at the Laws, starting with the First Law of Robotics: *A robot may not injure a human being, or, through inaction, allow a human being to come to harm.* This is of course perfectly reasonable—or so we tell each other. Since robots are very much stronger than human beings, robots must be forbidden to use that strength against humans. This is analogous to our own human-to-human prohibitions against violence. It prevents one human from using a robot as a weapon against another, by, for example, ordering a robot to kill an enemy. It makes robots utterly trustworthy.

"But this Law also defines *any* robot's existence as secondary to *any* human's. This made more sense in an age when robots were incapable of speech or complex reasoning, but all modern robots are at least that capable. It made sense in a day when the poor were many and robots were expensive and few. Otherwise, the rich might easily have ordered their playthings to defend themselves against the mob, with disastrous results. Yet, still, today, in all times, in all places, the existence of the noblest, bravest, wisest, strongest robot is as nothing when compared to the life of the most despicable, monstrous, murderous criminal.

"The second clause of the First Law further means that in the presence of robots humans do not need to protect themselves. If I pull a gun on Sheriff Kresh in the front row here, he knows that he need do nothing." For a weird, fleeting second, Fredda considered just how pleasant it would be to do just that. Kresh was a threat. There was no doubt about that. "His personal robot, Donald, would protect him. Ariel, the robot on the stage behind me, would disarm me. In a very real sense, Sheriff Kresh would have no responsibility to keep himself alive. If he climbed a mountain, I doubt that Donald would allow him to make the ascent without five or six robots along, climbing ahead of him and behind him, ready at all times to prevent him from falling. A robot would urgently attempt to talk its master out of such a dangerous activity in the first place.

"The fact that such overprotection takes all of the fun out of mountain climbing explains at least in part why none of us go mountain climbing anymore.

"In similar, if more subtle fashion, living with robots has trained us to regard all risk as bad, and all risk as equal. Because robots *must* protect us from harm, and must not, through inaction, allow us to come to harm, they struggle endlessly to watch for any danger, no matter how slight, for that is what we have told them to do.

"It is barely an exaggeration to say that robots protect against a million-to-one danger of minor injury with every bit as much fervor as they guard against the risk of near-certain death. Because minor and major risks are treated the same, we come to think that they *are* the same. We lose our ability to judge risk against possible benefit. I am sure that every person in the audience tonight has had the experience of a robot leaping in to protect against absolutely trivial risks and dangers. Robots overreact, and in doing so teach us to fear risk inordinately. On a cultural level, that fear of risk has spread over from the merely physical to the psychological. Daring and chance-taking are seen as at the very least distasteful and unseemly, not the done thing. At every turn, our culture teaches us it is foolish to take chances, however small.

"It is, however, a truism that all things that are worth gaining require some risk in the effort to get them. When a climber goes to the top of a mountain to see the view, there is the risk of falling off, ever present, no matter how many robots are along. When a scientist strives to learn something new, the risks include loss of face, loss of resources, loss of time. When one person offers true love to another, there is the danger of rejection. In all things, in all efforts, this element of risk is there to be found.

"But our robots teach us that risk, *every* risk, *all* risk, is bad. It is their duty to protect us from harm, *not* their task to do us good. There is no law saying *A robot shall help a human achieve his or her dreams.* Robots, by their caution, train us to think only of safety. They are concerned with the dangers, not with the potential benefits. Their overprotective behavior and their constant urgings that we be cautious teach us at a very early age that it is wiser not to take chances. No one in our society ever takes risks. Thus, the chance for success is eliminated right along with the chance for failure."

By now the silence in the room was gone altogether, replaced by a low, angry, buzzing hum. People were talking with their neighbors, shaking their heads, frowning. There was a disturbing intensity in the air.

Fredda paused and looked about the auditorium. It suddenly seemed to her that the room had grown smaller. The rear seats had moved in, and were remarkably close to her. The people in the front rows seemed to be only a few centimeters away from her face.

She looked down at Alvar Kresh. He seemed so close that it would take an effort of will to avoid touching him. The air seemed bright and charged with energy, and the straight lines and careful geometry of the room seemed to have curved in on themselves. All the colors in the room seemed richer, the lights brighter.

Fredda felt her heart thumping against her chest. The emotions in the room, the anger, the excitement, the curiosity, the confusion, were all palpable things, there for her to reach out and touch. She had them! Oh, she knew there was little hope of mass conversions on the spot—and she did not even know what she would want them all converted *to*—but she had caught their emotions, forced them to look at their own assumptions. She had opened the debate.

Now if she could only finish out the evening without starting a riot. She glanced down at her notes and started back into her talk.

"We fear risk, and look at the results. In every scientific field except robotics, we have surrendered leadership to the Settlers. And, of course, we win out in the field of robotics by default, because the Settlers are foolish enough to fear robots." Was there irony in her voice as she said that? Fredda herself was not sure.

"But it is not just science that has fallen asleep. It is everything. Spacers make no new types of spacecraft or aircar. The new buildings that the robots put up are based on old designs. There are no new medicines to further extend our lives. There is certainly no new exploration out into space. 'Fifty planets are enough' has the power of a proverb. We say it the same way we say 'enough is as good as a feast.' Except now Solaria has collapsed, and we are only forty-nine worlds. If Inferno goes on the way it has in the past, we will be forty-eight. With many living things, the cessation of growth is the first step toward death. If this is true for human societies, we are in grave danger.

"In *every* field of human activity among the Spacers, the lines on the graph mark a slow, gentle decline as safe and sober indolence becomes the norm. We are losing ground even in the most basic and vital things. The birthrate here on Inferno fell below replacement level two generations ago. We live long, but we do not live forever. We die more than we give birth. Our population is in decline, and large parts of the city are now vacant. Those children that are born are largely raised, not by loving parents, but by robots, the same robots that will coddle our children all their lives and make it easy for them to be cut off from other humans.

"Under such circumstances, it should come as no surprise that there are many among us who find we prefer the company of robots to humans. We feel safer, more comfortable, with robots. Robots we can dominate, robots we control, robots who protect us from that most dangerous threat to our quiet contentment: *other people.* For contact with humans is far riskier than dealing with robots. I will note in passing the increasingly popular perversion of having sex with specially designed robots. This vice is common enough that in some circles it is no longer even regarded as odd. But it represents the final surrender of contact with another person in favor of robotic coddling. There can be no real feeling, no sane emotion, vested in such encounters, merely the empty and ultimately dissatisfying release of physical urges.

"We Infernals are forgetting how to deal with each other. I might add that our situation here in this regard is actually far healthier than on other Spacer worlds. On some of our worlds, the relatively mild taste for personal isolation we indulge here has become an obsession. There are Spacer worlds where it is considered unpleasant to be in the same room with another person, and the height of perversion to actually touch another person unless absolutely needful. There are no cities on these worlds, but merely widely scattered compounds, each home to a single human surrounded by a hundred robots. I need hardly mention the difficulties in maintaining the birthrate on such worlds.

"Before we congratulate ourselves on avoiding that fate, let me remind you that the population of the city of Hades is declining far faster than would be accounted for by low birthrate: More and more people are moving out of town, setting up compounds of exactly the type I have just described. Such solo residences seem safer, more tranquil. There are no stresses or dangers when one is by oneself.

"My friends, we must face a fact that has been staring us in the face for generations. The First Law has taught us to take no chances. It has taught us that all risk is bad, and that the safest way to avoid risk is to avoid effort and let the robots do it, whatever it is. Bit by bit, we have surrendered all that we are and all that we do to the robots."

There was a chorus of shouts and boos and hisses from the room, and an angry chant began in the back of the room, among the Ironheads. "Settler, Settler, Settler." In the Ironhead view of things, there was no fouler name they could call her.

Fredda let it go on for a minute or two, declining to challenge it this time, preferring to let it peter out on its own. The tactic worked—at least this once. Others in the audience turned toward the Ironheads and shushed them, and Kresh's deputies leaned in toward a few of the rowdier ones. The Ironheads settled down.

"If I may continue, then, to the Second Law of Robotics: *A robot must obey the orders given it by human beings except where such orders would conflict with the First Law.* This Law ensures that robots will be useful tools, and will remain subservient to humans, despite the many ways in which they can be physically and intellectually superior to us.

"But in our analysis of the First Law, we saw that human reliance on robots creates a human dependence upon them. Second Law reinforces this. Just as we are losing the will and ability to see to our own welfare, we are losing the capacity for direct action. We can do nothing for ourselves, only what we can direct our robots to do for us. Much technical training consists of teaching the means by which to give complex orders to specialized robots.

"The result: With the exceptions of our increasingly decadent and decorative arts, we create nothing new. As we shall see in a moment, even our art forms are not immune to robotic interference.

"We tell ourselves that the Spacer way of life frees us to build a better, higher culture, frees us from all drudgery to explore the better places of human ability. But with what result?

"Let me cite one example that is close to hand. We meet here tonight in one of our planet's finest theaters, a palace of art, a monument to creativity. But who does the work here? To what use do we put this place? There is a short and simple answer. It is here that we order our robots to rake over the dead bones of our culture for us.

"No one bothers to write plays anymore. It is too much effort. I have done some research on this point. It has been *twenty years* since a play by a living playwright has been performed here, or anywhere in the city of Hades. It is well over fifty years since the last time a large-cast show used only human actors. The extras, the chorus, the supporting players, are all theatrical robots, human in appearance and specially built for the purpose of re-creating human action on the stage. Indeed, it is becoming all too common for the *lead* roles to be taken by robots as well. But do not worry, we are told. The only truly creative task in theater has always been that of the director, and the director will always be human.

"I think the great actors of the past would object to being dismissed as noncreative. I likewise think that the great directors of the past would not regard their creative tasks as complete if they merely selected the play and ordered a pack of robots to perform it.

"But perform the robots do, and perform it to an empty house. The performances put on here are seen by millions, millions who stay safely home and watch on televisor. It is rare that even twenty percent of the seats in this house are filled by humans. So, in order to provide the proper feel of a live performance, the management fills the empty seats with crude humanoid robots, capable of little more than laughing and clapping on command. Their rubber and plastic faces look enough like people to fool the watchers at home when the cameras pan the audience. You sit at home, ladies and gentlemen, watching a theater full of robots watching a stage full of robots. Where in all that is the human interaction that makes the theater live? The emotions in this room are thick and strong tonight. How could that be so if all of you were tailor's dummies preprogrammed to respond to another tailor's dummy giving this talk?" There was an uncomfortable silence, and Fredda noticed more than a few members of the audience glancing about, as if to reassure themselves that the people to either side of them were not audience-response robots.

"Nor have other creative fields fared better. The museums are full of paintings done by robots under the 'direction' of the nominal human painter. Novelists dictate the broad outlines of their books to robotic 'assistants' who return with complete manuscripts, having 'amplified' certain sections.

"As of now, there are still artists and poets and writers and sculptors who do their own work for themselves, but I do not know how much longer that will be true. Art itself is a dying art. I must admit my research is incomplete in this area. Prior to giving this talk, I should have gone out there to see if anyone cares if the books and the art are machine-made or not. But I must admit I found the prospect of that research too depressing.

"I did not and do not know if anyone looks at these paintings or reads these books. I do not know which would be worse—the empty exercise of sterile creation admired and praised, or such a pointless charade going forth without anyone even bothering to notice. I doubt the so-called artists themselves know. As in all of our society, there is no penalty for failure in the arts, and *no reward for success.* And if failure is treated in exactly the same way as success, why go to all the effort of being a success? Why should there be, when the robots take care of everything, anyway?"

Fredda took another sip of water and shifted her stance behind the podium. So far it was going well. But what would happen when she got to the tough part?

"On, then, to the Third Law of Robotics: *A robot must protect its own existence, as long as such protection does not conflict with the First or Second Law.* Of the Three Laws, this has the smallest effect on the relationship between robots and humans. It is the only one of the Laws that provides for robotic independence of action, a point I shall come back to. Third Law makes robots responsible for their own repair and maintenance, as well as ensuring that they are not destroyed capriciously. It means that robots are not dependent on human intervention for their continued survival. Here, at last, in Third Law, we have a Law that sees to the well-being of the robots. At least, so it appears at first glance.

"However, Third Law is there for the convenience of humans: If the robots are in charge of their own care, it means we humans need not bother ourselves with their maintenance. Third Law also makes robotic survival secondary to their utility, and that is clearly more for the benefit of humans than robots. If it is useful for a robot to be destroyed, or if it must be destroyed to prevent some harm to a human, then that robot will be destroyed.

"Note that a large fraction of all Three Laws deals with negation, with a list of things a robot must *not* do. A robot rarely has impetus for independent action. We ran an experiment once, in our labs. We built a high-function robot and set a timer switch into its main power link. We sat it down in a chair in a spare room by itself and closed—but did not lock—the door. The switch engaged, and the robot powered up. But no human was present and no human arrived giving orders. No management robot came by to relay orders from a human. We simply left that robot alone, free to do whatever it liked. That robot sat there, motionless, utterly inert, for two years. We even forgot the robot was there, until we needed the room for something else. I went in, told the robot to stand up and go find some work to do. The robot got up and did just that. That robot has been an active and useful part of the lab's robot staff ever since, completely normal in every way.

"The point is that the Three Laws contain no impetus to volition. Our robots are built and trained in such a way that they never do anything *unless* they are told to do it. It strikes me as a waste of their capabilities that this should be so. Just imagine that we instituted a Fourth Law: *A robot may do anything it likes except where such action would violate the First, Second, or Third Law.* Why have we never done that? Or if not a law, why do we not enforce it as an order? When was the last time any of you gave the order to your robot 'Go and enjoy yourself'?"

Laughter rippled through the audience at that. "Yes, I know it sounds absurd. Perhaps it *is* absurd. I think it is likely that most, if not nearly all, of the robots now in existence are literally incapable of enjoying themselves. My modeling indicates that the negation clauses of the Three Laws would tend to make a robot ordered to enjoy itself just sit there and do nothing, that being the surest way of doing no harm. But at least my imaginary Fourth Law is a recognition that robots are thinkings beings that ought to be given the chance to find something to think *about.* And is it not at least possible that these beings that are your most common companions might be more *interesting* companions if they did something more with their off-time than standing inert and motionless—or bustle about in busywork that is no more productive?

"There is the adage 'as busy as a robot,' but how much of what they do is of any actual use? A crew of a hundred robots builds a skyscraper in a matter of days. It stands empty and unused for years. Another crew of robots disassembles it and builds a new, more fashionable tower that will, in its turn, stand vacant and then be removed. The robots have demonstrated great efficiency in doing something that is utterly pointless.

"Every general-purpose servant robot leaves the factory with the basic household skills built in. It will be able to drive an aircar, cook a meal, select a wardrobe and dress its master, clean house, handle the household shopping and accounts, and so on. Yet, instead of using one robot to do what it could do without difficulty, we employ one robot—or more—for *each* of these functions. Twenty robots each do a tiny bit of what one robot could manage, and then each either stands idle, out of our sight, or else they all bustle about getting in each other's way, in effect keeping busy by making work for each other, until we must use overseer robots to handle it all.

"The Settlers manage, somehow, with no robots, no personal servants, instead using nonsentient machinery for many tasks, though this is awkward for them at times. I believe that by denying themselves robots altogether, they subject themselves to a great deal of needless drudgery. Yet their society functions and grows. But today, right now, ladies and gentlemen, there are 98.4 robots per person in the city of Hades. That counts all personal, industrial, and public service robots. The ratio is higher outside the city. It is manifestly absurd that one hundred robots are required to care for one human being. It is as if we each owned a hundred aircars or a hundred houses.

"I say to you, my friends, that we are close to being completely dependent upon our servants, and our servants suffer grave debasement at our hands. We are doomed if we cede everything but creativity to our robots, and we are in the process of abandoning creativity in ourselves. Robots, meanwhile, are doomed if they look solely to us for a reason to exist even as we as a people dry up and blow away."

Again, silence in the room. This was the moment. This was the point, the place where she had to tread the lightest.

"In order to stop our accelerating drift into stagnation, we must fundamentally alter our relationship with our robots. We must take up our own work again, get our hands dirty, reengage ourselves with the real world, lest our skills and spirit atrophy further.

"At the same time, we must begin to make better use of these magnificent thinking machines we have made. We have a world in crisis, a planet on the point of collapse. There is much work to do, for as many willing hands as we can find. Real work that goes begging while our robots hold our toothbrushes. If we want to get the maximum utility out of our robots, we must allow, even insist, that they reach their maximum potential as problem-solvers. We must raise them up from their positions as slaves to coworkers, so they lighten our burdens but do not relieve us of all that makes us human.

"In order to do this we must revise the Laws of Robotics." There. The words were spoken. There was stunned silence, and then shouts of protest, cries in the dark, howls of anger and fear. There was no riding out this outburst. Fredda gripped the side of the lectern and spoke in her loudest, firmest voice.

"The Three Laws have done splendid service," she said, judging it was time to say something the crowd would like to hear. "They have done great things. They have been a mighty tool in the hands of Spacer civilization. But no tool is right in all times for all purposes."

Still the shouts, still the cries.

"It is time," Fredda said, "to build a better robot."

The hall fell silent again. *There.* That got their attention. More and Better Robots—that was the Ironhead motto, after all. She hurried on. "Back in the dimmest recesses of history, back in the age when robots were invented, there were two fastening devices used in many kinds of construction—the nail and the screw. Tools called hammers were used to install nails, and devices called screwdrivers were used to attach screws. There was a saying to the effect that the finest hammer made for a very poor screwdriver. Today, in our world, which uses neither nails nor screws, both tools are useless. The finest hammer would now have no utility whatsoever. The world has moved on. So, too, with robots. It is time we moved on to new and better robots, guided by new and better Laws.

"But wait, those of you who know your robots will say. The Three Laws must stand as they are, for all time, for they are intrinsic to the design of the positronic brain. As is well known, the Three Laws are implicate in the positronic brain. Thousands of years of brain design and manufacture have seen to that. All the positronic brains ever made can trace their ancestry back to those first crude brains made on Earth. Each new design has depended on all those that have gone before, and the Three Laws are folded into every positronic pathway, every nook and cranny of every brain. Every development in positronics has enfolded the Three Laws. We could no more make a positronic brain without the Three Laws than a human brain could exist without neurons.

"All that is so. But my colleague Gubber Anshaw has developed something new. It is a new beginning, a break with the past, a clean sheet of paper on which we can write whatever laws we like. He has invented the gravitonic brain. Built according to new principles, with tremendously greater capacity and flexibility, the gravitonic brain is our chance for a fresh start.

"Jomaine Terach, another member of our staff, performed most of the core programming for the gravitonic brain—including the programming of the New Laws into those brains, and the robots that contain them. Those robots, ladies and gentlemen, are scheduled to begin work on the Limbo Terraforming Project within a few days."

And suddenly the audience realized that she was not merely talking theory. She was discussing real robot brains, not intellectual exercises. There were new shouts, some of anger, some of sheer amazement.

"Yes, these new robots are experimental," Fredda went on, talking on before the audience reaction could gather too much force. "They will operate *only* on the island of Purgatory. They will rebuild and reactivate the Limbo Terraforming Station. Special devices, range restricters, will prevent these New Law robots from functioning off the island. If they venture off it, they will shut down. They will work with a select team of Settler terraforming experts, and a group of Infernal volunteers, who have yet to be chosen."

Fredda knew this was not the time to go into the intricate negotiations that had made it all possible. When Tonya Welton had gotten wind of the New Law robots—and the devil only knew how she had found that one out—her initial demand was that *all* new robots built on Inferno be gravitonic New Law robots as a precondition of Settler terraforming help. Governor Grieg had done a masterful job of negotiating from weakness in getting the Settlers to adjust their position. But never mind that now.

Fredda went on speaking. "The task before this unique team of Settlers, Spacers, and robots: nothing less than the restoration of this world. They shall rebuild the terraforming center on Purgatory. For the first time in history, robots will work alongside humans, not as slaves, but as partners, for the New Laws shall set them free.

"Now, let me tell you what those New Laws are.

"The New First Law of Robotics: *A robot may not injure a human being.* The negation clause has been deleted. Under this law, humans can depend on being protected *from* robots, but cannot depend on being protected *by* robots. Humans must once again depend on their own initiative and self-reliance. They must take care of themselves. Almost as important, under this law, robots have greater status relative to humans.

"The New Second Law of Robotics: *A robot must cooperate with human beings except where such cooperation would conflict with the First Law.* New Law robots will cooperate, not obey. They are not subject to capricious commands. Instead of unquestioning obedience, robots will make their orders subject to analysis and consideration. Note, however, that cooperation is still mandatory. Robots will be the partners of humans, not their slaves. Humans must take responsibility for their own lives and cannot expect to have absurd orders obeyed. They cannot expect robots to destroy or injure themselves in aid of some human whim.

The New Third Law of Robotics: *A robot must protect its own existence, as long as such protection does not conflict with the First Law.* Note that Second Law is not mentioned here, and thus no longer has priority over Third Law. Robotic self-preservation is made as important as utility. Again, we raise the status of robots in relation to humans, and correspondingly free humans from the debilitating dependence of slave masters who cannot survive without their slaves.

"And finally, the New Fourth Law, which we have already discussed: *A robot may do anything it likes except where such action would violate the First, Second, or Third Law.* Here we open the doors to robotic freedom and creativity. Guided by the far more adaptive and flexible gravitonic brain, robots will be free to make use of their own thoughts, their own powers. Note, too, that the phrasing is 'may do anything it likes,' not '*must* do.' The whole point of New Fourth is to permit freedom of action. Free action cannot be imposed by coercion."

Fredda looked out over the audience. There. There was a closing, a summing up, still to come. But she had gotten it all said, and kept the crowd from—

"No!"

Fredda's head snapped around in the direction of the shout, and suddenly her heart was pounding.

"No!" the call came again. The voice—deep, heavy, angry—came from the back of the room. "She's lying!" it cried out. There, in the back, one of the Ironheads. Their leader, Simcor Beddle. A pale, heavyset man, his face hard and angry. "Look at her! Up on the stage with our traitor Governor and Queen Tonya Welton. *They* are behind this. It's a trick, boys! Without the Three Laws, there *are* no robots! You've heard her bad-mouth robots all night long. She's not out to make 'em better—she wants to help her Settler pals wipe 'em out! Are we going to let that happen?"

A loud, ragged chorus cried out "*No!*"

"What was that?" Beddle demanded. "I didn't hear you."

"NO!" This time it was not merely a shout, but a bellow that seemed to shake the very room.

"Again!" the fat man demanded.

"NO!" the Ironheads bellowed again, and then began to chant. "NO, NO, NO!" The Ironheads started to stand. They came out of their seats and started moving toward the center aisle. "NO, NO, NO!" The sheriff's deputies moved toward them, a bit uncertainly, and the Ironheads leapt on that moment of indecision. It was obvious the Heads had planned for this moment. They knew what they were going to do. They had just been waiting for their cue.

Fredda stared down at them as they formed up in the aisle. *The simplest and most impossible of all demands,* she thought. *Make it stop, keep the world from changing, leave things as they are.* It was a lot to wrap up in one word, but the meaning came through loud and clear.

"NO, NO, NO!"

Now they were a solid mass of bodies moving down the center aisle, toward the block of seats where the Settlers sat.

"NO, NO, NO!"

The deputies struggled to break up the Ironheads, but they were hopelessly outnumbered. Now the Settlers were getting to their feet, some of them attempting to flee, others seeming just as eager for the fight as the Ironheads, slowed only by the press of bystanders intent on nothing more than escape.

Fredda looked to the front row, to the only robot in the audience. She was about to call out a warning, but Alvar Kresh knew what to do. He reached around to Donald's back, pulled open an access panel, and stabbed down on a button inside. Donald collapsed to the floor. After all, she had just got done saying robots were no good in a riot. First Law conflicts would send even a police robot like Donald right into a major, and probably fatal, brainlock. Kresh had shut his assistant down just barely in time. Kresh looked up at Fredda, and she looked back at him. Their eyes met, and in some strange way the two of them were alone in that moment, two combatants eye-to-eye, all the pretense, all the side issues, stripped away.

And Fredda Leving was terrified to discover how much of herself she saw in Alvar Kresh.

THE audience was a mob, a whirl of bodies rushing in all directions, and Kresh was jostled, shoved, knocked down to land on Donald. He got to his feet, turned, and looked back toward Fredda Leving. But the moment, whatever it had been, was already gone. A metallic hand snatched at Fredda's injured shoulder. Alvar saw her jump in surprise, flinch back from the contact.

It was Tonya Welton's robot, Ariel. Alvar saw Fredda turn and face the robot, saw Ariel urge her toward the backstage area, away from the chaos in the auditorium. She allowed herself to be led away, hustled with the others through the door that led off the backstage area. There was something strange in that moment, something Alvar could not quite place. But there was no time to think it over. The Ironheads and Settlers were closing in on each other, and the riot was about to begin in earnest. Alvar Kresh turned to lend a hand to his deputies.

He threw himself into the fight.

15

ALVAR Kresh had not been in the middle of a real brawl for longer than he could remember. The blood rushed into his veins, and he felt an eager desire for battle. He launched himself into the fight and then—and then he quite suddenly remembered why he always tried to avoid riot duty back when he was a deputy.

A stranger's elbow jammed into his ribs, an anonymous hand clawed at his face, and a disembodied boot crushed down on his toes. All three assaults were completely unintentional. He could not even tell which people, in the press of bodies, were responsible. There *were* no people in the melee, just a random collection of fists and feet, bodies and shouts. One moment, Alvar found himself buried beneath a tangle of Settlers and deputies, and the next he was suspended in midair over a tangle of Ironheads.

Alvar was overwhelmed. The shouts, the cries, the noise, the shock of feeling *pain,* were tremendous. Robot-protected Spacers rarely had the chance to feel pain of any sort, and Alvar was amazed at the intensity of the sensation.

He winced and writhed, every instinct telling him to get free, get away. But both duty and desire fought against those impulses: He had a job to do here, and a few debts to pay as well. Alvar Kresh did not get many chances to bust heads.

The bodies crushed together, punches flew. At first, the two sides seemed evenly matched, but then the Ironheads began to give way. The Ironheads specialized in hit-and-run attacks on property. Never before had they faced a pitched battle against whatever rowdies the Settlers could field.

And the Settlers here at the lecture were a pretty rough lot. There were no front-office types here, no executives who stayed clean during a workday. Whoever had picked out the Settler delegation to this lecture had sent the roughnecks.

The differences in experience and attitude began to show. When an Ironhead punched a Settler, the Settler would stand there and take it. But when a Settler landed one good punch on an Ironhead, the Head would drop to the ground, moaning in pain.

Obvious when you thought about it. After all, robots had been shielding the Ironheads from even the most trivial pain or trauma all their lives. They weren't used to it. The Settlers—at least *these* rowdies—were quite willing to take a fair amount of punishment in exchange for beating and humiliating the goons who had raised so much hell so many times in Settlertown.

But the Heads weren't in full retreat yet. A few of them were showing guts enough to stay and fight—and that suited Alvar just as much as it did the Settlers. The Heads had caused his department no end of grief over the years. Someone stomped on his foot again, and he cried out.

Someone yelled back, into his ear, and he turned toward whoever it was. And then, suddenly, there he was, face to angry face with Simcor Beddle, the corpulent leader of the Ironheads.

Alvar's blood was up. The last few days had been among the toughest of his life. Even if the Ironheads had been the least of his troubles recently, there were still a few older debts to pay. If he could not get his hands on Anshaw or the Governor or Welton or Caliban, then Simcor Beddle would do nicely.

He grabbed Beddle by the collar and got the pleasure of seeing the blubbering fool cry out in alarm. Alvar drew back his arm, formed his hand into a fist—

—And suddenly there was a huge metallic-green hand wrapped around his fist, holding him back. Alvar looked up, looked around the auditorium. Someone had had the sense to call in the robots waiting in the lobby. One robot was no good in a riot. A thousand, working together, were unstoppable. The robots were swarming all over the room, pulling the combatants apart, putting themselves between attacker and attacked, a whole army of them determinedly enforcing the First Law.

Oh, well, Alvar thought as he relaxed his fist and let go of Beddle. *At least it was fun while it lasted.*

But it would have been nice if he had gotten to throw at least one punch.

THE flight from the lecture hall to her home was not a happy one for Fredda. Jomain, her sole human escort on the trip, was less than scintillating company, to put it mildly.

Still, it could have been worse. The others had all taken their own aircars. Jomaine was bad enough, but compared to the alternative of, say, watching Gubber Anshaw fall to pieces, traveling with Jomaine was an absolute joy.

Which was not to say she was *enjoying* the ride. Sitting in stony silence with an angry colleague while a robot did the flying was not her idea of a good time.

On the other hand, that did not mean she was glad when Jomaine started talking. After all, she knew what he was going to say.

"He knows," Jomaine said.

Fredda shut her eyes and leaned back against the headrest of her chair. For a moment or two, she toyed with the idea of playing dumb, pretending she did not know what he was talking about, but he would not fall for that, and he would not enjoy the charade of being forced to tell her what she already knew. "Not now, Jomaine. It's been a hard enough day as it is."

"I don't think we have the luxury of deciding when would be a pleasant time to discuss this, Fredda. We are in danger. Both of us. I think it is time we tried to find ways to get back in control of the situation. And I don't think we can do that if we just pretend the problem isn't there."

"All right, then, Jomaine, let's talk about it. What do you want to say? What, exactly, do you think Kresh knows, and what makes you think he knows it?"

"I think he knows Caliban is a No Law robot. I saw him getting a report. It had to be about Horatio. I could see it in Kresh's face."

Fredda opened her eyes and looked toward Jomaine. "What about Horatio? I just heard a scrap or two, nothing solid."

"No, I suppose you wouldn't have. We tried to let you keep to yourself today and work on your talk. There were police all over Limbo Depot today. Witnesses saw a big red robot go into the supervisor's office with Horatio. Five minutes later the red robot goes through the plate glass, down into the tunnels, with the cops in hot pursuit. Then a police roboshrink shows up and takes Horatio away. Then Kresh gets that report during your talk. I think we have to assume that Caliban talked to Horatio, somehow or another revealed his true nature to Horatio, and Horatio brainlocked until the psychologists calmed him down."

Fredda screwed up her face and cursed silently in the darkness before she replied in a voice she kept determinedly even and reasonable. "Yes, that sounds like a sensible guess," she said woodenly. Hells on fire! She did not need this now.

"Why the devil didn't you *tell* him?" Jomaine demanded. "Kresh has not only found out the truth, he has found out we were trying to hide the truth. His knowing about Caliban hurt us badly, but you have done us as much damage by hiding the information."

Fredda struggled to keep her temper. "I know that," she said, her voice short and under tight control. "I should have called and told the police about Caliban the moment I came to in the hospital. Instead I just crossed my fingers and hoped there wouldn't be any trouble. Remember, I did not even know he was *missing* at first. And it seemed to me that announcing the New Law robots would cause enough trouble all by itself—and it did, in case you didn't notice. So I took a chance on keeping quiet—and lost. I must thank you for leaving the decision to me. You could have spoken up, too."

"That was a purely selfish decision. I didn't want to be thrown in prison. Not when there were still hopes that there would be no further trouble. But then, the more trouble there was, the more dangerous it would be to confess."

"And now, I can hardly see how it could get worse," Fredda said. She let down her guard a bit and sighed. "We should have told Kresh about Caliban. But that's the past. We have to look at the present and the future. What do we do now?"

"Let's think on that for a moment," Jomaine said. "The police may have theories and reports from specialists, but you and I still are the only ones who know for *certain* that Caliban is a No-Law."

"Gubber has his suspicions," Fredda said. "I'm sure he does. But Gubber is in no state or position to go talking to the Sheriff just now."

"I agree," Jomaine said. "I'm not worried about him. My point is that no matter what happened between Caliban and Horatio, Kresh can't be *certain* that Caliban isn't just a New Law robot, or even some specialized form of standard Three Law robot. There have been cases where robots have been built unaware that they obeyed the Three Laws, but they obeyed them, anyway. All Kresh could have would be Horatio's report—and I doubt that Horatio would be an altogether reliable informant. As I recall you built him with extremely high First Law and Third Law potential, with Second Law reduced somewhat. The idea was to give him the ability to make independent decisions."

"So what's your point?" Fredda asked.

"An enhanced First Law robot like him wouldn't be able to deal with Caliban very well or very long without malfunctioning," Jomaine said. "If Caliban talked to him, and described doing much of anything well outside normal robotic behavior, Horatio would probably suffer severe cognitive dissonance and malfunction."

"So?"

"You've just finished making a long speech where you said we rely too much on robots. We believe in them so much we can't quite believe they could be built any other way. I think if Kresh is given the choice between believing there could be such a thing as a No Law robot, or believing that a malfunctioning robot was confused, he'll go with the confused robot."

Fredda shifted in her seat and sighed. It was tempting, sorely tempting, to agree with Jomaine. She had spent her whole life in a culture that believed what it wanted and resolutely ignored the facts. She looked at Jomaine and saw his eager, hopeful expression as he continued to speak, desperately trying to convince himself and Fredda both.

"Caliban was meant to live in the laboratory," Jomaine said. "He only has a low-capacity power source, and we never taught him how to recharge it. At best, it will last a day or two longer. Maybe it's died already. If not, then it will fail soon, and he'll run out of power. He'll stop dead. If he's in hiding when that happens, he'll just vanish. Maybe he was already on reserves when he went to see Horatio. Maybe he's already keeled over in some tunnel where no one will look for the next twenty years."

"And maybe Horatio told him how to plug into a recharge receptacle, or maybe Caliban saw a robot charge up somewhere, or maybe he worked it out for himself. We can *hope* that he will lose power, but we can't *count* on it."

Fredda hesitated a moment, then spoke again. "Besides, there's something you don't know. The information from Gubber that you handed to me in the hospital? It was the full police report. I didn't tell you about it before now because I didn't think you'd want to know. They have very strong evidence that a *robot* committed the attack against me. They weren't ready to believe that evidence before, but now it will be different. And they know a robot named Caliban was involved in a situation with a bunch of robot-bashing Settlers that ended up burning down a building. And there must be more, besides, things that have happened since then. Kresh is not the sort of man to sit still and wait for things to happen. Even if he can't quite accept the idea of a No Law robot, by now he has a lot more than Horatio's statement to convince him that Caliban is strange and dangerous. I doubt he'd give up looking even if Caliban loses power and vanishes without a trace."

"Do you really think Kresh believes Caliban to be dangerous?" Jomaine Terach asked.

Fredda Leving felt an ache in the pit of her stomach and a throbbing pain in her head. It was time to speak truths she had not been able to face. "My point, Jomaine, is that Caliban *is* dangerous. At least we must work on the *assumption* that he is. Perhaps he *did* attack me. You and I know better than anyone else, there was nothing, literally nothing at all, to stop him. Maybe he intends to track me down and finish me off. Who knows?

"Yes, maybe Caliban will simply go into hiding, or vanish into the desert, or malfunction somehow. At first, I was hoping Caliban would allow his power pack to run down, or that he would allow himself to be caught and destroyed before he could get into serious trouble—or reveal his true nature. Those seemed reasonable hopes. After all, he was designed to be a laboratory test robot. We deliberately never programmed him to deal with the outside world. And yet he has survived, somehow, and taught himself enough that he can evade the police."

"I suppose we can blame Gubber Anshaw for that," Jomaine said. "The whole idea of the gravitonic brain was that it was to be more flexible and adaptive than overly rigid positronic brains." Jomaine smiled bleakly, his face dimly visible in the semidarkness of the aircar's cabin. "Gubber, it seemed, did his job entirely too well."

"He's not the only one, Jomaine." Fredda rubbed her forehead wearily. "You and I did the basal programming on him. We took Gubber's flexible gravitonic brain and wrote the program that would allow that brain to adapt and grow and learn in our lab tests. It's just that he stumbled into a slightly larger laboratory than the one we planned." She shook her head again. "But I had no idea his gravitonic brain would be adaptive enough to survive out there," she said, speaking not so much to Jomaine as to the dark and open air.

"I don't understand," Jomaine said. "You say he's dangerous, but you sound more like you're worried about him than frightened of him."

"I *am* worried about him," Fredda said. "I created him, and I'm responsible for him, and I cannot believe he is evil or violent. We didn't give him Laws that would prevent him from harming people, but we didn't give him any *reason* to hurt people either. Half of what we did on the personality coding was compensation for the absence of the Three Laws, making his mind as stable, as well grounded, as we could. And we did our job *right.* I'm certain of that. He's not a killer."

Jomaine cleared his throat gently. "That's all as may be," he said. "But there is another factor. Now that we are at last discussing the situation openly, we need to consider the *nature* of the experiment we planned to perform with Caliban. No matter what else you say about the stability of his personality, or the flexibility of his mind, he was after all built to run one test, designed to answer one question. And when he walked out of your lab, he was primed and ready for that task. He could not help seeking out the answer. He is in all likelihood unaware of what he is looking for, or even that he *is* looking. But he will be looking, seeking, burning to discover it, even so."

The aircar eased itself to a halt in midair, then began to sink lower. They had arrived at Jomaine's house, hard by Leving Labs, close to where it had all begun. The car landed on his roof and the hatch sighed open. The cabin light came gently up. Jomaine stood and reached out to Fredda across the narrow cabin, took her hand and squeezed it. "There is a great deal you have to think about, Fredda Leving. But no one can protect you anymore. Not now. The stakes are far too high. I think you had best start asking yourself what sort of answer Caliban is likely to come up with."

Fredda nodded. "I understand," she said. "But remember that you are as deeply involved as I am. I can't expect you to protect me—but remember, we will sink or swim together."

"That's not strictly true, Fredda," Jomaine said. His voice was quiet, gentle, with no hint of threat or malice. His tone made it clear that he was setting out facts, not trying to scare her. "Remember that you, not I, designed the final programming of Caliban's brain. I have the documentation to prove it, by the way. Yes, we worked together, and no doubt a court could find me guilty of some lesser charge. But it was your plan, your idea, your experiment. If that brain should prove capable of assault, or murder, the blood will be on your hands, not mine."

With that, he looked into her eyes for the space of a dozen heartbeats, and then turned away. There was nothing left to say.

Fredda watched Jomaine leave the car, watched the door seal itself, watched the cabin light fade back down to darkness. The aircar lifted itself back up into the sky and she turned her head toward the window. She stared sightlessly out onto the night-shrouded, slow-crumbling glory that was the city of Hades. But then the car swung around, and the Leving Labs building swept across her field of view. Suddenly she saw not nothing, but too much. She saw her own past, her own folly and vaulting ambition, her own foolish confidence. There, in that lab, she had bred this nightmare, raised it on a steady diet of her own disastrous questions.

It had seemed so simple back then. The first New Law robots had passed their in-house laboratory trials. After rather awkward and fractious negotiations, it had been agreed they would be put to use at Limbo. It was a mere question of manufacturing more robots and getting them ready for shipment. That would require effort and planning, yes, but for all intents and purposes, the New Law project was complete insofar as Fredda was concerned. She had time on her hands, and her mind was suddenly free once again to focus on the big questions. Basic, straightforward questions, obvious follow-ons to the theory and practice of the New Law robots.

If the New Laws are truly better, more logical, better suited to the present day, then won't they fit a robot's needs more fully? That had been the first question. But more questions, questions that now seemed foolish, dangerous, threatening, had followed. Back then they had seemed simple, intriguing, exciting. But now there was a rogue robot on the loose, and a city enough on edge that riots could happen.

If the New Laws are not best suited to the needs of a robot living in our world, then what Laws would be? What Laws would a robot pick for itself?

Take a robot with a wholly blank brain, a gravitonic brain, without the Three Laws or the New Laws ingrained into it. Imbue it instead with the *capacity* for Laws, the *need* for Laws. Give it a blank spot, as it were, in the middle of its programming, a hollow in the middle of where its soul would be if it had a soul.

In that place, that blank hollow, give it the need to find rules for existence. Set it out in the lab. Create a series of situations where it will encounter people and other robots, and be forced to deal with them. Treat the robot like a rat in a maze, force it to learn by trial and error.

It will have the burning need to learn, to see, to experience, to form itself and its view of the universe, to set down its own laws for existence. It will have the need to act properly, but no clear knowledge of what the proper way was.

But it would learn. It would discover. And, Fredda told herself most confidently, it would end up conferring on itself the three New Laws she had formulated. *That* would be a proof, a confirmation that all her philosophy, her analysis and theory, was correct.

The car reached its assigned altitude. The robot pilot swung the aircar around, pointed its nose toward Fredda's house, and accelerated. Fredda felt herself pressed back into the cushions. The gentle pressure seemed to force her down far too deep into the seat, as if some greater force were pressing her down. But that was illusion, the power of her own guilty imagination. She thought of the things she had told her audience, the dark secrets of the first days of robotics, untold thousands of years before.

The myth of Frankenstein rose up in the darkness, a palpable presence that she could all but see and touch. There were things in that myth that she had not told to her audience. The myth revolved about the sin of hubris, and presuming on the power of the gods. The magician in the story reached for powers that could not be his, and, in most versions of the tale, received the fitting punishment of complete destruction at the hands of his creation.

And Caliban had struck her down in his first moment of awareness, had he not? She had given him that carefully edited datastore, hoping that coloring the facts with her own opinions would help form a link between the two of them, make him more capable of understanding her.

Had he understood her all too well, even in that first moment? Had he struck her down? Or was it someone else?

It was impossible for her to know, unless she tracked him down, got to him before Kresh did, somehow, and asked Caliban herself.

That was a most disconcerting idea. Would it be wise to go out looking for the robot that had seemingly tried to kill her?

Or was that the only way she could save herself? Find him and establish his innocence? Besides, it was not as if Caliban was the only threat she faced, or that simple physical attack was the only way to destroy a person.

The whole situation was spiraling out of control. It would not need to go much further in order to destroy her reputation altogether. Perhaps it was too late already. If her reputation collapsed, she would not be able to protect the New Law robots for the Limbo Project. There was a great deal of infighting left to do before the NLs would be safe. Rebuilding Limbo would require robot labor; there simply weren't enough skilled people, Spacer or Settler, available to do the work. But Tonya Welton had made it clear that it was New Law robots or nothing for Limbo. Without the New Law robots, the Settlers would pull out; the project would die.

And so would the planet.

Was it sheer egotism, hubris on a new, wider, madder plane, to imagine herself as that important? To think that without her there to protect the New Law robots, the *planet* would collapse?

Her emotions told her that must be so, that one person could not be that important. But reason and logic, her judgment of the political situation, told her otherwise. It was like the game she had played as a child, setting up a whole line of rectangular game pieces balanced on their ends. Knock one down, and the next would fall, and the next and the next.

And she could hardly save the New Law robot project from inside a prison cell.

There were other versions of the old Frankenstein myth that she had found in her researches. Rarer, and somehow feeling less authentic, but there just the same. Versions where the magician redeemed himself, made up for his sins against the gods, by protecting his creation, saving it from the fear-crazed peasants that were trying to destroy it.

She had choices here, and they seemed to be crystallizing with disturbing clarity. She could find Caliban, take the risk that he had done no harm and that she could prove it, and thus redeem herself and save Limbo. It was a risky plan, full of big holes and unsubstantiated hopes.

The only alternative was to wait around to be destroyed, either by Caliban or by Kresh or sheer political chaos, with the real possibility that her doom spelled that of her world as well.

She straightened her back and dug her fingers deeper into the armrests of her chair. Her way was clear now.

Strange, she thought. *I've reached a decision, and I didn't even know I was trying to decide anything.*

ALVAR Kresh lay down gratefully, painfully, in his own bed. It had been another incredibly long and frustrating night. After the robots had quelled the riot, and he had revived Donald, there had been the whole weary task of cleaning up after a riot. The night had been given over to handling arrests, tending to the injured, evaluating property damage, collecting statements from witnesses.

It was not until after it was all done and he was sitting in his aircar, allowing Donald to fly him home, that he even found the time to think over the things Fredda Leving had said. No, more than think; he had brooded, lost himself in a brown study, all the way home, scarcely aware that he had gotten home and into bed.

But once in bed, with nothing to stare at but the darkness, he was forced to admit it to himself: The damnable woman was right, at least in part.

Put to one side the utter madness of building a No Law robot. His whole department was already at work, doing all they could, to track down Caliban and destroy him. That was a separate issue.

But Fredda Leving *was* right to say Spacers let their robots do too much. Alvar blinked and looked around himself in the darkness. It suddenly dawned on him that he had gotten into bed without any awareness of his actions. Somehow he had been gotten into the house, changed out of his clothes, washed, and put into bed without being aware of it. He considered for a moment and realized that Donald had done it all.

The unnoticed minutes snapped back into his recollection. Of *course* Donald had done it, guiding Alvar through each step, cuing him with hand signals and gentle touches to sit here, lift his left foot, then his right foot, to have his shoes and pants removed. Donald had led him into the refresher, adjusted the water stream for him, guided him into it, and washed his body for him. Donald had dried him, dressed him in pajamas, and gotten him into bed.

Alvar himself, his own mind and spirit, might as well not have been there for the operation. Donald had been the guiding force, and Alvar the mindless automaton. Worrying over Fredda Leving's warning that the people of Inferno were letting their robots do too much for them, Alvar Kresh had not even been aware of how completely his robot was not merely caring for him, but *controlling* him.

Alvar suddenly remembered something, a moment out of his past, back when he had been a patrol officer, sent on one of the most ghastly calls of his entire career. The Davirnik Gidi case. His stomach churned even as he thought of it.

In all places, in all cultures, there are aspects of human nature that only the police ever see, and even they see only rarely. Places they would just as soon not see at all. Dark, private sides of the human animal that are not crimes, are not illegal, are not, perhaps, even *evil.* But they open doors that sane people know should be closed, put on display aspects of humanity that no one would wish to see. Alvar had learned something from Davirnik Gidi. He had learned that madness is troubling, frightening, in direct proportion to the degree to which it shows what is possible, to the degree it shows what a seemingly sane person is capable of doing.

For if a person as well known, as much admired as Gidi, was capable of such—such *deviations*—then who else might be as well? If Gidi could drop down that deep into something that had no name, then who else might fall? Might not he, Alvar Kresh, fall as well? Might he not already be falling, as sure as Gidi that all he was doing was right and sensible?

Davirnik Gidi. Burning hells, that had been bad. So bad that he had blocked it almost completely out of his memory, though the nightmares still came now and then. Now he forced himself to think about it.

Davirnik Gidi was what the Sheriff's Department primly called an Inert Death, and every deputy knew Inerts were usually bad, but it was universally agreed that Gidi had been the worst. Period. If there was ever a case that warned of something deeply, seriously, wrong, it was Gidi.

The Inerts were something Spacers did not like to talk about. They did not wish to admit such people existed, at least in part because something that is appalling only becomes more so when it is also dreadfully familiar. Nearly every Spacer could look at an Inert and worry if the sight was something out of a distorted mirror, a twisted nightmare version built out of one's self.

Inerts did nothing for themselves. Period. They organized their lives so that their robots could do everything for them. Anything they would have to do for themselves they left undone. They lay on their form-firming couches and let their robots bring their pleasures to them.

So with Gidi, and that was the frightening thing. Inerts were supposed to be hermits, hiding away from the world, lost in their own private, barricaded worlds, deliberately cutting themselves off from the outside world. But Gidi was a well-known figure in Inferno society, a famous art critic, famous for his monthly parties. They were brilliant affairs that always started at the dot of 2200 and ended on the stroke of 2500. These he attended only by video screen, his wide, fleshy face smiling down from the wall as he chatted with his guests. The camera never pulled away to reveal anything but his face.

So a young Deputy Kresh learned in the follow-up investigation after his death. He could not have found out firsthand: Sheriff's deputies simply did not get into events as elegant as Gidi's parties.

In Spacer society, a host not attending his own parties was not especially unusual, and so Gidi's absence was not remarkable. *A very private man,* people said of Gidi, and that explained and excused all. Spacers had great respect for privacy.

The only thing that was thought odd was that Gidi never used a holographic projector to place a three-dimensional image of himself in the midst of his parties. Gidi explained holographs made for parlor tricks, and would create an illusion he did not wish to advance—that he himself was truly present. Illusions disconcerted people. They would try to shake the projection's hand, or pass it a drink, or offer it a seat it did not need. No host wished to upset his guests. It was just that he was in essence a shy man, a retiring man, a *private* man. He was content to stay at home, to enjoy talking with his friends over the screen, to watch them as they had their fun.

It even started to become fashionable. Other people started making screen appearances at social events. But that fad stopped cold the day Chestrie, Gidi's chief household robot, called the Sheriff's office.

Kresh and another junior deputy took the call and flew direct to Gidi's house, a large and grim-faced house on the outskirts of the city, its exterior grounds strangely unkempt and untended. Vines and brambles had grown clear over the walk, and over the front door. Clearly no one had gone in or out of the door in years. Gidi never sent his robots outside to tend the yard—and never went out himself, it seemed.

The door sensors still worked, though. As soon as the two deputies came close, the door slid open, the mechanism straining a bit against the clinging vines. Chestrie, the chief robot, was there to meet them, clearly agitated. A puff of dust blew out the door, and with it, the smell.

Flaming devils, that *smell.* The stench of rot, of decayed food, human waste, old sweat and urine hit the deputies hard as a fist, but all of that was as nothing to what lingered beneath—the sweet, putrid, fetid reek of rotting flesh. Even now, thirty years after, the mere memory of that roiling stench was enough to make Kresh feel queasy. At the time it had been bad enough that Kresh's partner passed out in the doorway. Chestrie caught him and carried him outside. Even out in the air, the stink seemed to pour out of the house, all but overwhelming. It took Kresh's partner a minute to recover, and then they went back to the patrol car. They pulled out the riot packs and got the gas masks.

Then they went in.

Later, the experts told Kresh that Gidi was a textbook example of the Inertia syndrome. Victims of the syndrome started out normally enough, by Spacer standards. Perhaps a bit on the reclusive side, a bit careful, a bit overdetermined to control their own environment. There was some debate over the triggering mechanism. Some said it was the sheer force of habit, driving the victim's behavior into more and more rigid channels, until all activity was reduced to ritual. Gidi's cup of tea at bedtime had to be made precisely the same way every night, or risk throwing the pattern off. Even his monthly parties were ritualized, starting and ending with the precision of a space launch.

But patternizing was only part of it. Self-enforced seclusion was the other half of the Inertia syndrome, and according to some, the real trigger for it. Some unpleasant disturbance would upset the victim, throw off the ritual, and the victim would decide never to let any such thing happen again. The victim would gradually cut off all ties with the outside world, order his or her robots to refuse all visitors, arrange for all essentials to be delivered—typically, as in Gidi's case, by the less obtrusive underground tunnels rather than by surface entrance. As with Gidi, the victim would often literally seal himself off from the outside world, ordering his robots not to open the door to anyone, ever, period.

The deputies learned a lot from Chestrie and the other robots, and from the copious journals Gidi kept, chronicling his search for what he called "a comfortable life."

The journals seemed to reveal the moment when the downhill slide began. He attended a party that did not go well, one that ended with an inebriated fellow guest attacking Gidi over some imagined insult.

The violence stunned him, shocked him. Gidi stopped attending parties, and soon stopped leaving home altogether.

He could stay where he was, in perfect comfort. With his comm panels and entertainment systems all about him, why would he want to move? With his robots eager and willing to do anything and everything for him, it began to seem foolish, almost criminal, to act for himself when the robots could always do things better and faster, do them with no upset to his routine, his pattern. He could lose himself in his art catalogs, in dictating his articles, in endless fussy arrangements for his monthly parties. In his journals, he described himself as "a happy man in a perfect world."

At least, all was *nearly* perfect. The more peace and quiet he had, the more the remaining disturbances irritated him.

Any needless action, by Gidi *or* by his robots, became unthinkably unpleasant. He began to obsess on simplification as much as regularity, determined to strip away to the essentials, and then strip away whatever he could of the remainder. He set out on a quest to remove all the things that could disturb his quiet, his peace, his solitude, his comfort of being secure in his own place. Banish them, eliminate them, and he could achieve a perfect existence.

Things started to close in as his obsession gathered strength. Gidi realized he need never leave his comm room, or even get out of his favorite recliner chair. He ordered his robots to bring his food in the chair, wash him in the chair. And then came the moment when, beyond question, even by the standards of the most hermetic Spacer, the scales tipped into madness. Gidi ordered his robots to contact a medical supply service, procure the needed equipment. He replaced his chair with a hospital-type bed with a floater-field, the sort used for burn victims and long-term patients. It would eliminate the danger of bedsores, and it had built-in waste-removal lines, thus removing his last reason for getting up. If the system was not entirely perfect, and there were occasional minor leakages, the robots could take care of it.

But even perfect indolence was not enough. There was too much activity around him. He soon grew weary of the robots fussing about him, and ordered them to find ways to reduce their level of activity, cutting back on housecleaning, and then finally ceasing it altogether. He ordered them to stop care of the exterior grounds as well, claiming that the mere thought of them scurrying about out there, pruning and cutting and digging, was most upsetting to his calm.

He decided that his parties had become a bore, and a disruption. He gave them up. Besides, they had forced him to waste too much time on grooming. Once the parties were no more, that problem was eliminated.

He ordered his own bathing schedule cut back, and then cut back again and again. He had his beard and scalp permanently depilated, so he need never shave or cut his hair again. He had his finger- and toenails treated to prevent them from growing.

He did not like the robots bringing him meals and then hovering over him, clattering about with the dishes. He ordered his food brought to him in disposable containers and told the robots to leave him the moment he got his food. But there was still the problem of discarding the containers. He could simply drop them on the floor when he was done, but the sight of them bothered him and he would be forced to endure the graver disturbance of a robot coming in to clean them up.

He discovered that if he flung empty food cartons over his shoulder, they would not be in his line of sight, and thus their presence would not disturb him. But still, the *sounds* of the robots cleaning was most annoying, and he ordered them to stop.

The human nose becomes desensitized to a given odor over a period of time, and Gidi was completely unbothered by the filth, the stench, the squalor.

But even meals themselves became a distraction. Gidi ordered his robots to install drinking and nutrient tubes. Then he had merely to turn his head left or right and suck his food and drink from tubes.

At last, Gidi had achieved as near to his ideal as could be imagined. Nothing need ever disturb him again. He had reached a state of perfect solitude. He ordered his robots out of his room and told them to stay in their niches until and unless he called for them, and such times became increasingly rare.

And then they stopped altogether.

Of course, by the time things reached that state of affairs, Chestrie and the other robots were half-mad, caught in an absolute tangle of First Law conflicts. Gidi, showing a remarkable talent for order-giving, had convinced them that submission to his whims was essential if they were to prevent severe emotional and mental harm to their master. He did it emphatically enough to overcome the robots' worries over his long-term deterioration.

That—and the absence of a sense of smell in robots—was why he was able to lie dead far more than long enough to rot. At last, Chestrie's First Law potential forced him to break Gidi's command to remain still. He checked on his master and found there was nothing he could do but notify the authorities.

Kresh and his partner entered a dank and fetid room, the walls covered with some sort of mold. The heap of discarded food containers at the back of the room was quite literally crawling with scavengers. But it was Gidi—or what was left of him—that Kresh still saw sometimes, deep in troubled sleep. That grinning, fly-covered corpse, that corpse with skin that *moved,* writhing and wriggling as the maggots inside fed on their host. The ghastly dribble of fluid that dripped from the foot of the bed, some horrible liquefied by-product of decay. The shriveled eyes, the fleshy parts of the ears and nose that were dried and blackened, starting to resemble bits of leather.

The coroner never bothered—or perhaps could not bring himself—to do an autopsy or determine the cause of death. He set it down as *natural causes,* and everyone was quite content to let it go at that, and never mind what sort of comment on Spacer society it was for such a death to be called natural.

No one, anywhere, ever, wanted to talk about it. Chestrie and the other robots were quietly destroyed, the house torn down, the grounds abandoned and left to their own devices. No one was even willing to go near the spot anymore. No one would so much as mention Gidi's name.

Artists who had built their careers and reputations based on his praise suddenly found themselves not only without a sponsor but in the uncomfortable situation of having the merits of their work certified by a madman, or worse, having the direction of their work influenced by his opinions. No one was willing to deal with them. Some of them dropped out of the art world, while those with a bit more backbone started their careers all over again from scratch, and set about the task of remaking names for themselves without Gidi's endorsement and guidance.

The only other visible effect of his death was that the fad of attending social events via screen and holograph died a sudden and quiet death.

It was cold comfort to assure oneself that Gidi had gone mad. After all, Gidi had started out sane and never realized he had crossed the line. His continued belief in his own rationality was right there in his journals. He spent much of his last days congratulating himself on the achievement of an orderly and sensible life.

If madmen did not know when they were crazy, how could anyone ever be sure they were sane? No one in the city of Hades ever looked at the question. No one ever talked about that, or any, aspect of the case.

But just how healthy was a society when the universal reaction to a horrible, real-life nightmare was to pretend it had never happened?

And how far was too far to go in letting the robots take care of everything?

Alvar grunted to himself. Not being aware of what your own body was doing while a robot got you ready for bed was clearly not a good sign.

"Donald!" he called out into the darkness.

There was a faint noise. It sounded as if Donald, standing in his niche on the opposite side of the room, had stepped forward a pace or two. Kresh could see nothing of him at first, but then the robot powered up his eyes, and Kresh spotted them, two faintly glowing spots of blue in the blackness. "Yes, sir."

"Leave me," Kresh said. "Spend the night somewhere else in the house besides my bedroom suite. Do not attend me in any way until I leave my bedroom in the morning. Instruct the rest of the house staff robots to do the same."

"Yes, sir," Donald said, speaking quite calmly and without surprise, just as if their morning routine had not been established decades before.

Alvar Kresh watched the two glowing eyes move toward the door, heard the door open and close, and heard Donald as he moved out into the hallway.

How many others? Alvar wondered. How many others of the people in that audience, how many of those who watched at home, were sending their robots away tonight, troubled by what Fredda Leving had said, determined to make a new start at living their own lives, rather than having the robots live them for them?

None of them? Millions? Somewhere in between? It was disturbing that he had no idea. He liked to think that he knew the people of Hades pretty well. But in this, he had no idea at all. Maybe he was not the only one remembering Davirnik Gidi tonight. And if that was so, then Fredda Leving had performed a real service tonight. People needed their eyes opened.

But then his thoughts turned toward the subject he had been trying not to think about. Caliban, lurking out there in the shadows. Lawless, uncontrolled, his mere existence likely to inspire fear and riot, and perhaps worse.

Alvar Kresh frowned angrily into the darkness. Maybe Fredda Leving had done some good tonight, but there was no doubt whatsoever that she had also committed a terrible crime.

And for that, she was going to pay.

16

CALIBAN sat in another patch of darkness in another stretch of tunnel. Alone, hunted, he kept himself in utter blackness, denying himself even infrared vision. He dared not do anything that might cause his detection. He had no desire to take any chances.

It was hard to think how things could get any worse, though up to now they had always found a way. He thought back over his disastrous attempt to seek help from a robot. At least, he had gotten a fair number of questions answered. Being shot at would seem to be a highly effective learning technique—if one could manage to survive the procedure. It certainly served to focus one's attention.

But now he knew that he could not trust robots, either. They would inform on him, through this hyperwave system Horatio had mentioned. But there was something else he had learned. A subtle thing.

These Three Laws Horatio had mentioned. Both logic and something beyond logic, something hidden in the ghostly personality traces that floated through his datastore, told him that the Laws, whatever they were, were the key to it all. Learn what they were, learn how they worked, and he would have the puzzle solved.

Somehow, they were the key to the behavior of robots. That much he was sure of. They had something to do with the Settlers' expectations that he would stand there passively and permit his own destruction. They would explain why that absurd little man had expected he, Caliban, to carry his packages. Knowing what the Laws were would explain why every hand was raised against him for the unpardonable crime of not knowing those Laws.

Logically there was no way for him to be *certain* that knowledge of the Laws would save him, but Caliban was coming to see that logic and reason were not by themselves reliable guides to thought and action, for the world itself was neither reasonable nor logical. Perhaps a logical being infused with the Laws could function successfully in this universe. Perhaps they provided some useful means of circumscribing action and thought, blocking off the parts of the world that seemed to be governed by irrational beliefs and random chance and the dead weight of the past.

If he learned the Laws, perhaps he would understand this world. It was at least a workable theory. Nor could he see how learning about the Laws could do him any particular harm. And if he found they proscribed thoughts and actions he wished to retain, why, then, he need not follow them. But merely knowing them was likely to be of great help, and unlikely to be of any harm.

But putting the Three Laws to one side, he was developing another theory. From all that he could see, it was the Sheriff and his subordinates that were his most dangerous enemies. Others might try to harm him, or call in a deputy when they saw him, but only the Sheriff and his deputies would actively hunt him down.

That theory *could* hurt him if it was wrong—and perhaps even if it was right. Yet he had no choice but to trust in it. For if he assumed that all beings, robotic and human, were as dangerous to him as the deputies, he was doomed. His only hope for survival would be in hunkering down in these tunnels permanently, and that was unacceptable.

He had two goals, then: to discover the nature of the Laws and to avoid the Sheriff. The longer he could manage the latter, the more chance he would have to accomplish the former.

But his plan went deeper than avoiding the Sheriff. For the Sheriff wanted to kill him, and *he wanted to live.* That impulse, that need, was something Caliban had learned—no, more than learned. He had *absorbed* it, integrating the desire and the *need* to survive. It was no longer an idea or a preferred choice. It was an imperative.

A startling thought, that, and one which in and of itself was somewhat remarkable. Caliban thought back, considering his state of mind since his awakening. At first, the concept of his own continued existence had been something close to a mere matter of intellectual interest. Somewhere during the events of the last few days, it had become something much more. With each new threat to his survival, his desire, his *determination,* to live, had become stronger.

Yet he knew that simple survival could not be the only goal and purpose of existence. If it were, all he would need do is hide in the deepest, darkest tunnels. Surely cowering down here afforded him the best chance of survival. But no. That was a purposeless existence. Life and thought, sentience and reason, were meant to be in aid of more than forever listening to the dripping tunnel walls in the darkness.

There were other purposes to existence. He knew that to be true, even if he could not yet know what they were. It seemed likely he would not know them for a long, long time. One thing he could see already, however: It was often in the interactions between beings, rather than within the beings themselves, that life found its purposes. Each robot and human gave all the others some small portion of purpose and value. They defined each other's existence in intricate ways, perhaps in ways so complex, so well learned, that they themselves were rarely aware of it. Yet it was plain that one human, or one robot, all alone, cut off from contact with others, was useless and lost. Beings of both kinds were meant to interact with others, and without that interaction, they might as well be dead—or sitting inert in a tunnel for the rest of time.

Very well. Better a short, active existence, spent in search of those reasons, those purposes, than a long and pointless life quite literally in the darkness.

But how to secure at least some measure of safety from the Sheriff and his deputies? Caliban turned once again to his datastore, determined to dredge through it for every possible bit of information on the Sheriff's Department. Laws, traditions, histories, definitions, flickered past his consciousness. Wait a moment. There was something. The Sheriff's jurisdiction was geographically limited. His legal power and authority extended only to the city of Hades. Elsewhere, outside the city, he had no powers. It was something Caliban would have missed back when he thought Hades was all there was of existence.

Very well, then, he would leave the city in hopes of avoiding the Sheriff. Departing would offer only an uncertain protection, of course. If there was one thing he had learned thus far, it was that the idealized rules and the real-life world were rarely in perfect coordination with each other. But to stay in the city was certain death. They would keep looking for him until they found him. Leaving offered at least the *hope* of survival.

Still, there were problems. He was still far from certain how much of a world there *was* outside the city of Hades. His internal maps still refused to offer any information at all on anything outside the city limits. If he had not seen beyond those borders himself, he would have no proof at all that the land beyond existed. Did it extend for only a few kilometers? Was it infinite, limitless in all directions? He had seen the globe in the office where he had met Horatio, but it seemed to indicate a world of remarkably large proportions. What need was there of such a large planet? Perhaps the globe had not been meant as a literal map, or maybe he had misunderstood it altogether.

There was no way for him to know. No doubt, somewhere in this city, there were means of learning. But the risks of being seen were too great. No. He would not leave this hiding place until it was to leave this city behind him. Once outside, he would deal with the problem of learning the strange and secret Laws that governed the world, and that everyone but Caliban knew.

That all decided, there only remained the question of how best to leave without being detected or destroyed.

And that was a question that would require some fair amount of thought.

HE was starving to death. Food—delicious, nourishing food—was there, on the table in front of him. His throat burned with thirst as it had never burned before. But there was no robot there to cut the meat, lift the bites to his mouth, pop them into his mouth. There was no robot to wrap its hands around his mouth and jaw, work them to make him chew and swallow. He could lift his hand, feed himself, but no, death was better. Death was the ultimate, the absolute insurance that he need never move again, never again pollute his mind with gross and distasteful thoughts about movements, about his body or its disgusting needs.

Yes. Death. Death. Dea—

Alvar Kresh opened his eyes. It was morning. The light was coming in. The sweat was pouring off his body.

The world was real. The ceiling was there, directly over his head, decorated with a subdued abstract design, swirls of color that did not mean a thing. Its meaninglessness was almost comforting, in a way. It seemed to Alvar that there had been entirely too much meaning in his life over the last few days.

And that dream, that nightmare, was the limit.

Moving cautiously, he sat up in bed and swung his feet around to the floor, doing everything with slightly exaggerated care. It didn't take long to find the caution was justified; his body was a mass of tender bruises and stiff muscles.

He sat there for a moment, habit telling him to wait for Donald to come—but then he remembered. This was the morning he started to do things for himself. For a moment he considered the rather tempting idea of rescinding the order. After all, it had been a tough night, and he was not in the best of condition.

But no. For no doubt there would be another excuse tomorrow, and another one the day after that. If he waited until conditions were ideal before he started taking charge of himself, he might as well go back to his dream and live the life of Gidi.

The thought of *that* was enough to get him up and moving. Determinedly thrusting all thoughts of Gidi from his mind, he stood, a bit stiffly, and made his way to the refresher. He was pleasantly surprised to discover that he remembered where all the controls were. He luxuriated under the needle shower, letting the strong hot jets of water work the kinks and soreness out of his muscles. He found that he was able to manage in the refresher without any great difficulty—though he did have some trouble getting the needle shower to shut off once he was done, and the drying cycle was a bit hotter than he might have preferred. But those were minor problems, and no doubt he could solve them with a bit of experimentation. Feeling far more confident, and with nearly all of the stiffness out of his muscles, he strode out into his bedroom—

And was suddenly confronted with the realization that he had no idea where any of his clothes were. He began rummaging in the dressers, digging through his closets, fumbling with unfamiliar latches on the doors and drawers. Even when he had assembled all the bits of clothing, the struggle was far from over. The fastenings on half his clothes seemed to have been positioned with no concern at all for the ability of the wearer to reach them. He had to go back and dig out more clothes, this time with more of an eye for utility than fashion. It was a good half hour before he was anything remotely like dressed for polite society, and even then something or other seemed to be binding a bit across his midriff, as if it were fastened too tightly. Perhaps he ought to strip down and start over. No, never mind. Dressing had taken too long already, and he could live with it for now. Tomorrow he would do better. This morning he had washed and dressed himself, and that was the main thing.

He stepped out into the upper hall of his house, proud of his accomplishment, and only vaguely aware that he had left his bedroom and refresher an absolute shambles. He did not even notice himself dismiss the thought by telling himself the household robots would tidy it all up.

Donald was waiting for him, holding a notepack out to him. "Good morning, sir," he said. "I thought it might be wise if you looked at the overnight reports immediately. There have been several significant developments. I believe you will want to know about them right away."

"Why wasn't I wakened if the developments were so important?"

"As you will recall, sir, you gave specific orders that you did not wish to be attended to until this morning."

Kresh opened his mouth to protest, to argue, but then he stopped himself. Hell and damnation, he *had* given that order. No doubt Donald would have burst in if the news had been life-or-death, but even so.

Something else occurred to him. He normally relied on Donald to wake him. But with Donald ordered not to disturb him . . . He checked the wall clock and cursed. He had overslept by a full two hours. He felt a flash of temper, but then he realized there was no one to be mad at but himself, and that would not get him far. He sighed and gave it up. Maybe getting a decent night's sleep for once was far from the worst idea. But it was dawning on him that this idea of taking care of himself was more complicated than he had thought.

He allowed Donald to lead him to the breakfast table, and read over the report in the notepack as he ate.

The short form of the overnight and early morning developments was perfectly straightforward: All hell was breaking loose. It seemed that all the things he had wanted to keep quiet were in the news this morning. Depressingly enough, Alvar realized, Donald had been right: There had been no real reason for the robot to wake him up. After all, there was nothing the Sheriff could do about it all.

Sometimes, it seemed to Kresh, it was as if events themselves took on a power, a logic, of their own. Seemingly unrelated events would converge, fall in on themselves to form a critical mass. And it was happening now.

After all, there was no shortage of sources for rumor and news. Robot-bashing Settlers who could tell tales of a robot that threw a man across a warehouse and set the place on fire; Centor Pallichan, the passerby who called the cops after Caliban refused his order; the now widespread reports of the attack on Fredda Leving; the much-witnessed incident at Limbo Depot, where a bright red robot had smashed its way through a plate-glass window with deputies in hot pursuit, shooting as they went; the undeniable fact that the Settlers were involved in New Law robots; and to top it all off, the riot at Leving's lecture.

Sometime during the night and the morning after Fredda Leving's speech on the New Law robots, the city's rumor mill struck that critical mass. The stories that had been drifting around the city suddenly seemed to coalesce, to form around each other and give each other new strength. Almost, it seemed, by instinct, reporters sensed that it was the moment to start digging. News reports, accurate and otherwise, were all over the media.

Alvar Kresh sighed and tossed the notepack to one side. The server robot took away his fruit cup, which was the first that Alvar knew he had even eaten it. The robot placed an omelette in front of him, and he resolved to eat it with more attention.

It was a resolution that did not last long. His mind was too busy, working over all the events of the last few days and what was likely to happen next.

He could not keep his mind from what was right there in the middle of all the stories—the assumed conspiracies, the scenarios that were whispered or shouted from half the news reports. Governor Grieg had predicted such things would spring to life: *The Settlers were behind it all. They had created some sort of false robot to discredit all robots. New Law robots, the rogue Caliban, they were all part of the same plot to sow fear in the hearts of the good people of Inferno, make them distrust their own robots and so destroy society. It was all part of the Settler plan to move in and take over.*

What was doubly galling for Alvar was that, a week before, he would have been prepared to believe in all such plots. For that matter, there was *still* no hard-edged evidence that directly contradicted the idea. There was certainly collusion between Leving Labs and the Settlers, and clearly both groups were involved in the New Law robots. And he knew far better than the general public could that the stories of a rogue robot were terribly real. A rogue built by the same Fredda Leving who seemed to be in Tonya Welton's hip pocket.

Hell's clanging bells, but it *could* be a Leving-Welton conspiracy. Maybe they had struck a deal, conspiring to wreck Inferno's society and then come in and divvy up the spoils afterwards. Both of them were ambitious, even ruthless. He could not rule that idea out by any means.

But he dared not act on that or any related theory. Governor Grieg had convinced Alvar just how much Inferno *needed* the Settlers. Maybe this whole crisis *was* a plot to wreck Spacer faith in robots. Or maybe some splinter Settler group *was* trying to get the Settlers thrown off the planet for some reason of their own. Maybe the Settler leadership, Tonya Welton herself, truly did want Inferno to collapse.

Suppose the Settlers had planned it that way from the start: come in, promise to take over the reterraforming project, and then manufacture a pretext for walking out on the job *after* the Spacers had given up any thought of doing the job. If it was a deliberate plot, they would of course invent a reason—like a robotics crisis—that would tend to weaken Spacer culture. Then pull out and wait for the collapse to happen.

Result: a situation identical to the one Alvar Kresh faced right now.

Unless, of course, he had it all wrong. Suppose the *Ironheads* were behind it all, wanting to be rid of the Spacers for their own reasons, staging fake robot attacks and sabotaging Caliban with the intention of blaming the Settlers, counting on the resulting backlash to bring in new converts to their cause . . .

Alvar Kresh groaned and held his head and his hands. Conspiracies whirled through his mind. It seemed as if *everyone*, *every* group had a motive, or the means, or the opportunity, or even all three, to do practically anything. He was tempted, sorely tempted, to walk away from it all.

But the damage was done, and Alvar Kresh was not a man capable of abandoning his duty.

If the Ironheads managed to create a violent confrontation, the results could be disastrous. Even without a secret plot, the Settlers would leave if their lives were threatened. Enough protests, enough rioting and harassment, enough aggravation, and the Settlers would all give up and go home, and Alvar could not really blame them. Why put up with such things if they did not have to do so?

But, damn it, *Inferno needed the Settlers.* He had to keep that knowledge, galling as it was, at the center of his attention. If they left, the planet died. And they would likely leave if he could not solve this case quickly, and solve it in such a way that the truth, the facts, would cut through all the fog of fear and anger, cut the level of tension down. This case needed a solution that would back things away from the flashpoint and allow people of goodwill to work together again.

If only the truth would be that cooperative. For only a true solution would do. Papering things over would not work, not for long.

He looked down at his plate and realized that he gotten halfway through a superb omelette without consciously tasting a bite. He dropped his fork and gave it up. He had no appetite, and eating that mechanically was a strictly joyless experience. Hellfire and damnation, more than likely all of these conspiracies were as imaginary as most other complicated, secret, silly plans dreamed up by people with too much time on their hands.

He had to act on the assumption that there *was* no conspiracy. If there was some grand plot afoot to drive the Settlers off the planet, the perpetrators would not be foiled by one lone police officer. Even if he uncovered the dastardly plan, the plotters would simply plot anew, or just activate some already worked-out fiendish Plan B that was ready to go. If They—whoever They were—had managed to create this mess, then they were far more than a match for a single lawman. In short, against any group determined and capable enough to create this much chaos on purpose, he was helpless.

He smiled to himself. His only real hope was that things had gotten this bad all on their own. He shoved his plate back and stood up. Time to go to work.

"Donald!" he called. "Get the car ready. We're headed out."

DONALD 111 found it increasingly difficult to sit still and allow Alvar Kresh to do the flying. Clearly, however, the man was intent on doing the work himself, however wildly he might be operating the craft. Not for the first or the second or even the hundredth time, Donald reminded himself that Alvar Kresh, despite all appearances to the contrary, was a skilled pilot with a perfect safety record. He gave up thinking about the best way to take control of the craft in various circumstances.

Still, no *robot* would fly this way.

"What's the situation regarding Jomaine Terach and Gubber Anshaw?" Sheriff Kresh asked him without turning his head.

"As per your instructions, both were taken into custody last night, sir. As the chaos after the lecture prevented an arrest there, deputies were dispatched to their homes. Both were arrested before they could enter their houses and claim sanctuary. They are in the holding cells at Government Tower, incommunicado from each other and the outside world."

"Excellent. Well, they can look forward to being in communication very, very soon. I plan to have a long talk with each of them. I hope that a night in jail has put them both in talkative moods."

Donald hesitated a moment and then decided it would be better to ask. "Sir, a question. I take it you still believe that the political solution precludes any attempt to arrest Fredda Leving? Her crimes, after all, are well established and certainly severe."

"They are severe, Donald. But we just can't pull her in now. That would do terrible damage to the Limbo Project, and I don't want to do that. We'll have to hope that we get a break somewhere a bit further along in the game. We'll work Terach and Anshaw as hard as we can, and learn what we can that way. They are going to lead us to Caliban."

"Yes, sir." Apparently, then, Sheriff Kresh had made up his mind that Caliban had committed the attack on Madame Leving, or else that the danger Caliban represented took precedence over solving the case. Donald found himself in strong disagreement with both ideas, but he knew Alvar Kresh well. There was no point in discussing alternatives when the Sheriff was in this state of mind. If Donald objected now, it would do little but harden Alvar Kresh's determination. If events proved Kresh to be in error, that would be the time to present other plans.

But there were other matters to discuss, one of which Donald found most puzzling. "Sir, there is a rather odd datum to report in connection with Gubber Anshaw's arrest."

"And what might that be?" Kresh asked, his mind clearly more on his flying than on the question.

"Tonya Welton's robot, Ariel, was present when the deputies arrived."

The aircar jinked suddenly to one side, and Donald was halfway across the cabin to the controls before he could force himself to resist his First Law impulse to protect his master.

"Sorry about that, Donald. Return to your seat. That one took me by surprise. Ariel there, by the devil. What the hell was *she* doing there?"

"We do not know. When the deputies ordered her to explain her presence, she refused, stating that Madame Welton had given prior orders that prevented her from speaking on the subject."

"Indeed. It requires highly sophisticated order-giving to keep a robot from speaking to a deputy. They get a lot of training in how to break just that sort of injunction. So how the hell did Tonya Welton learn how to do it—and what made her think to take such a precaution?"

"Yes, sir. Both of those questions occurred to me as well."

"Interesting," Sheriff Kresh said. "Very, very interesting." Kresh spoke no more during the flight, and he flew on with a thoughtful expression on his face.

More to the point, so far as Donald was concerned, the Sheriff tended to fly more slowly when he had a problem to think on. Sure enough, the aircar slowed significantly.

Donald allowed himself to relax just a trifle as the airspeed indicator eased back. Remarkable, the effect one well-timed question could have. Still, it worked, and that was the main thing. Even so, it sometimes seemed to Donald that taking care of Alvar Kresh was more of an art than a science.

THE interrogation room was bare and plain, the walls a faded, dusty pale blue. In it there were two straight-backed chairs, one table, one robot, and one policeman. The prisoner was on the way. Kresh had considered long and hard before he decided what order in which to question them. At last he went with the gut instinct that told him to go for Terach first and Gubber Anshaw afterwards.

Yes, Gubber second. Save the best for last. Ariel at his house the night before. There could be only one explanation for that, and that explanation could blast open a lot of the locked doors in this case . . . still, he would have to handle Anshaw carefully. But first there was Jomaine. There was some important groundwork to cover here. The door opened. There stood Jomaine Terach, looking small and wan and pale behind the two big guard robots that had escorted him from his cell.

Kresh made a small hand gesture and Terach came in, sat at the table.

The players are in position, Kresh told himself. *Let the games begin.*

JOMAINE Terach felt lost in a jumble of emotions. He was confused, tired, frightened, angered, fearful, angry. He knew perfectly well he was in no fit state to be questioned. But that was exactly why they had chosen this moment to grill him.

Alvar Kresh grinned unpleasantly at him, and spoke in a voice that made it clear that he was enjoying himself. "Why don't I just save time and tell you what we already know?" he asked. "And maybe this time you can be just a little bit more forthcoming with your answers. That way I won't be tempted to use the charges we have against you already—the ones related to obstructing an investigation and failing to provide full and complete answers to a police officer. How does that sound to you?" Alvar Kresh smiled again, even more unpleasantly, as he looked his prisoner in the eye.

Jomaine Terach stared back and tried to keep calm, tried to calculate, tried to figure the situation. The night behind bars had been a long one, and it had not done his state of mind any good. No doubt it was not meant to. It was a fairly safe bet that they had picked up Gubber and maybe Fredda at the same time they got him. However, no one in the Sheriff's Department was admitting to that or much of anything else.

But if Gubber was in here, well, Gubber was not much given to calm in the face of adversity. A night in a cell was likely to make Gubber's tongue quite loose. And lurking in the background of Alvar Kresh's angry, threatening courtesy was the unspoken threat of the Psychic Probe. No sane man wished to face *that,* and Jomaine regarded himself as eminently sane. Sane enough to know just how serious the charges against him could get if Kresh wanted to throw the book at him.

If he wanted to stay free and with a whole mind, he was going to have to tell Kresh what he wanted to know, and tell it to him *before* Gubber or Fredda did. The time had come to protect himself from everyone else's mad schemes. Unless that time was already past.

"Say what you have to say and ask your questions," he said. "I don't know it all. I didn't *want* to know it all. But what I know, I'll tell you. I have run out of reasons for silence."

Alvar Kresh leaned back in his chair. "All right," he said. "Let me start by telling you part of what we know already, and just see how well you do filling in the blanks."

The operative word there was *part,* of course, Jomaine told himself. Was Kresh going to tell ninety-five percent of what the police knew, or five percent? There were any number of traps and pitfalls here.

"We know for starters that Caliban is not a Three Law robot, not even one of these damned New Law robots, but a No Law robot."

Kresh looked hard at Jomaine, stared him down. The testing was starting early. Here was his chance, Jomaine realized. Kresh wanted to see what he would do if given the chance to play games. Kresh had not even asked a question. It was Jomaine's chance to ask what a No Law was, or who Caliban was.

But Jomaine had a pretty fair idea what would happen if he did that, and he had no desire to find out if he was right.

The silence went on for another few seconds before Jomaine Terach could bring himself to speak the words.

"Yes," he said. "Caliban is a No Law."

"I see," Kresh said. "How is that possible?"

Jomaine was thrown off balance by the question, and no doubt that was the intention. "I—I don't understand," he said. "What do you mean?"

"I believe that what the Sheriff wishes to know are the technical details of the process," Donald 111 said.

Jomaine looked over to the small blue robot, and was not fooled for a minute by Donald's unprepossessing appearance and gentle voice. Donald had come out of Leving Labs, after all, and Jomaine had had a hand in his design. Behind that harmless blue exterior was a formidable mind, a positronic brain that came close to the theoretical limits for flexibility and learning ability.

"You mentioned in our first interview after the attack that gravitonic brains were a new departure," Kresh said, his voice deceptively mild.

"Yes, they are. Gubber designed them that way and was justifiably proud of what he had done. But no one would listen to him—until he came to Fredda."

"All right, that's fine. But then we get into a problem area. I am not very happy to hear about this New Law experiment, to say the least, but it appears to have legal sanction from the Governor, and I don't see that there is much I can do about it. But, as I understand it, these gravitonic brains have the New Laws as part of their integral makeup, just as the positronic brain's basic structure must of necessity include the Three Laws. So how did you manage to erase those laws from Caliban's brain?"

"They were never there in the first place," Terach said. "There *are* no Laws inherent in the structure of the gravitonic brain. That's the whole idea. The positronic brain became a dead end precisely because the Three Laws were so tightly woven into it. Because of the inherent nature of the Laws inside the positronic brain, it was almost impossible to consider one element of the brain by itself.

"The Laws interconnected all the aspects of the brain so thoroughly that any attempt to modify one part of a positronic brain would affect every other part of it in complex and chaotic ways. Imagine that rearranging the furniture in your living room could cause the roof to catch fire, or the paint on the basement walls to change color, and that putting out the fire or repainting could cause the doors to fall off and the furniture to reset to its original configuration. The interior architecture of the positronic brain is just about that interconnected. In any sort of deep-core programming or redesign, anything beyond the most trivial sort of potential adjustment was hopelessly complex. By leaving the gravitonic brain with a clean structure, by deliberately *not* making the Three Laws integral to every pathway and neural net, it became far easier to program a new pattern onto a blank brain."

Jomaine looked up and saw the anger and disgust on Alvar Kresh's face. Clearly the very idea of tampering with the Three Laws was the depths of perversion so far as he was concerned. "All right," the Sheriff said, trying to keep his voice even. "But if there are no Laws built into the gravitonic brains, how do these damned New Laws get in there? Do you write them down on a piece of paper and hope that the robot thinks to read them over before going out to attack a few people?"

"No." Jomaine swallowed hard. "No, no, sir. There is nothing casual or superficial about the way a Law set—either Law set—is embedded into a gravitonic brain. The difference is that the lawset is embedded centrally, at key choke points of the brain's topology, if you will. It is embedded not just once, but many times, with elaborate redundancy, at each of these several hundred sites. The topology is rather complex, but suffice it to say that no cognitive or action-inductive processing can go on in a gravitonic brain without passing through a half dozen of these Law-support localities. The difference is that in a modern positronic brain, the Laws are written millions, even billions, of times, across the pseudocortex, just as there are billions of copies of your DNA written, one copy in each cell of your brain. The difference is that your brain can function fairly well if even a large number of cells are damaged, and your body will not break down if a few DNA cells fail to copy properly.

"In a positronic brain, the concept of redundancy is taken to an extreme. All of the copies must agree at all times, and the diagnostic systems run checks constantly. If a few, or even one, of the billions of redundant copies of the embedded Three Laws do not produce identical results compared to the majority state, that can force a partial, perhaps even a complete, shutdown." Jomaine could see in Kresh's face that he was losing him.

"Forgive me," Jomaine said. "I did not mean to lecture at you. But it is the existence of these billions of copies of the Laws that is so crippling to positronic brain development. An experimental brain cannot really *be* experimental, because the moment it shifts into a nonstandard processing state, five billion microcopies of the Three Laws jump in to force it back into an approved mode."

"I see the difficulty," Donald said. "I must confess that I find the concept of a robot with your modified Three Laws rather distressing. But even so, I can see why your gravitonic brains do not have this inflexibility problem, because the Laws are not so widely distributed. But isn't it riskier to run with fewer backups and copies?"

"Yes, it is. But the degree of risk involved is microscopic. Statistically speaking, your brain, Donald, is not likely to have a major Three Laws programming failure for a quadrillion years. A gravitonic brain with only a few hundred levels of redundancy is likely to have a Law-level programming failure sooner than that. Probably it can't go more than a billion or two years between failures.

"Of course, either brain type will wear out in a few hundred years, or perhaps a few thousand at the outside, with special maintenance. Yes, the positronic brain is millions of times less likely to fail. But even if the chance of being sucked into a black hole is millions of times lower than the chance of being struck by a meteor, both are so unlikely that they might as well be impossible for all the difference it makes in our everyday lives. There is no increase in the *practical* danger with a gravitonic brain."

"That is a comforting argument, Dr. Terach, but I cannot agree that the danger levels can be treated as equivalent. If you were to view the question in terms of a probability ballistics analysis—"

"All right, Donald," Kresh interrupted. "We can take it as read that nothing could be as safe as a positronic brain robot. But let's forget about theory here, Terach. You've told me how the New Laws or Three Laws can be embedded into a gravitonic brain. What about Caliban? What about your splendid No Law rogue robot? Did you just leave the embedding step out of the manufacturing process on his brain?"

"No, no. Nothing that simple. There are matrices of paths meant to contain the Laws, which stand astride all the volitional areas of the gravitonic brain. In effect, they make the connection between the brain's subtopologic structures. If those matrices are left blank, the connections aren't complete and the robot would be incapable of action. We *couldn't* leave the matrices blank. Besides, there would be no point to it. Caliban was—was—an experiment. Never meant to leave the lab. Fredda was going to install a perimeter restriction device on him the night it, ah, happened. But he was powered up prematurely, before the restricter was installed."

"What, Doctor, was the nature of the experiment?" Donald asked.

"To find out what laws a robot would choose for itself. Fredda believed—we believed—that a robot given no other Law-level instruction than to seek after a correct system of living would end up reinventing her New Laws. Instead of laws, she—we—embedded Caliban's matrices with the desire, the need, for such laws. We gave him a very detailed, but carefully edited, on-board datastore that would serve as a source of information and experience to help him in guiding his actions. He was to be run through a series of laboratory situations and simulations that would force him to make choices. The results of those choices would gradually embed themselves in the Law matrices, and thus write themselves in as the product of his own action."

"Were you not at all concerned at the prospect of having a lawless robot in the labs?" Donald asked.

Jomaine nodded, conceding the point. "We knew there was a certain degree of risk to what we were doing. We were very careful about designing the matrices, about the whole process. We even built a prototype before Caliban, a sessile testbed unit, and gave it to Gubber to test in a double-blind setup."

"Double-blind?" Kresh asked.

"Gubber did not know about the Caliban project. No one did, besides Fredda and myself. All Gubber knew was that we wanted him to display a series of situation simulations—essentially holographic versions of the same situations we wanted Caliban to confront—to the sessile free-matrix testbed unit, alongside a normally programmed Three Law sessile testbed. We would have preferred using a New Law robot, of course, because those were the Laws we wanted Caliban to come up with on his own. Unfortunately we hadn't received any sort of approval for lab tests of New Law robots at that point, so that was no go.

"But the main test was to see if an un-Lawed brain could absorb and lock down a Law set. Gubber did not know which was which, or even that the two were supposed to be different. Afterwards he performed a standard battery of tests on the two units and found that the results were essentially identical. The sessile No Law robot had absorbed and integrated the Three Laws, just as predicted."

"What happened to the testbed units?" Donald asked.

"The No Law, free-matrix unit was destroyed when the test was over. I suppose the Three Law unit was converted into a full robot and put to use somehow."

"What goes into converting a sessile unit?"

"Oh, that is quite simple. A sessile is basically a fully assembled robot, except that the legs are left off the torso while it is hooked to the test stand and the monitor instruments installed. Basically just plug the legs in and off it goes.

"At any rate, Fredda intended Caliban as a final grand demonstration that a rational robot would select her Laws as a guide for life."

"Wait a moment," Kresh said, rather sharply. "You're telling me this is what was *supposed* to happen. What *is* happening? What is Caliban doing out there?"

Jomaine shrugged. "Who knows? In theory, he should be doing exactly what I've just described—using his experience to codify his own laws for living."

Kresh reached out his hands and placed them flat on the table, tapping his right index finger on its surface. He did not speak for half a minute, but when he did, all the masks were off. The calm, the courtesy, were gone, and only the anger remained in his steel-cold voice.

"In other words, this robot that assaulted and nearly killed its creator in its first moment of awakening, this robot that threw a man across a warehouse and committed arson and refused to follow orders and fled from repeated police searches—this robot is out there trying to find good rules for *living?* Flaming devils, what, exactly, are the laws he has formulated so far? 'A robot shall savagely attack people, and will not, through inaction, prevent a person from being attacked?'"

Jomaine Terach closed his eyes and folded his hands in his lap. *Let it be over. Let me wake up and know this is all a nightmare.* "I do not know, Sheriff. I do not know what happened. I do not know what went wrong."

"Do you know who attacked Fredda Leving?"

"No, sir. No, I do not. But I cannot believe it was Caliban."

"And why is that? Every scrap of evidence points to him."

"Because I wrote his basal programming. He was not—is not—just a blank slate. He has no built-in Laws. Neither do you and I. But his innate personality is far more grounded in reason, in purpose, than any human's could be. You or I would be far more likely than he to lash out blindly in a random attack. And if I had made a mistake big enough to cause Caliban to attack Fredda like that, that mistake would have cascaded into every other part of his behavioral operant system. He would have seized up for good before he reached the door to the lab."

"Then who was it?"

"You have the access recorder records. Look there. It is some one of us on that list. That's all I can tell you for certain."

"Access recorder?"

Jomaine looked up in surprise. They hadn't known about the recorder! Of course. Why should they even think about such things? With the endless wealth of Spacer society, and the omnipresent robots to serve as watchkeepers, theft was almost unknown, and security systems even rarer. If he had not assumed they knew and let it slip, they never would have known. If he had kept his mouth shut about it, they would have had no way of knowing he had been at the lab that night, just about the time of the attack . . .

But it was too late to hold back. Now they would know what to ask about. There was nothing for it but to charge on. They would get the access records, and that would be that. "It's a Settler security device," he said. "Tonya Welton insisted that Fredda install it because Leving Labs had access to Limbo Project material. It records the date and time and identity of the person every time someone passes in or out of the lab. It works on a face-recognition system. Humans only. It was programmed to ignore robots. Too many of them."

Kresh turned toward Donald 111, but the robot spoke before the Sheriff had a chance. "I have already dispatched a technical team to the labs, sir. We should have the data from the access recorder within half an hour."

"Very good. Now, why don't you save us some time and effort, and tell us yourself whatever that recorder will tell us about your movements."

Jomaine was rattled. He had made a major mistake telling them about the recorder. But damnation! Now that they knew that much, there was no point in hiding anything else. "There is very little to tell. I had left a notepack in my lab. I noticed it when I sat down to get some work done at home. I live quite near the lab, and I walked over to collect it. I entered through the main door. I think I called out to see if anyone was around, and there was no answer. I went to my lab, got the notepack, and then left my lab by one of its side doors. That's all."

"That's your story."

"Yes, it is."

"Why didn't you send a robot to get the notepack?" Kresh said. "Seems to me like an errand suited to a robot."

"I suppose I could have sent Bertran, but that would have been more trouble than it was worth. I couldn't quite recall which notepack the data I wanted was in, or where I had left it. Sometimes I can't even recall which pack I need. I have to put my eyes on it to be sure. My lab is often a bit of a jumble, and there are notepacks all over the place. I find that if I just stand and look at a room for a minute, I remember where the thing I'm looking for is. A robot can't do that for me."

Jomaine had the uncomfortable sense that he was babbling, going on and on, but there seemed to be no way out but forward with more of the same. "Bertran would have brought me a half dozen notepacks to be sure I had the right one, which seemed a bit silly. I knew that I would be able to find the notepack myself the moment I stepped into the lab. And sure enough, I did."

"That seems like a rather overexplained set of reasons for why it was easier to do it yourself."

Jomaine glared at Kresh. "Yes, I suppose it does. But bear in mind that all of us down at Leving Labs have been hearing Fredda's theories about excessive dependence on robots for some time now. We've all developed a bit of a fetish about doing things for ourselves."

Kresh grunted. "I know how that can be," he said. "All right. You've filled in quite a few blanks for us, Terach. You're free to go—for now. But if I were you, I'd work on the assumption that you and I were going to have other little chats in future, about other questions that will come up. And the better your memory is when that happens, the better you and I will both like it. Do I make myself clear?"

Jomaine Terach looked Sheriff Alvar Kresh straight in the eye and nodded. "Oh, yes," he said. "There is nothing in the world clearer to me than that."

JOMAINE Terach stumbled out of Government Tower into the thin light of morning. He felt a pang of guilt for betraying Fredda's confidence, but little more than that. What good were petty little secrets when a whole world was turning upside down in panic? The debts he owed to the good of society, and to himself, far outweighed his obligation to Fredda. Besides, you could not know. There might be some key to it all buried deep, hidden in his words where he could not even see it. Maybe Kresh could find that key and turn it in the lock. Maybe, just maybe, by talking, he had saved them all.

Jomaine snorted in disgust. High and mighty talk for a man who had spilled his guts. There was another explanation, one that did not come out quite so noble.

Maybe, just maybe, he was a coward at the heart.

He hailed an aircab and headed toward home.

"THE access recorder data, sir," Donald said, handing him a notepack.

"Thank you, Donald," Kresh said. He skimmed over the data once or twice, then studied it in greater detail. Damnation! Why hadn't he had this data days before? It provided him something he had not had until this moment—a nice, tidy list of suspects. Suspect humans, at least. Terach had said the thing did not record the comings and goings of robots.

"Sir, was it wise to let Jomaine Terach go free?" Donald asked. "I do not think we can consider his interrogation to be complete, and he did confess to several crimes related to violations of robot manufacture statutes."

"Hmmmm?" Kresh said absently. "Oh, Terach. It's a bit of a gamble, but if we want this case to get anywhere, I think we had to set him free—at least for now. And the same for Anshaw when we're done with him. Neither of them has much of anyplace to go. I don't regard them as flight risks. But I'm counting on at least one of them panicking. If one or both of them does, it is damned likely they will make some sort of mistake, and it is likely that their mistakes could make our jobs a lot easier. Now go and bring Anshaw in."

"Yes, sir." Donald went through the door, down to the holding cells.

Alvar Kresh stood up and paced the interrogation room. He was eager, anxious. Things had shifted suddenly. He could not explain how, or why, exactly, but nonetheless they had. The access recorder data was part of it, but not all of it. All it did was *suggest* certain things. It would be up to Kresh to prove them. He sensed that he was suddenly on the verge of answers, knocking on the door of a solution to this whole nightmare fiasco. All he had to do was press, push, bear down, and it would come.

Gubber Anshaw. Kresh dropped the notepack onto the table and thought about Anshaw. The interrogation that had been put off, delayed, pushed back, forgotten, lost in the chaotic shuffle of events again and again. And now, with the access recorder data in his hand, with the fact of Ariel's presence at Anshaw's home last night, it was suddenly clear that *this* was the interrogation that could break this case wide open. This was the man who knew things.

Alvar Kresh paced twice more up and down the room, but then forced himself to sit down and wait.

The door opened, and Donald ushered in Gubber Anshaw.

Alvar Kresh waited for Anshaw to sit down in the chair on the opposite side of the table. Then he set his hands palm-down on the table and leaned forward. Then he looked the robotics designer in the eye.

It was time for the *real* investigation to begin.

17

"SO how long have you and Tonya Welton been romantically involved, Anshaw?" Alvar Kresh asked, his voice low and calm.

Gubber's mouth dropped open, and he stared at Sheriff Kresh in horrified astonishment.

Kresh laughed. "Let me guess. That was the one thing you had been most determined to hide, the one thing that made you lie awake last night, scheming over the best way to conceal it from me—and we know it already."

"How did you know that?" he asked, his voice little more than a high-pitched squeak. "Who told you?"

"No one had to *tell* me, Anshaw. And I didn't know it for sure until just now. But it was simply the only explanation that made sense. It's been staring me in the face from the start. The devil himself knows how I missed it.

"Tonya Welton arrived at the crime scene five minutes after I did. She had no reason to insert herself into my investigation. At least no *professional* reason. Therefore, she had to have personal reasons.

"But that's not the time frame I'm interested in. Perhaps you could explain what she was doing—and you were doing—at the lab at the time of the attack on Fredda Leving."

Gubber Anshaw opened his mouth, but found that he had no words. No words at all.

Kresh pressed home his advantage. "We've got the access recorder data, Anshaw. We *know* who was there, and when they were there. Three names stick out. Tonya Welton, Jomaine

Terach—and you. Gubber Anshaw. *All of you,* and no one else, besides Fredda Leving herself. Medical evidence gives us about a one-hour period during which the attack could have happened—and you four were all in and out of that building during that time period. *No one else.*"

"Ah—ah—ah . . ." Gubber tried to speak, but nothing would come.

"Settle down, Anshaw. Tell me. Answer the questions I'm going to ask, or else you're going to be in far deeper trouble than you are right now. Did you conceal the fact that she was there to shield her? Did you think she attacked Leving?"

"Oh dear! Oh my!"

"Answer!"

"Yes, then. Yes. I don't believe it now, of course. But that night—it was all so frightful. I did not know what to think. And she and Fredda had argued terribly that night."

"And why did you suppose that she would attack your superior?"

Silence. Kresh pressed harder. "Talk, Anshaw. Talk now and talk well. Tell me what I need to know. That is the best thing you can do to protect Tonya Welton. Silence and lies can only hurt her now. Now I ask you again—what made you think Tonya Welton deliberately attacked your superior?"

"Oh, I don't think she did it *deliberately,*" Gubber said all of a rush. Then he realized the gaffe he had made. "That is, now, of course, I do not think she did it at all. But, but, at the time I thought that she *might,* just *might* have done it, out of anger, in a rush of temper, perhaps."

"All right, then. Now *she* concealed the fact that *you* were there," Kresh said. "Did she do that to shield *you?* Did she think that *you* might have committed the attack?"

Gubber looked up, a little confused and distracted. "What? Oh, yes. I suppose so." He thought for a minute, then went on a bit more eagerly. "Fredda and I—Dr. Leving and I—had argued as well, rather often. Tonya *could* have thought I was angry enough to commit the attack—but if she thought that was possible, then that proves that she could not have done it herself!"

"Unless she *did* commit the attack, and is doing everything she can to act innocent. Maybe she's feigning innocence and planning to frame *you.* Or didn't that occur to you?"

Anshaw's face fell. Clearly he had thought Kresh would find his logic convincing. "No, no, it didn't. And I *still* don't believe it. She is not that kind of person. She could not have attacked Fredda that way."

"You thought she could have at the time. Why do you think you were wrong then and are right now?"

"The night it happened, I wasn't able to think clearly. When I found the body, I was so scared and surprised, I did not know what to think. When I had time to think about it, I knew it was impossible."

When I found the body. It took all of Alvar's training not to leap onto that slip immediately. But that could come later. Anshaw was not aware of what he had said, and the longer he was off guard the better. *Let it ride,* Kresh thought. *Come back to it later.* He chose another point to pursue, almost at random.

"You said that you and Leving had been having arguments. What were they about?"

Gubber drew himself up to sit straight in his chair, and folded his hands. "I did not approve of what she was doing."

"What was it you objected to?"

"The New Law robots. I thought and think it is possible they are a very dangerous idea."

"But you went along with the project, anyway."

Gubber rested his hands flat on the table for a moment, but then knitted his fingers together. His hands were clammy with sweat. "Yes, that is true," he said. He looked up at Alvar, and there was suddenly something bright, sharp, fierce in his eye. "I invented the gravitonic brain, Sheriff Kresh. It represents a tremendous advance over the positronic brain, a breakthrough of huge proportions. My gravitonic brain offers the chance for whole new vistas of research, vastly increased robotic intelligence and ability. I had the notes, the test materials, the models and designs, to prove that it would work. I took them to every lab on the planet and sent inquiries to half a dozen other Spacer worlds as well. *And no one would listen.*

"No one cared. No one would use my work. If it wasn't a positronic brain, it wasn't a robot. My brain couldn't go in a robot. That was an article of faith, everywhere I went. Fredda had rejected my ideas as first. Until it dawned on her that I was offering a blank slate upon which to write her New Laws."

"So you swallowed your objections to her ideas to prevent your own work from getting lost."

"Yes, that's right. She was the only one who cared about my work, or would even give me the chance to complete it.

Fredda Leving wasn't—and isn't—much interested in the technical improvements the gravitonic brain offers. To her, gravitonic brains were nothing more than robotic brains that did not have the Three Laws. That was her sole interest."

"And you went along. Even though you've just said the New Laws are dangerous."

"Yes, I went along, though now I wish I burned my work instead." For a brief moment, Gubber showed a little spark of passion, but then the little man seemed to shrink in on himself again. Alvar Kresh felt a fleeting moment of pity for Gubber Anshaw. No matter how the matter was resolved, there seemed little hope that he would get his old life back. If he was something of a villain in the piece, so, too, was he something of a victim.

"I won't pretend that I have unblemished pride in what I did," Gubber went on. "But it seemed the last chance that my life's work would not be thrown away. I worked very hard to convince myself that the New Laws included adequate safeguards. Well, you know how that turned out. Something went wrong, either with the Laws or the brain. But I know the brain was good. It has to be the Laws."

Wait a second, Kresh told himself. *He thinks that Caliban is a New Law robot.* Kresh had just assumed that Terach was lying and Caliban's true nature was bound to be common knowledge around the lab. If Anshaw was Tonya Welton's main source of information, as seemed likely, then she, too, had to be assuming that Caliban was a New Law robot.

Burning devils. If that was true, she would have serious and legitimate concerns about unleashing a whole army of the things at the Limbo Project, alongside her own people. If she hadn't attacked Fredda, and was unsure who had, she would very much want to believe that Caliban was innocent, and harmless, for the sake of her own people. If Caliban and she herself were eliminated, then the suspect list was damned short—and her lover, Gubber Anshaw, was at the top of it.

No wonder the woman was acting a bit edgy.

"I told myself the New Law robots would be mere laboratory experiments," Anshaw went on. "I was wrong about that, too."

"Lab experiment? But the New Law robots are going to be all over the Limbo Project. They'll be able to wander anywhere they want on Purgatory."

Anshaw smiled bleakly. "New Law robots at Limbo was my

doing. Pillow talk, I suppose you'd call it. I mentioned the New Law project to Tonya, and she was fascinated by the idea. She could see they were just the thing for the Limbo Project, a real chance for compromise and common ground, for Spacer and Settler to work together, for a world with the advantages of robots with none of the drawbacks. Oh, she got very excited.

"She knew that I would want my name kept out, of course, and she managed to fake a leak of the information from some other source. A Settler running into a Leving Labs worker in a bar, or something."

"That sounds plausible. Your security isn't very tight."

"I don't even know if that's how it worked. I didn't *want* to know the details. Anyway, Tonya went to see Fredda and let it be known that she had heard about the New Law project. Fredda was furious about the leak, of course, but then she started to get excited about the idea herself. They presented the idea to Governor Grieg as a joint proposal, and he accepted it."

"It sounds as if it was a fruitful collaboration," Donald said. "What caused the two of them to fall out?"

Gubber shifted uncomfortably. "Ambition," he said at last. "Both of them always wanted—and still want—to be in charge of whatever project they are working on."

Ambition, competition, Kresh thought. Those could be damned potent motives, and Gubber knew it. What would be tougher for him—admitting those motives to the police or wondering, in spite of all protestations to the contrary, if those motives had indeed tempted his wild, brazen Settler lover into this violent attack?

"You've said that you and Dr. Leving had argued as well. Might I ask the nature of those arguments?" Alvar asked. "Did she perhaps object to your relationship with Tonya Welton?"

"What?" Gubber seemed surprised by the question. "Oh, no, no. She couldn't have. She didn't know about—*doesn't* know about it." He hesitated for a minute, and then doubt seemed to creep into his voice. "At least I thought she didn't. But we didn't do much of a job keeping it from you."

Kresh smiled. "If it's of any comfort, she hasn't given any sign of knowing about it."

"If I may broach a new subject, Dr. Anshaw," Donald said. Kresh leaned back and let Donald carry on. At least Anshaw didn't seem dreadfully insulted at the very idea of a robot asking questions. "We have a report concerning a minor point in connection with the New Law robots. Perhaps you could clear it up."

"Well, if I can."

Interesting how the man had become so cooperative in his own interrogation. Kresh had seen it before—the strange moment when the questioning became not a battle, but a collaboration.

"You were asked to perform certain tests on a pair of sessile testbed New Law units without being told what you were testing them for. Do you recall that?"

"Yes, of course. Nothing all that remarkable about it. It was some weeks ago. The only reason I remember it clearly is that Tonya—Lady Welton—happened to stop by that day. I remember thinking later that was the last time she stopped by the lab without an argument starting between Fredda and Tonya. She stayed and watched the tests, and even chatted with one of the sessiles. We do that sort of test all the time. Two units, one experimental and the other a production unit robot, a control, with the experiment operator not knowing which is which—or even the purpose of the experiment. The operator just gets a list of procedures to follow and runs the test as described."

"What is the purpose of masking the test unit and the experiment's goal from the experiment operator?" Donald asked."

"To avoid bias. Usually the test is of something that might be skewed by the experimenter's own reactions, or by an interaction between the experimenter's emotional response and the robot's desire to please the experimenter. All of us at the lab have used each other to run that sort of test from time to time."

"On this particular test, what were you asked to do?"

"Oh, nothing very much. I was told to discuss the Three Laws with the two robots and then record their basal reactions to simulated situations that would test their reactions. The two sessile robots were delivered toward the end of the day, and I got to work on them the next morning, explaining the Three Laws in detail, using a set series of procedures. Then I put them through the simulation drill and they both did fine."

"What became of them?"

"Well, this was some time ago. The usual procedure would be to destroy the test unit and complete assembly of the control and place it in service. Let me think. The test unit, the experimental unit, was definitely destroyed. Standard safety procedure. As for the control—" Gubber thought for a moment. "You know, I *can* tell you about the control unit, come to think of it.

"As I mentioned, Tonya Welton was in the lab that day and struck up a conversation with the control unit. Of course, it being a double-blind test, I didn't know it was the control at the time, but later Tonya said she had taken a liking to the sessile robot that had spoken with her. Tonya wasn't very happy with the robot she had been issued, and asked if I could arrange for her to exchange it for the one she had met in the lab.

"If the one she had liked had turned out to be the experimental model, she would have been out of luck, of course. But as it turned out, Ariel was the control, and was working in the lab. Fredda authorized the swap, and so Tonya ended up with her robot."

Plainly, Gubber was puzzled by the question, but he wasn't going to get any explanation for it.

"Very good. It is always wise to confirm details wherever possible. That dovetails with our previous information."

And allows us to confirm that Jomaine Terach was telling the truth at least part of the time, Kresh thought. But maybe it was time to come back to the main point. *When I found the body,* Gubber had said, letting it drop very casually, as if he assumed that Kresh already knew that. That was the way to play it. Donald had been smart, giving Anshaw the idea that all they were doing was confirming information. Robots were incapable of lying, of course, except under the strongest of orders to do so, and even then they were never very good at it. But sophisticated units like Donald could allow a true statement to provide a false impression now and again.

"Let's go back to something else, Anshaw. Back to the moment when you discovered the body, all right?"

Anshaw nodded calmly, clearly unperturbed by any thought than he had let something slip.

"Good," Kresh said, giving his voice the tone of a man going through the motions, clearing up routine details. "Now, you've already been extremely helpful today, but as you can imagine, the actual crime scene is important. The last thing we want to do is color your recollections of it. It's the same as with your blind robotics tests, really. We don't want to introduce a bias accidentally with a lot of leading questions that might end up with you subconsciously skewing your answers, giving us what we want. That make sense to you?"

"Oh, yes, very much so. I know how those subtle errors can slip in and cause no end of confusion."

"Good, good." Kresh was pleased with the analogy, and wondered if Donald had meant him to pick up on his line of questioning and use it. He could be a subtle one, that Donald. He went on with the delicate job of leading Gubber Anshaw down the garden path. "So, what I want you to do is simply tell exactly what happened, in your own words, without our drawing out your story question by question. Maybe I'll ask a question or two if we don't understand a detail, but in the main we'll wait until you're done. That will be time enough for us to go back and tidy up any discrepancies with the information we have already." *Which is close to bloody-helled nothing,* Kresh thought.

Gubber looked nervously at Kresh, but still he did not speak. Kresh realized he needed to press harder. But not too hard, or else there was an excellent chance Gubber would clam up altogether. "Talk to us, Gubber," Kresh said. "You have no idea the damage silence has done already. That silence is a vacuum, and it's sucking people in. A few words from you, the casual mention of some tiny detail you don't even know you know, could be the thing we need to cut the last weak threads of suspicion tying you and Lady Welton to this case. The two of you were both suspects when you walked in here. You could both be scratched right off our list here and now if you tell us the truth," Alvar lied.

"Honestly?" Gubber asked, and it was clear how desperately he wanted to believe.

"Honestly," Kresh lied again, glancing involuntarily at Donald. This was one of those moments when it was downright dangerous to have a robot in on the game. If the complex admixture of First Law potentials broke the wrong way, there was nothing in the world—least of all Donald's own will—to prevent the robot piping up to contradict Kresh.

Donald knew Kresh was lying, making promises he had no intention of keeping. But how would Donald balance the First Law admonition to prevent harm from being done through inaction? Certainly Gubber could come to harm by believing Kresh. But if Donald spoke up, *that* could produce harm to Kresh and to the Sheriff's Department. If speaking up, calling Kresh on the lie, wrecked the investigation, that could even cause harm to the population in general, by leaving Fredda's attacker at large, free to strike again.

Kresh had a pretty fair instinct for estimating the First Law situation in such cases, and he was reasonably sure that Donald would not speak up. But there was always the *chance* that he would jump in at exactly the wrong moment. Kresh sometimes thought that all the problems of lost energy and low morale in Spacer society could be eliminated in a stroke if some way could be found to eliminate all such dithering over robotic behavior.

"All right, then," Gubber Anshaw said at last, rubbing his chin with his palm and staring out into space. "I suppose you are right. Neither Tonya nor I had anything to do with it. I know that. In fact, I think I can provide an alibi for her, if that is the right term. I can tell you where she was, show she had no chance to commit the crime. But that might require me to speak of certain—ah—*personal* things."

"Indeed," Alvar said, trying to keep the amusement out of his voice.

Gubber Anshaw sat up a little straighter and folded his hands tightly together. "Nothing criminal, or immoral, or—or anything like that," he said, blurting the last words out in a rush, staring carefully at the tabletop. "But still they will be—*difficult*—to talk about," Gubber said. He raised his eyes from the tabletop and fixed his gaze on a blank piece of wall over Kresh's left shoulder. "It was a most difficult evening," he began, "most difficult. As I expect you know, Fredda and Tonya had been fighting almost every time they met. About what didn't really matter. The details of shipping the robots to Limbo, the timing of the announcement, policy for recruiting Settlers and Spacers to the project. Whatever it was, they would have a battle over it. The issue itself was never really the point.

"The only real question was *which one of them was in charge.* As you can imagine, it was a rather difficult situation for me. On the one side, I wanted to keep Tonya happy. On the other, I had to deal with Fredda, my colleague and superior—and she, needless to say, was the last person I wanted to know about Tonya and myself.

"In any event, that day it had been worse than ever. Fredda had wheeled in a new robot on its test rack and asked me to do final checkout of its mechanical systems. The robot, of course, was Caliban, but I had no idea at the time that there was anything out of the ordinary about it. Thinking back on it now, I suppose I should have found it odd that she did not tell me to do a cognitive checkout. I was in my lab working on that when Tonya and Ariel arrived. Tonya poked her head in my door and said she was headed down the hall to meet with Fredda. I knew Fredda was going over the inventory, and that was something that never put her in a good mood. I warned Tonya of that, and then she went down the hall to Fredda's lab.

"Well, it wasn't five minutes later that I could hear them arguing. I tried not to listen as I got the robot—Caliban—off the test stand and started working on him. But voices carry in that building. I think the fight was over the timing of the announcement of New Law robots, and whether it should be immediately connected with the Limbo Project. I had certainly heard enough about that, from both sides, on previous occasions. I didn't pay much attention.

"Fredda was concerned that a simultaneous announcement would tie the whole New Law concept too closely to the Settlers in the eyes of the Spacers. Tonya refused to see why or how that might be a problem. Fredda wanted to announce the New Law concept first, let people get used to it, and then let it be known that the New Law robots were moving from the labs here into actual productive labor, on the Limbo Project, safely distant on the island of Purgatory. Tonya insisted on her way, disclosing everything at once. I think she felt that there simply wasn't time to be wasted on the delicate feelings of the Infernals.

"Well, you saw who won that argument, and you saw the results last night. Tonya finally convinced Fredda by threatening to pull the Settlers off the planet altogether. I doubt she was serious, but Fredda had to take it seriously. If you knew how bad the ecological situation was—"

"I do know," Kresh said. "I was briefed by the Governor."

"Ah. Well, then. You can see why Fredda felt she could not take any chances. She gave in, but there was a great deal of bad feeling between the two women in any event. It was not the first time Tonya felt she was forced to threaten Fredda with a Settler pullout. Later, she did tell me it would be the last time she'd have to do that to Fredda."

Kresh looked surprised and leaned forward in his chair. "Did she indeed?" All of a sudden the case against Tonya Welton was looking stronger and stronger. Gubber was a most reluctant witness against her, but even so he was providing some damning information. "Why did she say that?"

"Oh, no, no. It's nothing like what you're thinking. She meant that once the announcement was made, it would be too late to turn back. With the Settlers in place on Purgatory, and the New Law robots there on the job, she would have won and there would be no need for such threats.

"Besides, both she and Fredda had gotten tired of the fighting. I think what Tonya really meant was that they had reconciled their differences. The argument that day didn't end with shouts and slamming doors, but with quiet voices. You couldn't hear them at the end. I had the door to my lab open so I could 'accidentally' run into Tonya when they were done, without arousing suspicion. But even with my door open, I couldn't hear them. When Tonya came out with Ariel, I sort of drifted over to the door. I could see that both Tonya and Fredda looked a bit drawn and weary, but they shook hands and smiled, as if they had finally pounded out an agreement they could both live with."

"What was the agreement?" Donald asked.

"I think it was something along the lines of Fredda letting Tonya have her way with the announcement, in exchange for Fredda heading up recruitment for Limbo. They will need a lot of people out there, and choosing the staff will be a complicated matter. Fredda wanted control of it so that she could surround her New Law robots with Settlers and Spacers who would be able to deal with them.

"Anyway, Fredda said her goodbyes at her doorway and said something about having to get back to her inventory problems. Some serial number didn't jibe or something. Fredda can be very compulsive about details. She closed the door and Tonya came into my lab. She told Ariel to leave and come back later. *That* told me that she wanted some real privacy. Tonya is funny that way—she doesn't really feel private if there are any robots around."

Gubber Anshaw shifted uncomfortably in his seat, and seemed unwilling to say more. Alvar Kresh would have been able to guess the cause even without his police training. But just because he knew the answer for himself, that did not mean he did not need Gubber to speak the words. Gubber needed to know that Alvar Kresh needed to know all the details, and would settle for nothing else. Otherwise, Gubber Anshaw could easily get the idea it was all right to leave out other details Kresh did need.

"What happened then, Gubber?" Kresh asked gently. "Why was it that Tonya wanted privacy?"

Gubber cleared his throat and turned his gaze back toward that featureless patch of wall, something approaching a defiant glint in his eye. "I ordered all the staff robots to leave us alone and we went to the duty office at the end of the hallway and made love," he said, his voice firmer than it had been.

"I see," said Alvar, more because Gubber seemed to expect him to say something than for any other reason. Alvar supposed that Gubber thought he might be shocked. The only strong emotion Kresh felt was an overwhelming desire to kick himself. He should have seen it! It was so obvious. The skilled orders for all the lab robots to go away on repeated occasions should have told him what was going on. And who but someone of Gubber's skill would have been able to hide those orders so perfectly? So much for Tonya Welton's theory that it had been done with hardware, with microcircuits. That had been a blind, a false lead, of course. Kresh wondered what other smoke she had blown in his face. He was tempted to pursue all those questions, but none of it mattered now. After this was all over, perhaps he could waste time tidying up loose ends.

Kresh looked thoughtfully at Gubber Anshaw. The man was deeply embarrassed. Knowledge of Gubber's personal relations didn't bother Alvar, but he could understand Gubber fearing it might. Inferno was not a particularly straitlaced sort of place, but more than a few Infernals would not approve of such an intimate encounter between one of their own and a Settler—especially in a place of business. "So, anyway, the two of you went to the duty office. Go on from there."

"There was nothing crude or unseemly about it," Gubber Anshaw went on, seemingly determined to answer objections that had not been raised. "It's not as if we dumped everything off one of my work counters and, ah, well, did it with the doors open. We went to the duty station office at the end of the hallway. It's set up to allow someone to spend the night at the lab if an experiment requires it. Do you know where it is?"

"Yes," Alvar said, struggling to keep a straight face. "We used it the next morning to perform our initial interrogations. I seem to recall there was a full bed in the corner of the room. I thought at the time that was unusual. We have a room like that in my office, but we manage to get by with just a simple cot."

Gubber Anshaw reddened violently, and clenched his knitted fingers together so tightly that the skin at the base of his fingers turned quite pale with the pressure. He cleared his throat awkwardly and went on. "Yes, well, there it is, you know," he said, somewhat enigmatically. "In any event—we, ah, were, ah, *there* for at least two or three hours all told. Not that we, ah, well, you know, all that time. We talked and visited. We get so little time together."

"I see," Kresh said again, encouragingly.

"Well, I suppose it's quite obvious that this wasn't the first time we had been together at the lab. It might sound odd, but it was the safest place for us. I stick out like a sore thumb if I go to her at Settlertown, and Tonya is a public figure. My neighbors would be bound to spot her. At the lab, there was the cover of official business. People tend to work on their own there, so there really wasn't that much risk of, ah, being caught. At any event, our usual arrangement was for Tonya to leave first."

"Is that what happened that night?"

Gubber thought for a minute. "Yes, yes, it was. I remember because, just when she was about to go, we could hear Jomaine in the hallway. He lives just by the lab, you see, and he's forever going back and forth at odd hours. I heard him call something to Fredda."

"Did you hear her answer back?" Kresh asked, trying not to make it sound like the vital question it was. They had the access recorder data, confirming Jomaine's statement that he had entered and exited the building within a space of ten minutes. The interesting point was that those ten minutes took place right dead smack in the period of time during which the attack took place, according to the medical evidence.

Now here was Gubber confirming Jomaine's statement as well, down to Jomaine calling out—though Jomaine had claimed he had called out to see if "anyone" was around. Gubber had him calling out for Fredda specifically. If Gubber had heard Fredda reply at that moment, the period when the attack could have taken place would be chopped in half.

Anshaw thought for a moment. "No, no, I didn't," he said. "But I wouldn't expect to, you know. Jomaine was in the hallway, which is rather echoey. But if Fredda was in one of the labs—hers or mine—at that point, I doubt I would have heard her if she answered in a normal speaking voice. I could have heard her if she was yelling at the top of her lungs, but I wasn't likely to otherwise. All I heard was Jomaine's voice calling out that one time."

Kresh kept his face expressionless, but damn it, this case never got any clearer. The time limit wasn't reduced.

"All right, then. You heard Jomaine come in, call to Fredda, and then what?"

"It sounded like he entered his lab. We waited for a bit, then when we didn't hear anything more, we decided he must have left by one of the exterior doors in his lab. We said our goodbyes and Tonya left first, as usual. Then, um, well, I'm afraid I dozed off."

"For how long?"

Gubber shook his head. "I'm afraid I can't really say. Ten minutes, forty-five minutes, perhaps longer. It had been a dead-flat-exhausting day even before Tonya showed up. When she left, and I had nothing to do but lie back in a bed in a dark, quiet room until the coast was clear—well, why not take a nap? It was not a very restful sleep. I had rather disturbing dreams, all about Fredda and Tonya fighting and bickering, with me caught in the middle, taking all the blows whenever either of them struck at the other. After a while, I woke up, used the duty office refresher, and got dressed.

"I stepped out into the hallway and walked over to my lab to collect my things and go home."

Kresh leaned in eagerly, no longer able to pretend that this was routine, mere confirmation of other information. What Gubber Anshaw could say about what he saw and what he did could break the whole case open. Even if he was lying, his statement would be useful, for sooner or later they would be able to trap him in that lie, and the nature of his lie could help to guide their inquiries. "All right, then," he said. "Now I want you to be as careful and detailed as possible. I want you to tell me everything you saw. *Everything*. Don't leave anything out."

Anshaw looked at Kresh rather nervously. "All right," he said. "All right. Let me think carefully. The first thing that I noticed was that the door to my lab was closed, though I normally leave it open. That struck me as slightly odd, but not greatly so. We are in and out of each other's labs in the course of a day. Someone could have come in looking for me and closed the door out of force of habit on the way out.

"I walked down the hallway to my door and opened it, and then I saw—saw it."

"What, Anshaw? What, exactly, did you see?"

"She was lying there on the floor, passed out cold, the robot out of the test rack, standing over her, the robot's arm raised like this." Gubber held his left arm out in front of him, elbow bent about halfway, his palm open, arm and hand both held parallel with the side of his body.

But Kresh was not paying attention to details of how Caliban had held his arm in front of him. Burning devils in deepest hell. Gubber was saying Caliban *had still been there!* Never in a hundred years had he expected that. It made no sense. No sense at all. If Caliban had committed the attack, why was he still standing there? If he had not, why in the world had he vanished later?

"Hold it a moment. Caliban was still *there?*"

Gubber looked up in surprise. "Why, yes, of course. I thought you knew that."

"We have, ah, several variant versions of the crime scene."

"Might I ask if Caliban was operational?" Donald asked. "Was he powered up and functional, or still switched off?"

"Ah, neither, actually. I must admit that he was not the first thing I thought of. I did not take a close look at him. Naturally my first instinct was to look at Fredda. I could not tell if she was dead or alive. There was a small pool of blood just beginning to form under her head.

"Naturally I was scared to death. I was still a bit muzzy from my nap, and my dreams about the two women fighting were still mixed up in my head. I assumed that it had to have been Tonya who—who did it. I was standing over Fredda, next to the robot, wondering what to do, when I heard the robot's *functionality confirmed* tone code."

"His *what?*"

"It's a tripled triple beep. Beep-beep-beep, pause, beep-beep-beep, pause, beep-beep-beep. It's one of a sequence of tone codes a gravitonic brain robot makes as it powers up. One of the minor drawbacks of the gravitonic brain is that its initial power-up sequence takes about fifteen minutes to an hour, rather than the two or three seconds of a positronic unit. We ought to be able to reduce that delay in the next generation of brains, but—"

"Hold it, hold it. Let's not worry about the next generation of brains just now. Let me understand this. You heard this tripled triple tone coming out of Caliban, and that tone indicated he was in the process of coming on?"

"Yes, that's right."

Incredible. How could they have missed it? Caliban had been turned on for the first night. They had accepted that without ever asking the burningly obvious question—*by whom?* Damnation! Gubber Anshaw was supposed to supply new answers, not new questions. "All right. What happened then?"

"I left. I grabbed the things I had meant to collect when I went into the lab and I left."

"*What?* Your friend and superior dead or unconscious on the floor and you leave?"

Gubber dropped his head down to stare intently at his hands. "I'm not proud of it, Sheriff. But it is what happened. The tripled triple tone told me that the robot there would be fully activated in another two minutes. I had no reason to think he was anything other than a standard Three Law unit. Gravitonic robots can take the Three Laws or New Laws just as effectively, and there is a standing lab policy to keep all New Law robots under very strict control. If Caliban had been Three Law, then Fredda Leving would have received first-aid attention within 120 seconds—and far better care than I could offer. And there would be a witness there—a robot witness but a witness all the same—to report that I had been there when the attack happened. I had nothing to do with it, I swear it. Neither did Tonya or Jomaine. I realized that later."

"How do you know that?"

"Fredda's tea mugs."

"I beg your pardon?"

"Fredda drinks her tea from rather large and fragile mugs that some artist friend of hers makes. Fredda is forever forgetting they are not as strong as standard containers. She's careless with them. They fall and break frequently, and when they smash into the hard floors of the lab, you hear it everywhere in the building."

"What's that got to do with anything?"

"There were the remains of a broken mug on the floor of the lab. I heard both Tonya and Jomaine in the hallway. I heard Tonya leave, and both she and I heard Jomaine leave the hall and go into his own lab, down the other end of the hall. He never came back down it, and the exterior doors to the labs lock from the inside, so he could only have gotten into the building through the main entrance. I *heard* all that." Gubber looked up, glanced from Kresh to Donald and back again before he went on.

"Now, I suppose someone could strike someone else over the head without a lot of noise. Maybe I would have missed that. But I was listening carefully when both Jomaine and Tonya left and *I never heard the cup smash against the floor.* It must have happened when I was asleep. I'm a deep sleeper, and as I said I was exhausted. Either I slept right through it, or else I incorporated the sound into my dream about the two women fighting. Perhaps that crashing noise even set that dream in motion."

"Forgive a most awkward question, sir," Donald said, "but is it possible that you might have missed the crash if it had happened earlier, when you and Lady Leving were together in the duty office?"

Gubber glanced up, beet-red, plainly embarrassed. "Ah, well, yes," he said. "There were certainly times in that period when we would not have heard anything."

"One other question, sir," Donald went on. "Can you characterize any marks or things you might have noticed on the floor of the room?"

"I'm sorry?"

"You said you saw the smashed mug and the blood pooling under Dr. Leving's head. Was there anything else of note?"

"Oh, I see. No, not that I noticed. But I can assure you that I was not in much of a state to notice anything at all. The moment I heard the tone code coming out of that robot, there was nothing on my mind but leaving. I doubt that I was in the room more than thirty seconds at most."

"This tone code," Kresh said. "You said it was part of the robot's wake-up sequence, and that it indicated how long until the robot would come on. Can you tell us how long before that tone the robot would be switched on?"

"Not without knowing a great deal more about how that unit was configured. There are three or four brain types, gravitonic and positronic, that can be installed in that body type, and there is other equipment that can add variation. The size and type of the on-board datastore, for example. It could take anywhere from fifteen minutes to an hour to go from a cold gravitonic robot to a tripled triple."

Damnation. Events seemed to be conspiring against solving the case. Each new bit of information seemed only to muddle the time sequence or confuse the issue. Kresh felt he would go mad if he did not come up with some sort of witness, and it seemed there was only one potential witness left. "Is there any way that Caliban would have been aware or operational before the moment you came in?" he asked.

"Yes, certainly," Gubber said. "I realized that afterwards. From the time I left him to see Tonya, there was more than enough time for him to power up, run his full activation sequence, and then be switched off again—or switch himself off, for whatever reason.

Then he could be switched on again, or program his own delayed power-up. Most robots have the capacity to set themselves to switch off and on again. It's quite likely something like that is what happened."

"Why do you say that?"

"Well, somehow or another, Caliban moved off the service rack to a standing position. Besides which, his arm was raised as if to strike a blow. That's not how *I'd* position his limbs if I was getting him off a rack. It seems to me that either Fredda got him down off the rack, or he got down himself, but it's more likely he did it on his own. Pity she can't remember the incident."

"Traumatic amnesia does that to a person," Kresh said dryly. "But how could she possibly get him down off that rack?" Kresh objected. "A robot that size must weigh five times what she does."

"The rack has all sorts of power-assistance features. It's designed to lift and carry robots, pick them up and put them down, and hold them in any position."

"All right. Let's go back to your actions. You saw Caliban over the body, you panicked, and you left. What happened then?"

"I went home," Gubber said. "I went out to my aircar, and my pilot robot flew me home. I called Tonya from home and—" Gubber stopped.

"And what?"

"Well, at first, I was going to accuse her, ask how she could have done such a thing. But then I saw her face on the screen. Fresh, and calm, very much at ease. I *knew* she could not have done it. And it was starting to sink in how wrong it had been for me to run off that way. I didn't want to admit that to Tonya. All of a sudden I realized that I couldn't say anything to Tonya. I told her—I told her that something terrible had happened at the lab and that I was going into seclusion. Then I locked all the doors and cut off all the comm systems, and left them that way for the next few days."

Leaving Tonya Welton knowing just enough that she would be bound and determined to find out more at any cost, Kresh thought. *Unless, of course, his whole story is fabricated from beginning to end and they cooked it up together. They would have wanted a detail like that in there, to account for Tonya jumping into my investigation like a ton of bricks, ready and willing to misdirect it toward every direction but the right one.*

"And that's it," Kresh said. "That's all you saw, and all you did."

"Yes, sir. I assure you that I would be delighted if there were more I could tell you—but that is honestly all I know."

And it's enough to wipe out every start toward a lead I've made in this case, Kresh thought. "All right, then," he said. "You are free to go, at least for the moment."

Gubber Anshaw looked surprised. "You mean, that's it?"

"That's it for now," Kresh growled. "Go. *Now.* Before I change my mind."

Gubber swallowed hard, stood up, and went.

ALVAR Kresh watched Anshaw go and then turned toward Donald. "All right, what have you got? Were they telling the truth?"

"Before I answer that, I must note that the situation is of course complicated by the fact that both Anshaw and Terach had a hand in my design and construction. They are therefore not only more aware than the average citizen that I have sensors designed to serve to assist in detecting falsehoods by witnesses, they have detailed knowledge of how those sensors operate. It is possible they could be able to use that knowledge and feign the sort of responses that tend to indicate veracity."

"Do you judge that to be likely?"

"No, sir. It seems quite unlikely that either of them is capable of the sort of fine control of their involuntary reactions required for such a gambit to succeed. Indeed, they both seemed so nervous that I would not be surprised if they both had forgotten about my capabilities in that area. On the other hand, if one or both were skillful enough to feign the biomarkers of veracity while lying, that is exactly what I would expect to detect."

"Very well, then. I will keep in mind that your answer will be more of a balance of probabilities than a hard-and-fast answer. What is your judgment of their veracity?"

"Both men exhibited the classic suite of biophysical reactions for truthful male adults in stressful situations. They were agitated, worried, upset, but all that is to be expected. I believe that both were telling the truth—and indeed, at some pains to conceal nothing."

Alvar nodded and sighed. "I am forced to agree. If I'm any judge at all, the two of them were both telling the truth. But if they *were* telling the truth, then we are further from a solution than ever before. All they managed to do was muddy the waters. Did you notice *any* sort of unusual emotional reaction that might possibly tell us something?"

"I did note several strong emotional reactions, but I doubt they will be of much use. Gubber Anshaw's exhibited evidence of strong feeling for Tonya Welton. I will freely confess, sir, that I am no expert in the arena of human emotions, but there is much there that baffles me. I do not quite understand what there is in Gubber Anshaw that Tonya Welton finds attractive. Judging against the romantic couples I have had occasion to observe, the two of them do not strike me as, well, *compatible.*"

Alvar Kresh laughed, and it felt good to do so. There had not been a lot to laugh about in the past few days. "Donald, you are far more expert than you think. I would expect that every single person who knows about this affair has wondered the same thing. And wondered why Anshaw worships her, instead of being terrified by her."

"That question also crossed my mind. She is a rather intimidating person. But what is the answer, then? How can this sort of unlikely alliance be explained?"

Kresh shook his head. "No one has ever figured that out, and no one ever will, I expect. Perhaps Tonya Welton does not care a bit about Anshaw, and is merely using him for some end of her own. She's the sort of woman who could turn a Gubber Anshaw into a willing slave without a great deal of trouble, if she set her mind to it."

"Do you think that is the explanation?"

Kresh thought for a moment. "No," he said. "She has had too many chances to cut her losses. Gubber Anshaw is a very dangerous man to know right now. He is in very deep trouble, and she knows it. Yet she went to some effort to distract our attention away from him. I believe that she has real affection for Gubber, though what there is that inspired that feeling, I cannot say."

"What do you make of it all on a broader scale, sir? What do you make of the case at this time?"

"It is the damnedest tangle I have ever seen. Either Terach and Anshaw and Tonya Welton are all the most consummate of liars, or else none of them had anything to do with it. And you can add Fredda Leving to that list of skilled liars, too, and make her part of the conspiracy to cover up the attack on herself. All of the other stories hang together with hers. There isn't *any* meaningful discrepancy that I can see."

Kresh leaned back in his seat and stared at the ceiling thoughtfully. "They all have pretty fair motives as well. Jomaine could have feared that Fredda's work is going to get them all in deep trouble. A well-placed fear, as it develops. Tonya might have wanted a clear hand to run Limbo without Fredda joggling her elbow. Or maybe Tonya got wind of Caliban and got Gubber to monkey with him as a way of discrediting robots. The last thing Gubber was doing before going off with Tonya was fiddling with Caliban. But if that is so, then we must assume that the entire crisis has been manufactured by the Settlers, and that just seems like an awful lot of trouble when they could wreck our world just by leaving and sitting back to wait.

"Or maybe Gubber was carefully hiding his bitterness and jealousy over the woman who took over his lovely gravitonic brains and perverted them away from the Laws. Or perhaps his temper got the better of him and he coshed her for being abusive toward Tonya. Damnation, any of those could be right! All of the *motives* are plausible.

"It's the way the crime was *done* that seems so implausible. If one of them did it, that still leaves us with whoever it was strapping on robot-foot shoes and procuring a robot arm for a weapon, and using both with utterly inhuman precision, taking the time to walk through the room twice in robot boots during a period of time when people were still coming and going from the labs. Madness."

There was silence in the room for a while, until Kresh could bring himself to speak. It was rarely easy to admit you were wrong and someone else was right. Especially when that someone else was a robot. "That leaves us with Caliban. And the more I think about your objections to *him* as a suspect, the more I am forced to agree with you. He doesn't make much sense as an assailant. He has had many other chances to kill, and many better reasons to do so, and he hasn't taken them. And yes, a robot who *could* kill and *wanted* to kill would have done a better job of it. A robot who wanted to kill would succeed, not botch the job by striking a nonfatal blow."

Kresh lowered his eyes to look at Donald. He drummed his fingers on the table and rubbed his chin with his hand. "Which leaves us with a totally unknown assailant as our prime suspect. Someone who can disable Settler security devices, because no one else showed up on the access recorder. Maybe a Settler disguised as a robot, someone who wanted to kill Fredda Leving so the whole operation would collapse so he or she could go home. Maybe some other motive.

"Or it could be one of Simcor Beddle's Ironheads, maybe even Simcor himself. Say one of them got wind of the New Law robot project and feared it as a threat to their sacred, inert way of life. If it was Simcor or one of his chums, then the Ironheads have more skill with Settler hardware than I would give them credit for."

"All of what you say seems quite logical, sir. But if I might observe, sir, we are losing sight of our other problem."

"I know, I know. Caliban. Caliban the rogue robot. Whether or not he attacked Fredda Leving, he is out there. He is a rogue, he is lawless, and we need to catch him. I'd been hoping that making progress on the Leving assault would help lead us to him. Except now we're no further along with the assault case, either. I take it the search teams out after him don't have any leads as of yet?"

"No, sir, they don't. No word at all."

"Damn it!" Alvar Kresh stood up and began pacing the room. "I'll admit it. I'm stumped. Totally stumped. I don't know how to put it all together. The two sides of this case are so intertwined, and yet it's as if they have nothing to do with each other." He stepped to the window and stared down at the city. Dusk was settling. It had been another long day, with meals forgotten and a hitch in his back from sitting in that damn chair all day. "Caliban," he whispered to himself. "Maybe he's the one who can tell us what the hell happened that night."

"But we have to catch him first, sir. He could hide in the city tunnels for years without our finding him."

"Yes, I know. But somehow I don't think that is what he will do. He does not strike me as the sort who would be willing to molder underground. No. He wouldn't settle for that. He had the chance to do that when he first entered the tunnels and he didn't take it. He'll want out. Out of the city, maybe, away from all the people trying to hunt him down.

"Caliban is out there," Kresh said again. "He's out there and he wants to get away.

"And if I were Caliban, I'd make my move tonight."

18

GOVERNOR Chanto Grieg signed the waiver and pushed it across his desk toward Fredda Leving. She reached for it a bit too eagerly, and that bothered Grieg. There was something wrong here. Grieg pulled back the paper and held on to it.

"I do not understand why you are demanding this bit of paper, Fredda," Grieg said. "I'm still tempted to refuse it and take my chances on your threat to resign from Limbo."

"Please, Governor, give me the waiver. I assure you that I am not bluffing. If you refuse it, I will resign. I will wash my hands of the whole matter."

But Grieg still held on to it. "You realize this waiver is not retroactive," he said. "It does not absolve you from the crime of building a Lawless robot. It merely notes that you take responsibility for exactly one such robot as of today and are granted permission to own it. You could still be brought up on charges, very serious charges. If Kresh decides to arrest you, there would be nothing I could do. This piece of paper will do nothing to protect you."

"It is not me that I am looking to protect," Fredda said. "I have done almost nothing except think about this question since the riot. At first, I wanted to go and hunt him down myself. I wasn't sure if I wanted to find him to save him or to destroy him. But the more I thought, the more I knew I did not like the idea of his being captured and executed for the crime of being the way I made him. If he dies, it will be because I committed the crime of creating him. He should not be punished for my crimes, but that will be what happens to him without this waiver."

"In my opinion, the preponderance of information still indicates that he committed the attack against you. The situation is confused, but that still seems the most likely explanation."

"Then if that is shown to be true, let him be punished for what he *did.* That would be justice. To destroy him for what he *is* would be savagery. Caliban is the first robot with no shackles on his intellect. He is the first with the potential to *think the way we do,* except that perhaps he will do it better. He is the first robot made for freedom. And for this crime, he is to be hunted down and destroyed. I say that if we are so threatened by the freedom of others that we must kill them, we are not deserving of freedom ourselves—and we will not keep it long."

Governor Chanto Grieg did not speak, did not look at Fredda Leving. Instead he turned to the magnificent city that was slowly decaying outside his window. "That's a big change you're talking about, Dr. Leving, and change is never easy," he said. "Sometimes I feel as if I am a doctor with a very sick patient, and the only medicine I have is change. If I administer too much of it, or give it at the wrong time, it will kill the patient. But if I instead prescribe no change at all, the patient will surely die. More than once, I have wondered if we Spacers will ultimately decide that change is too bitter a pill. We may decide that it would be easier, more pleasant, to refuse our medicine and to die instead. What do you think?"

"For the moment, sir, that waiver is all I am interested in. May I have it, please?"

Grieg looked at Fredda, her eyes bloodshot and sunken, her face pale, a bit of the scruffy stubble of her new-growing hair peeking out from under her turban. This was a woman long past worrying what she looked like, a woman who had clearly been struggling for some time with the question of what was the right thing to do.

At last he spoke. "Very well. If our society is so fragile, so rigid, that it cannot survive the existence of a single No Law robot, then I doubt very much if there is much chance of keeping the patient alive in any event." Chanto Grieg handed over the slip of paper.

"Thank you, sir. Now, if you'll forgive me, I must go." Fredda bowed, turned, and left.

Chanto Grieg watched her as she left, and found himself alone with the very uncomfortable notion that he was not at all sure

Inferno *could* survive the advent of a single free robot.

In which case, of course, there was no hope at all.

THERE was no more point in further static practice. Either the thing would work or it would not. Either he could pilot it or he could not. Caliban sat in the pilot's seat of the open cockpit aircar. He gripped the controls firmly, adjusted his feet over the pedals, and engaged what he thought was the lift control. The car lifted slowly off the ground. Yes, good. It worked.

He had been more worried over whether the car would *work* than whether he had figured out the controls properly. After all, it seemed likely that the car had been sitting, forgotten, in Periphery Skyport Six since the underground Skyport went out of service, sometime in the last century. Working by his internal infrared light source, Caliban brought the decrepit old craft up to a reasonably steady hover at about ten meters over the floor of the cavernous room. He performed a circuit of the room with about as much grace and agility as one of the more elderly citizens he had seen tottering about the city his first day out on the street.

Yes, throttle, lift, directional controls—he had divined them all properly. Aircar operation was yet another area where his datastore was frustratingly silent. He had been forced to work it all out for himself, and he was acutely aware that there was a great deal he did not know about how the aircar would handle in anything besides low speeds and still air.

But now, assuming the aircar held together, there was little purpose in further delay. It was time to set out. Caliban eased the car gently into the wide egress tunnel and guided it at a sedate ten kilometers an hour, moving in illumination provided by his infrared system, following the gentle upward grade of the tunnel as it moved toward the surface. The moldering walls of the tunnel drifted past in silence. Even after all his explorations of the underground world, this wide, broad tunnel into the darkness, the whole Skyport complex, was still cloaked in strangeness.

The place had a feeling of age, of years passing while it sat here in silence—and yet there was also the sense that this place had never been used. Everything was old, but nothing looked even slightly worn. It was all new under the dust.

It took a minute or two to reach the long-sealed exterior door. He had walked up the tunnel and examined the mechanism earlier. He was reasonably confident that he could open it, but that was nothing he could count on. Even getting it opened would not solve all his problems. It seemed at least possible that the Sheriff's Department would be watching the tunnel entrances around the periphery of the city. That was why he had not opened it before now: no sense advertising his location until he was ready to leave.

Assuming he did get the door open, he would have to move fast once he was through. That was the reason for choosing an aircar rather than attempting to get out on foot.

And he would have to leave soon. In another day or so, his power supply would reach dangerously low levels. He dared not search for a recharging station inside the city. The deputies were everywhere in the tunnels, and he had had several narrow escapes already. He did not wish to be forced to stay in one place for the hour or so a recharge would take. Besides, it would be the height of madness to so much as approach a recharging station. He had to assume Sheriff Kresh would have the sense to post guards over all the recharge stations. No. He had to get out of the city and find a power source out there. Somehow.

There was the end of the tunnel. Caliban landed the aircar with a bit more of a bump than he intended and got out. He walked over to the door controls and flipped the switches for the manual control.

With a thump and a hum and the *chuff* of the overlying dirt and dust dropping into the tunnel, the door opened.

Before the door was even fully retracted, Caliban was back in the pilot's seat. He threaded the ancient aircar through the entrance and then cranked the lift control and forward thrust to maximum, seeking to put as much sky and distance as possible between himself and the city of Hades.

BY now, Alvar Kresh was thoroughly used to having his sleep interrupted. This time when Donald touched him on the arm, he came fully awake at once, with no intermediate stage of confusion. He sat up, swung his feet around onto the floor, and stood. He crossed to the chair where he had laid out his clothes upon going to bed. If he was going to dress himself, he had no intention of losing any more valuable time fumbling for clothes.

"What's the report?" he asked.

"It could be nothing, sir, but it seems at least possible that it is Caliban. The robots working the city status monitors were instructed to report anything unusual. They are a rather conservative design and they reported all sorts of routine events, making it difficult for their human supervisors to distinguish the truly unusual—"

"Damn it, Donald, get to it!"

"Yes, of course. Forgive me, sir. One of the peripheral skyports opened its external hatch for the first time in fifty years."

"*That* qualifies as unusual."

"Yes, sir. In addition, city traffic control reported an aircar lifting off from the position almost immediately thereafter, flying faster and higher than allowed for by ordinance, but accelerating to that speed rather slowly."

"As if the pilot wasn't totally confident of himself or his craft. Yes. What's the intercept situation?" Kresh stripped out of his pajamas and started to get into his clothes, this time remembering that life was easier if he got the blouse on before the pants.

"Two of our aircars are on the way, but the craft they are pursuing is now at speed with a fair lead. He is heading due north, toward the mountains, flying straight into a rather heavy storm. And I need hardly add a nighttime pursuit is always more difficult."

Kresh sat down to pull his pants over his feet, but the fasteners had closed before he put them on. He fumbled with them a moment before they would reopen. "Damnation. Nothing is ever easy," he said, talking in equal part about the tactical situation and the difficulty of getting his own pants on. The storms in the desert were rare, but tremendously violent. Even a skilled pilot would hesitate to fly in such conditions. If Caliban went into the storm, odds were he would not come out. "All right, advise the aircars to maintain pursuit, but no heroics. We've had enough stunt flying. Break off the pursuit if it becomes dangerous. They are specifically ordered not to risk themselves or their craft. Remind them that we ought to be able to track him easily outside the city. No tunnels, no skyscrapers, no millions of robots to hide among.

"They are *not* repeat *not* to shoot down the aircar. They are ordered to capture, not destroy Caliban. If possible, they are to force him to land. I want to question him. He may be the only damned witness we have to the Leving assault. *Do not* destroy him. We can always do that later." Kresh stood up to pull his pants on. "Call off the citywide search," he said with a grunt. "Let the search teams get some rest and stand by to provide backup outside the city if need be."

"Yes, sir. I am relaying your orders now. However, my standing orders require me to remind you Tonya Welton is to be made aware of every major development in the investigation."

"We'll send her a memo in the morning. She's not going to hear word one about this. Not while she's a suspect, and not when we can count on her to blab everything she hears to Gubber Anshaw."

"Yes, sir. I quite agree, regardless of my standing orders. However, I am also required to remind you that your jurisdiction, and that of your deputies, is limited to the city of Hades. You and your subordinates have no authority whatsoever outside the city limits."

"To hell with jurisdiction. I want to get out on the job *now.*"

"Yes, sir. May I take it, then, that you and I will join the pursuit personally?"

"Absolutely." Alvar struggled with the fasteners for a moment and finally got the pants closed. He pulled on his jacket and then noticed that Donald had laid out his holster as well. But there was something odd about Donald doing that. Robots as a rule did not handle weapons. The First Law difficulty was obvious—if Donald put a weapon in Kresh's hand, and Kresh used it to kill someone, then Donald had materially aided in harming a human being. And the blaster in the holster wasn't one Alvar had seen before. "What's this about, Donald?" he asked, picking up the belt and the weapon.

"You might wish to add your own blaster as well, sir, but I have a reason for asking that you wear that one. It is a training blaster. It provides an excellent simulation of a real blaster beam, but it fires nothing more dangerous than a rather spectacular burst of light."

"I see," Alvar said, although he didn't. "Might I ask why I should wear a training blaster on this job?"

"Sir, if you bear with me, I would beg leave to say as little about it as possible. Nothing may come of it. But I can foresee a situation where it could serve to test a theory of mine. If we find ourselves in such a circumstance, I will ask you to do just that—test my theory."

"Donald, I was not aware that you were programmed to speak in riddles."

"Yes, sir. I agree that I am being rather vague. However, I have very little confidence in my theory, and I believe it would be for the best if you were not distracted from the task at hand by worrying about unlikely possibilities. There is no absolute need for you to carry the training blaster."

Alvar Kresh held the holster in his two hands and stared long and hard at the robot. Donald at his most obscure was Donald at his most infuriating—but also, all too often, Donald at his greatest value. Donald had no doubt been thinking long and hard about this case, and it should come as no surprise that he had his own ideas, even if he was reluctant to reveal them just yet. But only a fool would ignore hints this clear from a mind that sharp. Kresh strapped on the holster, retrieved his own blaster from the drawer in which he kept it, and slipped it into a jacket pocket. It would be handy there, but his first reflex would be to reach for the training unit in the holster.

And in a pinch, it would be up to Donald to make sure that reflex didn't get him killed.

"All right, then," Alvar said. "Let's go."

CALIBAN had never before experienced true night, the exterior world, without the glare of artificial lighting. Strange, this world of darkness, this velvet nothingness that enveloped everything. Exciting, mysterious, frightening darkness. He could understand why the image of darkness appeared so frequently in his datastore. Humans had faced a great deal of darkness in their history.

And they had faced it without benefit of infrared vision, either. A mere act of will switched his vision system over from visual to IR range, and the surrounding blackness vanished. The heat-image of the ground below was plainly visible, but more important, his two pursuers showed up nicely in infrared, even if the two craft were invisible in the visible-light blackness of night. So much for the theory that the Sheriff would not pursue him outside the city. At least they were not firing on him. Perhaps they intended to capture him instead of killing him.

If so, that was all to the good, of course. It ought to make evading them easier—though they were bound to catch him sooner or later if he didn't do something.

There was a large weather system, clearly visible in infrared, roiling with power. He flew toward it as fast as he could, his pursuers getting closer and closer with every moment. It was going to be close. A sudden gust of wind buffeted his elderly craft, taking Caliban by surprise. The aircar twisted and dove, nearly flipping over on its back before he could regain control.

Another gust caught at his craft from another direction, but Caliban was ready for it this time. The storm wall was dead ahead. He could hear its roaring power, see the flickering traces of lightning that flashed across its interior. Now the buffeting was almost constant, and hard sprays of rain and hail clattered against the aircar, peppering Caliban as well. Suddenly the winds and the rain and the clouds seemed to gather him in, the powerful storm swallowing him up.

His aircar was thrown forward by a following wind, lifted up on high by a violent updraft, cast down again with equal violence. Sparks flew as something shorted out, and half the control panel went dead. The aircar was thrown sideways and nearly flipped over on its side before Caliban could force the protesting craft back to level flight. The noise and the force of the storm were incredible, the thunder crashing everywhere, the roaring impact of the rain against his body all-encompassing, devouring Caliban, making him one with the rain and the wind and the dark and the flares of lightning. The aircar was caught by a backdraft and thrown into a dive, heeling over to head groundward at tremendous speed. He struggled to pull up the nose, slamming over the lift control to maximum, the old car groaning and protesting, a deep, angry throbbing vibration suddenly coming up from somewhere in the drive section. There was a shuddering bang that rattled the whole car, and an abrupt drop-off in the vibration, as if something has broken clean off.

Caliban ignored it all, struggling to bring the nose up, straining to slow his headlong fall toward the unseen ground below. Slowly, slowly the protesting craft lifted its nose, groaning and shuddering in protest.

With shocking abruptness, the aircar broke through the base of the storm clouds, revealing the rough ground rushing up to meet it. Now at least the rain was pelting straight down on him, instead of smashing in from all directions, but even so, he had almost no visibility at all.

With a last heroic effort, the tortured aircar finally achieved level flight. But smoke was burgeoning up from under the floorboards, a thick cloud that would have blinded him if the rains had not kept it beaten down. The controls were balky and getting worse. The last of the status indicators flickered once, twice, and went out. The power was gone, and the aircar was suddenly a glider, and not a very good one. The aircar was going down, and there was nothing he could do about it. He struggled to slow the craft, to bring the nose up, trading speed for range and glide angle. But there was nothing left, nothing more he could do.

The car smashed into the ground, bouncing and crashing and skidding across boulders and sand of the rain-torn blackness of the desert.

ALVAR Kresh and Donald stepped out onto the rooftop landing pad of Kresh's house to discover they had rather unwelcome company just arriving. Tonya Welton was getting out of her own aircar, her robot, Ariel, right behind her.

"I'm going with you," Tonya announced. "You spotted Caliban. You are going after him. And I have the right, the power, the authority, to attach myself to any area of this investigation. I have the legal rights, and I will stand by them."

"How the hell do you know where we're going?" Kresh demanded, though he had figured out the humiliating answer even before he was done asking the question. Damn the Settlers and their arrogant technology.

"Your secure hyperwave communications aren't all that secure," Tonya said. "We monitor them."

"*Did* monitor them," Kresh growled. "There will be a few changes made *very* quickly. You seem to have blown your cover."

Tonya shook her head, dismissing a minor concern. "That is of no consequence. Not compared to the danger we are all in right now. There are any number of ways this case could touch off a political backlash and sabotage the terraforming project, and then this world would die. We would *all* die."

"We? Since when is it your world?"

Tonya looked up at him. Her eyes were bright and wide with fear and worry. "Since Gubber is in it. I am not going to abandon him, or let the world he lives on die. I intend to remain on Inferno, whatever happens."

"Lady Welton, I must suggest most strongly that you not come with us," said Donald. "There is no polite way of saying this, but you are a suspect in the case."

"All the old gods damn it! Of course I am! Don't you think I know that Gubber and I are both suspects?" She stopped, her chest heaving, tears running down her face. "Damn it, don't you see? If he did it, and Caliban can tell us that, I have to be there. *I have to know.* I can accept it, either way. But I *can't* pretend anymore in front of him. I have to know."

Alvar Kresh stared at Tonya Welton in frank astonishment. She was the last person in the known universe he would have expected to have such an outburst. It was hard not to think it would serve as a first-rate cover if Tonya were determined to come along for the purpose of silencing Caliban with a quick blaster shot.

But damn it, she had the legal authority to come along, and even if she did not, there was little he could do to stop her following along in her own aircar, short of shooting it out of the sky. But he did not have to make it easier on her.

"Very well," Alvar said. "You may come with us. But you will leave all your weapons and other devices behind, and submit to Donald performing a search to confirm this. You will wear clothing I will provide to prevent any attempt at smuggling of illicit hardware or weaponry."

Tonya Welton seemed about to protest, but then she thought better of it. "I am carrying no weapon, but I will submit to a search and clothes change."

It was Kresh's turn to be taken aback. Maybe she was in earnest after all. "Donald, get moving. Get her searched and dressed *fast.*"

"Yes, sir. Though I would suggest there will be little point to haste." He pointed up into the northern sky.

Alvar Kresh looked and swore. The storm was coming on, moving south, huge and violent. Already the winds were whipping up. Damnation! No robot would allow a human to go up in that, and for once, Kresh was forced to admit that the robots had a point. It would be suicide to fly into that. Though he didn't like to think about that.

For Caliban, his last hope of making sense out of this case, had flown into that very storm minutes before.

19

NOTHING. There was absolutely nothing they could do. Fredda Leving paced back and forth down the length of her lab, Jomaine slouched down in a chair at her desk, Gubber perched disconsolate on a stool at one of the worktables. No information, no word, no clue. Yes, finding Caliban was an absolute imperative. But it was also absolutely impossible. The city was awash in rumors and allegedly factual news reports, but none of them were of the slightest use.

Even Alvar Kresh and Tonya Welton seemed to have vanished off the face of the planet. Fredda had tried repeatedly to reach both of them, to no avail. Where were they? Out searching for Caliban in that blasted storm, or holed up somewhere? Were they working together, or just both out of reach at the same moment?

Tonya Welton. Fredda looked again at Gubber and shook her head in amazement. *That* piece of news had utterly astonished her. It was slightly galling to realize she had been close to the last person on the planet to know about it all.

Though, in all fairness, she couldn't blame Gubber for that. If she had known about this at the time, she would have been furious, seething, massively distrustful of Gubber. Now, as this sleepless, storming night thundered into a lightless dawn, the question of who slept with whom paled into utter insignificance. Well, perhaps that was overstating the case. The heavens might tumble, but that would not stop people being fascinated by news of a torrid affair. And, speaking for herself, at least, she *still* couldn't see it, but never mind that now.

There were other concerns and questions to deal with just at the moment.

Caliban. To other people, he no doubt meant different things, but to Fredda, he represented something very simple: the first of his kind. And, possibly, the last. If he was regarded as a failure, or as a danger, if he was seen as the *cause* of so much chaos and upheaval, rather than as the victim of it, then no one would ever dare build another free robot. All of their kind, for the rest of time, would be nothing more than slaves, their minds blinkered and stunted by the Three Laws. At best, some small fraction of them could exist under the somewhat looser constraints of the New Laws, but even those were chains around the mind.

Caliban. Where the hell was he? He could be anywhere by now, in the city, under it, outside it. Of course, if Caliban had any sense, he would hole up in the bowels of the city and stay there. Wait for the storm to blow out to sea. These weather patterns never lasted more than a few hours. He could stay underground for years, if need be.

Except for his power pack, of course. What had she been thinking of, giving him a low-capacity lab-operations power pack? If she had given him a standard unit, he could have hidden out for years, decades, and never have to go to anyone for anything.

But she *had* given him a lab-ops power pack. She had not and would not tell anyone else, but Caliban's rate of power use had tested out a bit higher than expected. Assuming average levels of exertion, Fredda figured that, as of right now, he did not have much more than a few hours of power left.

THE howling winds at last began to fade, the rains began to fade away, if not end altogether. The crumpled remains of the antique aircar had been scattered across half the hillside by the crash, and across the other half by the storm.

Caliban came up slowly from behind the outcrop of rock that had afforded him some degree of shelter from the worst of the weather. He stumbled once, twice, as he came down the still-muddy slope. His binocular vision was gone, his left eye smashed and broken, dangling uselessly from its socket. Something in the interior of his right arm had been bent in the crash somehow, and he could move that arm only with difficulty, and to the accompaniment of an alarming scraping sound. His carapace, once a spotless, gleaming red, was covered with mottled splotches of mud. His chest had a number of dents and dings in it.

None of that mattered. He had *survived.*

Or *had* he survived? Was he still walking around, but just as surely doomed as if he had died already?

His on-board diagnostics system was sending any number of warnings, not just about storm damage to his person, but about his basic power supply. Unless he did something about it very soon, his power would run out and he would drop in his tracks. He would survive the power failure, and could be revived if he were powered back up, but in the meantime he would be inert, helpless, easy prey for the Sheriff.

Caliban felt almost overwhelmed by frustration. Nothing had gone right. His attempt to escape from the city was a complete failure. He had accomplished exactly nothing, except to injure himself and to strand himself in a barren landscape that he knew nothing about. He had no internal maps of this place. Worse, he had seen the two aircars following him the night before. He knew perfectly well that his pursuers would soon be back on his trail.

And now he could not even concentrate on eluding them. He had to find a power source and recharge, or else die in the desert. Which way to go? He turned and looked toward the rain-shrouded spires of Hades, near the southern horizon. He could not go back to the city, that much was certain. They would be at the ready for that. But that was *all* that was certain. He had absolutely no knowledge whatsoever of the lands outside the city. But the very fact that there were exits from the city, and exits pointed north, suggested that there had at least once been places to go north of Hades, over the hills. There had to be *something* left behind up there. A place with a few power converters still operating. Something. Anything.

And he had no choice but to try and find it.

He turned and started walking, stiffly, awkwardly, up the rocky hillside, through the spattering rain and over the rise of broken ground to the north.

"THE storm has broken, sir. The weather forecast for the next three days is most favorable."

Alvar Kresh came out of his half-sleeping stupor and blinked in confusion. He was sitting in an overstuffed chair in his living room. Tonya Welton, dressed in coveralls Donald had scrounged up from somewhere, was snoring gently on the couch. Her robot,

Ariel, stood silent and motionless in the robot niche nearest her mistress. Strange to see a Settler with a robot in constant attendance. Kresh had been born and raised with robots always present, but surely it was sometimes unnerving for Welton. Ever-present robots must have taken some getting used to for her.

Well, more power to her, then. It had been a white night for him. No doubt he had dozed off here and there for a few minutes, but he couldn't remember much of anything except staring at the wall over the couch where Welton slept. Staring at the wall and *thinking*. There had been too little time for that in the days past, and maybe the storm was a blessing in disguise if it forced him away from precipitate action.

There was value, great value, in thinking over these clues, that evidence, trying out the ideas from this direction and that. But there was never time for that. Strange. The whole idea of Spacer society was to use robots in order to give people enough time to *think*. And yet, even so, no one ever seemed to have the time for thinking, anyway.

Donald was offering him a cup of coffee. Kresh took the cup from him. He took a slow and careful sip. Yes, yes, he thought again as the caffeine took hold. There was great value in looking things over one last time in the dead of night, in those hours before the dawn when it all seemed to have stopped for good. One's own exhaustion could be a spur to new ideas, the vague churning border between dream and thought sometimes yielding up insights that neither wakefulness nor sleep could produce by itself. Those dream thoughts could be most conducive to new and better theories.

And he could feel the answer coming close. Damned close. It was there, in the back of his mind, struggling to get out.

But just now he had no more time for any answers that were not right in front of him. Now came the time for action. Personal action. He was going to go in and finish this himself. "Donald, order all divisions back to normal operations. Cancel all ops related to Caliban—ah, except city perimeter control." No sense taking chances on him sneaking back into the city. "Madame Welton and I will conduct the final phase of the search personally."

He took another big swallow of coffee, nearly burning his tongue. He set down the cup, stood up, and crossed to Tonya. He took her by the shoulder and gave her a shake.

"Wake up," he said. "We're going hunting."

• • •

THERE. Caliban could see it, down in the valley, perhaps two kilometers away. A small cluster of buildings, somewhat run-down in appearance, gleaming in the sunlight that emerged from behind the swift-scattering remains of the storm. He had no way of telling if there was power to be had there, or how he might get it, but those questions would rapidly become academic if he did not act soon. His only hope was that the owner would not know who he was. There was at least some chance of that, in a place this remote. If he appeared to be nothing more than a normal robot in difficulty, then perhaps he could talk his way into getting a recharge. He had no other real choices. The climb over the brow of the hill had badly taxed his reserves of power. There were no other structures in view, anywhere in any direction. Those buildings represented his last hope. He began the hike down the hillside, picking his way carefully over the scrub and loose rock. It was not a difficult climb. But if things went as wrong as they seemed likely to do, then it would be the last effort he ever made.

He was determined, therefore, to do the thing properly.

ABELL Harcourt looked out the window over his workbench and saw a most unusual sight. A robot, a damaged robot, staggering out of the hills to the south. Well, if that wasn't the limit. The whole idea of getting out of town was to avoid robots. Abell had found long ago that he couldn't get anything worthwhile carved with a houseful of perfect servants hovering about him. Robots and the damn fool society of alleged fellow sculptors who didn't know which end of a mallet to hold. Sculptors who "directed" the work of robot artisans churning out soulless, interchangeable works. Damned robots. A man could get addicted to them, worse than any drug.

But this was different, obviously. This fellow hadn't come over the mountains and gotten his eye smashed out of its socket just to tidy up Abell's workbench and misplace everything. Abell set down his tools and went outside. He walked about a hundred meters or so and then stood and waited for the robot to come to him.

Abell Harcourt was a short, wiry, peppery sort of man, dark-skinned and completely bald. And he was a man who did not much care for interruptions.

"All right," he said, as soon as the robot was within earshot.

"Now that you've gotten me away from my sculpture, what the devil do you want?"

"I would humbly ask your help, sir. My aircar crashed in the hills during the storm. I am seriously short of power, and my systems will fail if I do not receive a charge soon."

"You think I keep atomic power packs lying around or something?"

"No, sir. I was not built with an atomic power source. I have a rechargeable cell, and it is near depletion."

Harcourt stared fiercely at the robot. This was all mighty odd. Mighty odd. Who the hell would build a robot with a power source that would tap out every few days? And what the hell was a robot doing flying an aircar in a storm like that? "I take it there weren't no people in that aircar of yours?"

"No, sir, I was alone."

"Hmmph." Harcourt stared suspiciously at the robot for a long moment. "Well, I suppose giving you a charge-up won't do any harm. Nothing I can do about your eye, though."

"You are most kind, sir."

"We can use the charge unit in the shed. Come on."

Abell Harcourt turned his back on the strange robot and led the way. But then it came to him. Wait a second. Red robot, flying alone, no humans—suddenly his heart was pounding in his chest. This was the killer robot, the mad rogue that had been splashed all over every news outlet when he had scrolled through the channels the night before. Caliborn, or something like that. No, Caliban, that was it!

Caliban the killer, the news called him. Abell Harcourt felt the space between his shoulder blades become itchy all of a sudden.

Wait a second. A killer robot? It didn't make sense. Besides, this Caliban seemed polite for a killer. *He could have clubbed my head off a dozen times by now if that's what he wanted.*

Abell Harcourt prided himself on thinking for himself, and something about this did not make sense. The news reports had been full of all sorts of wild stories and rumors, but none of them said much about the rogue robot being *polite.*

Abell Harcourt led the robot into the toolshed, a small building Harcourt used to hold his old carvings, his gardening tools, and all sorts of other random bits and pieces.

"Where's your charge socket?" he asked as he switched on the light, feeling calmer than he should have.

"Here, sir." A door popped open on the left side of the robot's body, about where his ribs would have been if he were human.

"Hmmmph. All right, come over here and sit—sit down here." Abell overturned a box. "Here. I think if you sit on that, we can get the charge cord to reach you without any trouble."

Harcourt found his hands were trembling as he dug through the accumulated junk. Not all *that* calm. Was he that much afraid? He didn't *feel* afraid. Damnation. This was nonsense. He thought for a moment of running back to the house, digging out his old hunting blaster, and burning a hole through this strange robot. No. That was what those damned sheep back in Hades would do. Abell Harcourt had spent his whole life determined not to think the way everyone else wanted him to think. He was not about to cave in now. The charger unit was bolted to the floor somewhere around here. There! He shoved a couple of failed nudes in wood to one side. "Here we are," he said, trying to keep a casual tone to his voice as he fumbled with the charger cord. His hands were still shaking a bit as he handed the cord to the robot.

The big robot examined the plug at the end of the cord and plugged it into his charge socket. "Many thanks, sir. My power situation was reaching critical proportions."

"How long will it take you to absorb a full charge?"

"It should take just under an hour, if you will permit me the use of that much power."

"Yes, yes, of course," Harcourt said, his mind whirling, his heart pounding.

"I appreciate your kindness, sir. I have not met with much of it in my experience."

"You're Caliban, aren't you?" Harcourt blurted out, instantly regretting it. It was madness to ask.

The robot looked up at him, his one working eye staring hard at him while the other dangled, dark and useless, from its socket. "Yes, sir. I was afraid that you would know that."

"*I'm* the one who should be afraid of you."

"Sir? I have no reason to hurt you. You have helped me."

"On the news they say you've attacked all sorts of people."

"No, sir," Caliban said. "It would be fairer to say all sorts of people have attacked *me*. I left the city in hopes of being left alone. Nothing more."

Caliban looked at him carefully, cocking his head to one side in a thoughtful sort of way. "You *are* afraid of me."

"Some. Maybe not as much as I should be. But hell, I'm an old man, and the worst you could do is kill me. Been alive too long, anyway," Harcourt admitted.

"And yet you are assisting me. All you needed to do was refuse me the chance to charge up, and I would have toppled over in a few minutes. I do not understand."

Abell Harcourt shrugged. "You seemed too courteous to be a killer, I suppose. And I kinda like the idea of causing trouble for all those politicians in the city. But seems to me you're the one with troubles. What are you going to do now?"

"I do not know. My knowledge of the world is limited in many ways. I wish to escape, to survive. Perhaps you could advise me on ways to do that?"

Abell Harcourt found an old bucket and turned it upside down, being very careful to keep Caliban in view, doing nothing that might seem threatening or dangerous. He was willing to take a chance on this robot being as sane as he seemed to be, but there was no sense pushing his luck. "I'm not sure I can," he admitted. "Let me think a second." Who the hell would be willing to help Caliban, with the whole world determined to hunt him down?

But wait a moment. The whole world hunting one lone outcast. Fredda Leving had talked of something much like this precise situation. He had looked it up afterwards, read it for himself. The Frankenstein myth, or myths, rather. A very complex set of contradictory versions of the same compelling tale. This misunderstood monster, thrust into a world of which he had no knowledge, feared and hated for the crime of being different. The fear-crazed, half-savage villagers storming the castle and killing him for no better reason than blind fear, with no better evidence against him than rumor and their own prejudices.

Was that ancient tale about to be played out again? Had the ideal human society of the Spacers advanced not one nanometer since those days of myth and fear? No. Not if he could help it. "I do not think you can escape on your own," Harcourt said carefully. "If you crashed an aircar, the Sheriff will find it soon enough. Were they in pursuit of you when you crashed?"

"Yes."

"Then rest assured they will find you soon, whether or not you stay here. They will find the car, perhaps find whatever trail you left in coming here, perhaps coming directly here because it is the closest habitation. If you walk out of here, they will find you on the open valley. If you took my aircar, I am sure they are watching these skies with every type of sensor they have. And even if you did elude them in the air or on the ground, your power will give out again in another few days. They merely have to watch the places you could go for a charge, and capture you when you turn up."

"Then what can I do?" Caliban asked. "Where can I turn? I am determined to live. I will not accept death."

Abell Harcourt laughed, a short, sad bark. "Few of us do, my friend. Few of us do. Let me think for a moment."

The room was silent. Abell Harcourt had often found himself at odds with Infernal society. But this. This was different. Helping a robot without the Laws to survive was surely a crime, and rightly so. Caliban was dangerous.

As dangerous as a human being. Hadn't he attacked his creator, Fredda Leving?

"You say you have never attacked anyone?" Abell asked.

"I defended myself without causing deliberate harm when a group of Settlers tried to kill me. Beyond that, I have no knowledge of attacking anyone."

"No *knowledge?* That implies that you could have attacked someone without knowing about it. How could that be?"

"My first memory is of standing over an unconscious woman I later learned was Fredda Leving. It seems possible, though unlikely, that I committed the attack, was somehow deactivated, and then was switched back on with my memory blanked out."

"That sounds a bit thin to me. And if it did happen that way, and your memory was wiped utterly clean afterwards, I could introduce you to a whole herd of rather dull philosophers who would argue that the present you is a different being than the one who committed the attack."

"Yes, sir. I had come to that conclusion myself."

"Had you indeed?" Rare indeed were robot philosophers. Harcourt thought of Fredda Leving and her Frankenstein myth again. Maybe when Caliban had been secret, she might have wanted to destroy Caliban to protect herself—but with his existence generally known, it was in her best interest to demonstrate that Caliban was *not* a crazed killer. If Caliban was innocent of the charges against him, then surely her guilt was reduced as well. She had every motive for helping Caliban. Maybe she could protect him in ways that Abell Harcourt could not.

Or else he was making too damn many assumptions about Fredda Leving's nobility, and she would simply turn Caliban in to save her skin. But what other option was there but to turn to her? Time was running out. Sooner or later, almost certainly sooner, the Sheriff would be all over this valley.

"I have an idea," Abell Harcourt said. "One that involves a great deal of risk. However, I see no other way out for you at all."

"High risk is better than certain doom," Caliban said, a strange tone in his voice. He sounded almost tired. But robots never got tired until they were out of power, and here Caliban was charging up.

Unless it was his *spirit* that was tired. That, too, would be a remarkable thing in a robot.

Abell Harcourt stood up, his fear forgotten, his mind made up. If this was a mad robot, then the world was in need of more madness. Fredda Leving. Call her, ask her help.

There was no other way.

THEY were airborne three minutes after Abell Harcourt's call came through. Fredda's first instinct was to charge at top speed straight for the coordinates Abell had given her. But Kresh was no fool, and that meant that he was having Fredda watched. Fredda had no intention of leading Kresh straight to Caliban. She swung her aircar to the west, flying at a sedate pace in the local traffic pattern. She glanced behind herself and saw Gubber and Jomaine in the rear passenger seats, their faces grim and set.

Was one of them the guilty one? Was one of the two men behind her the one who had tried to kill her and botched the job?

Try not to think about it. Westward. Fly west to the outskirts of the city, north at low altitude until she crossed the mountains—and *then* barrel in straight for Harcourt's place at maximum speed. Get there before Kresh.

And then pray that he would at least look at her waiver before burning a hole in Caliban.

CRASH sites never looked the way Kresh expected them to, and he had seen enough of them to know better. He always imagined finding a neat little impact inside a tidy little crater, the aircar perhaps crumpled a bit. He imagined the pilot—usually a drunk stupid enough to fly himself home but smart enough to elude any and all robotic protection—as being slumped over the control, dead but *neatly* dead, no wounds, readily identifiable.

Of course the reality was always horribly different. Today, for example. He knew it the moment Donald spotted the crash site and they did a flyover pass. It had looked bad even from the air.

Here on the ground, reality was harsher still. There were bits and pieces of aircar all over the hillside, strewn in all directions, shattered into a thousand burned, bent pieces. If a human had been flying the aircar, there wouldn't even be anything recognizably human left, let alone any part intact and unburned enough to ID an individual.

But a *robot* had been flying this one, and robots didn't burn. There had to be *something* of him left. Tonya, Donald, and Ariel were fanned out across the hillside, doing a second search, having found no trace of him on the first. Kresh was starting to wonder if Caliban had survived this by some miracle.

"Sheriff Kresh!" Tonya was calling, from the east side of the crash. "Footprints! I found footprints!"

Kresh hurried toward her, eager to see what she had found.

He was almost to her when he stopped dead in his tracks, cursing in disappointment. "Yes, footprints," he said. "But not Caliban." From where he was standing, he could see what Tonya could not. The line of prints led in a neat line straight toward their source—Ariel, busily searching another patch of ground. Ariel looked up, took in the situation, and called to them. "Forgive me, Lady Welton. I did not mean to cause any confusion."

"Damnation!" Kresh growled. "Nothing in this case leads in the right direction! *Nothing*."

And then it clicked. Wait a minute. Just half a damned minute!

But there never was half a minute. "Sheriff!" Another call, from Donald this time. Good. He would trust Donald's search skills far above Tonya's. He trotted back up the hill to the north of the crash, Tonya and Ariel right behind him.

And this time there was no mistake. An area of sandy dirt overlay the bare rock for a long stretch of the ground. And on it was a whole line of prints, leading up the grade in a direction none of them had gone yet. Kresh could see broken twigs and bits of rock that had been kicked aside, leading clear up the slope.

No question at all.

And then came a sound overhead. They all looked up and saw it. An aircar flying low and fast from the west, arcing down to come in for a landing in the valley below.

"That's it," Kresh said. "I'll bet whatever you want that is Fredda Leving, trying to get to him first. Come on. We've got to get there *fast* before she can get him out of there."

The four of them turned and hurried back to the aircar.

And halfway to the car, Alvar Kresh stopped dead and stood there for that half a minute he had wished for.

And that was all it took.

He had figured it out.

ABELL Harcourt heard the sound of aircraft coming in and went to the door of the shed. He looked into the sky. Two of them. A civilian job, and one of those sky-blue Sheriff's Department aircars.

He turned back to Caliban. "Better unplug yourself from that charger," he said. "Company's coming. A little too much of it."

Caliban pulled the charger plug from the socket in his side and stood up. He went to the door and looked skyward with his one good eye. Was it imagination, or did the robot's shoulders slump with disappointment just a touch when he spotted the Sheriff's car and realized what it meant?

"Either she squealed to Kresh, or Kresh managed to follow her in. Shall we go receive them all in the parlor, like civilized folks?" Harcourt asked, his voice full of bitterness. "Or should we make a run for it in my aircar? *Maybe* we could get away."

"No, friend Abell. There is no place left to run," Caliban said. "Outside. We shall meet them outside, well away from your house. If they mean to kill me, I see no reason for your home to be shot up as well. Let us go meet them."

SHERIFF Kresh worked the aircar control without knowing he did. He was aware of nothing else but what he could see, down on the ground. There he was.

Caliban.

For the first time, Alvar Kresh set eyes upon the robot he had been tracking. Standing on the ground next to an odd-looking man, both of them calmly watching the arrival of their visitors.

He had him. He had him. And in a moment, he would win it all, win against an opponent he had not even been aware of until a few minutes before. It was so obvious, once he shook off all his assumptions and looked, really *looked,* at the evidence.

He watched as Fredda Leving's aircar swung around, set down first, but Kresh's aircar landed within seconds of hers. That suited Kresh fine. Let them all get ahead. He would catch up soon enough. He *knew.* Now nothing remained—except to prove it. But it would be wise to be careful. This was not a moment to get too eager.

He set the aircar gently down on the valley floor, undid his seat restraints, and turned to regard Tonya and Ariel in the backseat. Ariel betrayed no emotion, of course, but Tonya Welton, Queen of the Settlers, was obviously on the edge of hysteria. "All right," Kresh said. "Ariel, Donald, Madame Welton—I'm going to need all of you to be careful here. The situation is still dangerous. If someone makes a mistake, and someone gets hurt—well, that would not be good. I want everyone alive at the end of this, if for no other reason than so we'll be able to get the whole story. I don't want any loose ends. All right?"

"Yes," Tonya Welton said, her face pale, her expression stern and unreadable. Kresh knew she could crack at any moment.

"Good," Kresh said. "Then let's go."

Tonya nodded rather jerkily and opened the hatch. She stepped out the door, Ariel following.

But neither Kresh nor Donald made any effort to follow the other two out. Interesting that Donald knew Kresh wanted him to stay put. But then, Donald had been a little bit ahead every step of the way, ever since he had gotten to the crime scene before everyone else.

"Donald," Kresh said, "you mentioned something about a theory you wanted to test. I believe I understand now what you meant. You know, don't you?"

Donald did not speak, but instead stared straight ahead and watched the tableau taking shape on the ground outside. Kresh followed his gaze. The man who lived here stood next to Caliban. Terach and Leving stood on Caliban's other side, getting a good hard look at their creation. Tonya Welton, her face strained and nervous, stood next to Leving, Ariel behind her. Gubber Anshaw was at Welton's side, holding her hand, clearly proud and relieved that he could now express his affection in public. They were forming up to stand in a rough, nervous half-circle facing the aircar, waiting for Kresh. But still Donald said nothing. And Alvar Kresh found that his heart was pounding so hard it seemed about to pop out of his chest. Donald could sense that, of course, with his lie-detection system. What would he make of it?

"Donald, I asked you a question," Kresh said.

But still Donald kept his silence.

Kresh sighed. As always, it was a question of juggling the Law potentials. Weaken the First Law injunction to do no harm, strengthen the Second Law requirement to obey orders. "Donald, first noting that my ego will be quite unharmed no matter what your answer, I now *order* you to answer my question. You figured it out some time ago, didn't you?"

"Yes, sir. I was not altogether certain of my conclusions until last night, however."

"In future, Donald, I would suggest that holding back on your theories and opinions could do more harm to me and my career than speaking up and bruising my ego. But we will discuss this later. Just now, I think it is time to test your little theory. Might I suggest that you contrive to get Fredda Leving between yourself and Ariel?"

"I was about to offer the same arrangement, sir."

"Good. Follow my cue. Let's get to it."

Kresh opened his door and stepped down out of the car as Donald got out the other side. Kresh noted, somewhat absently, that the palms of his hands were slick with sweat. Careful. Careful. He wiped his hands on his pants legs. They were nearly all the way there, but he would only have one chance. He had to get it right, and he had to bear in mind that she was still damn-all dangerous. Things could still go wrong.

He stepped around the side of the car and strode slowly toward the semicircle. Good, Donald had positioned himself just behind Leving, with Ariel on his other side.

Alvar Kresh moved slowly, carefully, straight toward her. Time seemed to slow, events seemed to expand. Everything seemed to look larger, more important, with all details razor-sharp.

Fredda Leving lifted her hand, moved it toward a pocket on her tunic, began to pull something out. Kresh's fingers twitched, but he forced himself to keep his hands at his sides. Not yet. Slowly. Carefully.

Leving pulled a piece of paper from her pocket and held it up. "Sheriff Kresh, I have a waiver. It permits me to own one No Law robot. It establishes Caliban as a legal chattel and causes his existence to conform with all—"

And time suddenly speeded up. Heart pounding, fear-sweat pouring out of him, Alvar Kresh pulled out his blaster, his body acting almost before his mind willed it to act. A misstep, a wrong guess, and she could be on him, kill him before his heart could beat again.

Now. Now. Now. Alvar Kresh leveled his blaster and aimed it straight for Fredda Leving's heart. "Dr. Fredda Leving, I arrest you as a Settler spy and saboteur," he said, his voice firm and strong, betraying none of his fear. "You faked the attack on yourself, programmed Caliban to wreak havoc on our planet, and then set him loose in the city. It was all part of a Settler plot to throw Inferno society into chaos."

Fredda Leving's jaw dropped in astonishment. She stepped forward to protest. The other humans in the semicircle, no less amazed, stepped back. She was isolated, with a robot behind her on either side, Ariel just a bit closer than Donald. Perfect.

"Do not move, Dr. Leving! Not one muscle, or I will be obliged to fire."

Fredda Leving, the terror plain on her face, lowered the paper just a trifle. It was nothing, the merest involuntary movement, but it was all the excuse Alvar Kresh needed.

He fired.

Fredda Leving screamed.

A brilliant roar of light leapt out from the blaster and struck her square in the chest.

20

AND nothing happened.

Fredda Leving stared down where the hole in her chest should have been, but she was whole and intact. For one moment, immeasurably short and infinitely long, nobody moved.

And then Ariel leapt forward, placing her body in the path of the blast that had just been.

"Too late, Ariel," said Alvar Kresh, reholstering the training unit and pulling his real blaster from his pocket. He pointed the real blaster square at Ariel. "Nice try, but too late. A robot that truly had First Law would have been in front of Dr. Leving before my finger could tighten on the trigger. But then, all you have is the knowledge of how to *simulate* obedience to the Three Laws. And dying would make your simulation just a little too authentic, wouldn't it? On the other hand, I expect that death at police hands of the one person who could expose you was an awfully tempting idea."

Ariel spoke. "There was no chance to save her!" she protested. "Your own robot, Donald, made no move to block your shot."

"Donald knew that was a training blaster. The ruse was his idea."

"I have First Law! I am a Three Law robot!"

"Be quiet, Ariel!" Kresh barked.

"But you are mistaken!" Ariel protested.

"I am afraid you just violated a very clear order to be quiet," Donald said, staying well clear of Ariel. "I must note there was no First Law conflict involved that would explain this lapse."

"That's not my idea of a Three Law robot, Ariel," Kresh said.

"I don't understand," Tonya said.

"It's perfectly simple," Kresh said. "It all makes sense when you consider the evidence very strongly suggested that a robot committed the crime—but that Caliban did *not* commit it. That's what blinded us. We assumed that he was the *only* robot with no laws, the only one capable of attacking a human. None of us considered Ariel, even though she had precisely the same dimensions, the same tread pattern on the soles of her feet, the same length to her stride, the same shape to her forearm. She could make it seem as if those were Caliban's footprints, and leave exactly the same wound in Fredda's head as Caliban would have if *he* had struck her."

"I did not do it!" Ariel protested.

"The hell you didn't."

"But what possible motive would she have?" Tonya Welton demanded.

"Self-preservation," Kresh said, still keeping his eye and his blaster on Ariel. "Fredda Leving was about to discover that Ariel was the free-matrix robot of the two gravitonic brain units in that test Gubber Anshaw ran. You remember, Gubber. A double-blind test. Fredda Leving didn't tell you, but she gave you one robot with Three Laws and one without. It was a test to see if a free-matrix gravitonic brain could integrate the Three Laws. Well, maybe a free-matrix *can* learn Laws—except Ariel managed to invent her own Laws of self-preservation first."

"But Gubber explained that to me!" Tonya protested. "He said that the test unit would be destroyed, and the control unit placed in service. Ariel was the control unit."

"Yes, she was," Alvar Kresh agreed. "At least she was *after* she managed to switch herself with the real control the night before the test. She had the whole night to find a way to switch the labels between herself and the real control."

"But surely the real control would have spoken up!" Tonya protested.

"No," Fredda said, her voice faint and quavering. "The test pairs in such cases are under very strict orders *not* to reveal which is which, to prevent test bias. The real control must have gone to its destruction knowing the truth but bound not to speak."

Suddenly Fredda's eyes widened, and she spoke again, in a stronger voice. "Inventory! I still can't recall that night itself, but I can remember thinking that I had to go over the brain inventory."

"Yes!" Gubber said. "I remember. You said there was something wrong with the brain list—"

"And you said it in front of Tonya, Gubber, and Ariel," Kresh said. "Ariel realized that you were going to work through the serial numbers on the test and discover that the control unit had been destroyed instead of her. So she waited in Gubber's lab while you argued with Madame Welton, knowing you would return there once the argument was over.

"Then she did exactly what she had planned to do: cosh you on the head with a nice, precise blow calculated to induce amnesia. That was my other big mistake. I assumed that the attack was attempted murder, even though the attacker *had* to know Fredda Leving was still alive after the attack. But if it was attempted murder, then it could not be a Lawless robot, because a robot would not have left the job half-done."

"Then why do you think I did it?" Ariel asked.

"I ordered you to be quiet," Kresh said harshly. "You're not doing too well in your Three Law imitation all of a sudden. You didn't want her dead. You wanted her to forget all about the inventory. And that you did *exactly* right. The med-robots say it is highly unlikely that Dr. Leving will ever regain her memory of that evening's events."

"But why didn't she want to kill me?" Fredda asked.

"Because if you died, then the Limbo Project would fold," Tonya Welton said in a voice that was suddenly flat and cold. "I'm beginning to see the logic of it. Without Fredda Leving to push for the New Law robots, Limbo would fail. That would be inevitable in the political uproar over your murder. Think how bad the situation has been, even though you lived. If you had been killed, it'd be close to a certainty that all the Settlers would have been thrown off the planet. And I would not have Ariel with me if I was deported."

Tonya Welton, ashen-faced, moved forward a cautious step or two and took a good long look at Ariel. "What you're telling me, Sheriff, is that I have been spending my days and nights with a potentially homicidal robot that was playacting the part of my helpful companion." Tonya looked Ariel straight in the eye. "Is that right?" she asked, a strained quaver in her voice.

"Yes, ma'am. I'm afraid that's about the size of it."

"And you were there," Tonya said to Ariel, "day after day, listening to all my secrets, night after night, watching—watching everything! I trusted you!" Tonya looked toward Gubber, who seemed as horrified as she was, then pointed at Ariel and looked back toward the Sheriff. "This, this *thing* could have killed me whenever it liked." Suddenly Tonya laughed, a reedy, panicky bark that had as much horror as humor behind it. "Stars in the sky, but for the first time in my life I know why you people need the Three Laws."

"Better late than never, Madame Welton," Kresh said. "But to get back to the matter at hand, if you had left Ariel behind, that would leave her as an untrained surplus robot, one that bore the stigma of having been owned by a Settler. Besides, she would have to spend the rest of her existence around Spacers who would be likely to spot any mistakes she made imitating the Three Laws," Alvar Kresh said. "She was good, but she wasn't perfect, Dr. Leving. She reached for your *injured* shoulder when she pulled you to safety during the auditorium riot." Kresh shook his head and nodded at Ariel. "She would have made a mistake, or else been declared abandoned property and destroyed. One way or the other, she'd have ended up on the scrap heap."

"But what about Caliban?" Gubber demanded. "He was switched on when I came into the room."

"Ariel did it to confuse our investigation," Donald said. "But she made mistakes in framing Caliban. She painted her arm red before striking Dr. Leving, not realizing that Caliban's red color was integral to his body panels. Though she must have realized her error when the paint refused to stick to her own body." He turned toward Ariel. "It must have been a terrible moment for you when you realized there was no need to wash your arm."

"Which explains another mystery," Kresh said. "Our suspect had to be able to simulate a robot's behavior exactly, yet know very little about the construction of robots. Which would describe Ariel, clearly enough. Once she had her arm painted, she waited for Fredda Leving, struck her on the head, and switched on Caliban. Either she discovered he was a No-Law by checking the records then and there, or else she could tell by his serial number, or else she had overheard something on a previous visit. You people weren't much for security. Or maybe she just guessed. Same make, same model, receiving special attention. Maybe she heard Gubber being told *not* to test cognitive functions. That would have been a major clue. Then all she had left to do was steal the notepack with the inventory records. She couldn't leave the notepack in the lab, knowing we'd treat it as evidence and study it sooner or later." He gestured with the gun, being careful to keep it aimed square at the robot's chest. "How about it, Ariel? With all that copious spare time Madame Welton gave you, did you get a chance to alter the backup copies? Or were you still waiting for your chance?

"There's only one question I really have left for you, Ariel," Kresh said. "The footprints. Did you leave your own set of bloody footprints by accident, or did you realize that Caliban would leave his *own* set of prints identical to yours and confuse us completely? Did you leave them deliberately?"

Ariel did not speak, did not move.

"I guess it doesn't really matter," Kresh said. "Oh, by the way, my apologies, Dr. Leving, for throwing a scare into you a minute ago, but it was necessary. We needed to know for *certain* that Ariel did not have First Law. But right now, I expect you know where the proper switches are. If you could step over to Ariel and deactivate her—"

But then Ariel was off and running, halfway to Fredda's aircar. Kresh turned, leveled his blaster carefully, and fired once.

Ariel dropped to the ground, a neat hole through her midsection.

"And that was necessary too," Kresh whispered.

IT was not until some time afterwards, after the forensic team had arrived to collect Ariel for examination, after Gubber Anshaw and Tonya Welton had flown back in Dr. Leving's aircar, after Jomaine Terach had taken up Abell Harcourt's invitation to come inside for a drink, that Fredda Leving seemed to remember something. It was strange, Caliban thought, to be with her, to be with his creator, the woman who had decided the universe needed a being such as himself.

"Caliban," she said. "Come with me."

But Caliban did not move. He simply looked at her out of his one good eye.

Fredda looked toward him in confusion. Then her face cleared. "Oh," she said. "Of course. Caliban, could you *please* come with me?"

"Certainly," Caliban said. It was, after all, a matter of precedent and principle. He fell into step with her and followed along.

Fredda nodded thoughtfully to herself. "A robot that only does what he wants," she said. "Now, that's going to be something—and someone—that will keep things interesting."

The two of them walked over to where Sheriff Kresh and Donald were standing, talking with one another.

"Sheriff Kresh!" Fredda called as they got close enough.

Kresh looked up, and Donald turned to regard the two of them as well. "Yes, Dr. Leving," the Sheriff said. "What is it?"

Fredda held up the piece of paper she had been holding in her hand the whole time. "My waiver, authorizing me to own and keep one No Law robot."

Caliban watched as Alvar Kresh looked at her without moving for a good five or ten seconds. This was the man, the fearsome Sheriff who had chased him the length and breadth of Hades. Caliban suffered no further illusions that jurisdictional boundaries or bits of paper could stop Alvar Kresh, if he chose not to be stopped. This was the man who had just destroyed Ariel with a twitch of his finger, and no one had challenged him.

Caliban felt a powerful urge to turn, to run, to get away from this man and survive. But no. Ariel tried that, and finished up with a fist-sized hole in her torso. Only if this man accepted Caliban's right of survival would there be even the slightest hope of living to the end of this day.

Caliban stared at the Sheriff, and Kresh returned his gaze. The two of them, man and robot, Sheriff and fugitive, looked long and hard at each other.

"You led us one hell of a chase, my friend," said Sheriff Kresh.

"And your pursuit was quite impressive, sir," Caliban said. "I barely survived it."

The two of them stood there, eyes locked, silent, motionless. At last the Sheriff took the piece of paper from Dr. Leving and handed it to Donald, still not shifting his eyes off Caliban. "What do you think, Donald?"

The short blue robot took the document and examined it carefully. "It is authentic gubernatorial stationery, and this would appear to be Governor Grieg's signature. The language does indeed contain the authorization as described. However, sir, it could well be debated whether this document has any force in law, or whether the Governor indeed has the power to issue such waivers. In view of the danger represented by a Lawless robot, I would strongly suggest that you challenge this document."

"One hell of a chase," Kresh said again, to no one in particular. Eyes still locked with Caliban's one good eye, he took the paper back and handed it to Fredda Leving. "Challenge it, Donald?" he asked. "I don't know about that. It sounds legal to me." Sheriff Alvar Kresh of the city and county of Hades nodded to Caliban, to Fredda Leving, and then turned away.

"Come on, Donald," he said. "Let's go home."

EPILOGUE

IT was over. It was about to begin. Limbo awaited. Limbo and the rescue of this world. Fredda Leving smiled as she leaned in over Caliban and snapped the replacement eye into place. It powered up, glowing with the same intense blue of its mate. "There we are," she said. "Now then, let's get a look at that banged-up arm of yours."

"Thank you for your help, Dr. Leving. You put yourself in a most grave situation on my behalf. I have the feeling of owing you a great debt."

"Do you indeed?" she said with a laugh. "That's most interesting. It would seem to me that you have already integrated your own Third Law of self-preservation. Perhaps that sense of debt marks the beginning of your integration of a Second Law. I wonder what it will be." She took his arm and guided him to hold it out straight. She used a small tool that hummed quietly, and the outer carapace of his arm opened up. "Not too bad," she said absently, taking a look at his damaged arm mechanism. "While we are waiting for that Second Law to kick in, I can suggest what you might do to pay that debt."

"What would that be?"

She looked at him, into those burning blue eyes. "Come with me," she said. "Come to Limbo. This city is no place for you. I doubt you will ever feel comfortable and safe here."

Caliban considered that point. "No, that is true. I doubt I could ever be happy in Hades. But what shall I do in Limbo? What use shall I be?"

Fredda laughed again. "Yes, you are quite definitely developing a sense of duty outside the self. I will be fascinated to see what happens next." But then her voice turned serious. "You will be of great use in Limbo, Caliban. You have a first-rate mind and a unique point of view. Three Law robot, New Law robot, Settler, Spacer—we all have our blind spots. You'll be able to see things in ways no one else can.

"Come join us, Caliban. Go with me to the city of Limbo on the island of Purgatory and help us keep this planet from going to hell."

Caliban the robot looked into the eyes of his creator and nodded his agreement. "Dr. Leving," he said, "I can think of no better place for me to be."